*continued . . .*

"Ms. Potter has no equal when writing romantic adventure . . . One plot twist after another . . . a cast of memorable characters . . . I couldn't put this book down. I was spellbound . . . This incredible historical is an exciting spin-off to *The Heart Queen* and *The Black Knave*, but it stands beautifully on its own. This trilogy is on my keeper shelf, as are all Patricia Potter's books, to be savored over and over again. You don't want to miss this one."  —*Old Book Barn Gazette*

"The story line is loaded with action yet enables the audience to understand what drives both lead characters and several key secondary players . . . a robust romantic adventure . . . [a] powerful tale."  —*BookBrowser*

## The Heart Queen

"Potter knows how to play on the heartstrings and she makes marvelous music in this poignant, tender, yet action-packed, romance. The complexities of relationships, secrets, betrayal and murderous plots blend well in this spin-off from *The Black Knave*."  —*Romantic Times* (Top Pick)

"This is a book that is difficult to put down for any reason. Simply enjoy."  —*Rendezvous*

"Exciting . . . powerful . . . charming . . . [a] pleasant page-turner."  —Harriet Klausner

"Potter is a very talented author . . . if you are craving excitement, danger, and a hero to die for, you won't want to miss this one."  —*All About Romance*

"Potter's story gives us action and pure excitement. Her characters are strong and intelligent, and she tells a truly romantic tale. This is what romance is all about . . . Terrific . . . You'll be thoroughly satisfied and wanting more. Truly delightful."  —*Old Book Barn Gazette*

# The Perfect Family

"The reader loses all sense of time as they become entangled in a web of mystery Ms. Potter spins in *The Perfect Family* . . . Flawless characterizations . . . You are holding a work of art when you pick up a book by Patricia Potter."

—*Rendezvous*

# The Black Knave

"Well-drawn, memorable characters, compelling action, and Machiavellian political intrigue add to a story that Potter's many fans will be waiting for." —*Library Journal*

"Patricia Potter has taken a classic plotline and added something fresh, making her story ring with authenticity, color, exciting action, her special humor, and deep emotions. *The Black Knave* is *The Scarlet Pimpernel* with twists and turns that make an old story new." —*Romantic Times* (Top Pick)

"I couldn't put it down! This one's a keeper! Pat Potter writes romantic adventure like nobody else." —Joan Johnston

"A fabulous romantic tale of intrigue and daring . . . will keep the reader spellbound through each twist and turn."

—*Rendezvous*

"A rousing tale of intrigue, danger, and forbidden romance that engaged my interest from first to last page . . . a most satisfying read." —*All About Romance*

# Starcatcher

"Patricia Potter has created a lively Scottish tale that has just the right amount of intrigue, romance, and conflict."

—*Literary Journal*

"Once again, Pat Potter demonstrates why she is considered one of the best writers of historical novels on the market today . . . Ms. Potter scores big time with this fabulously fine fiction that will be devoured by fans of this genre."

—*BookBrowser*

# Dancing with
# a Rogue

## Patricia Potter

**BERKLEY SENSATION, NEW YORK**

DANCING WITH A ROGUE

A Berkley Sensation Book / published by arrangement with the author

PRINTING HISTORY
Berkley Sensation edition / July 2003

ISBN: 0-425-19100-1

A BERKLEY SENSATION™ BOOK
Berkley Sensation Books are published by The Berkley Publishing Group,
a division of Penguin Group (USA) Inc.,
375 Hudson Street, New York, New York 10014.
BERKLEY SENSATION and the "B" design
are trademarks belonging to Penguin Group (USA) Inc.

PRINTED IN THE UNITED STATES OF AMERICA

10  9  8  7  6  5  4  3  2  1

# Prologue

Something terrible was about to happen.

Gabriel felt it in every nerve of his ten-year-old body as he heard the door shut securely behind him.

He stood still, clutching the piece of paper his father had just given him. *Remember, his father had said. Remember these names. Someday you will reclaim our honor. Someday . . .*

His father's voice faded away . . .

His father's face was fixed in his mind, but it wasn't the face he knew so well. The one usually wreathed in smiles and laughter. He loved his wife and his son. He was a good and honorable man. Everyone told Gabriel Manning that.

Yet moments ago, his father's face was painted with grief and bitterness.

Everything in Gabriel's world had changed in the past few days.

His parents were not wealthy, but unlike many of his friends his mother and father loved each other. He was the firstborn and only surviving child. Of the two other children, one died during childbirth and the other of a lung ailment. The loss of the two made their love for Gabriel that much stronger.

But now something black and wicked had affected the world he so loved.

They'd tried to keep it from him. At first, anyway. But he saw things: secretive sessions in the study, the maid in tears, a number of the servants suddenly dismissed after years of service, a father who no longer had time for him, his mother's face aging in front of him.

And then this afternoon his father had called him into his study.

His usually jovial face was lined. Tears were in his eyes.

"Sit down, Gabriel," he said.

Stunned by his father's evident despair, he did so.

His father looked down at a paper on his desk. His hands shook. Then he very carefully sealed it with wax and handed it to Gabriel.

"Keep this," he said. "Keep it until you are twenty-one. Then I want you to open it and consider what is inside."

Gabriel looked at it, knowing deep within that his life was changing forever.

"Swear it," his father said. "Do not tell your mother about it. Do not show it to anyone."

Gabriel knew his eyes opened wide. "But why?"

"Your mother would not approve. But she is not a man. She doesn't understand the requirements of honor."

Gabriel thought his mother would, indeed. She was the most admirable woman he'd ever known, much more so than any of his friend's mothers. But his father's piercing stare kept him from protesting.

He nodded.

"You will hear things, Gabriel. People will call me a thief. Perhaps a traitor. I am neither. A fool, perhaps, but not a traitor. Never a traitor."

"I know." Gabriel wanted desperately to comfort him, but those were the only words that came to him.

"I cannot go to prison. Or to a penal colony. I cannot put your mother through a trial."

He hesitated. "You must be very strong, Gabriel. I have made arrangements to send you and your mother to America.

Look after your mother. Protect her. Always know I loved her, and you, more than life itself."

His head dropped. "This letter names men I brought into the company so we could expand. They betrayed me, and they betrayed England, though I can't prove it."

He stood and went over to where Gabriel sat. "You will have to be a man hence. I am so sorry. I wanted you to have everything. I wanted you to have the shipping company."

Gabriel's heart stopped beating for a moment. There was such sadness in his father's voice. "Come with us to America."

"I must stay here. Now you go to your mother."

Gabriel knew protestations would gain him nothing. He recognized the finality in his father's voice.

They heard the clatter of a carriage outside. His father went to the window. Gabriel followed behind him. A carriage stood in front of the house. Four men in dark clothes took the first steps up to the door.

His father stiffened.

"Go, Gabriel. Always remember I am an honorable man and I loved you with all my heart." He hesitated, then said, "My honor—our family honor—depends on you, son." A tear rolled down his cheek. "It is a heavy burden. I should not . . ." He stopped. "Go, boy. Go to your mother."

Gabriel did not want to leave.

"Go, my boy," his father said, his voice cracking. "For God's sake, go."

His father never swore. Never. Stunned, Gabriel reluctantly left the room, the letter clutched in his hand. Once outside, he heard a key turn in the lock of the door behind him.

A pounding came at the front door of the town house.

Gabriel saw William, the last remaining member of the staff, hurry to open the door, but he lingered where he was. He wanted to be near his father.

Then he heard the snap of a gunshot inside the room.

"No!" he screamed.

He was still screaming as men rushed into the hall, smashed open the door; and he saw his father on the floor, blood pouring from his head.

# Chapter One

It was the irony of all ironies.

Gabriel Manning stared at the words on the official document that had just been delivered after months of delay. He had probably been responsible for some of the delay, he and his American privateer, which had captured more than a few British ships.

And now it seemed that the country Gabriel had so recently fought and long blamed for killing his father had made Gabriel Manning a peer of the realm.

He chuckled, but it was a mirthless sound. A marquess, by God. He was a marquess. His enemies were handing him the weapon he would use to skewer them.

He hesitated outside the office of the man who had made everything possible. He knew his news would not be happily met on this first meeting in many months.

Gabriel clutched the missive from a barrister in London, a barrister charged with informing him of the inheritance but who was obviously not eager for him to travel to England to collect it. A barrister whose name he remembered.

*There are no funds left,* according to the letter. *Only an en-*

*cumbered estate that is heavily indebted. I will be pleased to
sell what is possible to sell and send the proceeds to your account. There is no need for you to make the long and difficult
journey to England.*

Oh, but there was need. A very great need.

The war with England was over. He'd spent the last year
as a privateer captain and had taken his share of prizes, most
of which he turned over to the American government. He
knew that on the cessation of hostilities, he would be given a
captaincy with the Samuel Barker Shipping Company.

He'd earned the berth the hard way, as had so many American sailors. He'd toiled at the shipyard since he was eleven,
squeezing in hours of reading at night. His father had always
told him he would never succeed without education.

His father would have been proud. But not proud enough.
Gabriel had not yet fulfilled the vow he'd made.

The piece of parchment his father had given him two
decades ago had gone around the globe with him. One day he
would bury it at his father's grave, but only after he'd accomplished his father's charge.

Gabriel had one of two things he needed to carry out a plan
he'd been formulating for years. The war with England had
interfered temporarily, but now this title would give him the
entrée he needed.

But he needed more funds. He'd handed back prizes to the
American government, which had been in dire need of funds.
He had saved most of his life and had accumulated nearly
twenty thousand pounds, but he suspected it would be less
than what he needed.

He'd expected to have several more years to exact justice,
but the title wouldn't wait. If he didn't claim it, according to
the barrister, a distant cousin was next in line.

He hadn't meant for this news to be his homecoming to
Boston.

But the letter had awaited him at the office of a solicitor.
And now he had to tell Samuel, the man who had hired him,
taught him, even fathered him to a certain degree.

He knocked and the door opened immediately.

"So you have returned in one piece," Samuel Barker,

owner of Samuel Barker Shipping Company, said as he clasped his hand with unusual warmth. "Gabriel, I am glad to have you back. You worried me, my boy. I heard about the chances you took." He smiled as broadly as his New England heritage allowed. "I have that command and a part ownership in the company ready for you. I've had the papers drawn."

A knife sliced through Gabriel. He knew a command was his. Samuel had talked about it for several years. He had not known about a part ownership in the company. It had been a dream, not reality.

Gabriel handed the letter he'd received from England to Samuel, who read it quickly, then searched Gabriel's face. "What are you going to do?"

"I have to return to England," Gabriel said. "I have to clear my father's name."

"I cannot postpone the sailing of the *Cecilia* to Japan. It must leave in two weeks."

"John Garrett, my first mate, is available and qualified to captain her," Gabriel said, the knife turning ever so painfully. But he had no choice. A voyage to Japan would take months. He could not wait that long.

"Do you plan to stay in England?" Samuel asked.

"I have no desire to make it my home."

Barker nodded. He knew something of Gabriel's background. Gabriel had told him during a drunken conversation years ago. "I do not want to lose you. I missed you this past year, but your record is outstanding. You will be of great benefit to this firm."

Samuel strode to the window of his office that overlooked the Boston harbor. "I'll give the *Cecilia* to Garrett for this voyage. And find a ship for you when you return."

Gabriel swallowed hard. Samuel had become a second father to him these last ten years. Now he saw the disappointment on the man's face. He'd been so uncharacteristically eager to relate the news.

Yet Gabriel knew he could never really proceed with his life until he had accomplished the one thing his father had requested—no, bade—him to do. And now he'd been handed the means through which he could accomplish it. He could not give up this one chance.

Samuel turned to him. "Do you need money?"

"No, I have prize money left."

"If you need anything . . ."

"Only your friendship."

"You will always have that, Gabriel. I never had a son. If I did, I would want him to be like you."

*No, he wouldn't. He wouldn't want a son of his blood to be obsessed with revenge.* Not revenge, he reminded himself. *Justice.* Yet he knew the difference, and the recurring nightmare of that night so long ago made it revenge.

He felt humbled by Samuel's faith, and yet even that would not deter him.

"Do what you have to do, and return to us," Samuel said.

Gabriel nodded and left the room, feeling the affection following him. But he wouldn't dwell on it. He had too many other things to do.

He would need more funds, and he would not take them from Samuel. He knew exactly the man who could help him.

The best thief in Boston.

## Paris
## *1815*

"It's so dangerous, *ma chère amie*."

"I know," Monique said, "but I will never rest until I meet him. And destroy him."

Monique Fremont applied the final touches of theatrical paint for her last performance in France as Danielle, her friend and hairdresser, completed the elaborate coiffure, which took two hours to complete.

Monique bore the ritual patiently. Tomorrow she would begin a new performance, one she'd planned for years. The masquerade would begin in earnest and end, she prayed, in a denouement that would destroy an English earl.

She'd had an excellent offer from an English theatrical

company in London. It was an offer she'd hungered after, and, more importantly, it was the means to an end.

When Danielle finished positioning the last of the cascading curls and nodded with satisfaction, Monique took one last look in the mirror. She adjusted the dress, which just barely covered her nipples.

No sign of Merry Anders remained. No sign of the thin waif who'd taken care of her mother after her beauty faded and her protectors disappeared. No sign of the English child who had taken the name of Monique Fremont when she'd entered the theater.

She wondered whether she resembled her father at all. Her mother said not. Monique prayed not, for that might ruin everything.

She did look like her mother. Black hair. Gray eyes that her mother's lovers had called luminous. She was taller, her mouth wider, her cheekbones not as pronounced. Her chin was more determined.

Her mother had once been a classic beauty. On the other hand, Merry had been called "fascinating" rather than pretty. It had not been her looks, she knew, that had made her one of Paris's most famous actresses. It was her vitality, critics proclaimed, the way she projected herself that made beauties beside her look pale and dull. One critic said she was radiant with life.

They didn't know it was not life.

It was the need for revenge.

Those same scribes had been moaning because she had accepted an offer to join a theater in London. How could she possibly leave French connoisseurs for English bores who could never appreciate the subtleties of her performances, the wit that crouched within every word?

The house was a sell-out tonight. Every hopeful suitor would be in attendance as well as the older cavaliers who had tried so hard to seduce her. She'd had more offers than she could count from would-be "protectors."

No one would suspect that the worldly Monique Fremont, who had appeared from virtually nowhere, was still a virgin, that she looked upon most men as fools and the others as libertines. It was an opinion honestly reached after watching a series of protectors use, then discard, her mother.

No one she had met in Paris had changed that opinion. She saw lust, not love, in their eyes despite their declarations. She saw greed and jealousy and arrogance and condescension and stupidity.

And she'd earned the title of Ice Queen because she'd fended off so many proposals. She knew that most supposed she had a secret lover or a tragic lost love. It certainly couldn't be the admirers' own lack of attractiveness.

Though she had not consciously intended it, her wariness of men had protected her these past years. The mystery surrounding her had drawn reluctant respect and made her appear even more desirable.

Men always wanted what they couldn't have. Women, on the other hand, managed on what they *did* have.

She'd never heard her mother complain, or yearn for a different life. What was, was.

Monique had a completely different philosophy, developed through years of staving off her mother's protectors and learning the tricks of a thief during those lean times her mother had no one but her.

It hadn't been until one of her mother's "friends" saw her mimic several famous personalities that she had been trained and nurtured as an actress, first as a bit player, then as an ingenue, and finally as a leading lady.

But her mother never lived to see that triumph. She'd died of consumption four years earlier, having never seen London again, as she'd longed to do. Lack of money—and fear—always stopped her. She'd lived in fear, in truth, which was mainly why she had taken protectors, each succeeding one a little less attractive, a little less generous, a little less kind.

Men had used her all her life, yet she'd still hoped for her knight to appear.

In Monique's opinion there were no knights to be found. She'd decided long ago that a woman must make her own way, determine her own future, and never, ever, depend on a man. After her mother's death, Monique saved most of her earnings, choosing to live in small but safe lodgings and investing in English ventures through an *avocat*. She didn't trust French investments. French politics were too volatile.

"There, " Dani said. "You look *magnifique*."

"*Merci,*" Monique said, knowing that she must stop thinking of herself as Merry Anders. She must be Monique Fremont through and through. "We will leave immediately after the performance."

"*Oui,* all is ready. The coach will be waiting."

Monique nodded, then looked closely. "Are you sure you want to go with me? It could be dangerous."

"I am sure," Dani said in accented English. "I've been practicing my *Anglais*."

Monique had her reservations about thrusting Dani into harm's way, but the young woman had served as maid, dresser, friend, and confidant for seven years. They had met when Dani, a slight fourteen-year-old thief, was caught picking pockets inside a theater. She looked starved, abused, and terrified. Monique had convinced the theater owner not to turn her in to the police and had asked her if she'd wanted a position. Dani had been reluctant, obviously expecting Monique to take advantage of her in some way. In the end, Monique had employed her and taken her under her protection, teaching her to read and write and then to speak well.

It had taken months to earn her trust, but Dani eventually told her that she had been raped repeatedly by her stepfather and that she'd fled to the streets and joined a group of young thieves, stealing to survive.

Over the next seven years, they had become friends as well as mistress and servant. Slowly, over time, Monique had told Dani of her own dismal background and some of her plans.

Dani had no intention of being left behind. She had skills that might be helpful.

A knock came at the door five minutes before she was to go on stage. Dani straightened out the wrinkles in Monique's costume, an indigo-blue gown that highlighted her gray eyes and flattered her less-than-rounded body.

She took one last glance in the mirror. Her cheeks hadn't needed paint. They were already flushed from anticipation.

One life would be ending and another beginning. At long last she had the money, influence, and reputation to repay a debt.

She lifted her cheek and glided out the door Dani held open to the standing appiause of an overbooked house.

# Chapter Two

## London

Gabriel stood on deck of the ship as it wended its way down the Thames. The first buildings of London loomed before him.

*London.*

Good memories. Ugly memories.

Unfortunately, the latter overshadowed the former.

Captain Adams strolled over to him as the ship passed. "Remember anything?"

"Some," Gabriel replied neutrally. Adams knew he had been a boy here. Little else. He didn't know about the scandal or the pain that followed it. To Adams, he was the representative of an important Boston shipping company.

"I enjoyed having you aboard."

Gabriel nodded. It wasn't a compliment. It was a duty. Gabriel was known to be a favorite of Samuel Barker, the owner of this ship, and Gabriel hadn't been the world's most compatible companion. He'd been preoccupied and impatient.

"I thank you for the courtesy you've shown me," he said. "It has been a pleasant voyage."

And except for the reason he was making the voyage, it

had been. The summer weather had held, the seas had been calm, the wind fair. They had made record time.

Unfortunately, he'd not been in the mood to enjoy it.

Instead, he had prowled along the decks at night and sharpened his newly honed skills in his cabin.

He could open any door with a picklock. He played at opening locks constantly, as well as practicing sleight of hand.

Riley, an Irishman who now owned his own disreputable tavern on the Boston waterfront, had taught him the finer points of being a gentleman thief, including disguises and opening safes. He'd also taught him to climb the walls of buildings, something that came easily to a sailor.

Gabriel watched as the anchor dropped, and a boat was lowered to take the captain into London. Once the formalities were through, he planned to visit the solicitor who had contacted him. He would find out from him how to insinuate himself into the ton.

And whether an American, even with a British title, would be welcome.

But he already knew he would be received where he wanted most to be received. He knew the arrogance of his opponents. He had engaged a solicitor before the war to work with a counterpart in London to obtain information. The London solicitor had given him a very lengthy report on the three men who interested him.

They were all on the fringes of the ton. Not quite accepted, yet tolerated because of their titles and pedigree. And power. No one knew the exact source of their power or their wealth. The solicitor added that any queries into their business were squelched and that those who openly spoke against them recanted or disappeared. Their fellow peers feared them. No one dared touch them.

Only one was currently married. Another—the Earl of Stanhope—was a widower twice over, and rumor had it that he'd killed at least one wife.

Gabriel would feel no hesitation in bringing these men down.

His title would admit him to many homes. Others wouldn't

resist the temptation to host an American barbarian. At the very least, he would prove a curiosity to the jaded members of society.

They had no idea of how much of a barbarian he was.

Paul Lynch, the manager of the London theater group that had lured Monique there, had been waiting on the dock as she disembarked from one of the smaller ships. Others, she noticed, anchored along the river, dependent on longboats to take crew and passengers ashore.

Dani followed her with a hatbox. A seaman easily carried her heavy trunk.

She turned back to the sea. A ship under an American flag was anchoring not far from them. Her gaze swept over the deck, skimming past a man at the rail, then returning to him.

His hands were clasped behind him, a stance she associated with captains and officers, yet he wore no uniform. Not even a coat despite the cold wind sweeping the harbor.

Instead, he was clad in only a shirt that billowed out in the wind. His dark blond hair was short and windblown, his stance tall and straight with confidence. She couldn't see the color of his eyes from where she stood but for some reason she thought they would be green.

*Ridiculous thought.* She wasn't even sure why he'd captured her attention. Yet even as she turned to her escort, the figure remained in her mind.

Lynch offered her his arm. "Mademoiselle, you will not regret making this decision."

He was a pompous man with an unctuous air. Yet he operated one of the most successful theaters in London, second only, she'd heard, to the famous Drury Lane Theater.

She gave him a smile. *"Merci."*

"We will begin rehearsals on a new play tomorrow," he said. "We have been waiting for you."

"I look forward to returning to work," she said in the unaccented English she'd perfected.

He looked pleased. "I will have the carriage at your residence at noon tomorrow. Perhaps you would have a late supper with me this evening?" he added hopefully.

*"Merci,"* she said. "But I am very tired." She saw the disappointment in his eyes. "But tomorrow, *oui*." She inwardly winced at the sudden gleam in his eyes. She didn't want an admirer in the manager of the theater. He was her employer. She didn't want any complications. But she did want information about the theater's clientele and about Thomas Kane, the Earl of Stanhope.

Lynch offered his arm, and she accepted it. The carriage was a public one. The driver jumped down from the box to help the seaman tie down her trunk on the carriage roof.

Lynch held the door open and offered assistance first to Monique, then to Dani. "I will take you to your rooms. I'm sure you will be pleased with them." Acceptable lodgings had been part of her contract.

"And the schedule, monsieur?"

"We will have rehearsals for three weeks and then the opening. It is an amusing play," he said quickly.

"I read it," she said. "I agree with you."

He seemed to slump with relief. "It is a farce. We are not licensed by the Crown to perform drama, but I hope to change that. If this play is successful, then I will apply for a license."

"The Prince of Wales—Prinnie—will be in London when we open," Lynch continued. "He has remarked to friends that he looked forward to your arrival. Your fame precedes you here," he said, his hand touching her skirt.

In minutes, it would be up her skirt. She moved away and gave Lynch a stare that had quelled greater men.

His gaze dropped. "I hope you will think of me and the other members of the company as your family."

"I'm sure I will," she said, knowing she would do no such thing. She planned to keep to herself until she made the acquaintance of Stanhope. No tinge of scandal could touch her.

She had to be the unobtainable Ice Queen. Stanhope, according to her sources, always wanted what he couldn't have. The longer he couldn't have it, the more obsessive he became.

Monique knew she had to be careful. Her mother had called him a very dangerous man. He had tried to kill her mother, then had hunted her like an animal after she had escaped him. If he discovered Monique's true identity, he might well try to do the same to her.

She peered out at the shops and town houses as the carriage clattered through busy streets. She had never been to London, though her mother had often spoken wistfully of it and of several cousins who had helped her escape it. Monique had vowed to try to find them and give them help if they were in need, but they could never know who she was, not until Stanhope was either in prison or dead.

*Stanhope.* Her father.

"We are nearing the theater," Lynch said. "I thought you might like to see it before going to your rooms."

She would be expected to be interested, and she made the suitable exclamations. But what she really wanted to know was the location of Stanhope's residence, the clubs he attended, and the identity of his acquaintances.

She decided to ask. "A friend of mine in Paris said I should look up the Earl of Stanhope."

The smile left Lynch's face. "He is one to stay away from, mademoiselle," he said.

"I am surprised at that," she said. "My friend told me that he was most generous."

Lynch paused, as if reluctant to say more. Then, "There will be many men who will be standing in line for moments of your time. Wealthy, well-placed gentlemen. I can help you make wise decisions."

"Ah la," she said, taking a fan from her reticule where she also carried a handkerchief as well as some coins. She opened the hand-painted Brise fan. "You are making him sound very dangerous. And interesting. I want you to send him several tickets for the new play."

"Mademoiselle Fremon. . . ."

"Monique," she said. "Please call me Monique. There should be no formalities between friends, and we will be friends, *oui?*"

"I truly hope so," Lynch said, his hand back on her lap.

"Then I must really insist that you send the earl an invitation."

Her employer muttered to himself.

"What was that, monsieur?"

"I will do as you wish, but please consider my warning. Stanhope is not an admired man."

She blessed him with a smile, then returned to the subject much on her mind. "Are there places of entertainment where I can meet interesting people?"

His sharp glance studied her. "Interesting or dangerous?"

She fluttered the fan again. "Both."

"I wish to protect my investment in you," he said in a plaintive voice.

"Monsieur, I am twenty-five years old. I have worked for my living since I was seven. I have a small pistol and I know how to use it."

His face went white. "A scandal . . ."

"A scandal would increase your attendance," she replied easily. "Now where might Lord Stanhope go for a nightly entertainment, or would you not know?"

"I would not." It was obvious he felt affronted that his advice was not being given due consideration. "I think it is only right that I tell you there are rumors surrounding Stanhope. Some say he killed his wife."

"I am not his wife, nor am I interested in his protection. We merely have a mutual friend. No more, and la, you worry too much, Mr. Lynch, though it is rather sweet."

She touched his cheek playfully with her fan.

The carriage drew up to a narrow town house across from a park.

Lynch looked at her nervously as she stepped down from the interior. "It is not large, but the rooms are charming. I am leasing them from a lord who kept his . . ." He stopped suddenly.

"Mistress," she finished for him. "Is that correct?"

"Yes."

"You do not have to be embarrassed. I am French," she reminded him. "I am certainly aware of such arrangements."

He released a long breath of air, and she suddenly realized he feared she would be insulted.

She needed someone on her side, someone who could help

if she got in trouble. "It looks very pleasant," she said. "I appreciate your assistance."

"We want you to be happy." He paused. "How is it you speak English so well? Almost without an accent?"

She'd known that question was coming. "I am an actress," she explained. "I must be able to mimic many accents."

"Our audiences will be charmed. We have many French here."

"I know," she said sadly. "It is so . . . triste that they have lost their homeland. But now that Napoleon is defeated, perhaps they can return home."

"Perhaps you, too, will choose to make your home here."

"Perhaps," she said.

"I heard that Napoleon attended your performances."

"*Oui,* he came to see me perform several times. A little man, yet there was something about him . . ."

Before they reached the door of the town house, a small but very straight woman opened it and curtsied. "I have been expecting you, miss," she said. "I'm Harriett Miller, the housekeeper. Everything is ready for your arrival. I hope it meets with your satisfaction."

Her back was stiff, her expression neutral. It was obvious she didn't know what to expect, or if she would even be allowed to keep her position.

Monique gave her a quick smile. "I'm sure everything will be fine," she said. "There's just my maid, Dani, and myself. We are not very demanding."

The smile apparently lifted a burden from Mrs. Miller, because her shoulders relaxed. Her expression didn't change, and Monique wondered whether she disapproved of serving an actress or a French woman, or a combination of both.

Actresses were admired and even invited to grand events. But the admiration stopped short of total acceptance. Most were considered loose and a definite threat to women whose husbands were wont to stray.

"Would you like to inspect the rooms?" Harriett Miller asked.

"*Oui,*" she said.

The town house was small, yet the decor exceeded her expectations. The rooms had a tranquility to them; the furniture looked comfortable and flowers filled vases throughout. Her bedroom was decorated in shades of rose, light and pretty and feminine. A room to the side featured an unusually large tub. A gift from a lord to his mistress? Regardless, she eyed it with delight.

She returned downstairs, where Lynch was waiting for her.

"You were right," she said. "It is perfect."

"Then I will leave you to get rest," he said. "I am told Mrs. Miller is a fine cook. A carriage will pick you up at twelve to meet the rest of the cast and to read through the play. Then later . . ."

He bowed and left the "then later" to her imagination.

Soon after, she had replaced her tightly laced corset and heavy dress with a dressing gown.

Dani served the tea Mrs. Miller had prepared and sat down with her mistress.

"And now it begins," she said.

"*Oui,*" Monique agreed. "Tomorrow morning, we will go shopping for some new gowns. Dressmakers are notorious gossips. Perhaps we can find out establishments frequented by the Earl of Stanhope. I do not wish to wait until the play opens to do so. I also want to know who his friends are—if he has any."

"I will talk to Mrs. Miller and other servants in the houses around us," Dani said.

"Be very careful," Monique warned her. "I would never forgive myself if something happened to you."

"I am just a maid," Dani said. "No one even sees me."

"I don't think that's quite right," Monique said. Dani could be a real beauty if she tried. Her hair was a soft copper and her eyes a cool blue, but she pulled the former back in an unflattering knot and wore spectacles to shade the pain in those eyes.

Her loose, almost dowdy clothes hid a fine body. Like Monique, she was wary of men. Even under Monique's protection, she felt vulnerable. She'd been used as a child. She didn't intend to be used as an adult.

Dani met her gaze. "We can still go back," she said. "It is

your . . . papa. Perhaps it is better that you leave the past as it is."

"I cannot, Dani. He tried to destroy my mother, then kill both of us. I could never come back here as who I am if he's still alive, and I hunger to know England. My mother loved it so . . ."

"Then I am with you," Dani said. "Tomorrow, we begin."

Monique nodded. Since that afternoon, another image had intertwined with her reasons for wanting to remain in England. Inexplicably, the gentleman aboard the American ship had remained in her thoughts, the picture of him so clearly outlined in her mind. But she would not mention him to Dani. That would make him too important.

And he *wasn't* important. She was not interested in romantic nonsense. She'd had no more than a fleeting glance at him and probably would never get another one.

But why did the image linger inside her? Why had it made an impact? Fate?

Ridiculous. She didn't believe in fate.

## London

Gabriel grew impatient as the *Cynthia*'s crew waited for their turn to dock and unload.

He'd thought about taking one of the tenders to shore but the man he was about to become wouldn't do that.

So he paced the deck, wondering about the men he would soon meet. Would they recognize him? His name?

He looked down at his clothes, the shirt and breeches, and knew he needed to go below and dress. The new marquess would never wear such informal clothes. No, he would be a peacock, a strutting American impressed with his new status.

As he waited, his mind wandered back to several hours earlier when he'd watched passengers disembark from another ship. One was a woman dressed in a ruby-red gown with a flamboyant hat designed to attract attention. He couldn't turn away as she was met by a gentleman, then as she'd turned to gaze out at the harbor.

It was almost as if their gazes had met, though he knew that was impossible. The distance was too great. And because a bonnet had shaded part of her face, he couldn't make out much of her features other than an overall impression of vitality and assurance.

He liked confidence in a woman. He always had. He was not attracted by artful giggles or coy helplessness. But because he was committed to the task his father had set for him, he had not allowed himself the luxury of a courtship, much less marriage. It wouldn't have been fair.

It had never bothered him. But now . . .

He'd been oddly struck by a longing so strong and deep—and unexpected—that it was a body blow. It had rolled over him like waves and even at that distance he'd felt a need to find her. To look into her eyes and try to fathom why his body felt warm and . . .

The woman had turned and the moment had gone. He would probably never see her again. He probably wouldn't recognize her if he did.

But he knew that was a lie. He would recognize that assurance anywhere.

Damn, he didn't need a distraction, especially not a momentary whimsy.

He went below to his cabin. He would be a different man when he emerged again.

Gabriel rented a carriage and left for his solicitor's office. His belongings would stay aboard ship until he decided where to have them sent.

He had not informed the solicitor, Reginald Pickwick, that he planned to make the trip to London. Pickwick was the son of the man who had betrayed his father, just as three peers of the realm had. It was ironic, he thought, that Pickwick, father and son, had remained employed by the Manning family despite the fact the firm had been at least partly responsible for the scandal thirty years ago.

He wondered if this Pickwick was still associated with Stanhope and his friends.

Probably.

*Scoundrels hung together.* Now he would like to see them hang individually.

He had the address on the missive he'd received, informing him—quite curtly—that he was heir to the title of Marquess of Manchester. It had gone on to say the estate was bankrupt, but the property was entailed. He would be pleased to lease the property and pay off the debts. No need for Gabriel Manning to make the voyage.

But the title was the one thing Gabriel wanted. And so was a look on the face of the man who tried to persuade him not to leave America.

He reached the solicitor's office and stood outside for a moment. Gabriel's suit was ill-fitting and not in the best of taste, but obviously made of expensive cloth. He wore gloves and carried a cane.

He looked, he hoped, like a lout with more money than taste. And sense.

Gabriel used the cane to rap on the door. An arrogant, impatient rap.

A man he assumed was a clerk opened it.

Gabriel had the letter in his hand. "I am the Marquess of Manchester," he said. "I wish to see this Pickwick."

The man frowned at the obvious condescension. "He is busy."

"He is busy, *my lord,*" Gabriel corrected. "I wish to see him to claim my rightful inheritance."

The haggard looking clerk continued to stand there.

Gabriel pushed him aside and stepped into the hallway. He waited until the man closed the door. "Please announce me."

"He . . . he is busy," the clerk said again.

"I would think a marquess would be an important matter."

"Ah . . . this is very unusual, but I will ask him."

Several minutes later he was ushered into an office. Reginald Pickwick rose from behind a suspiciously clear desk.

He was probably fifteen years older than Gabriel, which would make him approximately forty-eight. He would have been a young man when Richard Manning had killed himself. He'd probably clerked or been a partner in this very office. Gabriel wondered what happened to the elder Pickwick.

Curiosity wouldn't help his role at this point.

There didn't seem to be anyone with him. Gabriel refrained from mentioning the obvious. Empty desk. No client.

Gabriel flopped down in a chair without invitation. He folded his legs as the solicitor eyed him with barely restrained contempt.

Which was just fine with Gabriel. He wanted the solicitor to think him an American bumpkin. Even more, he wanted the solicitor to pass on the information to the men who would think they could use him as they had used his father.

"I want to see the estate," he said.

"It is in sad repair, and there are no funds," the solicitor said. "I thought I had made that clear in the letter." He looked down his very long nose and sniffed as if he smelled something not to his liking.

Gabriel grinned at him, chafing at the discomfort of the ill-fitting mismatched suit he'd purchased in Boston for just this occasion. But it was obviously making the impression he wanted to make.

"Ah," he said, "but I have funds of my own, and, now that I am a peer of your illustrious country, which, I might add, has just been defeated by mine, I plan to make my way in society. Perhaps even make a marriage. I am told English gels admire titles. Even empty ones." He made sure arrogance laced every word.

Pickwick's throat wobbled with indignation. Finally he found words. "What is your business?"

He studiously avoided the words, *my lord,* Gabriel noticed.

"Commerce, my good fellow. I am in commerce, but now I intend to stay here and marry a fortune. You would not know of any good investments while I seek a bride, would you?"

A vein fluttered in the man's neck.

Gabriel took some pleasure in that. Pickwick was sweating. And in a cold room. Why?

"I take it I now have the title?"

"It came to you on the death of your cousin," Pickwick said. "Your father's family had no other male heir."

"No gels, either?"

"A few daughters. Your cousins. They married well. They

were mentioned in the will, but the title and house are entailed; they go to the next male heir." He leaned forward. "Your grandfather always meant to disown your father, but the entailment is very clear and he could not find a legal means of accomplishing it."

Gabriel grinned. "It is official, then?" he asked with mock ingenuousness. "You get to call me 'my lord.'"

Pickwick looked as if he were being forced to drink poison.

"I would like to hear it," Gabriel demanded, inwardly telling himself not to overplay his hand.

"My lord," Pickwick repeated obediently in a choked voice.

"Now that sounds mighty good." Gabriel stretched his legs out.

Pickwick swallowed, then, obviously trying to control himself, said, "I can try to let the estate. I have been making inquiries. I had thought to save you a voyage. I never thought you would wish to return . . ."

Gabriel drew his brows together. "I don't know why."

"Your father. Many still remember him," Pickwick said. "They may not welcome you. He was seen as . . . a traitor."

"Did they shun my uncles?"

"No, but—"

"Then why should I be penalized for something my father did?"

Pickwick squirmed in his chair. "I am just advising you that you may wish to make provisions for the property, and return to your business. You would have some income."

"I thought I had explained. I don't need income, and I rather fancy being a lord. I will stay at the Polten for the next few days, but I will need your help in finding more permanent lodgings in London as well as a tailor. Perhaps some gaming clubs. Most certainly introductions."

The man's face paled.

"I will make it worth your time."

"Why?"

Gabriel gave him another blank look.

"You would have your title, whether or not you live in America, and I understand the colonies appreciate a title."

"They are not the colonies any longer," Gabriel replied. "And they are not very fond of the British right now. Difficult to believe I am one of you." He kept his tone light. In truth, he'd been less fond than most, and that was saying a great deal.

"Your father . . ."

"I hardly remember him."

"I do," Pickwick said, watching him closely. "He came to our house several times."

It took all Gabriel's willpower to maintain his casual pose. He shrugged. "It happened a long time ago."

"What do you know about what happened?"

"Only that my father killed himself and we left London."

"Your mother told you nothing of your father's . . . ?"

Gabriel kept his expression bland. "She didn't speak of him."

"Is there any way I can convince you to leave England?"

"No," Gabriel said. "I intend to take my place here. It is my birthright," he continued pompously. "Will you give me the assistance I need or should I find a new solicitor?"

"Have you ever been to a gaming hell?"

"I've gamed."

"That is not what I mean. Stakes are high in London's clubs. You will be laughed out of London if you can't match their wagers. And God help you if you do not pay your debts."

"We do play cards across the sea," Gabriel boasted. "I win quite frequently."

Pickwick looked skeptical, but Gabriel saw the beginning of a gleam in his eyes. The implication of unlimited money was beginning to overtake his distaste for his client. Some of the contempt had faded in his eyes, replaced by greed he tried not to show.

The bait had been taken. "You will find me suitable lodgings of good address. Within five days. No more. And I would like to go gaming tonight. Would you arrange my admittance to the suitable clubs?"

"That might take some time."

"Then some 'hells,' I understand you call them."

"I will try to arrange something," Pickwick said.

"Now that's what I expected. I will be here at eight."

He rose without giving Pickwick more time to reconsider. "I will let myself out. We can finish our business later. I expect to hear of several possible town properties tonight."

"But . . ."

"I feel sure you are up to the task."

He opened the door and smiled at the stuttering behind him.

# Chapter Three

The interior of the building was dark and hummed with the sound of quiet muffled voices. A haze of smoke clouded the figures sitting around tables or standing in small groups.

Monique paused in the door of the club, the theater manager on her arm.

It had taken all her powers of persuasion to convince him to bring her after they had finished the first rehearsal earlier this afternoon.

This was, she'd been told, one of London's most notorious gaming hells. Titled gentlemen attended, but they were usually men who had been refused entrance for one reason or another at the more respectable clubs. Women were admitted, but "decent women" wouldn't consider stepping inside.

She was an actress and as such did not need to care about "decent."

She wore a dress that came close to being scandalous. It was a dark blue velvet which barely contained her breasts.

Lynch had protested at first. But after a rehearsal that had delighted him and a supper during which she urged wine upon him, he had finally agreed to take her to one of the city's many gaming establishments.

And though he claimed reluctance, it was obvious he did

not object.to having her on his arm. She knew, though, that she would have to use all her diplomatic powers to fend him off tonight.

One face peered up. Startled. Then more faces turned toward her, as if a wave swept through the room. Voices stopped. Several chairs toppled as their occupants suddenly stood.

She stood as the center of attention, allowing glances to wander over her dress, her face. She smiled slightly, then turned to Lynch. "I think I would like to play a game of chance."

He stood like a man struck dumb.

"Mr. Lynch?" she chided gently.

Before he could respond, several men approached, their faces showing a variety of expressions. Curiosity. Interest. Lust. She looked for someone nearing fifty, a man with dark eyes.

It would be too much luck to find him here, she thought. *Be patient.*

But her name would be on many lips on the morrow, and that was what she wanted.

"Lynch," one of the men said. "You sly fellow. Who is this vision?"

Lynch's eyes brightened. "This is the newest addition to our company, the celebrated Monique Fremont. She will be starring in our next play. Mademoiselle Fremont, I have the honor to present Lord James Sutcliff, Sir Jonathon Kyler, and Mr. Thomas Bryden."

They crowded closer, each extending extravagant compliments and undressing her with lustful eyes.

But then by being here, she was proclaiming her availability.

Sutcliff was obviously the youngest, a gay young blade several years younger than she, and obviously wealthy, handsome, and all too confident. Kyler was older, probably close to fifty, with a paunch and a face marked by veins that proclaimed him a heavy drinker. The third, Bryden, was the most interesting. Polite, watchful.

"France's loss is our gain," Bryden said. "I have heard of you."

"I am flattered, monsieur."

"I understand that you met Napoleon," he added.

"*Oui*. He is a man like any other," she said, noting the serious glint in his eyes. Admiration and something else. And how did he know about her acquaintance—such as it was—with Napoleon?

Sutcliff's gaze had undressed every inch of her and was now centered at the point where her dress covered her left nipple. Just barely. "London is indeed graced," he said. "And we are doubly honored that you would visit this establishment. Are you interested in the cards?"

"*Oui*," she said. "Very much. Monsieur Lynch told me the very finest players are patrons here."

"Whist? Hazard? Which is your game?"

"Faro," she said with a smile, watching as eyebrows arched.

"I would be pleased to stake you," Sutcliff said.

"Thank you, but I can stake myself," she said.

He looked startled, as if unused to refusals.

Bryden smiled. "That must be a first, my lord," he said.

Sutcliff looked crestfallen, then a smile returned. "I will bet on your wagers, then, mademoiselle. I know you will bring me luck, and it's been deucedly poor lately."

"If you wish," she said with cool indifference. Her gaze circled the room, pausing to study each player, either sitting at a table or standing around a wheel. She wondered whether any one of them was her father. But that would be too much luck. Right now, she wanted to announce her presence in London and initiate talk about the famed and mysterious actress who spurned potential lovers.

If everything she'd heard about him was correct, he would seek her out.

Sutcliff offered her his arm.

She gave him her brightest smile, then turned to the theater manager and took his arm. "Monsieur Lynch," she said with a deep chuckle, "is my protector tonight. I am new in your city, and I am not quite sure of your rules."

"I will be honored to teach you," the third man—Kyler, she remembered—said. "Supper, some evening."

"*Merci*, but Mr. Lynch said he intends to keep me very busy with rehearsals. Perhaps you will attend one of the performances."

She swept past them to the faro table, leaving the three men looking thunderstruck.

The play had started.


In the wee hours of his second day in London, Gabriel continued to throw away money at various gambling hells he insisted that Pickwick introduce to him.

He wanted to appear the fool, and he was sure he did. He was loud, boastful, and a poor loser.

He made sure everyone knew he was a marquess.

He wore a cravat not quite tied properly, a waistcoat in a shade too bright a blue, outdated knee breeches and a wig he knew had gone out of fashion. Tonight—as he had last night—he looked to be a man trying to appear a gentleman, and failing. He openly boasted about his title and wealth and drew contempt at every stop.

Pickwick had managed to get him into one of the less prestigious of the men's clubs, but after an hour of losing he turned to Pickwick, speaking loudly. "Do you not know of a place where a gentleman can win?" It was a clear implication, and horrified faces—none more so than Mr. Pickwick's—glared at him.

Once outside, he turned on his host for the evening. "Dull and stuffy," he said. "Do you not know of something more . . . entertaining?"

And thus they started the second night of roaming gambling hells. Pickwick didn't gamble. He stood in the shadows, obviously trying to disassociate himself as much as possible from his loud companion. It was obvious he hated every moment, but greed overtook distaste.

Gabriel had planned carefully. He knew exactly how much he would risk. He wanted to do it in the first few days.

Once his reputation as an oaf was made, no one would realize he was making steady gains.

*He was a bloody good gambler.*

But after visiting one club and two gambling hells last night, and three more this night, he'd lost nearly three thousand pounds and hadn't yet met the men he wished. He'd hoped that Pickwick would know their haunts and lead him to one. But thus far, no luck. Yet he knew he couldn't ask Pickwick to arrange a meeting. That would be a warning to someone who had gotten away with thievery and treason for more than twenty years.

They had to come to him.

Steal from the father; why not steal from the son? Gabriel thought that might be an attractive prospect for someone as arrogant and larcenous as he had been told Stanhope was.

It was in the wee hours of the morning when he and Pickwick arrived at the last of the gambling hells he intended to frequent this night.

They emerged from a carriage as two people departed from the entrance of yet another club.

One of the two was a woman. He hadn't seen another woman in the establishments he'd frequented, but he supposed it was not that odd. A courtesan, perhaps even a rebellious daughter of a member of the ton.

But as his gaze riveted on her, a shock ran through him.

She was striking. Dark hair framed a face that could never be dismissed lightly. Her gaze met his. In the soft glow cast by a gaslight above, he saw gray eyes widen as if she recognized him.

They had never met. Yet he would swear she was the woman he'd watch disembark from the French ship.

He stepped forward and bowed, "Miss . . . ?"

The man at her side tried to hustle her along. She halted and tilted her head in question. "Do I know you, monsieur?" she asked.

"No, " he said. "Though—"

"Then I ask you to step aside." Her companion inserted himself between him and the lady. Since Gabriel was at least half a foot taller and a good deal more muscular, it was an act of courage.

"I did not mean to intrude," he said.

Her lashes fluttered for a moment as if she was confused, but nothing else about her showed indecision.

He couldn't help staring at her, wondering what there was about her that had captured his attention as no other woman had.

*Do not forget why you are in London.*

But wasn't staring and being a bore exactly what he should be doing?

Trouble was, it wasn't an act.

Damn it, why did he feel like a schoolboy with his first crush? She was a woman, nothing more, and quite obviously not a lady if she was emerging from a gambling hell.

Yet she appeared the epitome of what he felt a lady should be, her body carried with an elegance and grace that couldn't be feigned. Her chin was high, and her eyes danced with life.

*Who was she?*

A bore would ask. But he discovered he didn't want to be a bore. Not with her.

*Play your role. One slip and you might well fail.*

"Monsieur?"

"I am the Marquess of Manchester," he said, bowing again, suddenly wishing he was better dressed. He looked like a peacock.

"How nice for you," she said, but her eyes were curious, as if she saw beneath the pose.

"And you are . . ."

At the mention of his title, the thin little man next to her dropped some of his hostility.

"Monique Fremont," he said. "She will be the star of my next production at the new theater on Charles Street. I am Mr. Lynch, the manager of the company."

An actress. He found his breath returning to him. So that was why she had such presence. And why she dared enter a hell patronized totally by men.

"My pleasure," he said. "I will be at the first performance."

"You had better hurry to obtain seats," her companion said. "The play should sell out quickly."

"I can understand why," Gabriel said, his gaze fastened on

the woman again. She wore a loose gray cloak, but even so he could see the swell of her breasts.

He couldn't help but study her face more closely. Not beautiful. But very arresting with the angular bones and wide mouth and great gray eyes. It wasn't the physical appearance that fascinated him so much as the amusement in her eyes and the blinding smile that suddenly lit her face.

A hand tugged at his sleeve, reminding him of his reluctant companion. "My solicitor, Mr. Pickwick," he finally said.

Pickwick bowed with an awkward eagerness that seemed totally out of character. He'd been complaining all evening, and now he was practically beaming.

Did the woman do that to everyone? He didn't want to think so. He wanted to believe that smile was meant for him alone.

But then she turned away, and she and her companion entered a carriage. It clattered down the street, leaving him and his companion standing alone.

"A fine looking woman," he said.

Pickwick seemed transfixed. "Yes," he said.

"But just a woman," Gabriel added, knowing he was trying to convince himself.

"I think not," Pickwick said soberly. "A woman like that is trouble."

Monique didn't understand the heat that suddenly coursed through her body when the odd marquess accosted her.

He had been far too familiar, far too bold, and he looked a wastrel, the type of man she usually despised. He had no sense of fashion, though his clothing was obviously expensive. And the wig . . . abominable.

He was another noble with too much money and too little sense. And an odd accent. She thought it could be American. But he had introduced himself as a marquess.

Something familiar tugged at her mind. She had seen him somewhere before.

The image of the man on the ship returned. Ah, but *he* was a man. The short cropped hair, the shirt and tight breeches. Nothing like the mismatched noble. And yet . . .

Perhaps it was the way his gaze lingered on her, not lustfully as did that of so many men, but with a different kind of appreciation.

She was imagining things.

Besides, she had other things to worry about tonight, mainly her escort, who was inching closer and closer to her in the carriage. She had fended him off last night as being too weary from the journey.

She had the same excuse tonight. She had worked hard at the first rehearsal today. The play was a comedy and called for sparkling repartee. Her leading man, Richard Taylor, was competent, but he, too, had hands that never quite knew where they belonged.

It wasn't under her dress.

Between learning lines, and taking measure of her fellow thespians and fending off questions, she was quite exhausted, especially after a night visiting gaming hells.

She had won consistently. She was a good player, although she had feigned incompetence. She'd been taught by fellow thespians in Paris and was usually blessed by good luck. Tonight the dice had been good, the cards better. Everywhere she went, she attracted attentive onlookers.

Tomorrow, Lynch told her, she would probably be in all the papers. The new French actress who defied convention and had amazingly good fortune at the cards.

"Your name will be on every tongue tomorrow," Lynch said, as if reading her mind. He still hadn't decided whether the notoriety would be good or bad for his new production. She had finally convinced him it would be very good.

They arrived back at the town house and Lynch stepped down, then offered his hand. She took it and easily descended.

She paused at the door and turned around. She saw in his face that he expected an invitation inside.

*"Merci,"* she said. "You have been so very kind."

"The night is still young."

"The night is very old," she replied. "And I wish to do well for your play."

"You will do very well. Richard likes you and that is very rare. He usually hates the leading lady."

"He's very good. As are the rest of the players."

"I try to find the best," he said, his gaze taking on the brooding, hooded look that men usually thought was sexy. "Can we not go in and have a glass of brandy?"

"I have had so much champagne that I am spinning," she said.

"Then I will help you inside."

She ignored his suggestion and rapped on the door. In seconds it opened and Dani stood on the other side.

Monique leaned over and kissed Lynch lightly on the cheek. "You are so kind," she said. "But Dani can help me now. And there is a rehearsal tomorrow, is that not so? You will want me to have the proper rest, *non*?"

"Yes, but . . ."

By then she was inside and closing the door.

Danielle winked.

"I am getting too old for this."

"You will never be old, mademoiselle. Did you find what you were looking for?"

"Not yet, Dani, but I'm still baiting the trap."

"Would you like something to eat?"

"I would. And some tea. I want to read the lines again. It *is* a good play. Clever. I think it will be a success."

"All your plays are a success," Dani said loyally.

"*Oui,* but this one . . . is far more important."

"And when you finish?"

They had not talked about the "after" of this play. It would be tempting fate.

"I don't know," she said honestly. "I haven't thought about it."

And she hadn't.

"You will stay here?"

"Possibly. England was my mother's home. But . . ."

"But?"

"We are after a very powerful and ruthless man. I am not thinking ahead."

Dani helped her off with her dress and into a night robe, then disappeared toward the kitchen.

Monique took the pins from her hair and started brushing

it. Her thoughts were on the man she so wanted to bring to his knees. What would she feel when she met him? The man who had given her life, then tried to take both her mother's and her own.

Then they drifted again to the marquess she'd met outside the gaming hall. She wondered why. There was nothing of interest about him. Nothing at all. Nothing but that fraction of a second when . . .

Nonsense. Nothing but nonsense.

She sighed, feeling suddenly lonely. She seldom did that. She refused to let loneliness into her life. It was a defeating emotion.

But now she felt alone and lost. Not even the prospect of Dani's tea stemmed the wave of foreboding that suddenly swept over her.

# Chapter Four

The line stretched out of Gabriel's new lodgings and down the block. He never would have expected such a response from one small advertisement for a valet and housekeeper.

He hadn't asked Pickwick to help him in this. He wanted servants he could trust.

Several of the applicants gave the army and sea as their last employment. The war with America had ended and so had the one with France. Soldiers and sailors were frantic to find means to feed their families and themselves.

Others were qualified servants who had lost employment through no fault of their own and presented extensive references. Some applicants he wouldn't trust farther than he could throw them.

His attention riveted though on a tall, stocky man with a quiet countenance and a face both determined but weary.

Sydney Smythe was a former army sergeant. His eyes had been without hope when he'd entered Gabriel's study, but he didn't embellish his qualifications as so many others did.

Gabriel had always been an astute judge of character and he knew instantly that this was his man. When Gabriel had asked whether he'd ever served in a household before,

Smythe said simply, "No, milord, but I am a hard worker and I learn fast."

"And why choose this work now?"

"There is no other, milord."

"I would not wish an unhappy valet."

"Milord, I would be the happiest man in London. I have a mum and sister who are hungry."

His brown eyes had not pleaded. Gabriel sensed he was not a man to plead, but hope was beginning to shine in his face. Through it all, dignity remained solid. Smythe was the type of man he would have liked at his side during the war.

"Well, I've not been a gentleman before, Sydney, so perhaps we can learn together."

The man stood there, disbelieving. "Milord?"

"You are employed, Smythe. Two pounds a week."

A muscle in the man's throat pulsed. "But that . . . is too generous, milord."

"I ask only one thing from you," Gabriel said. "Total loyalty. Can you give me that?"

"Yes, milord."

Gabriel believed him.

"Then you can dismiss the rest of the men and interview the women for the post of housekeeper."

The man stood there for a moment.

"Yes?" Gabriel said.

"My mum. She's a fine cook."

"Can she clean?"

"Yes, milord."

"Tell her to come by in the morning. I will talk to her."

"I . . . I . . ." The man seemed to shake slightly. "Thank you, milord. I will do my best for you."

"Then do not be too curious, Smythe," he said. "That will be thanks enough."

"No, milord. No." He started to back away. "I can start today."

"Just turn the others away, and bring your mother in the morning. You can begin then." He fished in the drawer of his desk, taking out several coins. "You will need some clothes. See if you can find something today."

."What would you prefer?"

Gabriel waved his hand. Smythe still wore the worn remnants of a uniform. "I care not." He paused. "And get your family something to eat. It can come from your first month's wages."

For the first time, the man's face broke into a smile.

"Yes, milord. Thank you."

Gabriel turned away. In truth, he was humbled by the poverty and desperation he'd seen today.

He wondered whether the man's gratitude would continue when he heard the rumors about his employer being a wastrel and an American upstart. Or even caught wind, somehow, that he had been a member of the American forces that had so recently defeated his country.

Yet, oddly enough, he'd felt an instant affinity for the man. Of course, others standing in line had been desperate too, but there was a dignity in Smythe that conveyed a sense of honor. Gabriel thought he would be loyal.

He didn't want to pretend twenty-four hours a day.

And what would he do for those hours spent away from the gambling hells?

Gabriel had worked nearly every day since the moment his father had killed himself. He had made himself useful on the voyage to America and earned a few farthings. And when they had arrived in Boston, they were taken in by his mother's sister.

Her husband had been a wealthy banker but had been barely tolerant of his wife's relatives. Gabriel had decided the first day he would at least try to repay the charity. He had gone to school and worked every spare hour at a shipyard doing every menial job no one else was willing to do.

Eventually his uncle accepted him, even came to respect him, but Gabriel had stubbornly rejected help. He never forgot all the slights, the discourtesies that had eroded his mother's spirit day by day. He was seventeen the day his mother died. He'd left his uncle's house the next day.

He'd been befriended by the owner of the shipping company where he had worked, and he was offered a seaman's post. He'd worked hard enough to catch the eye of the captain, who promoted him. In eight years he'd become a first mate, and had just been named captain when war with Britain broke out. He'd become a privateer, then an officer in the navy.

He liked work. He liked being occupied, and being merely a gentleman was not to his liking.

But being exactly that would fit the portrait of a man ripe for the picking. He would have to squander his hours.

At least tomorrow he would have a cook. He hoped she was a good one.

He spent an hour dressing, trying to tie his cravat into an elaborate knot. He swore frequently. He'd never cared much about appearances and had always tied his neckcloth rather carelessly. He doubted whether his new valet would have much more expertise than he.

The London dandy treasured his cravat. No self-respecting new lord could do less. Pickwick had assisted him the last two evenings.

Now he was on his own. Tonight he would troll alone. He'd decided Pickwick didn't want him to find the men he was seeking. Which probably meant Pickwick knew exactly what happened all those years ago.

He finally achieved the result he wanted with the cravat. Not quite perfect. But pretentious.

He added a quizzing glass to his attire, letting it dangle from a buttonhole. Then he chose one of the canes he'd recently purchased, tucked it under his arm, and sallied forth.

Gabriel knew he would represent a target. He was big, at least in height, and—when he wished—he could intimidate the hell out of most people. But in these clothes, and with the vapid expression he'd perfected, he would be the prime mark for thieves. They might be in for a bit of surprise. He'd learned brawling early in his career at sea.

He planned to take supper at a tavern, then he would begin prowling on his own through London's clubs and gambling hells. He now knew most of the rules, where he would be accepted and where not. He might even try to take on a club where he knew he would be barred.

A fine ruckus was what he needed.

He locked the door of the town house behind him. He'd been very careful as to what he'd brought with him. He wanted nothing to give him away, to reveal, in truth, that the new Marquess of Manchester was also one John Manning, a respected and feared American captain.

For that one reason, he'd used his middle name—John— since the days he'd left his uncle's home. He'd known then what he was going to do.

The plan had festered for a long time.

Now he was Gabriel again, a simple American who had just fallen into luck.

He walked the streets, sometimes reaching for his quizzing glass to ogle a lady or a carriage in the street. It took a certain amount of practice to keep the bloody thing in his eye.

With every lady he passed, his thoughts returned to the actress, Monique Fremont. Every other woman looked colorless. Dull. Lifeless. She had literally brimmed with life, her eyes full of amusement that was part real humor and part sardonic. Unusual for a woman.

He wondered whether she had felt the same jolt of awareness he had, but then why would she? He was a fop. A dandy. A useless man with a title he'd neither earned nor deserved.

His thoughts turned again to Pickwick.

Pickwick had been efficient about the lodgings Gabriel had just let. He'd been efficient in obtaining the services of a good, if supercilious tailor. He'd also been helpful in introducing him to London's nightlife, though Gabriel would have sworn that there were places he was not being taken for Pickwick's own reasons.

Gabriel found a lad hawking one of the city's newspapers, gave him double the amount demanded, and entered a tavern, where he chose a seat by the window.

Gabriel had been checking the newspapers for several days, finding this one to be the most likely to contain gossip. He ordered an ale and a meat pie, then glanced through the paper.

His attention focused on a column about London society, pausing only when he saw his name.

ALL OF LONDON IS DISCUSSING THE AMERICAN WHO HAS

USURPED AN OLD AND HONORED TITLE. HE HAS BEEN SEEN IN MANY OF LONDON'S NOTORIOUS GAMING ESTABLISHMENTS.

The account continued to say the new marquess had been seen losing large sums in some of London's most notorious clubs. It scorned his clothes, his speech, and his manners. Wealth and title did not equate class, it concluded.

Gabriel smiled as he read. A wealthy American ready for the plucking.

He wondered how long it would take.

His gaze wandered to a column where theatrical announcements were listed. He looked for any notice of a new play. He didn't see one, nor did he see the name of the French actress.

Nonsense. He should be concentrating on three men, not on a woman who frequented gambling hells. She was probably looking for a protector, and he sure as hell couldn't get embroiled in that kind of situation.

*A woman like that was trouble.* He suspected that Pickwick was right. And God knew he needed all his wits about him.

He dismissed her from his mind, wondering why she kept intruding there. He'd always had the ability to focus in on one objective and ignore distractions. And that was all she was. A minor distraction.

Still, he couldn't help but wonder whether he might encounter her again during his tour of the clubs tonight. He didn't like the tingle of anticipation he felt. Not at all.

Thomas Kane, the Earl of Stanhope, leaned back in his chair and took a long appreciative draw on his cigar, then dangled it in his fingers as he gazed at his companion.

"So he did decide to take the title?"

"So it appears, Thomas." Sir Robert Stammel couldn't disguise the tremor in his voice.

*Weak,* Stanhope thought and not for the first time. Stammel needed constant reassurance. But his very weakness made him valuable. He was afraid of his own shadow, but more afraid of Stanhope.

"He realizes there are no funds attached?"

"Wicky says he claims he has funds of his own. At the rate he's losing at cards, I would guess he has a fortune."

"He's paying his gaming debts?"

"Thus far. He's said to be obnoxious, but thus far he's been good for his losses."

"Where did he get his money?"

"Wicky says he has been raised by a wealthy family in Boston. Supposedly from there."

"And Pickwick thinks he intends to stay?"

"Wicky says he's looking for an English bride."

"Hummmmm." Stanhope rose from the chair and went to the window of his country home, located some twenty miles from London. He looked out at the manicured lawn below him. He loved that lawn. It was orderly. It was also a useless extravagance.

He liked useless extravagances. They were symbols of money and power. Of freedom. His father had hated extravagances.

He turned back to Stammel. "I have a marriageable daughter," he said. "A marquess would be a good match for her."

Stammel looked startled. "Surely you are not suggesting . . . Pamela."

Stanhope shrugged. "She is quite pretty when she takes care with her appearance. She might be good bait."

"She is your daughter."

"Sentimentality, Robert? I never would have suspected you of it." He raised an eyebrow.

Stammel blinked rapidly. "I just thought . . ."

"It is time that the little country mouse became useful." He paced the room. "I have never thought her attractive enough to be useful." He paused, then said thoughtfully, "Perhaps a man who wants an alliance with a wealthy family can overlook a bluestocking with little looks. The season begins next week. I want invitations for her. Invitations that will include this new marquess. "

Robert sighed heavily, surrendering just as Stanhope knew he would. "She has not been introduced at court."

Stanhope shrugged. "I will have a coming out at a small

soiree at my home. Say she was ill when the presentations were made at court."

"But the ladies at Almack's . . ."

"I do not care about them. Nor do I care if she is accepted there. Neither, I suspect, will our American mark. He wants a good English wife. I will give him one. Pamela will not defy me."

Stammel tried again. "Maybe this Manchester knows something about what happened years ago? Maybe it would be best to stay away from him."

Stanhope fixed his companion with a stare he knew froze most people. "He was ten years old! A spoiled brat."

"He found his father's body, for God's sake."

"From what you say of this fop, he could not care less." Stanhope paused, then looked at his companion thoughtfully. "Yet it wouldn't hurt to make queries."

"It will take two months at least."

"One of our ships leaves for Boston on Thursday. Have the captain make queries about him."

"In the meantime, perhaps we should stay away from London?"

"I will be bloody damned before I allow a Manning to keep me from London and my club. No one spoils my plans. The theater season is starting and I hear there's a new French actress. Henry met her at a gambling hell. Said she was spectacular." He rolled the cigar between his fingers.

Stammel returned to the previous subject. "He might remember your name. Or your face."

"I only saw the brat once. And we were victims, remember?"

"I think we should stay away from him. I have a feeling—"

"You always have feelings, Robert. Nothing ever comes of them. Besides, I think this might be an interesting opportunity."

"No," Stammel replied. "It's too dangerous."

"Then you can stay in the country with your wife."

Stammel winced. He disliked his wife and seldom stayed in the same vicinity. He was in residence here for that very reason. But he also knew Stanhope didn't like anyone staying here when he was away. "You like playing with fire, Thomas. I do not."

Stanhope shrugged. "Do as you wish. I'm sure that Henry will be as interested as I am in this new marquess."

He watched Robert squirm. Unlike himself, Robert had grown fat and lazy, and, as he prospered, thanks to Stanhope, he had grown more and more timid. He was no longer hungry.

But he was addicted to Stanhope. Addicted to Stanhope's power, and Stanhope knew how to use that tether.

"We will return to London tomorrow."

"I hope you know what you are doing," Stammel said.

Stanhope shrugged. He liked the idea of a second-generation addle cove. He had sheared one self-righteous Manning. It would be interesting to shear another.

Monique was tired. She'd spent the last two days in rehearsals that lasted late into the night. And her sleep was interrupted by nightmares. In the past few weeks, she often woke drenched in sweat.

She carefully removed the paint from her face in the dressing room. Dani had left earlier at Monique's suggestion. There was little reason for her to sit around hour after hour. Lynch always made sure there was a carriage waiting to take her home.

Monique stared at herself in the mirror. For a moment she thought it the face of a stranger. The girl in her was long gone. If, indeed, it had ever been there.

She couldn't remember a carefree moment, a second when she had not worried about her mother and their survival, not until she'd become a successful actress, but even then the past haunted her.

She wondered whether she could ever love a man after what she had seen and learned, and experienced. Perhaps when she gained a measure of justice.

She had not returned to the gambling hells in the past three days. She had made her presence known. Now she would wait.

In the meantime she worked tirelessly in rehearsals. She'd

heard that London audiences could be raucous and critical. It wouldn't fit her plan at all to be hissed off the stage.

So she'd thrown herself into the part. Her role was that of a wife who decided to have an affair to teach her wandering husband a lesson. She plans to take a lover but none suit. And every attempt to be "caught" ends in farce.

It was witty and clever and she and the principle actor played well off each other.

His blond hair and blue eyes contrasted with her dark hair, and unlike many actors he was tall. His off-stage comments, though, were often a little too amorous for her taste. He made it obvious he was seldom refused and considered her attempts to keep the amour on stage but a ploy.

She'd tapped him with her fan more than several times when he'd repeatedly attempted to press his attentions.

A knock came at her dressing room. Probably her leading man again.

She tried to curb her impatience as she rose and went to the door.

A man stood there. Older. Distinguished looking. A warm smile on his lips. It didn't quite reach his eyes.

He bowed. "Mademoiselle, I am the Earl of Daven," he said hopefully after a short silence. "We met the other night when you were . . ."

"Not being a lady," she finished.

"But you could be nothing else," he said extravagantly.

*Daven.* She knew from her research, he was one of Stanhope's friends. Her trolling had netted a fish. "*Merci,* monsieur. You are too kind."

"I was hoping you would take supper with me tonight."

"I am sorry, my lord, but I have a previous engagement."

Anger flickered in his face, and she suspected he wasn't usually refused.

"Then tomorrow night?"

"Also engaged, my lord."

"Is that for all succeeding nights as well?" he asked.

"Not necessarily, monsieur. But I have just come to your wonderful city and I have many friends who preceded me. Is it unusual that I wish to see them?"

"But you were at a gambling hell . . ."

"A foolish decision, to be sure, but I had heard so much about them I wanted to see for myself. And I had not yet found my friends. Now I have."

"You are encumbered?"

"*Non,* my lord. But neither will I risk my reputation and future without knowing more about my acquaintances."

"My title is a long and noble one," Daven said.

"I am sure it is, monsieur, but that does not mean the man holding it is as honorable. And now if you will excuse me . . ."

The man looked stunned.

Richard appeared beside him, as if summoned.

"Monique?"

"Richard, this is the Earl of Daven. Monsieur, this is Richard Taylor, who is my husband in the play."

Richard seemed singularly unimpressed, and she liked him all the more for it. He looked at Daven with suspicion, then at her. "Are you ready to leave?" he asked.

He'd said nothing about accompanying her home, and she appreciated the unexpected gallantry.

"*Oui, merci.* I just need my cloak." She looked back toward Daven. "I hope you return for the play, my lord," she said with a brief curtsy. She saw puzzlement in his eyes. And jealousy.

She also knew from his expression that she needed to be careful. He was not a man to toy with. Neither was the man who gave her life, then tried to take it. No wonder they were friends.

From now on, she would carry the small gun a friend had given her.

"You will excuse me, my lord?"

He looked displeased, but nodded. "I do hope you will have supper with me in the future," he said.

"We will see, my lord. I hope you will attend the opening of our play. And bring your friends."

"I will do that," he said.

Under the glare of the younger Richard Taylor, he backed

away, his gaze still on her. Consuming her. She felt a chill run up her back.

Then he was gone.

*"Merci,"* she said to Richard.

"I will accompany you home. I did not like the looks of him."

"He is a lord with an important title," she mocked.

He grinned. "I heard." The smile disappeared. "Be careful, Monique. His kind thinks everyone and everything belongs to them."

"I know. I will be careful."

He looked at her for a long moment. "You will permit me to take you home, then."

*"Non,"* she replied. "Mr. Lynch has a carriage waiting for me. I will be fine, truly, I will."

"I will accompany you to the carriage then."

"That is kind."

"I want to keep you safe. You are the finest actress I've played with. No fruit will be thrown at us."

"I have heard of this English custom. Have you ever had fruit thrown at you?"

"Unfortunately, yes. But I attributed it to the play, not to my efforts." His eyes were merry. And mischievously amorous.

"I will allow you to walk me to the carriage," she said.

"Ah, progress."

She handed him her cloak and waited until he helped her on with it, then left her dressing room and walked through the darkened theater. Richard stayed with her as they exited the door. As promised, a carriage and driver stood in front.

She glanced around. No one lingered, yet she felt as if someone was watching her.

She shook off the feeling as she allowed Richard to assist her inside the carriage. She looked around as the carriage clattered down the street.

As the carriage passed the next street, she saw a man standing in the shadows. Though she could not see him, she knew his gaze followed her carriage.

For the briefest second she wondered how wise this quest

was. But it was too late now. She was committed and she would stay the course.

Gabriel finished the last of an excellent meal in solitude.

He had known he would have to play a waiting game, but it had become more and more difficult. He wanted the three to come to him. That was the only way the plan might work.

In the meantime he had to play the role of a fool, and he was becoming damn well weary of it.

So far his bait had not been taken.

He did, though, finally have food worth eating.

Sydney Smythe's mother was everything the new valet had claimed. In the two days of her employment she had proved to be a good cook and housekeeper.

The only problem, he thought, was that she was too good and too kind. She had already started mothering him.

It had been a long time since he'd had mothering. The essence of his mother had disappeared when his father died. She'd become an empty shell, depending more and more on the wine bottle for solace.

Martha Smythe was of lean stature. She wore a nervous smile. Her hands had clenched tightly during the interview.

But once she had the position, she'd begun to show her nurturing nature. Piece by piece, Gabriel had learned her story.

She had been a merchant's daughter who'd fallen in love with a soldier and married against her family's wishes. She'd had two stillbirths and four live ones, two of whom died in childhood. Only Sydney, who'd followed his father's path into the army, and his sister, Elizabeth, now twelve, survived.

Martha had relied on Sydney's small contribution and her own meager earnings. She'd mended and washed clothes as well as baked pies for a nearby tavern that had also employed Sydney. When it burned down, they both had lost their main source of sustenance. They had reached the end of their very tiny savings when Sydney, in desperation, had decided to try for a position for which he was entirely unsuited . . .

It was, Gabriel thought, a small piece of fate.

At the end of the interview he had asked about the daughter. Martha planned to walk the long distance between her small room and Gabriel's.

"This house is large enough for both of you," he said. "There are several rooms above, and she can help you with the cooking."

The gratitude in her face nearly unhinged him.

So now he had a household he really hadn't wanted.

And a young girl would move in with them tomorrow.

He wondered if things weren't getting out of hand. The more people around him, the more danger for him.

Yet, he hadn't felt he had a choice. He knew what it was like to have nothing.

The problem was he didn't expect to be here long. He planned to return to America as soon as he'd taken care of matters here.

Where would that leave Sydney and his mother?

He grabbed his cane. He needed a walk. A long one.

He started out, wondering where to go. He remembered the actress. Monique. The theater where she would perform was not that far from his town house.

Gabriel had resisted the temptation for five days.

He decided not to resist any longer. He would just walk by. Surely she would not be there at this evening hour.

At least it was a destination.


Flowers were delivered to both Monique's lodgings and the theater. So many flowers that they filled the entire town house.

Most were from the Earl of Daven.

They left her unmoved. The only reason she had anything to do with Daven was that she'd been told he was a friend and companion of the Earl of Stanhope.

She ignored them and went up to her bedroom to read awhile before leaving for a rehearsal. She'd just picked up the book when she heard the knocker downstairs. Annoyed, she put the volume down. She truly enjoyed Walter Scott and his adventurous romances.

She went down the stairs and watched as Mrs. Miller

opened the door and accepted yet another bouquet of flowers for which she would have to find a vase.

After Mrs. Miller shut the door, Monique looked at the bouquet of the most beautiful roses she'd ever seen. Not as elaborate as Daven's had been. Not an ostentatious number of blooms, but perfect in every way.

She looked at the card and the bold black handwriting scrawled across it. *"For gracing London with your beauty."* It was signed by Lord Thomas Kane, Earl of Stanhope.

She held the card for a long moment as she stood in the hallway of the town house. Then she dropped it as if it had just exploded into flames.

Her father.

Harriett Miller, the housekeeper, hurried over to her. "Oh, miss. These are so lovely."

Monique wanted to tell her to throw them away. But servants talked. And throwing away a bouquet from an earl would, no doubt, become a topic of conversation. Still, she wanted them somewhere she wouldn't see them often.

"Put them in the dining room," she said. She rarely ventured there, taking most of her meals in the bedroom with Dani.

"But . . ."

Monique's glare stopped the protest immediately.

She stood against the wall for several moments. This is what she'd wanted. What she'd planned all these years.

But now she wondered whether she could really complete the masquerade she'd planned. What would she do when she saw him face-to-face?

Would he recognize a daughter of his blood?

Would she have any feeling other than the hatred she'd learned from her mother?

Planning was easy. The execution, she realized now, was going to be far more difficult.

"Mademoiselle?"

Dani appeared from her room, where she had been cleaning one of Monique's dresses. It was uncanny the way her friend always knew when she was distressed.

She tried a smile. "Everything is going as planned. I just received flowers from Stanhope."

Dani regarded her solemnly.

Monique wondered if her face was pale. She would have to be a far better actress than she had been today if she was to carry this off.

"We can go back to Paris," Dani said slowly. "You know Monsieur Fayssoux would be more than delighted."

"England is my home," Monique said. "And my mother needs justice."

"Not at your expense."

"It has begun. I cannot put the genie back in the bottle."

Dani sighed. "Then we must go and make you beautiful. He will probably be there tonight."

"*Oui,*" Monique said. "You must make me very beautiful."

# Chapter Five

Gabriel limped down the street outside the Earl of Stanhope's town house.

He looked like an old man, stooped and battered.

No sign of life appeared within the house. He had gone by several times yesterday and again today.

But then most of the town houses appeared vacant other than a servant or two. The season would not begin for another few weeks, and the influx into London was several days away.

He had watched a servant leave twenty minutes earlier, probably to go shopping. It was a good time to get into the house and explore it.

He looked around. A carriage clattered down the streets.

He sank down on a step as if his legs would no longer carry him, then, when no one was in sight, made his way to the gate. It was locked, but he took only seconds to open it with a pick, and he entered the garden.

It was exquisite. Who cared for it while the earl was in the country? A full-time gardener, no doubt. Yet he'd watched all morning and seen no one.

He went to the servant's entrance and rang the bell. No one came.

After a moment he used the two picks he'd obtained in Boston. A twist of his fingers and he was inside the house.

He paused to adjust his eyes in the gloom of the interior hall.

The walls were lined with portraits. He paused to look at them, seeking an insight into the character of the man. The men looked grim, the women joyless.

He moved through each room carefully, always aware there could be an unexpected retainer still in the residence. No one on the first floor. He went down the steps to the basement. The kitchen and what appeared to be a servants' area were also empty. Satisfied no one was in the residence, he continued his search of the house, stopping in what was certainly Stanhope's office.

A huge desk dominated the room. The surface was clear.

He tried the desk drawer. Locked. He used the small tools again, opened the drawer, and rifled through the contents. Personal correspondence. Invitations. Household sums. Nothing of importance.

He found Stanhope's seal in a box near the back of the drawer and pocketed it, replacing the box. Hopefully he could return it before Stanhope noticed it was missing.

Gabriel had what he wanted. Still, he inspected the rest of the house, leaving the master suite to the last.

It was far too elaborate for his taste. Closed red velvet curtains darkened a room dominated by a huge four-poster bed. A large wardrobe sat against the opposite wall.

Gabriel absorbed the essence of the room, trying to fathom the man who so easily destroyed others. Then he moved around again until he found what he was looking for.

*A safe.*

Combination lock this time. He knelt next to it and sandpapered the tips of his fingers to make them more sensitive. Pressing his ear against the lock as Riley had taught him, he turned the knob, listening for the click of a tumbler. Left, then right, then left again. After several tries, he found the combination and the safe opened.

He reached inside. A box contained a necklace of emeralds. Several thousand pounds in banknotes. Shipping contracts. Why here? One he studied with interest and memorized the names on it. Then he replaced everything as it was.

He rose and went to the window, moving the curtain only slightly.

More people were on the street. He saw one woman heading directly for the town house.

Would she come in the back?

Swiftly he moved down the steps, then waited. He heard a turn of the lock at the back, and he went to the front door.

Locked, of course, and he didn't have time to use his tool. He should have unlocked both of them just in the event . . .

He swore silently and ducked into the office as he heard footsteps moving toward him. They passed him and went up the stairs, probably to the third-floor servants' quarters.

He hurried to the back, through the garden, and turned left on the street.

Gabriel patted the seal in one of his pockets. And smiled.

He'd accomplished his mission.


Stanhope wondered whether his flowers had been delivered. They had been sent from his own gardens prior to his arrival in London.

They were his finest.

He knew Daven. Daven never knew when enough was enough.

He wondered how his gift would be received compared to Daven's and whether the man had made any headway.

Stanhope had a thousand pounds wagered on who would get the French bitch in bed first. And he didn't like to lose.

It would be, he thought, a most entertaining season.

He had a servant out delivering invitations for a soiree at his home to announce his arrival to the social scene. Some families would not accept them, but others would, either out of fear or in hope of doing business with him. His interests were far-flung, including a shipping empire, banking, and interests in mines in Wales and the north of England.

One invitation had gone to Gabriel Manning, the new marquess. Stanhope was curious as to whether he would accept it or not.

He wanted to issue one to Monique Fremont, but that would not sit well with the wives of the men he had invited. His reputation among the ton was not the best since his wife died of a suspicious illness. Rumors swarmed about her death.

But his parties were also celebrated. He always had the finest food, the best wine and spirits, the most celebrated musicians.

He would outdo himself this time. He wanted to impress the new marquess.

Then he would turn his full attention to Mademoiselle Fremont.

Perhaps he would even visit the new theater this afternoon and take a glance at this woman that had so transfixed Daven. Daven had a taste for less-than-acceptable women. But they were always beautiful.

He might even invest in the theater company. He hadn't done that before, but if the woman was all that Daven said . . .

He called his valet to help him dress and tie his cravat.

While waiting for Ames, he regarded himself in the mirror. Not bad for a man in his fifties. His hair was still dark, as were his sideburns. He took pride in not requiring dye, as did so many of his acquaintances. He knew he looked like a man ten years younger than his actual years.

Ames arrived, breathless.

Stanhope glared at him for not being immediately available, and the man's hands shook as he tied Stanhope's cravat into the fashionable *orientale* style that was damnably uncomfortable. Then Ames helped him pull on his highly polished Hessian boots.

"Do the cravat again," he demanded. "It is not quite perfect."

"Yes, milord," Ames said in a quivering voice. Ames had been with Stanhope only six months. Most of his servants did not last that long, but since the war ended servants were readily available.

He tolerated Ames's clumsy attempts for another thirty minutes, then proclaimed it barely acceptable. He pulled on a pair of spotless gloves—God help every servant in the house

if there was the merest discoloration—and told Ames to see
that his horse was saddled.

A few moments later he lifted himself into the saddle and
guided the horse toward Haymarket and the theaters.

Monique saw two men in the back of the theater. She recognized Daven instantly.

She knew immediately that the second man was Stanhope.

She didn't miss a cue as she tore her gaze away from them
and toward Richard, forcing a gaiety in her voice. When she
turned again, she saw the two men in conversation with Paul
Lynch.

She concentrated on Richard. It was a trick she had learned
long ago, to wipe away everything except the character she
was playing. She even felt the attraction she was supposed to
be feeling. For two hours she would be the wronged wife who
responded with revenge and humor and a wounded soul.

For the rest of the rehearsal she was able to keep her mind
on only the lines. Her stomach felt a haven for butterflies, her
legs were rubbery. But she was the mistress of her fate in the
play, and she was bloody determined to be the same outside
the theater.

The rehearsal concluded. Mr. Lynch appeared seemingly
out of nowhere.

"Monique?"

"*Oui,* monsieur?"

"The rehearsal is going well. You are everything I hoped
you would be."

"*Merci.*"

"There is someone you wanted to meet. An earl,
Monique." He looked embarrassed. "He offered to invest in
the company."

"I did not know you needed investment," she said.

He looked uncomfortable. "Investors always help. They
tend to bring their friends."

"Who is this potential investor?"

"The Ea—rl of Stanhope," he stuttered.

"The man you warned me about?"

He shifted on his feet. "You did say you wanted to meet him and this seems . . . fortuitous, would you not say?"

Greed had obviously overtaken his sense of protection. She expected no more.

"I will see him," she said, "and I will be most pleasant. For your sake, of course. But then I am always pleasant unless someone makes me otherwise."

She watched as he digested the warning.

"No one has ever proved anything against the Earl of Stanhope."

"Do you vouch for him now, Mr. Lynch?"

The man's face turned even redder.

"I will expect my carriage to be waiting."

He nodded.

She left him without another word and went to her dressing room, where Dani waited.

"He has taken the bait, Dani. He wants to invest in Lynch's company."

Dani was already taking pins from her hair. "You are making him wait?"

"*Oui*. Our lord needs a little humility, I think."

"Do not twist the tail of the tiger, mademoiselle."

"Oh I plan to do a great deal of twisting."

A knock came at the door, and Monique exchanged a look with Dani. "Answer it," she said.

Dani opened the door a slit, peering out.

A voice obviously accustomed to obedience boomed into the room. "I wish to give my compliments to Miss Fremont."

"She is changing clothes," Dani said cooly. "It must wait."

"I am the Earl of Stanhope. Lynch said . . ."

"I do not care if you are Father Christmas. You must wait." She closed the door and turned back to Monique.

"We will take our time, Dani," Monique said.

"Of course," Dani said as she unbuttoned the back of Monique's dress.

Monique expected impatient knocks at the door, or even a broken door. She knew about Stanhope. She knew from her mother, and she knew from local London gossip. He wasn't a man who liked to be kept waiting.

Which was exactly why she was making him wait.

So she was surprised at the silence outside her dressing room as Dani helped her put on another dress, and brushed her hair back. Adding just a small brush of paint to Monique's cheek, Dani stood back and nodded her approval.

Monique picked up her fan in her hand and opened the door.

A man dressed in riding clothes was sprawled in a chair outside the dressing room.

"My lord," Monique said, bobbing just enough to make the curtsy look slightly mocking.

He bowed. "I am Thomas Kane, the Earl of Stanhope." His gaze ranged over her like a buyer about to purchase a turkey for supper. A chill ran down her back as his nearly black eyes glittered with something close to malice even as his lips curved into a smile. If she had any doubts about her mother's tales, she didn't now. Here was a man who disliked women, perhaps even hated them.

She knew he had to be near sixty years of age, but he looked younger. He would have been a handsome man were it not for the coldness of his features, the arrogance in the way he held his head as if he alone ruled the world. He was of middle stature, not tall but not short either. Close to her own height. His lips seemed to have a permanent smirk.

"I am honored, my lord," Monique said. "Monsieur Lynch said you were considering investing in our small play."

"Not the play," he said. "Nor Mr. Lynch. You, my dear. You were spectacular."

"Oh, posh. We are not so ready. But *merci,* my lord."

"I hope you will have supper with me."

"Oh, but then Lord Daven would be very unhappy with me. He also asked and understood that my time is consumed by rehearsals. It is my art," she said dramatically.

"He is my friend, and I do not think he will object."

"That is very generous of him, but I do not socialize with investors, my lord." She started to brush past him.

He neatly maneuvered his body to block her. The chill down her spine grew colder.

"Then perhaps I should withdraw my support," he said.

"You may do whatever you feel best," she retorted.

His face changed. Surprise, then annoyance, and finally something else. He studied her for a long moment.

"I believe I will keep my investment with Lynch," he said slowly. "And how much would it cost me for you?"

"I am not for sale, monsieur, and you *are* insulting. Please leave."

She wondered how insulted she should be. She wanted to be unobtainable because from what she had learned of him, he couldn't resist a challenge. And yet . . . she knew he was no one to play with. He had tried to kill her mother. He might have killed his wife.

Still, to accomplish her goal, she had to have access to his home. And safely. She saw now that it would be much harder than she first believed.

He still didn't move. Finally, after seconds that seemed like minutes passed, he stood aside. "I intended no insult," he said smoothly. "I am accustomed to making it clear when I want something."

She stared at him. "You make things much too clear, my lord. I do not know how you regard actresses in London, but I assure you I am not looking for a protector. I am not what you call here a cyprian and most certainly not a doxy that you can tumble in bed. I do the choosing, not the . . . gentleman." She let enough of a pause pass before the last word to tell him she wasn't sure she considered him as such. "And now if you will excuse me, my maid and I would like to leave."

He finally stepped back, but his eyes said he was none too pleased. "I did not intend to offend," he said, though it was obvious to her that he was struggling to contain his anger. "I hope you would not hold it against me."

"I will consider that an apology," she said, "and accept it." She allowed herself a small smile. "I hope you will attend our opening performance."

"You may be sure of it." He bowed slightly, and, with the same arrogance with which he'd appeared, he turned around and left.

Monique heard Dani's sigh behind her, as if she had been holding her breath for a long time.

"My lady, he is a bad one. I was afraid . . ."

"That he would hit me?"

*"Oui."*

"A man like that commits his violence behind closed doors," Monique said.

"Perhaps we should return to Paris. I am afraid for you."

*"Non.* I have taken that first step. I am a challenge now, one he has to win."

"And then?"

"And then I will find a way to prove he is a murderer."

Dani was silent.

Monique willed herself to relax. She could control Stanhope. She just had to make sure she was never alone with him.

Dani helped her on with her cloak. In minutes she would be back at the town house and Mrs. Miller would have tea prepared. And a bath.

What a lovely thought.

She sent a lad outside to fetch their carriage.

A crowd of young bucks lounged outside as they left the theater. They had been gathering there the last few days as word of her arrival circulated. But this afternoon there were more than a few, each one craning their necks. One approached her.

"Mademoiselle, I was hoping you may consent to supper with me," the young man said in deplorable French.

*"Merci,* but I cannot," she replied in perfect English.

He looked surprised. Several others started to crowd in around her. Dani tried to move closer but was blocked.

"Please let my friend through," she said.

Instead Dani was pushed backward and Monique's unwelcomed suitor pressed closer to her.

She looked around, and toward the back she saw a tall familiar figure. It was the marquess she had met at the gaming hell, the one that eerily reminded her of the man who had attracted her attention at the harbor.

But now, as before, he had none of the presence she'd seen in the man who had dominated the deck of the ship, standing as if he owned all he surveyed. A quizzing glass was in one eye and he languidly held a walking stick. He remained in the back of the group, but his gaze on her was intelligent and searching just before his expression went blank.

"Pardon me," she said to the man blocking her as the rented coach clattered toward her. She made a move for it, but the buck who had asked that she accompany him to supper stood in front of her.

"I am sure you would not regret it," he said. He grasped her elbow.

"Release me," she demanded, but by then the group of men had closed in.

"She said 'release' her," a familiar voice said. It seemed lightly spoken, but an edge of menace lay underneath. She looked up, startled to see the Marquess of Manchester slicing his way through the crowd like Moses through the Red Sea. Oddly enough others parted for him.

She wondered why. He looked like such a dandy.

"Miss Fremont," he said. "I must apologize for my tardiness."

He looked at the man who still had his hand on her arm. "I believe the lady asked you to release her," he said.

The man holding her arm hesitated, then dropped his hand to his side and backed away. Silently, Manchester watched. He *knew* her assailant would back away.

Despite appearances to the contrary, she once more had the impression of strength.

"*Merci,* my lord," she said. "You *are* late," she scolded, taking his cue.

The words made the crowd back away even farther.

She looked around for Dani and saw her fighting to get back to her.

"Monsieur," she said. "My friend . . ."

Before she could blink, he gathered Dani to his side and brushed away any more would-be suitors. In seconds, he had cleared the way to the carriage and helped her and Dani inside. Without asking her consent, he joined them, taking his place on the opposite seat. "They could follow," he said blandly.

She didn't know what to say. She knew she should tell him to leave despite the fact that he had come to her aid. She wasn't sure at all that she wanted to share the intimacy of the carriage with him.

The carriage driver hesitated before closing the door. "To your residence?" he asked her.

"*Oui,*" she said. "And then you can take this gentleman where he wants to go."

She waited for him to give a location, but he didn't. Instead, he lounged against the back of the seat, his long legs stretched out comfortably. His quizzing glass was still in his eye, and she wondered how he controlled it.

He had taken off the tall beaver hat he wore and now he tucked it next to him. "Infernal thing," he said. "Hot as hell."

"Then why wear it?"

"Do not all the well-dressed gentlemen in London?" he asked.

She looked at his clothes, which were not quite right. She couldn't quite understand why. They were of good material, and the fit was right, but . . .

"I do not know, monsieur. I have not seen all the well-dressed gentlemen in London."

He grinned at that. "Now that is a surprise, considering the number of admirers waiting outside the theater."

"Why were you there?"

"I'm an admirer also," he said. "Like the others, I hoped to lure you out to supper."

She raised an eyebrow. "You do not look like a man who loiters around theaters."

"Why not?" he said.

She studied him for a long time. "How did you manage to make those men back away?"

He shrugged. "They are of little consequence," he said dismissively.

Monique didn't care for that answer. It had a haughty indifference for others, even rude others. "I still don't know why you were there."

"I was thunderstruck the other night upon meeting you. And now look at how fortunate I am." He turned his attention to Dani. "And who is this young lady?"

"Danielle," Monique said. "She is my friend."

Dani gave her a quick glance, then glowered at the man sitting across from them. It didn't seem to bother him.

Monique narrowed her eyes. Something didn't ring true. He was not the type of man to lurk in doorways, looking for a woman. He was the kind to storm inside.

She wasn't sure how she knew that. His manner—except for those brief moments when he'd come to her assistance—was bold but not particularly attractive. He was overdressed and she abhorred such pretensions as quizzing glasses, not to mention the elaborate cravat he wore. She liked simplicity in a man.

The image of the man on the ship returned. She hadn't really seen the sailor's face. This man's thick sandy hair seemed darker.

He seemed intent on keeping the silly quizzing glass in his eye.

"You were not, perhaps, on a ship a few days ago? An American ship?" She surprised herself by asking the question. She'd meant to daunt him with silence.

He unfolded his legs and she noticed how long and well-formed they were. She forced her gaze upward even as a surge of heat flooded her.

"Monsieur?"

"You have good eyesight, mademoiselle. I was on the *Cynthia*," he finally replied after obviously weighing his words.

"You are newly come to London then. How is it you have a title?"

It was a rude question, but she was fascinated with him. And she had never been averse to asking what she wanted to know.

His accent *had* been odd, and she was usually good at accents.

He smiled. "My uncle died without heirs and his title came to me, the son of the black sheep of the family. I do not think the ton is pleased."

A twinkle flashed in his eyes, as if he were sharing a small humorous secret. Then it was gone as quickly as it had appeared, and he seemed to mold his face into indifference as a sculptor might do with clay.

"You are from America?"

"Since I was ten."

"You do not have much of an accent."

"My mother was a Londoner," he said. His smile faded as he said it.

He was as unlike the man she'd met at the gambling hell as an actor was often different from his roles.

"Do you miss your home?" Her intended snub had all but disappeared. He interested her as no man had in a long time, silly quizzing glass notwithstanding.

As if he fathomed her thoughts, he took it from his eye and dropped it carelessly into a pocket. "Bloody uncomfortable things," he explained.

"Then why wear it?"

He gave her an arch look. "It is fashionable, I am told."

"If it were fashionable to jump in front of a carriage, would you do it?" There was the slightest bite in her voice. She didn't want to be disappointed with the man across from her.

Or maybe she did.

"Perhaps," he said, his lips twisting in a wry smile that belied the word.

He was confusing. As if he was slipping in and out of roles.

Knowing she should turn away and look out the window as the carriage paused in the crowded street, she still couldn't take her gaze from him. A hank of gold hair fell rakishly over his forehead, ruining the well-groomed look, and it made him look more appealing, more approachable. His eyes were a startling green, a color more vivid once he'd stopped squinting to keep the quizzing glass in his right eye.

The carriage started moving again, and she looked out. For some odd reason she really didn't want the short journey to end. She was enjoying the mystery. Worse, she was enjoying him.

That didn't happen often. Nor did the expectancy that hung in the air between them. Her heart beat just a little faster, her blood flowed just a little warmer. She felt alive in his presence. Challenged. She hadn't ever felt quite that way before.

Then, thank the saints, the carriage drew to a stop in front of her town house. "I am staying here," she said, breaking the almost palpable tension between them. "I do appreciate your assistance."

"May I walk you and Danielle to the door?"

She liked the way he included Danielle. And the fact that he remembered the name of a servant. Be careful, she warned herself. "Would it matter if I said no?"

"Yes," he said simply.

Again he surprised her. Perhaps that was the challenge. He wasn't doing or saying what she'd anticipated.

She nodded her head in response.

"I would still like to take you to supper." He glanced quickly at Dani, who eyed him suspiciously. "You and your maid."

She was tempted. She wanted to know more about him. She wanted to know why he was wearing the garments of a dandy when he was obviously so much more at home with simplicity.

Once again he didn't fit the image of someone who cared about what others thought.

But the warmth flowing through her body, the unexpected tug in a place that usually did not respond in such a manner warned her off. She had a mission. She had to keep her head clear.

"Thank you, but no," she said. "I am tired, and so is Dani. We plan to retire early."

"Would you consider some other time?"

"I have none until the play opens, monsieur," she said, effectively cutting him. She waited for an angry reaction.

There was none. Only the barest shrug, indicating he had tried and was not devastated that he'd not been accepted.

"Then I will accompany you to the door and return to my own lodgings."

"No gambling tonight?" The question surprised her as much as it appeared to startle him. She was prolonging the meeting. She knew it and couldn't help it.

"No, I have lost too much," he said. But again there was something wrong. There was no regret. No worry. Just an off-hand comment.

"I am sorry," she said.

He grinned. "You need not be sorry for my faults, mademoiselle, and meeting you made it a small price to pay. But I hear you are lucky in cards. Perhaps you would teach me a little about the games."

A twinkle lit his eyes again and she sensed in that moment he didn't need help.

Before she could ask any more, the coachman had opened the door and the marquess stepped out. He offered his hand to Dani first, then held out his hand to her and caught her with the other hand as she stepped down.

Her face was within inches of his as he looked down at her. She felt his breath, heard the quickened beat of his heart. She suddenly noticed that his hands were no longer gloved and his skin burned her arm as her cloak fell behind.

Fire whipped through her as she looked up at him, her own gaze lost in his. They were deep and impenetrable. So full of secrets and shadows that a knot of apprehension twisted her stomach.

Yet she couldn't step away, could hardly breathe at the unexpected need stabbing at her.

He leaned closer and she smelled some elusive male scent. She thought he was going to kiss her, and she was startled at how much she wanted exactly that. His lips passed her cheek with a feather touch, then he took a step back and dropped her hand.

"You are beautiful, mademoiselle. Much too beautiful." His eyes glittered with intensity. They were no longer coolly amused. Instead they were like small green flickers of flame.

"Who are you?" she whispered. Her legs were barely holding her up. She felt weak and stunned, and that had never happened to her before.

"I told you. I am merely a man claiming an old and honorable title."

"I don't think so," she said. "You are not what you want people to believe."

"Am I not?" he said. "Or perhaps you just inspire me to be more."

She felt Dani's arm on hers. "We must go," Dani said.

Monique caught her breath, then nodded. She took an experimental step. Her legs did not fail her, as she thought they might seconds earlier.

She nodded to the Marquess of Manchester and forced herself to turn and mount the steps of the town house without looking back.

She didn't have to look back. Everything about him was engraved in her mind.

# Chapter Six

After leaving Monique's rooms, Gabriel refused the offer of the coachman to take him to a place of his choosing. Instead, he retrieved his beaver hat from the seat and walked away from the town house.

He knew the location.

If he had any integrity, he would not return.

Damn, but she sent his head whirling. He had never met a woman who intrigued him so. He liked her directness, her lack of usual feminine wiles. He liked her wry sense of humor when she'd asked if he would step in front of a carriage.

An actress. He'd never met one before in person, but he had always enjoyed the theater when he'd had time. Which wasn't often. He enjoyed Shakespeare and dramas rather than farces. Darkness had always suited him more than light.

That had been true even at sea. He was attracted by sunsets and evenings and even the deepest night when all that one saw was the white tips of rushing waves, and the stars and moon above. He even liked the storms that tested him, his command, and his ships.

His purpose now was dark, and if he had honor, he would not bring anyone else into it. He had been aware from the beginning that he risked imprisonment, even death.

His father's honor, that last plea he'd made, was worth his sacrifice. He didn't have the right, though, to bring anyone else into his battle and risk their life and livelihood.

How close he had come to kissing her. He restrained himself only because something told him that once he took that step, he couldn't turn back, that it would be the beginning of a long journey he couldn't take.

He walked the mile easily, enjoying the brisk London air. He wondered whether it was because he'd been a lad here; part of him felt as if he was returning home. The streets were dirtier than those of Boston but cleaner than many of the ports he'd visited.

Yet while the city streets were familiar, the strictures of society were not. Perhaps he hadn't been so aware as a lad, or perhaps his father's own connection to a titled family had protected him. But he truly disdained a system that valued name above deed, gamesmanship above industry.

He had to admit that his impressions were driven by three men, three men who had thieved their way to riches and were protected by their name and titles.

He reached his rooms and went up the steps. The door opened before he reached it, and Smythe, resplendent in new dark clothes, opened it and bowed as he came in.

"If you do that again, I might have to discharge you," Gabriel said. He had told Smythe several times not to bow, but the man insisted on doing it anyway.

The man's face paled.

"No, Smythe," Gabriel said. "I will not discharge you, but I wanted to make a point. No more bowing. No more curtsies from your mother or sister. I am not royalty."

"But my lord . . ."

Gabriel surrendered. Smythe was a soldier through and through, and used to courtesies that embarrassed Gabriel.

Smythe took his gaudy waistcoat. Gabriel untied the cravat and pulled it off, handing it to him.

"My lord is not going out again tonight?"

"I think not," he said.

"A letter arrived for you," Smythe said. "I put it on your desk."

Gabriel frowned. He hadn't been in London long enough to be sent a letter. "From America?"

"No, my lord. Delivered by a footman. I did not recognize the livery."

"Thank you," Gabriel said.

"Would you be having supper? My sister made a fine supper."

"I would, indeed," he said. "I will take it in the study."

"Yes, my lord."

Gabriel despaired of ever getting his one manservant to drop the "my lord." It made him feel bloody uncomfortable. He left Smythe and went into the study. He read the elegant invitation to a soiree at the home of Thomas Kane, the Earl of Stanhope.

He sat down in the chair and stared at the invitation. The event would be in six days. A personal note was at the bottom in tight neat handwriting: "Welcome to London."

A knock came at the door, and he said "Come."

Smythe had a bottle of port on a tray. "My lord?"

"Please," Gabriel said. "Then you can help me with these dratted boots."

Smythe's stern face relaxed for the first time since he'd returned. It was clear he was still wondering at his luck in obtaining a post and terrified of losing it. He obviously worried about his skills and removing boots was an easy enough one.

Gabriel suspected that being dismissed was one of the few things that terrified the man.

If he'd fought Napoleon's armies, he certainly was no coward. Neither did he look like a man impressed by other men who had not earned his respect. Gabriel wanted to engage him about his service, but then he would be giving something of himself away.

And so he waited as Smythe helped remove the Hessian boots that were all the fashion in London.

"Thank you," he said after Smythe had neatly pulled them off.

"Should I serve your supper now?" Smythe asked.

"Yes," Gabriel said. "And then you are free the rest of the evening."

Smythe didn't move. "I could prepare a bath, your lordship."

Gabriel realized that Smythe wanted to keep busy, that he probably felt that was the key to continued employment.

"A good suggestion. In an hour. Then I plan to retire."

Smythe hesitated. "Are my clothes adequate, my lord? Would you prefer a uniform?"

"No, I do not. The clothing is very adequate."

"I would not wish to embarrass you."

"If anything, Smythe, *I* will embarrass you. You are a gentleman's gentleman, and I am not much of a gentleman. To most of London, at any rate," he said.

Smythe didn't say a word, and Gabriel knew he'd probably heard some of the rumors about the bumpkin American.

He took a sip of port. He wanted to ask Smythe to join him, but that would probably really unhinge the man.

He put down the glass. "How are your mother and sister? Is the room adequate?"

"Yes, my lord," Smythe said. "It is warm and comfortable."

"Where is your sister?"

"She is reading, my lord."

"What does she like?"

"Everything," Smythe said proudly. He hesitated. "I bought her a book with part of the money you gave me for clothes."

"Has she had any schooling?"

"The rector taught her to read and sums, but then he died, and the replacement did not feel a girl needed any more than that."

"I have some books I brought with me from America," he said. "Tell her to see me in the morning and she can borrow some."

A muscle moved in the man's throat.

"We did not want her to bother you, sir."

"Anyone who reads is not a bother, Smythe," Gabriel said. "I will see about finding her someone to help with lessons."

"I will pay it out of my salary," Smythe said.

"We will talk about that later, and now I am well and truly hungry."

"Yes, my lord."

"Once more, Smythe, I detest this 'my lord' business. It's all right when someone is here, but when I'm alone I would just as soon prefer something less formal."

Smythe looked puzzled.

Gabriel knew the man would never call him Gabriel. "Mr. Manning will do quite nicely," he said.

"I will try to remember, my lord." But this time there was amusement in his voice.

"Thank you, Smythe."

Monique looked through the bouquets of flowers expressly for one from Manchester. It had been three days since he had accompanied her from the theater.

It was maddening at how much she wished for flowers from *him*.

Instead, they continued to be delivered from others in astonishing numbers.

There were twelve bouquets in all today, including one from Stanhope. A small box accompanied it.

She opened it to find a fine silver comb with onyx stones. The card said, "I could not resist." It was expensive, but not overly so.

*The first gift from her father.* If he but knew.

She handled it gently, then scrawled a note, thanking him but saying she could not accept such an expensive gift.

It was meant, she knew, as a promise. This gift now. Others would follow.

She rang for Dani and showed her the comb.

Dani grimaced. "What are you going to do?"

"Return it."

"He will not like that. He is not a man to be thwarted."

"I am aware of that."

"What about that other gentleman? The one in the carriage?"

Monique shrugged.

"I liked him."

"He is a dandy," Monique said dismissively. "Another aristocrat who believes he can take what he wants."

"I do not think so," Dani said.

Monique turned toward Dani, who was generally suspicious about men. "Why?"

Dani shrugged. "Small things. His courtesy for me when I meant nothing to him. And the way he listened to you. He did not sit there and tell you how important he was, nor did he try to press you when . . ."

"I might have allowed him," Monique said. "Perhaps he is just more clever than most."

"He is clever," Dani agreed. "But I do not think in a bad way. Not like Lord Stanhope."

"Well, he is gone now. And he has not made a call in the last few days. It was just a pleasant flirtation for him."

"I think not," Dani said. "His eyes . . ."

"I never knew you to be a romantic before," Monique said.

"*Non,* I am not," Dani admitted. "Still . . . he is interesting."

"He was a distraction," Monique said. "A momentary entertainment, but now we must concentrate on the matter at hand. Do you suppose Mrs. Miller can find someone to deliver this box?"

"*Oui,*" Dani said. Then she paused. "There is no rehearsal tonight. Should we stay in?"

"No, I think we will go to Vauxhall Gardens tonight. I hear there will be fireworks tonight, and booths with punch and ham. Many people will be there, I'm told."

"I think I would like that, too."

Dani's reply surprised Monique. Usually Dani hid inside, reluctant to go among strangers. But perhaps the tension was affecting her, too.

"Good, then it is settled. I will wear my gray muslin dress and a cloak. I can always hide under the hood if need be."

Dani gave a rare laugh. "You can never hide. You float along the ground and every head turns."

"Well, I shall try. For this night at least," Monique said gaily, suddenly excited by an adventure that had nothing to do with Stanhope. A few moments of carefree fun. "And you," she said, "you must wear something pretty, too."

"I have nothing," Dani said.

"Yes, you do," Monique said. "You can wear one of mine. We are much the same size. And you would look very pretty in blue."

"I do not want to look pretty," Dani said, her eyes darkening.

Monique hesitated. "I will be with you every moment. You cannot hide forever."

"I like hiding."

"Well tonight, we will be together. . . . Please."

The rebellion slipped from Dani's eyes. Then she smiled. *"Oui."*

Vauxhall Gardens was like nothing Gabriel had ever seen before. He had never been there as a lad. His father had considered the behavior there licentious, he remembered. He hadn't known exactly what the word meant, but he'd remembered it.

But tonight there was to be an orchestra and singers and fireworks, and the night was a perfect English evening. No fog, only a cool breeze.

He would not have thought about it if he hadn't met with Elizabeth Smythe this morning.

Smythe had brought his sister down to him as he ate breakfast. She had shyly presented herself to him. Elizabeth was a thin sprite of a child with huge eyes and a reserved nature. He bade her to sit down and join him for breakfast. She obviously didn't want to do it, but he was tired of eating by himself at a large table while others served him.

"It would be a kindness," he said.

She looked as if she wanted to escape.

"Your brother said you like to read," Gabriel said. "I like people who read and I thought you might share some of my books."

Her eyes opened wide. "Truly?"

"Truly," he said.

She finally took a seat as her mother served them, her chin bobbing nervously.

But the moment Elizabeth started talking about books, and geography, her blue eyes lit like a sky filled with stars. They sparkled and glowed. "I want to go around the world," she said. "But first I want to go to the colonies and see the Indians."

"Some of them are very fierce," he said.

She regarded him for a moment. "But do they not have reason?"

"Yes, indeed they do," he said.

He'd wondered whether his small collection of books would be too difficult for her, but now he realized she had one of those rare minds that soaked up knowledge like a sponge.

"And where would you like to go here in London?"

"Oh," she said, excitement vibrating her small body. "The fireworks at the Gardens. That would be marvelous. My uncle said he would take me when he had time."

He looked at Smythe, who had just walked in with a steaming plate of eggs, much too much for him alone, but then Smythe and his mother seemed determined to fatten him.

"When is the next fireworks?"

"Tonight, my lord," Elizabeth said.

"Then I think you should go."

Smythe looked stricken, even mortified. Gabriel realized how truly desperate the family must have been.

Suddenly he too wanted to go, and not for the fireworks. God knew he'd seen enough shot streaking through the skies to ever enjoy a fireworks display. But he realized how lonely he was, and the thought of an evening with a family was suddenly very appealing.

"I would like to take you and your mother and Elizabeth," he said.

"That . . . would be unseemly, sir."

"I am an American. I can be unseemly," he said. "Or anything else I want to be. Smythe, you have no idea how much pleasure it would give me."

Elizabeth looked up at Smythe with pleading eyes. "Please, Sydney. Oh, please."

Caught between his sister and employer, Smythe gave a deep sigh and surrendered. "As you wish, my lord."

"We will leave at seven," he said. "And Elizabeth can visit my study and borrow any books she wishes."

Smythe nodded solemnly. "Thank you, Mr. Manning."

*Mr. Manning.* Well, he had accomplished something today. He finished his meal, then stood. "I need your help with that blasted cravat," he said. "I have some business this morning. I will rent a carriage for tonight." He glanced at Smythe. "Unless you have a brother or nephew who can help us."

Smythe allowed his lips the smallest of smiles. "No, sir. I will engage one."

Vauxhall Gardens was all that he had heard described, and more. There was a fee at the entrance, and he paid for the four of them. They must be an odd group, he thought. He had decided he couldn't completely discard his new personality, so he wore a gaudy waistcoat of a bright pattern against a green background. He fixed the quizzing glass in his eye and chose his most elaborate cane.

Elizabeth looked surprised when she saw him, but she said nothing. Mrs. Smythe looked uncomfortable as well, but she was dressed in what must be her best dress. An old worn bonnet covered graying hair. She held Elizabeth's hand tightly and admonished her over and over again not to let go.

The gardens were filled to overflowing with fashionable families as well as groups of ladies and couples.

Gabriel took pleasure in watching shy Elizabeth come to life, her eyes glowing as they moved around. Smythe looked uncomfortable in his new clothes and Gabriel knew he felt uneasy about socializing with his employer. Still, Smythe's eyes softened as he, too, watched Elizabeth, and Gabriel saw the gratitude in them.

Smythe's mother looked just as awed. If she felt uncomfortable among the fashionably dressed, she said nothing about it. Since others had servants watching over children, he suspected that many thought the child was his and the Smythes his servants.

In truth, he was enjoying every moment with them. He felt a kinship with Smythe as a soldier, even if the man was unaware of it. He liked Smythe's mother, who was one of those women who endured without bitterness and even with a bit of humor. He was enchanted by young Elizabeth and her intellectual curiosity.

He'd seldom taken any time to relax, to enjoy the pleasures of a family. After his father's death, there had been little family life left. His mother had stayed in her room and grown frail and bitter.

This was a respite from the tension of the past few days, the balance between boredom and anticipation as his plan bore fruits. He would be a guest at Stanhope's home, and then he would be in position to implement his plan.

For these few hours, at least, he intended to enjoy the park, the city, and give a few hours' pleasure as well. It had been a long time since he had done that, too.

He stopped at a booth and purchased punch and ham for each of them, then found a table for them to sit. He kept a close eye on Elizabeth. He read the London newspapers each day, looking for mentions of the three men who had betrayed his father and mentions of himself. There had been several of the former, one of which mentioned the soiree to which he had been invited and several not so flattering to himself. Among other reports was one about assaults in the Garden, and he was determined that nothing would happen to his young companion.

Her eyes glowed as she ate the ham and gazed at the well-dressed men and women sauntering and parading down the pathways. He noticed the equally watchful looks of her brother and mother and their very carefully phrased remarks and quick sideways glances at him as if afraid he disapproved of something. He was part of them, yet not a part. He knew that he made them uncomfortable, and as he watched Smythe place an arm around his young sister, he felt a raw stab of loneliness. He didn't know when last he had touched someone with that kind of affectionate intimacy. His mother had for all practical purposes died with her husband. Since then, he'd had no time—or heart—for gentle thoughts or attachments. Love and hate, he'd believed, could not coexist.

Still, he'd never felt the kind of emptiness he did now, nor had he ever wondered whether revenge was worth the toll it required. He had gone too far, though, to leave the path he had taken. He knew every night would be haunted by the face of his father when he had pleaded with an uncomprehending lad.

He finished his meal quickly, a habit he'd formed early, and rose. The others started to do the same, although they had not quite finished.

"Stay and finish," he said in a voice he suddenly realized was much too harsh, more like the voice in which he issued orders aboard ship. He softened his tone. "I am just taking a short stroll."

They sank back in the seats, a relieved look on the three faces. He knew regret again. He doubted that he would ever be anything more than "milord" and employer to them.

He fixed the quizzing glass in his left eye and sauntered among the diners. His gaze was abruptly caught by the sight of two women sitting at a table, their backs to him. One had a bonnet over bright red hair. The other's hair was covered by the hood of a cloak. Heat rushed through him like a burst of electricity. Though he couldn't see her features, he knew instinctively by the tilt of her head and the animation in every movement that she was the actress who had occupied so many thoughts in the past few days.

He hesitated, wondering whether he should approach, and damned himself for even considering such a move. She had made far too strong an impression on him.

Nor, did he particularly want her to see him with his quizzing glass, and it wouldn't be wise to discard it just now. He did not know the crowds of men and women, but unquestionably some would be of the ton, and he would invariably meet them in the coming days. He had built his image too carefully to tear it down now. In truth, this outing had been a poor idea, but he'd needed a respite before the next stage of his plan.

He couldn't tear his gaze away, though, and remained there as he saw her back stiffen slightly as a well-dressed older man approached her. Monique's back was still toward him, and he studied the face of the man as he bowed, then said something in a low voice.

Gabriel didn't quite know why but something about the

man raised hackles on his back. There was arrogance in every movement, but there was something in his face and in his eyes that gave him pause. It might have been the dark emptiness in those eyes or the way his lips parted in what was obviously meant to be a smile but was more a sneer.

The fellow's smile changed into one of triumph as he sat down, obviously at the woman's invitation.

Disappointment settled deep inside him. It was as if he'd just discovered that a gem he treasured had a flaw he had not expected. His reaction was unreasonable. He knew that. He understood that. Gabriel had accompanied her home and had never attempted to call again, although an unspoken invitation had been in her eyes despite her words. He'd sensed that the invitation had been as reluctant as his own momentary lapse of judgment.

She certainly didn't owe him anything and could speak with whomever she wished. She could also choose her own companions, and yet this man was at least old enough to be her father and there was something about him that . . .

Was she looking for a protector? A wealthy one?

He waited. Perhaps the man was a patron of the theater. Yet, she flirted with him, using a fan to signal her availability. Then she stood and took his arm, and the two of them walked together toward the concert area, the maid trailing behind the couple.

So, the innocent was not so innocent after all. He had thought—to hell with what he'd thought. He turned back toward the rest of his small party and saw that they had finished with the meal. They too were looking toward Monique, who was disappearing down the pathway.

"Who is that?" Elizabeth said, and he realized she must have seen his face. He'd noticed before that she read moods well. She listened and watched.

"An actress," he said.

Her mouth formed a perfect *O* and her eyes were curious. Her mother admonished her by touch. "She did not mean to be impertinent," her mother said.

"Asking questions is never impertinent," he replied. "One never learns anything without them."

Mrs. Smythe looked uncertain about that answer, but merely nodded. Gabriel suspected Elizabeth would receive a lecture later.

"Let us go and hear the music," he said.

But for some reason, his heart was no longer in it. A light had just inexplicably dimmed.

Monique agreed to accompany the Earl of Stanhope to the concert area.

She'd been startled to see him, and her plans for a relaxing evening fled. Her heart had nearly stopped for a moment as he approached.

But this was a safe place with all the people promenading. She instinctively knew he was a man she could not refuse often. His arrogance would not allow continued refusals. She had to keep his interest.

She gave him a practiced smile that promised nothing, but she saw the flicker in his eyes. Let him think he'd won this round.

He barely glanced at Dani, unlike the marquess who'd saved her from an awkward situation. This man had only disdain for a servant.

She wished she could stop thinking of the marquess. He certainly had shown no more interest in her, and, even if he had, no marquess would be attracted to an actress as anything but a mistress. She would never be any man's mistress. Never. The memories of her mother were far too painful. Her mother had been forced into prostitution by the very man walking next to her.

"How do you like our gardens?" Stanhope asked.

*"C'est si belle,"* she said.

"So are you," he said.

She played with her fan. "You are . . . most amiable, monsieur."

"You are the talk of all of London. Every eye is on you."

"I think not, monsieur."

"Ah, a modest woman."

Her stomach was queasy. She'd never imagined she would

feel the fear he evoked in her. There was something distinctly evil about him, and it sent quivers up her back.

His blood ran through her. Was she anything at all like him? Was her quest for vengeance as wicked as his actions?

Justice, she told herself. She was seeking justice. How many women other than her mother had he destroyed?

"Do you have a family, monsieur?" she asked.

"A daughter," he said.

"Oh, is she here in London with you?"

"She stays with her aunt," he said shortly. "She needs a woman's influence."

"But surely the season . . ."

"Pamela is rather shy."

"And your wife?" She already knew the answer, but she wanted him to say it. She also wondered about her half sister. What kind of life did *she* have?

"Mary died ten years ago," he said shortly.

She ignored the warning in his voice. "You have not re-married?"

He stopped and looked down at her. "I enjoy the company of beautiful women," he said.

"And that excludes marriage?" she said, fanning herself.

"I like new challenges." His eyes glittered with a brightness that was frightening.

"And then you discard them?" she asked.

"There are no complaints," he assured her.

A chill ran through her. She took another step, but his hand stopped her from moving farther. "I pay whatever is necessary to get what I want," he said.

"Money is not important to me."

"Money is important to everyone."

"Truly, monsieur? More important than anything else? Than your daughter?"

"You can do anything if you have money," he said. "My daughter is fortunate. She has the finest in clothes, in jewelry. I can give the same to you."

"That is most flattering, monsieur," she said, ignoring his title. "But for the moment I am most satisfied with my life. I enjoy the theater. I have no need of anything more."

Surprise flickered in his eyes.

"I would like for you to visit my house," he said. "You will like it."

"It would not be . . . proper, my lord. A visit to your home alone and I would be known as your mistress."

He seemed to hesitate, then said, "Then will you come if there are others there? I am planning a soiree at the end of the week. I would be most pleased if you could attend."

She raised an eyebrow. "An actress, my lord?"

He shrugged.

"May I bring an escort?"

"Who?"

"It would be someone respectable," she assured him.

He hesitated.

"We will make it some other time, then."

"You may bring whomever you wish," he said after a momentary pause. "And now will you attend the concert with me? I have a supper box."

"You like music?"

"Yes," he replied.

That surprised her. One thing they apparently had in common. She didn't want anything in common.

They strolled to the concert area, and she realized her hood did not give her the anonymity that she'd wanted. But now she did not care. Her carefree evening with a friend had been destroyed, and now she was playing a role again.

He helped them into the box and started to close the door on Dani.

"If Danielle doesn't join us, I will not stay," she said.

Stanhope looked startled, irritated, then reopened the door and placed a chair at the back, as far from the two of them as he could.

A chamber orchestra played Mozart. Music usually enthralled her, but tonight she was too aware of the man next to her and the many sly glances directed their way.

It was what she wanted. Part of her plan.

But with every passing second, she wondered whether she could really do what she had planned all the years she had cared for her mother, watching as desperation and grief and

shame ate away at the beauty Monique remembered. She stole
a glance around. It caught a man standing not far away with
what looked like a family group. A pretty young child. A
woman whose clothing spoke of a lower class. The child's
eyes glittered with excitement, and her hair was the same
color as the marquess's. She looked up at Lord Manchester
with adoration.

Her blood froze as her gaze met Lord Manchester's and
locked. The warmth of the other day was gone, and yet an
emotion burned deep within. He seemed as unable to look
away as she did. She didn't miss a quick flash of contempt,
though.

Then she heard a cough next to her.

She turned her attention back to Stanhope.

A lump formed in her throat. Was the child a by-blow of
the Marquess of Manchester?

And why should she be surprised if she was?

Still, she felt a sickness deep inside. She knew the pain of
being a bastard child.

"Who is that?" Stanhope's displeasure was clear in the
way he emphasized the last word.

"The Marquess of Manchester," she replied. "He gave me
some assistance several days ago."

Stanhope visibly stiffened, and he turned to study the small
family group several aisles away. "An odd group. I did not
know he had a child."

Monique shrugged indifferently. "I did not talk to him at
any length. I know nothing of his personal life."

Stanhope's eyes questioned her statement, and she wondered how much she had given away in that too-long glance
at Manchester. She was slipping. She usually was excellent at
hiding emotions.

It was just that she'd thought Manchester, despite his
dandy pretensions, had been different from the men she'd
known.

"He is a gambler," Stanhope said, "and not a very lucky
one from the rumors."

"I do not read gossip," she said.

Someone frowned at them for talking during the music,

and she gratefully lapsed into silence. She did not look back again toward the marquess, but she was more than a little aware of his presence.

She tried to lose herself in a Mozart concerto, but her skin tingled with awareness. She used her fan to cool skin too warm for a cool night.

Then the concert was over and the sky exploded with fireworks. Rockets transformed the dark blue velvet of an English night with trails of molten gold, then spectacular bursts of color. She used the distraction to turn around.

The Marquess of Manchester was gone.

# Chapter Seven

The day following the concert Gabriel left his town house for the waterfront.

He left dressed in some plain but warm garments he had purchased in Boston. Within an hour he'd found a disreputable drunk who didn't blink when asked for an exchange of clothing. Alcohol, no doubt, convinced the man that Gabriel was a fool.

The clothes were soiled, but Gabriel had dressed in dirty clothes before. Working in the wet hold of a ship taught one not to be overly concerned with niceties. A down-on-his-luck sailor wouldn't own even the least of Gabriel's wardrobe.

He wanted to know more about Stanhope's shipping company. The shipping company that once belonged to Gabriel's father.

He had purposely not shaved that morning, and he'd rubbed a bit of dirt on his face. He knew sailors. Hell, he'd been one much of his life. He knew how to talk to them, how to become one of them.

His first stop was a riverfront tavern.

He quickly discovered that the sailors had no love for Stanhope's company. Despite the fact that the company initially offered sailors a higher than ordinary salary, life, apparently, was hell on the ships. The food was usually rotten, the discipline harsh, the ships kept in poor repair.

Many sailors had been drugged, then taken to the ships.

Yet nothing seemed to touch Stanhope. There were rumors of important connections, but no one could identify exactly who that protection was.

Gabriel wondered whether the earl had the same connections twenty years ago.

In one tavern that appeared to be patronized by a particularly villainous looking group of ruffians, he broached the subject of duplicating a seal. After bargaining, he promised to pay twenty pounds for a duplicate.

It was a fortune in this part of London.

"'Ow do I know ye can pay?"

The man had a patch over one eye, and the other one had larceny in it.

Gabriel shrugged.

"'Ow did someone like ye get that much blunt?"

"None of your affair."

The man eyed with him a malevolent glare, then held out his hand for the Stanhope seal.

Gabriel shook his head. "I want to meet with the . . . artist."

"'Ow do I know ye won't cut me out?"

"Faith, my good fellow. Faith."

"I am not yer good fellow."

"I can see that, which is why I chose you," Gabriel said with a grin he knew was as fearsome as his companion's. He had learned from the best. "Now do you wish to earn a fee or not? If not, I will find someone who will."

"Who are ye?"

Gabriel just looked at him. "I need a seal. Nothing more. And you should know that if you tell anyone about me, I'll be forced to protect my privacy." He made his voice as brittle and hard as hail striking cobblestones.

"Ye play fair wi' me, I will do the same," the man said, obviously making up his mind. "Come wi' me."

They left the tavern together. Gabriel followed the man

through some alleys. Then he stopped. "Put this over yer eyes."

It was a dirty scarf. Gabriel wasn't enough of a fool to be led around London's dark allies blindfolded.

"No," he said.

"He'll kill me if I take ye to him."

Gabriel didn't like the looks of the area, nor the shadows. He grabbed the bandit by his rough jacket. "Then tell him I can be trusted. I can find out who you are. Where you live. You betray me and I will kill you. If you do not, I will make it worth your while. I will have more work for you."

The man barely nodded his head.

"Your name?" Gabriel asked.

"Jack."

"Just Jack?"

"Jack Pryor."

"And if I ask around, what will I learn about Jack Pryor?"

Jack didn't say anything.

"Are you married, Jack?"

"Do I look the nodcock?"

Gabriel arched an eyebrow. "Let's get on with it."

The man didn't move. "You talk strangely."

"I've been a sailor fifteen years," Gabriel said.

"Let me see your hands."

Gabriel held them out. Calluses were quite evident. That was why he usually wore gloves.

Jack nodded with satisfaction. "Follow me."

Gabriel did so, marking streets as he went. It was a good exercise for a mind plagued since last night with the sight of Monique and Stanhope.

He had not known who the man was until he heard someone in the crowd whispering his name—and not in a complimentary way.

Monique Fremont and Thomas Kane, the Earl of Stanhope. The very image of the two together had made him queasy. So queasy that he had hustled his guests to the side of the park with the excuse that he was thirsty. He had brought them all punch before their journey home and he had listened to Elizabeth chatter with excitement.

For once, she'd lost her shyness in her excitement. The outing had been worth every pence and every moment for the joy that transformed her face into something truly remarkable.

But he couldn't get Monique Fremont's elegant face, graceful bearing, and cool gray eyes from his head. He had not last night. He couldn't do it today. Not even this trip into the bowels of London's dark side darkened the brightness of the mental image he had of her.

Not even the memory of her smiling up at the man he hated most in the world.

He had vowed to erase that image by taking the next step in the ruination of Stanhope.

He wondered whether it would be the ruination of himself as well.

He shook the notion away as they arrived at a print shop. Jack went in, stayed several moments, then emerged and motioned for Gabriel to accompany him inside.

The space was completely filled with tables, where broadsheets of one sort or another were filed high. There was a workbench with trays of type scattered over it. There was a bench in front of it.

An elderly, frail-looking man with glasses perched on his nose sat in the midst of what looked like chaos. He looked as if a wind might blow him over, but then as Gabriel studied him closer he saw that what looked thin was actually wiry. There was strength in that small body. The glasses and face made him look benevolent until Gabriel looked closer into his eyes.

They were like mirrors. They studied him like he was a bug on the wall. Then, "You want Stanhope." No question was in the statement.

Gabriel did not reply for a slice of a moment.

The man seemed to force himself to take his eyes from him. He turned to Jack. "Go and watch outside."

Surprisingly, Jack immediately did as he was told.

Once he was gone, the printer looked at him for a long time. "Why?"

Gabriel shrugged. "Why what?"

"Jack recognized the seal. You want something from Stanhope. What and why?"

"I am doing a favor for someone."

"The only reason someone would want another's seal is to forge a document."

"I could think of other reasons."

"You dress like a common seaman. You don't talk like one."

"I could, but then I would be insulting you."

"You're Manchester. You look like your father and I heard you were in London."

"Yes." There was no reason to hide it.

"Stanhope framed your father and stole the company."

Gabriel narrowed his eyes. "How did you know that?"

"I know everything that happens on the London docks," the printer said flatly.

"Did you know my father?"

The man nodded and fixed an unblinking stare on Manchester. "Why do you want the seal?"

"I have a use for it."

"I hear you gamble. Why should I trust you with something that could bring the runners to my business?"

"Do you think I'm a fool?"

"To come here alone with Jack, yes."

"He and I came to an understanding."

"An understanding like that can get you killed."

"I can take care of myself," Gabriel said.

"I think you can," the printer said slowly. "So why play the fool?"

Gabriel didn't reply.

"You look like your father but you are not like him. He trusted people."

"And it killed him."

"I will make your seal."

"I might also need some documents forged."

The printer nodded. "I can do that." He stood, and his head came to Gabriel's chest. "I'm Winsley," he said slowly. "Your father helped me start this business. Stanhope has ruined more people than your father. I would like to see him destroyed. You might be the person who can do it."

"It's said he might have important friends," Gabriel said.

"No one claims him as such," Winsley said. "But no one seems to be able to call him to accounts, either."

"Can you sell stones for me?"

"Stolen stones?"

"*Found* stones," Gabriel said.

"Don't be too ambitious, young Manning."

"I haven't been young since I saw my father on the floor, blood pouring from his head."

"I will do what I can for you. When do you need the seal?"

"As soon as possible. I hope to return it before it is missed."

"A few days then," Winsley said.

"Should I come here?"

"No. Someone will bring it to you."

Gabriel nodded. "I will have your money then."

"I am pleased to see you were not foolish enough to bring it with you."

"I have been at sea a long time. I know seaports."

"You are not an ordinary seaman."

"I was for a number of years. I captain a ship now."

"Ah. I suspected as much. Even in those clothes, you have the look of a leader."

"I hope to hell not."

"You let your guard down."

"I will have to watch that."

"You put me at risk, too."

Gabriel looked around the shop. It was covered with dust. "Then why are you a forger?"

"I asked some questions about Stanhope. He nearly destroyed my business, warning away people. Some people he couldn't warn away."

*Luck or coincidence? Or did Stanhope's business dealings affect far more people than he'd thought?*

Or could it be a trap? Perhaps Stanhope had missed the seal and sent Jack to spy on him.

Perhaps. . . .

He wondered whether his eyes showed what he was feeling.

But the man only turned away, effectively dismissing him.

Gabriel went into the front of the shop. Jack was there, waiting.

"I can find my own way back," Gabriel said, handing him a half of a crown.

"Did ye get what ye wanted?"

Gabriel shrugged. "My thanks for your help."

"I don't want yer thanks. I want yer blunt."

Gabriel looked at him. "I suspect you will have a great deal more."

He headed for the door, then the street, glancing around him as any sane man would do in the immediate area.

But even as he did, he was thinking ahead. Tomorrow would be Stanhope's soiree.

First he must go back to his lodgings and change clothes. Hopefully no one would see him, but if they did he would explain he'd been attacked. Then a trip to the tailor's to pick up the new doeskin trousers and waistcoat he had ordered for Stanhope's affair. He had ordered the best. Perhaps he would attend a hell tonight, this time to win. He'd learned in the past few weeks which were the honest houses. A stroke of luck would not be noticed in light of his losses.

Then the soiree tomorrow and a slight bit of larceny.

He wondered whether Monique Fremont would be present.

He tried to tell himself she would be a distraction to Stanhope and that was all to the good.

He also wondered if she knew Stanhope's reputation, whether she knew that some believed he had killed his wife. He wondered whether he should warn her.

It was her business, not his.

Still . . . he was a gentleman, and he would not want harm to come to her.

Monique wondered who she could get to take her to the soiree at Stanhope's home. She needed someone who would not keep a very close eye on her.

There was Mr. Lynch, of course, but he would take her

offer as an invitation. So would the would-be suitors that hovered around the theater.

All the way through the rehearsal, she considered the actor that played her husband. That would, she knew, displease Stanhope, yet instinct told her that it would be a wrong move. It would humiliate Stanhope. She didn't want to do that. Not until all was ready for the final humiliation.

Her mind ran over possibilities. Lynch or Richard?

Lynch was unusually critical during the rehearsal. "Where is that sparkle, that zest?"

She tried to brighten her smile.

Richard leaned over after Lynch left them. "I think he had a bad night. You should see his wife. And hear her. She always suspects all the actresses of being after him. He must have arrived home late last night. She might even show up today."

She smiled back. "I am warned."

"There's someone else in the theater," he said.

She turned her head quickly and saw a man standing in the shadows toward the back of the theater. For a moment she thought it was Stanhope, then she noted he was taller, leaner.

She turned back to Richard and recited her next line.

She had not forgotten the contempt on the marquess's face last night when he saw her with Stanhope, nor the sickness in her belly when she saw the child.

For a moment she wanted to flee. Instead, she looked at Richard as he said something.

"Bloody hell," Lynch shouted. When she looked at Richard, she saw puzzlement in his eyes as well.

"Sorry," she said. "Give me the cue again."

He did, and she responded as she always had before, the words coming out. The anger she felt fueled her. She saw from Richard's face that she had seldom acted better as she exchanged repartee.

She concentrated on every line. The dress rehearsal would be in three days, then the play would open three days later. Dear God, it had to be good. She had to be the darling of London, wanted by everyone, not a flop colored by rotten food.

Even Lynch was silent as they came to the end.

The house was filled with lights.

She turned toward the curtains. She would make it clear to the stagehands that no one was to be allowed near her dressing room.

Dani was in the wings. Her gaze was fixed on the back of the theater. "The marquess. He is here."

*"Oui,"* Monique said. "I saw him. I do not want to see any more of him."

"But did you not say you needed an escort?"

Monique narrowed her eyes. Dani looked innocent, but there was a gleam in her eyes.

If Monique didn't know better, she would believe Dani was turning her hand toward matchmaking. But Dani distrusted men every bit as much as she did.

"He would make a good protector," Dani said.

"He had a child with him," Monique said. "He must be married."

Dani shrugged. "Perhaps the child is not his."

"What man escorts a child not his own?"

"You do not need to stay with him, but I . . . I think he would make you safe." Dani's eyes pleaded with her.

"He may not wish to go. He has not made any attempt to see me, and he did not look approachable last night."

"Perhaps he did not like seeing you with that man."

*Jealous? Unlikely.* He had not called on her again, nor tried to see her again. It was an unusual feeling for her, wanting someone who did not want her.

*Wanting someone.* That was unique in itself. She had vowed long enough never to be dependent on a man. Yet she didn't seem able to slow the quickening beat of her heart, nor cool the blood that turned warm when she saw him.

A gambler, Stanhope had said. So he knew of him, even if he had not made Manchester's acquaintance. But a marquess would be welcomed in nearly everyone's home. As for the gaming, she'd learned since arriving here that every young lord gambled.

"Shall I bring him?" Dani asked.

"Lynch has probably ejected him from the theater," she said.

"Not if he has funds," Dani said with a disdain that amused Monique.

"I suppose he bribed some of the guards outside."

"*Oui.*"

Monique considered Dani's proposal. Maybe Manchester would be the perfect foil. A marquess would no doubt excite Stanhope's obvious competitiveness. And she'd already discovered that despite the fop appearance, he could handle problems.

*And you really want to see him again.* She hated that little voice inside her.

She hated the way she felt.

But maybe if she saw more of him, she would realize he was nothing more than another useless aristocrat who felt it his right to gamble away his heritage and perhaps destroy the people who depended on him.

"*Oui,*" she said.

Dani gave her a triumphant smile and slipped out the door.

Monique brushed her hair and placed a bonnet on it to keep from piling it up with pins. At the last moment she pinched her cheeks and bit her lips to bring more color into her face.

Her eyes, she noticed, were not their usual gray calm but more like that of the thunderheads prior to a storm.

"Drat the man."

She stood when the knock came and she took the few steps to the door. When she opened it, he stood there, his hat in one hand while he whirled a cane with the other.

No flowers. No candy. No extravagant gift.

He was even taller than she remembered. His green eyes danced with curiosity.

His hair was properly dressed, and she didn't like it. She liked it more when it looked tousled and wild.

For a moment they just stared at each other, the attraction vibrating in the air, the electricity a palpable thing.

Then he broke it with a bow that was more mocking than respectful. "Mademoiselle. I did not know if you would be here after a late night"

"I might say the same, my lord. I thought you might be gambling tonight."

"I expect to do that," he replied. "But I felt it my duty to warn you about your companion last night."

"Warn?"

"He has not the best of reputations."

"Neither do you, my lord."

"But I have never been accused of murder."

"And Lord Stanhope has?"

"Privately."

"I am sure you have been called things that are not true." Drat but his eyes were green. They were not dancing any longer, but instead intense, almost willing her to bend to his will.

She would bend to no man's will.

*"Merci,"* she said, then eyed him speculatively. "Perhaps you can be of some assistance to me."

He looked surprised. "If I may."

"I have been invited to the Lord Stanhope's home. A social . . . occasion, I believe. But I would like an escort."

His mouth crooked on one side. A strange smile. Oddly pleasant. "I too have been invited. It would be my honor to accompany you."

Relief flooded her. And anticipation. And something else not quite as benevolent. She shrugged away the latter.

The relief was real. She had not wanted to be alone in Stanhope's town house. The anticipation was there because she would have an opportunity to study the house.

And another kind of opportunity.

And the something else. She sensed this man could be dangerous. Not to her physically. But certainly in other ways.

She ignored the warning. "You are very kind, my lord."

"It will do my reputation no harm to have you on my arm," he said. "I do not know about your own."

"An American bumpkin, you mean."

"You read the newspapers."

"I hear gossip."

"They can think what they like. They sneered at Americans in 1776 and again a few years ago. They discovered a strength they hadn't understood."

"And do you have a strength they wouldn't understand?"

His expression was enigmatic. He didn't reply. Or perhaps he had.

"How long do you plan to stay in London?" she asked after a moment.

He didn't answer immediately. She realized their voices had lowered and become husky. She was not only warm now. She felt as if her skin was sizzling. Where *was* Dani?

He leaned closer and she smelled the clean scent of soap, not the heavy perfume so many men affected. His eyes were as startling green as emeralds, and his mouth . . .

His mouth touched hers with a firmness combined with gentleness, more of an exploration than a conquest. She found herself responding, rising on her tiptoes. He moved closer and their bodies stretched against each other and she felt her own begin to ache in sensuous and unfamiliar ways.

His kiss deepened, and then she heard a purr come from deep in her throat and felt, rather than saw, him smile. She looked up, and he was smiling with those eyes she once thought so aloof.

His arms went around her and drew her even closer to him. She felt the heat of his aroused body, the steady drumbeat of his heart, and the whispered promise of his breath.

*It's a lie.*

She pulled away and looked up at him. Her lips felt swollen, and she knew her cheeks must be rose colored with heat and emotion.

"You take liberties, my lord."

"Aye," he said. "It seemed the thing to do. The invitation was there."

The words were like a dash of freezing water.

"You saw what you wanted to see, not what was there," she said in as cool a voice as she could imagine.

"I think not."

"You are arrogant."

"Are not most lords?"

The heat of passion was being replaced by the heat of anger. His answers were cool and dispassionate, almost as if that electricity had struck only her. And yet when she glanced down at his hands, she saw they trembled slightly as one leaned on an ornate cane.

She moved away to the mirror. Her worst fears were realized as she saw the flush of her face, the hair that had escaped the bonnet and fell down the side of her face. Even worse, the way her breasts thrust against the bodice of her dress, the nipples very obvious through the cloth.

She wanted to tell him he would not be needed tomorrow after all. She wanted to tell him to go to hell.

Revenge on Stanhope. That should supercede any other emotion, even this arrogant man.

She'd always been able to twist them around her fingers. She was very good at manipulation.

She suspected this man could not be manipulated.

"I must go," she said. "You will still accompany me tomorrow?"

He bowed again. "Most certainly, mademoiselle."

She nodded.

His eyes were an enigma as he reached the door. He looked back once at her.

"Be careful of Stanhope," he said. "I came to tell you that."

But as he disappeared outside, she wondered exactly who she had to be the most careful of.

# Chapter Eight

Stanhope oversaw every preparation critically. Every food item, every flower arrangement was inspected. Any bloom with the slightest imperfection was removed, each platter not perfectly arranged was sent back to the kitchen, the slightest speck of dust incited rage.

Pamela attracted the most displeasure. At his summons she had arrived yesterday and had crept around the house like a mouse, her brown eyes red and swollen. His daughter had never been a beauty, but—dressed and her hair well arranged—she was acceptable.

He had ignored her for years. He had thought she might be of some use to him, but she had always feared him, and he'd never respected timidity. Nor did he like women. They served their purpose in satisfying his physical needs, and he enjoyed the attention that having a beautiful woman on his arm gave him.

Mostly, they were a bloody nuisance, of little intelligence and loyalty. His mother had run away with a lover when he was six years of age, and he'd had little use for his father's mistresses in the following years. One had seduced him, taught him the physical pleasures, then tried to steal from him. He'd not informed his father, but had broken her arm and threatened worse.

He had seen fear then, and it had given him a sense of power that was stronger than any emotion he'd ever known before. He'd learned how to enhance fear, how exquisite it was to see fear change into terror. It gave him surges of pleasure that satisfied a deep hunger inside him, a hunger that had never been quenched in any other way.

Except once. He tried not to think of that any longer. There had been one woman long ago . . .

He had thought himself in love. For once in his life, he'd felt loved for himself.

She was unsuitable. He'd known that, but he thought he could keep her safe somewhere.

And then his father had discovered she was with child. And his father had killed her.

He'd never allowed anyone to touch his heart again, not even a daughter born of a union his father had arranged. He'd hated Francis the moment he'd met her. She was loud where Mary had been quiet, had atrocious taste in her wealth where Mary had exquisite taste with very little. She brayed where Mary had a clarion merry laughter.

But that was a quarter of a century ago. He'd locked away the pain as he had locked away every other emotion except a need for power.

He looked at his daughter and wondered why his daughter's fear didn't please him as it had in the past. He told himself it was because he needed her to be attractive.

He looked for her, but she was not in the living quarters. Probably dribbling more tears in her bedchamber with her maid, who was as meek as she. God, he hated meek women. They offered no challenge.

He shouted for the butler and instructed him to tell one of the maids to fetch her. He would be damned if he would go up to her. While he waited, he poured a drink, then took one last look at the large sitting room, where a string quartet would play. The front of the room had been cleared and rearranged. The quartet was said to be the finest in London, and he'd gone through all the music with them. He wondered whether

Monique Fremont had a voice worth hearing. Many actresses did. Perhaps he would ask her.

The image of her face came back into his mind. A flicker of some recognition, some odd familiarity ran through him. He tested it, searched his mind for a clue. Another theater, perhaps, but no, he would remember that. Strange that he hadn't felt it before, or recognized it. He had an extraordinary memory for faces, a talent that served him well. But as much as he searched his memory, he couldn't place that face in another time, or place.

A timid knock came at his door. "Come in," he shouted loudly enough to be heard several rooms away.

Pamela entered, wearing a plain afternoon gown. Its bright yellow did nothing for her brown hair and light brown eyes. She looked sallow and unappealing.

"Did your aunt choose that?" he asked.

"No," she said with the slightest hint of defiance. "I did."

Despite his earlier thought about meek women, her momentary boldness annoyed him.

"There is no excuse for abominable taste. You look like a dead fish. I have guests coming tonight, one a very eligible marquess, and I want you to look as if you have at least one breath of life left inside you." He glared at her, and she flinched.

Still, she dared open her mouth. "I do not want a marquess."

"Do you think I care what you want?"

"No, but I hoped . . ." Her voice died away.

He did not like the feeling he was getting. "You have not let that young buck . . ." Twenty-five-year-old images flooded back. Not her, too. The devil take it, he wouldn't have it. He would not allow history to repeat itself.

"No!"

Her denial was too sharp.

"If he has ruined you, I will see him dead and banish you to some place you will not want to go."

"No one has touched me," she said.

"I would have a doctor confirm that," he said.

She went white. "You would not . . ."

"I will," he said again, his voice rising. He could barely contain his fury. What in bloody hell had his sister been thinking?

"I will do anything you want," she said, her voice rising.

"Then get dressed and you'd bloody better have that worthless twit of a maid do something with your hair or she will be on the street tonight. And you will be charming for the Marquess of Manchester tonight."

Her shoulders bowed slightly, the short bout of rebellion gone.

"Pamela?"

She curtsied. "Yes, Father."

"I suggest you begin now. It will take some time to make you presentable."

She started to back out.

"Pamela!"

She froze but didn't look back.

"I expect you to bewitch the marquess. If you do not, we will be talking to that doctor, and I will make queries in the village. There are always those who see everything."

She bolted from the room.

His gaze followed her footfalls. He would instruct his butler to start making additional queries immediately. Something had given his daughter new boldness. He would know what it was.

Dressed in tight doeskin trousers, peacock-blue waistcoat, and an elaborate cravat that felt as if it were stretching his neck about two inches, Gabriel arrived at Monique's town house and knocked at the door.

In seconds it was thrust wide open by the redheaded maid named Dani, who wore a welcoming smile on her lips.

He couldn't help but smile in return. "Is your mistress ready?"

"*Oui*, monsieur," she said. "And she is beautiful. I made sure of that."

"I think she is always beautiful."

"*Mais oui,*" she agreed. "She really does not need me. She . . ."

"She is grateful for your loyalty," said a musical voice be-hind Dani. "And you are right, monsieur, Dani is responsi-ble."

He stepped inside and for the briefest moment he felt his breath had been stolen away.

Her hair had been piled in curls with one long dark curl falling down around her left cheek and framing it. Her dress was midnight blue and made her gray eyes appear luminous.

She was, simply, the most seductive and intriguing woman he'd ever met. He reminded himself that she had been with Stanhope, staring up at him with the attention a woman gives a man when she intends seduction.

The reminder of his disappointment—even dismay—was like a festering wound, and he resented that. He didn't want to care about anyone now, especially a woman who was ob-viously looking for an advantageous situation, even someone like Stanhope.

He still tasted her lips, felt the softness of her body against his. Her response to his kiss had been instinctive, surprised, then ever so receptive. His gut tightened whenever he allowed himself to think of those few passionate moments.

It would be pure hell accompanying this woman tonight when she incited painful reactions in his body and clouded his senses. He would need every one of them tonight. He had re-ceived Stanhope's seal earlier today, though not the forgery, and he wanted to return it to the desk. Hopefully, the earl would not have missed it yet.

His gloved hands brushed her skin as he helped her with her cloak. From the burning of his skin, he might as well have had no cloth between them at all. He wondered if she felt the same blazing feeling as he did, and knew immediately from the way she flinched away from him that she did.

He saw in her eyes that she did not want this heated at-traction any more than he did.

Because he wasn't wealthy enough?

Well, he wasn't. He was spending every penny he had to honor his father's request.

He had a title, and the position of captain waiting for him

when he returned. Nothing more. This was obviously a woman that went after larger game.

He swore to himself and then wondered whether the words were audible because she looked up at him and her eyes darkened.

"We should go," he said.

But they stood there, unmoving, as if inertia had wrapped around them, and neither could break loose.

"We should go," he said.

"Yes." Not *oui*. Of course, she spoke perfect English, but usually she had a charming French accent. Now it was gone. He knew how difficult it was to maintain a role when emotions ran high. And, the devil take it, emotion roiled and boiled around them like a hurricane at sea.

Part of him wondered. It was only one word, and yet it was a telling word. That she chose that one instinctively rather than the one she should have grown up with.

Another piece of a puzzle.

It didn't matter, he told himself. Nothing mattered except exposing Stanhope for what he was. He forced himself to take a step back, then she released a long breath. Her throat moved slightly, and it was like the flutter of a fragile bird.

She was no fragile bird, he reminded himself. She was a calculating woman who'd made it clear that she had designs on an older, monied lord.

When he'd moved, her gaze dropped as if he had broken some invisible binding.

He took a deep breath and stood back for her to lead the way to the rented carriage. She stood, waiting for him to open the door and offer his assistance. Christ, he would be there in that intimate interior with her. He remembered that first time. He'd almost ravished her then.

His body started reacting again and he felt his already tight britches grow even snugger. His blood warmed and thickened as he opened the door and gave her his hand. She stepped lightly into the carriage despite the skirts.

He moved to the seat opposite her, knowing that it would not be wise to take the cushioned seat next to her. Her light scent filled the carriage, and he thought how pleasant it was.

"*Merci,* my lord," she said.

"My pleasure," he said and not as easily as he had hoped.

"I did take your warning yesterday," she said.

"Then why are you attending tonight?"

"Why are you?" she challenged.

"He has a shipping company," Gabriel said. "I have business I wish to do."

"With a man you do not trust?"

"If I was a woman, I would not trust him," he said. "I am not. I can watch over myself."

"And you do not think a woman can take care of herself?" She took her fan in hand and tapped her dress with it. "I have been taking care of myself since I was seven. I am supremely good at it."

He shrugged. "Then so be it."

The carriage clattered through the streets. The air outside was cold, but the temperature in the carriage was charged. Hell, it was damn heated.

"You speak English very well," he probed.

She looked at him sharply.

"You have a British background?" he persisted.

"*Non.* An actress learns accents."

"I said nothing about accents."

"You are being rude."

"Am I?"

"You are judging me. Neither you or anyone else has that right."

"No," he agreed. There *had* been accusation in his questions. She was right. He certainly had no right to pass judgment on anyone.

But her eyes told him he was not being relieved of guilt with that one word.

"What kind of business do you have with Lord Stanhope?" She obviously hoped to turn the conversation toward him.

"I have an estate and no income," he said lightly. "I am told Stanhope is looking for investors and promises a huge return."

"Even if he killed his wife?" she said, slightly mocking his charges.

He stiffened. He had never told her that Stanhope had been accused of killing his wife, only that he had been accused of murder.

"Yes," he said. "And what would you know of it?"

She lifted one shoulder. It was not quite a shrug. "I do hear things, monsieur."

They were back to *monsieur* again.

The atmosphere in the carriage grew tense again. "And you, my lord, do you have a family?"

He was startled, then suddenly realized that she must be referring to young Elizabeth. "No," he said. "I do not. No wife. No children. I have never felt the need for attachments."

"Then last night . . ."

"That was the daughter of my housekeeper. She expressed a desire to see the gardens. She was well chaperoned by her mother and brother."

"Oh," she said, and he saw that little flutter in her throat again as her gaze searched his face as if searching for the truth. Or a truth. "I would not think a lord would care that much about his employees."

"I have learned that loyal servants are important."

She didn't say anything for a second, then she sighed. "Who are you?"

"I told you. The Marquess of Manchester, newly arrived from America."

"That I believe."

"And what do you not believe?"

"That you are a fool?"

He bowed slightly. "I thank you for that."

"Then why are you pretending to be one?"

He arched an eyebrow, regretful now that he'd left the maddening quizzing glass in his rooms. It was far more effective in showing disdain for a comment. "Now you give me too much credit. I am but myself. The papers call me an American bumpkin and I suppose that some believe it to be so."

Her expression expressed disbelief.

"I am, in truth, a gambler," he added, "and often not a very good one."

"Then why . . . ?"

"Are you not one yourself? You must understand the compulsion to wager on the turn of a card."

"It depends on the stakes," she replied.

"Exactly. The higher the stakes, the stronger the compulsion."

"And what do you consider high enough stakes, my lord?"

"Oh, an easy life, I suppose," he said, yawning.

"You have not had an easy life?"

Bloody hell, but she was quick. He was glad he wore gloves and had every time she had seen him. His calluses would quickly give him away. "Easy enough," he said. "But fortunes are built on gambles."

"And fortunes are lost."

"Yes." Even he was aware that his voice had a tinge of bitterness that shouldn't have been there.

The carriage came to a stop. A second later the coachman opened the door.

Gabriel stepped down and once more offered his hand to Monique. For a moment she hesitated as though she too feared another touch. Then she reached for his hand and stepped down, immediately turning toward the steps, where other fashionably dressed men and women were mounting and going through a door held open by a servant in livery.

Every eye, though, turned toward them, and it was as if a scene had been locked in time. A tableau of perfectly still performers.

Then movement started again. Eyes turned away.

She gave him an odd little smile, as if they shared some intriguing secret and took his arm and gracefully ascended the stairs.

The marquess was more and more an enigma.

He displayed himself as one thing. But his actions—at least with her—seemed to belie that role.

She doubted if others would notice. They would not care enough to do so.

She didn't care either, she told herself. But since she herself was playing a role, she recognized the slightly off-balanced errors of someone else. He too was an actor, at least at the moment, but she did not know why.

She didn't want to know, as long as he didn't get in her way. Perhaps he used the facade as a defense. Or maybe he was trying to expand his wealth and thought playing a fool might give him more insight.

It didn't matter as long as he stayed out of her affairs.

Once she escaped the interior of the coach, she felt herself relax. She was always at her best when actually playing the role rather than anticipating it. She knew exactly what she had to do tonight.

The first step would be to rid herself of her escort.

Stanhope was standing just inside the door, a pretty young lady beside him. His smile—cool and calculating, she thought—faded for a moment when he saw her, and her companion. Almost as quickly as it faded, it returned.

"My dear," he said. "It was so good of you to join us." He turned to Manchester. "And the Marquess of Manchester. I saw you the other evening at Vauxhall Gardens. Miss Fremont told me you had been of assistance to her."

The man next to her preened. There was no other word for it. And he preened exceptionally well. Monique was impressed, especially since she sensed he had probably never done so before.

"I am indeed honored to be invited," he said. "Mademoiselle Fremont was kind enough to consent to come with me. The most beautiful woman in London accompanying me to the home of such a famous and successful man is truly dashing. I am just agog with London." He saw the flicker of distaste in Stanhope's expression at his misuse of words.

The girl beside him, though, did not change her expression. A tight smile did little to enhance a fragile prettiness.

Stanhope turned to her. "May I present my daughter, Pamela? She is here from our country house for the season. My dear, the Marquess of Manchester and Miss Monique Fremont. She is opening in a new play in a few days."

Pamela's eyes flew open for a moment as she acknowledged the introduction. They lit for a moment, then the life left them.

*Her sister.* Something moved deep inside her as she stared into the pale blue eyes of her half sister. She searched Pamela's face, looking for similarities to her own. Would Stanhope see any?

She stopped when her gaze returned to Pamela's eyes again. Sad. Hopeless. No spark of joy.

Of course not. She lived with a man who was a monster.

Monique wondered whether he had killed Pamela's mother, or whether there had been another wife. Lynch had only said rumors suggested he had been responsible for his wife's death.

She wanted to take the young woman in her arms. She wanted to take her away from the man who stood at her side. Instead, she merely curtsied. "Lady Pamela."

The girl smiled shyly.

"Please enjoy the evening," Stanhope said abruptly, ending the introductions. His eyes ran over her as if he owned every inch. "There is music in the drawing room and food in the dining area." He turned to her companion. "I would like to speak to you later," he said.

"At your pleasure," Manchester replied.

She forced herself to look away. Lord Manning knew what Stanhope was, and yet he was willing to do business with him. She wondered whether he was fully aware of what his host was capable of. Was he intending to fleece him? Why else masquerade as a Sapscull? If so, she feared he was choosing the wrong person.

It was none of her business now. He was her escort, nothing more. She need have nothing else to do with him after tonight. She didn't like the way he made her feel, the new hunger he aroused in her.

He was a distraction she did not need.

And perhaps a danger to her sister. If Stanhope intended to use her . . .

She hesitated a moment in front of her half sister. "I hope I will see you again."

Pamela smiled again, a sad small smile.

Stanhope looked from his daughter to her, then back again. "Perhaps I will take her to see your play."

"I will make sure you receive two excellent seats," she said.

Stanhope turned then. "Perhaps Lord Manchester would like to accompany us." He looked expectantly at the two of them.

"Yes," Manchester said. "That would be most pleasant."

Monique looked from one man to another, then at Pamela. The smile had disappeared and something like fear had replaced it. Manchester's acceptance had prompted it. But why?

*No.* The answer was there in the calculating look in Stanhope's eyes. For some reason, Stanhope was using his daughter—her half sister—as bait for Manchester.

Manchester looked oblivious, but his gaze settled on Pamela. That seemed to make her even more uncomfortable.

Then another couple came through the doorway and Stanhope turned away, as, obediently, did his daughter.

She and Manchester walked into the library where there was less of a crowd than in the dining room. "She is pretty," Monique observed once they were out of hearing of her father. She wanted an answer. She wondered if there was more resemblance between them than she'd thought.

"Is she?"

"You appeared to like the idea of accompanying them to the performance of the play."

"You promised good seats," he replied glibly. Too glibly.

She stopped, looked at him intensely. "You can have a good seat anytime."

"I find it convenient to go with our host. Unless you have a reason I should not."

She had no reason to give him. She couldn't say that Pamela was her sister and she would not allow her to be hurt. She couldn't say her father had tried to kill her mother, and herself. She couldn't say that she was intent on bringing him to some kind of justice.

*Jealousy.* No. She would not give him that satisfaction, particularly since there would be absolutely no truth in it. She cared nothing about him. Nothing.

*"Non,"* she said. "I simply thought you might enjoy supper after the performance." As soon as she said the words she

regretted them. But she suddenly feared for the young girl, who looked so vulnerable and unhappy.

"I would," he said. "I shall see it twice."

She wanted to kick him. But she couldn't show her interest in Pamela.

"Will you bring me a glass of champagne?" she asked. She wanted him to leave her. He was much too disturbing. And she had things to do.

"Will you stay here?"

The dratted man could read her mind. "Yes," she lied.

His eyes crinkled with amusement. "I will find you," he said. He gave her a crooked grin that said he knew she was lying. He turned and followed a crowd of people heading in another direction.

She stood there for a moment, aware of the furtive glances cast her way. They must wonder why she was here.

She stepped back in the shadows. Aristocrats and their ladies. She and Manchester were the outsiders. Novelties. Welcome for entertainment value.

*Manchester?* Where was he?

She thought about going up the stairs, but she had no reason and the hallway was filled. She would be noticed.

Then she smiled to herself. Maybe she would wait for him after all.

She'd planned to spill something on her gown. But she would enlist an unsuspecting Manchester in the charade.

She smiled at a woman who frowned at her, then sniffed and whispered loudly to her escorts, "Another of Stanhope's whores."

Her husband shushed her.

Monique simply smiled sweetly. She didn't really care what any of these people thought. She blamed them nearly as much as she blamed Stanhope. They didn't care if a merchant's daughter was destroyed by one of their own. For a moment her mother's hopeless face was stark in her mind.

"Miss Fremont?"

Manchester's voice closed that particular door and she turned around, her hand outstretched as she reached for the glass she knew would be in his hand.

Her fingers brushed it and the contents splashed over her dress.

"Oh," she exclaimed.

His expression didn't change.

"My apologies," he said, but he didn't look apologetic. One dark eyebrow was arched in question.

"You are clumsy, my lord."

"So I have been told."

"Will you ask someone to help me?"

"Of course."

He turned toward Stanhope, but not before she saw that infernal amusement in his face.

He knew she'd spilled the champagne deliberately.

# Chapter Nine

She had spilled the champagne deliberately. If there was one thing she was not, it was clumsy.

The question was why.

Gabriel mused over that as he reached Stanhope, explained that he had clumsily spilled wine on Miss Freemont and she needed assistance.

Stanhope looked down at his daughter, a slight sneer on his lips. "My daughter can help her. She's very domestic." He looked down at Pamela. "You will be happy to do so, won't you, my dear?"

Pamela Kane's eyes brightened but Gabriel didn't know whether it was because she really wanted to be of help or to get away from her father. She looked terrified of him.

He bowed slightly. "I would be grateful. I wish to redeem myself in her eyes. I was unforgivably bird-witted."

"She is beautiful," Lady Pamela said wistfully.

He wanted to say she too was quite an attractive young lady and, in truth, had much of the same facial structure as Monique. Her hair was lighter, and her eyes blue rather than gray, but . . .

He dismissed the notion as fanciful. Perhaps he looked for Monique in other women now.

Pamela did not meet his gaze as she stared at someone or something behind him. "I will fetch Annie. She's my maid and ever so good about removing stains."

He pasted an eager smile on his face, then he led the way to the place he'd left Monique.

She wasn't there.

They looked in the dining room, then the other rooms, avoiding only the hallway where her father continued to greet newcomers. Music was now coming from the library.

"Perhaps the kitchen, my lord," she suggested. "She might have thought someone there could help her."

"Lead the way," he said, though he knew very well where it was.

She went ahead of him, avoiding other guests. He realized she was happy to have an excuse not to be on display.

He didn't want to like Stanhope's daughter. Maybe it was her evident vulnerability and her obvious fear of her father that made him want to protect, just as he'd found himself drawn to young Elizabeth. Perhaps because he'd had no sister, no one but his mother and he hadn't been able to do anything to help her.

But Stanhope was going to pay for what he had done to his father. Nothing had to get in the way of that. It wasn't only for his father, but for all the others the man had swindled and betrayed and murdered.

He wanted to take everything from Stanhope. His money. His power. His reputation. His life.

Perhaps he would be doing young Lady Pamela a favor also.

He vowed that in doing one, he would ensure he was doing the second.

Monique was not in the kitchen. They went upstairs to the withdrawing room, where several men were in deep conversation. They instantly quieted when he approached, but he recognized one as the Earl of Daven, whom he'd seen at several gambling hells.

He knew from his own search of the home that the only rooms remaining were the master suite, two additional bedrooms—one of which supposedly was Pamela's—and the study, which had been closed.

Where did she go? And why?

Then he saw her emerge from the master suite. Her eyes widened when she saw him.

Pamela moved toward her. "Father wanted me to help you."

"Thank you," Monique said, then looked wryly down at her dress. "I thought I should find something right away. I hope you do not mind my wandering about. I thought I might find a water pitcher."

An excuse. Nothing more. She could have also found it in the kitchen, but Gabriel didn't say anything, merely raised one brow to indicate his disbelief. He knew the moment he did that it was a mistake. The Marquess of Manchester would never have been so aware of someone else's deceptions.

Was she a thief as well?

The idea interested him. Intrigued him.

Yet she was a successful actress. Would she risk everything for a bauble or two?

Maybe she had searched for a servant, and decided to try one of the bedrooms.

"I was afraid the material would stain. It is my favorite gown."

He bowed slightly. "I can easily understand why. But you would be lovely in the simplest of garments."

"You flatter me, my lord."

"I speak only the truth. You are a woman of many facets."

Sparks crackled between them. He was barely aware of Pamela, who stood next to him.

"I am but a simple actress."

"I think you are anything but simple," he replied.

"And the Marquess of Manchester?" she said in a low voice. "What is he?"

"The marquess is enchanted," he replied, ignoring the nuance.

She gave him a disdainful look.

Pamela backed away, whether because of the words or the evident tension that had thickened between them, he did not know. He only knew he was alone with her and that he longed to reach out and touch that black curl.

Instead, he hardened his voice. "Has no one ever told you not to wander alone in strange houses?"

"But I'm not alone, am I, my lord? There is a houseful of guests."

Her gray eyes were large and innocent looking. And yet her body was tense. *She's an actress.*

But it was her business, not his, and he had his own plans. He knew he couldn't become involved with any petty thievery she might undertake to enhance her salary.

He certainly was no saint himself. Yet he felt a sinking sensation in his gut. He was surprised at the depth of his disappointment. He'd felt it a few nights ago when she'd flirted with Stanhope, too.

He was a thief, too. He'd stolen Stanhope's seal. Or borrowed it.

Just long enough to get it duplicated. Winsley had made his cast. The forged seal should be ready in the next few days.

Even now he felt the weight of the original in an inside pocket of his evening coat, which he wore over a very snug waistcoat. He'd meant to find a moment to replace it in Stanhope's study and pray he'd not needed it.

He needed all his skills to do it, and here he was, staring like a damned fool at a woman who was probably as devious as himself.

"Would you like to go to the drawing room?" he asked. "Since you were at the Vauxhall Gardens, you must enjoy music."

"I do. Very much."

Her tongue moistened her lips, and he felt a burning, untamed need inside him. He wanted her more than he'd ever wanted another woman, and God help him that was the last thing he needed.

He forced himself to turn around. "I will escort you back, since you seem to get lost."

"Does my gown look presentable?" she asked, a husky note in her unsteady voice.

Did she feel the same heated pull?

"It is every bit as lovely as the woman who is wearing it," he said.

She gave him a small smile. "You are a flatterer, my lord," she said, that husky sound still evident. Her gray eyes were smoky, elusive, challenging.

He held out his arm, and she placed her own arm on it. Then she looked up at him. "You do not have to look after me, my lord."

"Would you prefer the earl?"

She didn't answer that, just lifted her chin and moved ahead.

He looked down on her dark hair, clasped by a silver comb. A gift from an admirer? The sweet smell of roses drifted enticingly upward. He wondered whether the dark curls were as soft and silky as they looked.

Then they were at the stairs. He looked down. Guests seemed unaware that two of their number had disappeared and oblivious to the waves of attraction radiating between them.

He forced his eyes straight ahead and away from the woman at his side. When they reached the bottom of the steps he turned toward the library and saw Stanhope there.

The earl's dark eyes were like pieces of black onyx. The side of his mouth twitched, but Gabriel knew it wasn't any kind of smile. A muscle jumped along his tightened jaw. He was furious, but trying to hide it.

He stepped forward. "My daughter said all was well, Miss Fremont."

"Yes." She smiled at Stanhope. Gabriel cringed at the smile. It appeared spontaneous and real, but then he'd learned exactly how good an actress she was.

"May I borrow her for a while?" the earl asked, offering his arm. "I would like to introduce her to some friends. Perhaps my daughter can show you our gardens."

Gabriel turned and saw Pamela. He hadn't noticed her. It was almost as if she was hiding herself.

"It would be my pleasure," he said, relinquishing Monique with the contradictory emotions of regret and relief.

He moved out of the way as the earl offered Monique his

arm, and she looked up at Stanhope with admiration shining in her eyes, just as those same eyes had shone up at him just minutes ago.

Gabriel managed a smile and turned to Pamela. She really would be a pretty young lady if apprehension did not constantly cloud her face. She looked as if she expected to be struck.

"You really do not have to see the gardens," she said shyly.

"But I would like to," he replied as gently as he could without completely disregarding his role of fool.

She looked stricken but nonetheless obediently led him out the front and around to the back of the house.

He had been impressed with the garden the day he'd taken the seal. Now lanterns highlighted the well-tended beds of flowers.

"I am surprised that your father is such a fancier of gardens," he said.

She stumbled, and he reached out to assist her. He wondered whether it was her nervousness. And he also wondered why her father had asked her to escort him. He didn't think he looked like a flower lover.

"I—I—" she stuttered, and he realized she was terrified of him.

He looked down at her. "I do not bite, my lady."

"Father . . . Father thinks . . ." She could not go on.

"He thinks what?"

Although it was too dark to see, he knew her face was probably red with embarrassment. If he hadn't hated Stanhope before this moment, he certainly would now. He wondered why Stanhope was throwing his daughter at him, despite the fact that the child was far too young for him and obviously had no interest in him at all.

"Do you usually live in London?" he asked, trying to make her feel at least a little more comfortable.

"Oh no, my lord. I live with my aunt in the country. My father sent for me this week. He usually . . ."

"He usually what . . . ?"

"He usually doesn't care what I do," she said softly, then flinched again, as if that brief comment would bring blows.

But Stanhope *had* wanted her to come this week and had even suggested they walk together at night in the garden. Or was it just to keep Gabriel away from Monique Fremont? There was no question that Stanhope lusted after her.

Bloody hell, what man wouldn't?

"Where does your aunt live?"

"A dower house in Leicestershire. She is widowed."

"Do you see your father often?"

"No," she replied.

He saw her shiver. "You should have brought a cloak," he said. He took off his evening coat and put it over her shoulders.

"We should go back inside." But she didn't say it with any real conviction, and he suspected she was relieved to be outside the view of her sharp-eyed father.

But he did not want to go inside. He didn't want or need that feeling of almost feverish excitement every time he saw Monique, particularly since he questioned her honesty and honor. Still, she always made him feel more alive than at any other time in his life.

"I suppose we should return," she repeated after an awkward moment. He couldn't comfort her. The Marquess of Manchester would not do that, and he couldn't afford to make mistakes now, not even to ease her disquiet.

Still, he did not want to force her to return to an untenable situation, either. She was so fragile.

He looked at her again and had that same odd feeling of familiarity. She certainly didn't have Monique's vibrant and confident presence, but there was a delicacy about their facial bones and a similarity of build. He had even seen her lift her chin, just as he had seen Monique do.

Nonsense, he told himself.

"But you would rather stay out here?" he finally asked, trying to rid himself of softness. It was impossible.

"I don't like those people," she blurted out.

Neither did he. Most of them had looked at him and Monique with undisguised contempt. Of course, that was what he'd planned, but it didn't make him like them any better.

"What *do* you like?" He shouldn't be asking these questions. He knew that. But she was obviously lonely. Lost. Even frightened. And he found he couldn't walk away from her. Even if she was Stanhope's daughter.

Or perhaps because she was.

"Home. My aunt." She started to say something but stopped before he knew what it was.

"A young man?"

Terror replaced fright on her face.

"Why don't we make a bargain, you and I?" he said.

"What kind of bargain?" The question was suspicious.

"Your father obviously wants to make a match between us. I can . . . call on you and perhaps it would benefit both of us. I will make no demands on you."

"Why would you do that? I saw the way you looked at Miss Fremont."

"I am trying to establish myself in London. I am looked upon as an outsider, most likely because I am. If I am calling on the daughter of a respected noble . . ."

"And Miss Fremont?"

"I think her interest lies elsewhere."

"My father?"

She was obviously not as naive as he thought. "I think so," he said wryly.

She looked at him for a long time, judging his face, weighing his words. Then she nodded. "It's what my father wants. I do not know why. He has never . . . indicated any interest in me before." She paused. "He must want something from you."

He shrugged carelessly. "Is it a bargain?"

"How do I know I can trust you? You are an acquaintance of my father's."

"Because as enchanting as you are, my dear, you're too young for me."

Her eyes didn't leave his eyes. "What do you want from him?"

"An investment. A business arrangement. Nothing that will hurt you," he said. At least, he hoped to hell not.

"You will not want anything from me?"

"Only the pleasure of your company."

"My father says I am dull and unappealing."

Another reason to ruin Stanhope.

"I think he is very wrong."

"You are different," she said.

"Different?"

"Different from what I thought when I first met you. You seemed . . ." She stopped in midsentence.

"I am learning my way in London," he said. "I am American and don't always understand your customs. Perhaps you can help me? You can tell me who everyone is and explain all these titles, and . . ."

"I do not know many people in London," she said, still resisting.

She was reluctant, obviously not quite ready to trust him. Yet what better way to get to her father? Especially if her heart was with some young man, which he suspected it was. He would not be toying with her. It would be a mutual arrangement, pure and simple. Still a niggling moment of conscience prodded him. While he would not be toying with her, nor was he being honest.

"You can call it off whenever you wish," he said.

She finally nodded. "Then you will disappear? Jilt me?"

"Or you can jilt me," he said. "Whatever would be easier for you."

A little life came into her face.

"Do you swear?" she asked, the hope in her voice striking a chord in him. "A little time . . ."

"I swear. You can be my instructor on English manners and tradition. I will protect your heart."

A smile lit her face, making her extraordinarily appealing. He hoped her young man was worthy of her.

"Let us go inside," he said. "You are chilled."

"I've been cold since I arrived here," she said. "But it's the chill in the heart, not the air."

He took another look at her. Not the timid mouse. Someone much too wise for her years. Just as he had been.

He waited for her to lead the way to the steps, then the door. There he took his coat back and carefully buttoned it.

They entered into a hall blazing with lights. The sound of Mozart drifted from the library.

Gabriel saw Stanhope and Monique together in a corner. Her dress showed no sign of the stain now, and she lifted her head and laughed. He hadn't heard her laugh like that before. Like chimes of music.

And for Stanhope.

Gabriel led Pamela past them, pausing in front of Stanhope. "You have a truly delightful daughter," he said. "I would like to see more of her." He smiled at Monique.

The affair seemed to drag on interminably after that.

Stanhope had said he wanted to speak to him privately, and Gabriel wanted to know the earl's intentions. He also wanted to get inside the study. The seal in his pocket was growing heavier.

But it was not difficult to talk to Pamela. Once her fear faded, she was a charming companion, intelligent and well read. Some young man would be very lucky.

He saw Monique leave Stanhope's side. "Please pardon me," he said to Pamela, "I must speak to your father."

Her eyes shadowed again.

"About business, Lady Pamela. Not about you."

"Be careful," she whispered.

How much did she know about him? he suddenly wondered. But though he would reluctantly use her, he wouldn't ask her to betray her father. No matter how much he wanted Stanhope, he wasn't going to make her live with that kind of guilt.

He knew what guilt was. Perhaps if he had not left his father's study that day . . .

He stood and walked over to Stanhope, swaggering a little as he did so, like a man who'd had too much wine. "You said you wished a private conversation, my lord."

A flicker of disgust crossed Stanhope's eyes, then he inclined his head sightly in consent. "My study," he said. "It is toward the rear."

He started for the hallway, expecting Gabriel to follow him. He did.

The study was as Gabriel remembered it, the desk as clean

as it had been. Hopefully in the few days since he'd taken the seal, Stanhope hadn't needed the damned thing.

"My lord?"

"I understand you might be looking for some investments," Stanhope said as he sat down in the chair at the desk.

"Yes. I feel I should invest in my new country," he said piously.

"Very loyal," Stanhope said.

"I can be. To people I trust."

Stanhope opened a humidor and handed him a cigar. Then he handed him the oil lamp to light it.

"You know your father and I worked together. I was devastated to see what happened to him."

Gabriel took a deep draw on the cigar. It was the only way he could keep from leaping on the man across from him and pummeling him. But he had a more agonizing end for the Earl of Stanhope.

"I am sure you did what you could to help him," he said.

"We offered money. We engaged the best barrister that could be found. Perhaps he could have explained, if he had not . . ."

"Shot himself," Gabriel said. "Yes, it was the final disgrace. We could not even bury him properly."

"You were . . ."

"Ten. He kept everything from us, of course."

"Well, perhaps now we can have a more successful partnership. Your father would approve, I think."

Gabriel smiled and took another deep draw of the cigar. He almost choked.

"Do you have something in mind?" he finally asked.

"I'm outfitting several ships," Stanhope said. "Now the war is over, trade should increase, both with the United States and France. You can help us in the colonies."

"I don't think they are colonies any longer," Gabriel said with a disarming smile. "They really do not like the reminder of their recent . . . relationship with England."

"Renegades and ruffians," Stanhope said dismissively. "If we had not the French to contend with, we would have made short order of them. We will have them back someday. Mind my words."

"You have plans, then?" Gabriel asked.

Stanhope shrugged, as if reminding himself he was talking to an American. But apparently Gabriel's birth in England and his recent title made him an Englishman, even if he was still considered a great fool. "I would like to purchase a new ship. I would make an interest available to you."

"Oh, that sounds jolly," he said, pasting a greedy smile on his face. "What kind of ship?"

"You leave that up to my manager," Stanhope said. "In England, fine gentlemen do not get involved with their businesses. They just invest."

Gabriel knew he couldn't look too much the idiot. "Americans do not hold that view," he noted. "If I invest," he said, "I would want to see the ship and see manifests." He was well aware how easily it would be to forge manifests, both by Stanhope—and by himself.

He could see the calculation in Stanhope's eyes. "Exactly how much do you have to invest?" the earl asked.

"How much do you need?" he replied shrewdly.

Stanhope looked at him with appraising eyes, evidently weighing greed against caution.

"Fifty thousand pounds for a minority interest."

Gabriel raised an eyebrow. Even a fool would see through that. "Minority?"

"I retain control of everything I own," Stanhope said.

"Then we have nothing to talk about."

"You do have the funds?" Stanhope said.

Gabriel faked indignation. "Of course." And he would. Soon.

"I think we can work out an arrangement," Stanhope said. "Perhaps joint shares, but my manager will see to day-to-day operations."

*And would steal Gabriel blind.*

Gabriel nodded. "I have funds on the way. I sent an order to my bank in Boston."

He held the cigar up in his fingers as a salute.

"I will have the papers drawn," Stanhope said, standing

and reaching over to clasp Gabriel's hand. "Now I must get back to my guests."

"You have a very charming daughter," Gabriel said. "May I hope to have your permission to call on her?"

Stanhope stilled. "You must understand how precious she is to me."

"I have only the most honorable of intentions," Gabriel said, praying that Pamela would not contradict him. He was sure the girl would be interrogated.

"Then, of course, you have my permission, my good fellow. We hope to see a lot of you around here. Your father would be pleased."

*Yes, he would. Very pleased.*

"And now I really must return," Stanhope said.

"Would you mind if I stayed and finished my cigar? It really is quite excellent."

He saw Stanhope's glance move around the room as if wondering whether there was anything that should not be seen. Then he shrugged. "Of course not. We are business partners, possibly family. Take your time."

Then he was gone.

Gabriel waited until Stanhope walked through the door, then closed the door behind him. In seconds he had the desk drawer open. Nothing looked disturbed from the last time he'd inspected it. He was not going to replace the seal if it appeared someone had searched through the desk.

But apparently Stanhope had been too busy with his homecoming and soiree. Gabriel replaced the seal in the box at the back of the drawer, closed and locked it, then went back to his chair, sat down, and enjoyed the very fine cigar.

# Chapter Ten

Monique sipped on champagne offered by several admirers who surrounded her, including the Earl of Daven and Lord Robert Stammel. She took turns being a coquette, fluttering her fan first at one, then the other.

All in all, it had been a successful evening. She had an opportunity to see Stanhope's sleeping quarters, had even quickly searched the area. She found diamond cravat pins, jewel-encrusted snuffboxes, and a safe. Unfortunately, she did not know how to open it, but Dani would.

As a small token she picked up a diamond cravat pin.

No more. Not yet. She wanted things to disappear slowly. She wanted to spread distrust between him and his partners. She wanted them to turn on one another.

The stain on her dress had disappeared. She'd worn that particular gown purely because stains did not show. She had not wanted to leave the house, only the public rooms.

She glanced between two of her admirers. Stanhope was returning to the room and heading straight for her. She had seen the marquess and earl leave together.

She licked her lips. It was a nervous mannerism she tried to control, but she also knew slightly moistened lips were seductive to many men.

The other men stood aside for Stanhope. It was clear he dominated any gathering. "My dear, would you care to join me in the library for the music?"

"Of course," she said, accepting the arm he offered. "These gentlemen were kind enough to bring me champagne. My . . . escort appears to have abandoned me." She pouted slightly.

"He and I had some business," Stanhope said. "He asked me to look after you."

"It's very kind of you."

"He just asked to call on my daughter," Stanhope said, stopping to watch her face.

She kept it motionless. She had seen Manchester and her . . . half sister enter together. Pamela's face had been flushed, and one of the buttons on Manchester's evening coat was undone. Pamela had given him a hesitant, sideways look, as if they shared some kind of secret.

Monique's heart had dropped. Not for herself, she quickly assured herself. It was Pamela she worried about.

Manchester had told her he hoped to do business with Stanhope. Was he going to use Pamela to do it? For some reason, she had not thought him that kind of man, but what really did she know about him?

He seemed to be a chameleon.

She wondered whether she should warn the girl, but with what excuse? It was none of her affair, or shouldn't be.

Drat him. No, damn him!

She was aware of Stanhope's eyes still on her. She gave him a brilliant smile. "And what did you say?"

"He is a marquess," Stanhope said. "It would be a fine match. He insists that his intentions are entirely honorable."

She said nothing, just fluttered her fan.

"You seem to know him, my dear. Do you think he is an honorable man?"

"I have no idea, my lord. He did help me at the theater, but I barely know him and certainly have no interest in him. He is not worldly enough for my tastes. Too much the American bumpkin. Isn't that what people said? That is why I consid-

ered him the perfect escort for tonight. He would not be . . .
possessive."

"That is good to hear, mademoiselle."

"Oh, posh. You surely did not think . . ."

"In truth, I did not know what to think, and I would not
want him playing with my daughter's heart."

Neither did Monique, but she thought her concern was far
more sincere than his own. He was ready to throw Pamela to
the wolves—or wolf—for some reason of his own. She decided she would try to warn Pamela some way.

She wondered where the Marquess of Manchester was at
this moment. He appeared to have completely disappeared,
and she certainly couldn't ask her companion. She quietly
fumed even as she heard the lovely notes of a sonatina.

She looked around the room and saw Pamela sitting with
two older ladies, her fan clutched tightly in her hands. The
flush in her cheeks was gone, and she looked pale again. Her
eyes were fastened on the musicians, but Monique wondered
whether she was really listening. She seemed to be in a world
of her own.

Manchester *was* an attractive man when he took the dratted quizzing glass from his left eye and removed the ridiculous beaver hat . . .

*Stop thinking of him.*

"I would like to see more of you," Stanhope said as the
sonata came to an end.

"I will be very busy when the play opens," she said.

"I have the date marked."

"I hear British audiences can be very critical."

"I do not believe you have anything to worry about, my
dear. They will love you."

"You are kind, my lord."

"To those I like," he said with a patently false smile on his
face. She wondered whether he really believed it was not obvious.

"I thought I would have a country party this weekend," he
continued. "You can rest before the play opens. I already
checked with Lynch. He also thinks you need a diversion."

"You just arrived in London, *oui*?"

"Yes. But my country home is less than a day's journey, and I would like you to see it."

She did want to see it. But she would be in his territory then.

"I cannot," she said. "I have other commitments this weekend."

His face mottled with anger. She saw him struggle with it, saw his one hand clench his cane until his fingers were white.

"But, " she said after a moment's silence, "I too would like to see you again. Perhaps a supper."

His face cleared slightly.

"I truly would like to see your home. But the play opens next week and I do need the rehearsals. I want to stay here in London and I cannot do that unless the audiences like me."

Her eyes pled with him.

He nodded and moved closer to her, obviously completely oblivious to the other people in the room, including his daughter. "You would not have to act," he said. "I can take care of you."

"And then you would grow tired of me, and what would I do?"

"I cannot imagine anyone growing tired of you."

"Ah, sweet words now."

"You do not believe me?"

"I believe no man, my lord. My mother was deserted by one. That is why I have learned to care for myself."

"Then what are your terms?"

She looked at him for a long time. "Your two friends have also made offers," she said.

"I will better either one."

"Ah but money is not everything," she said. "I like to know the man."

"I'm one of the most powerful men in England," he boasted.

She raised an eyebrow, which she knew how to do very dramatically.

He gave her a small smile. "You are not impressed?"

"As I said, my lord, I believe no man."

"What do you want?"

"Time to decide among you."

He seemed to weigh her words even as she watched him struggle with anger, lust, and pride. A potent combination, and a dangerous one.

Yet he was also a competitive man. She'd noticed that, too.

"How long?" he finally asked.

"A month, and I expect no demands during that time." She held her breath.

"And if you do not need a month?" he asked. The challenge won, as she'd hoped it would.

She smiled. "I am promising everyone a full month."

"And they have agreed?"

"No, I have not asked them yet."

"What if they do not wish to play your game?"

"Then it will be none," she said. It was a game of chance. She had thrown the dice. The question was whether or not he would accept the wager.

"Done," he said.

She gave him her most brilliant smile.

She had done well tonight.

Monique looked across the room at her half sister. And the feeling of triumph was short-lived.

In truth, her stomach twisted at the thought of Pamela with Manchester. Together.

Because of Pamela?

Or because of her own disappointment?

That was a truly disturbing thought.

The journey back to her lodgings was tense.

Manchester acted as if nothing had happened. When it had been time to leave Stanhope's home, he'd suddenly appeared at her side.

Ever the excellent escort.

An American oaf? Why did that ring increasingly false?

And where had he been during much of the evening?

Unfortunately—even amazingly—she felt the tiniest sensation in her lower stomach when his leg brushed hers as he entered the carriage.

"Did you accomplish what you wished?" she asked.

"Yes, and you?"

Drat, but his eyes were intense.

*"Oui."*

"I noticed you and the earl seemed to enjoy one another."

"He is a wealthy and powerful man."

"Yes."

There was an uncommon amount of agreement between them.

"What did you think of Pamela?" She could have kicked herself for asking the question. It just came out.

He looked at her for a moment, his eyes clear in the light of the lantern hanging inside. "She is pretty enough."

She wanted to slap him. "Enough for what?"

He yawned.

She wanted to murder him.

"Lord Stanhope said you asked permission to call on her."

"Yes."

She really hated those one-word sentences.

"Why?"

"Because it is a good alliance," he explained patiently, as to a child, as if surprised that she should even ask. "You should know about alliances," he added. "I noticed that you were paying a great amount of attention to the good earl." The latter sentence had the least bit of bite to it.

"He was our host."

"Yes," he acknowledged once more with that maddening agreeability.

She turned away and looked out the window as the carriage clattered down the road.

She wanted that thrill back, that moment when she sensed victory. She wanted to revel in thoughts of Stanhope's downfall. Instead, she only saw Manchester looking down at Pamela.

"She's very young," she suddenly said.

"Who?"

He was being deliberately obtuse.

"Pamela."

"Young wives are the best wives."

"She's an innocent and you don't care anything about her."

"And you do?"

She started to respond and stopped. Some new note had entered his voice. Curiosity, yes. But something else.

"I just met her," she said.

"She reminds me of you."

Shock ran through her body, and she stiffened. "She looks nothing like me."

"No," he agreed, putting the quizzing glass in his eye and ogling her. "It's something . . . more subtle. Your bodies, the way you tilt your heads . . ."

"I do not see any similarities at all," she said huffily, hoping he would think she just didn't care for the comparison.

"My imagination, perhaps," he agreed again.

"Does she . . . agree to you calling on her?" she asked.

"Now that is a personal question, mademoiselle. But I would think my suit would be welcomed. I have resources. I have a title."

"She's a child."

"Oh, she's much more than that," he said.

The carriage came to a stop in front of her town house. She waited for him to move. He didn't.

"You did not take my warning about the earl, mademoiselle. I don't think you should be lecturing me." There was an anger in his voice she hadn't expected.

She started to move, but his arm pinned her down. "You are playing with fire."

"It is my concern, not yours."

"You are right there," he said, "but for some reason . . ."

Their voices had lowered to little more than husky whispers. The air in the closed carriage was sparking, hissing, crackling. Threatening to ignite.

He suddenly leaned over and kissed her. But it wasn't like the other time. His lips pressed roughly against hers and she felt his teeth nibbling at them. There was a wildness about the kiss, an anger she hadn't anticipated.

She fought it for a moment. He was obviously a cad, ready to exploit a young girl for his own financial benefit.

And yet . . .

And yet fire started building in her belly and she felt herself respond to the sizzling hunger that he roused in her. One of his fingers traced the lines of her face as if he were memorizing each one of them, then his hand moved down. It snaked inside her cloak and caressed her left breast. She felt it tighten and swell in reaction to the merest brush of his skin.

She wondered only for a fraction of a second when he'd taken off his gloves.

His hand left her breast, and she knew a longing ache that was stunning. How could she want someone like this? Especially someone like him. She'd spent a lifetime avoiding men like him. Men who used women.

She started to move, but his mouth wouldn't release her. Instead his tongue made its way into her mouth and teased her until she was mad with longing.

She had thought the fireworks always between them would have been quenched by his behavior tonight. Perhaps even her own. Instead the air was explosive, filled with the hot expectancy of a pending lethal storm.

Breathlessly, she found herself waiting for his next overture, for the next seduction. She found herself opening her mouth to him as she heard a low moan rumbling through his body.

Then he let her go, almost as if he were pushing away something distasteful.

She felt humiliated beyond belief that she had just permitted what had happened, and even wanted more.

His face looked as startled as she knew hers must.

Then he rapped the carriage box with his cane.

And she slapped him as hard as she possibly could.

Gabriel felt the blow, and it was more powerful than he thought could come from such a feminine young woman.

For a moment he'd almost succumbed to her. God knew there had never been a woman who so attracted him before. He'd known she was as unwilling a participant as he in the damnable attraction that always flamed between them, though he didn't quite understand why she was seducing the much older Stanhope and his friends rather than what appeared to be a wealthy lord with a title.

He was more than a little perturbed by her choice.

His face stung as he heard the coachman, summoned by his rap, descend from the box.

He made his voice cool. "Have a good evening, mademoiselle."

She sat as still as any stone creation, looking as surprised at her own actions as he had been.

Monique Fremont totally befuddled him. Unmanned him.

He wanted to despise her. She was obviously playing one lord against another. The reason could only be wealth.

Yet each time he found himself alone with her, he could barely control his body, which had always been so disciplined.

Always before he had paid for love, or it had been given freely but without emotional attachments. Never had he felt this gut-wrenching desire that nearly overwhelmed every other thought.

The door opened. The coachman stood aside for him to descend, then help his lady out.

Instead, he sat there.

She gave him an odd little smile and climbed over him. "Thank you for your courtesy tonight." The words were poisoned with irony.

He took off his beaver hat. "Any time, mademoiselle. I enjoy small plots."

Her lips tightened and she turned away.

He still felt the imprint of her hand against his face.

Gabriel stepped out of the coach, watched as the coachman escorted her to the door. It opened almost the very instant they reached the top of the steps.

She didn't look back at him. Her body was stiff, her head high, as if she were a queen. Arrogant and proud. Dismissive.

He knew he had been an oaf for not accompanying her to the door. But he feared that if he did, he might well not be able to stop what he barely stopped a moment ago.

He turned away and looked at the fog-misted road. He wanted to walk home, hell, he had to walk home. London was encased in fog now, and he needed the cool mysterious mist to cleanse him of a fire he did not want. He forced himself to turn away from the town house. He paid the carriage driver liberally and shook his head as the man asked where he wanted to go.

"Be careful, gov'nor," the driver said as Gabriel headed toward his own lodgings.

The theater was packed. Outside, vendors were hawking their usual wares of tomatoes and other gross objects often used to demonstrate displeasure with a performance.

Gabriel sat in a box next to Pamela. Her father and the two other men that Gabriel now thought of as "The Group" accompanied them.

He'd known she was good. He'd stood in the back of the theater and watched her rehearse.

But that didn't prepare him for the illumination of her presence when she walked on the stage, nor the way she captivated every man and woman in the theater.

She was, in a word, breathtaking. The stage makeup made her face almost translucent. Her eyes sparkled and her quick witty repartee was delivered with a charming confidence that was irresistible.

Within two minutes of being on stage, she'd stolen the heart of every man and made every woman envious.

"She truly is remarkable," Pamela whispered to him.

"Yes," he said.

"She is the most sought after woman in London," Henry Worth, the Earl of Daven said, "and she has consented to have supper with me tomorrow night after the performance." He shot a triumphant look at Stanhope.

The last line of the play was uttered, and the theater erupted in applause. No rotten fruit tonight. The audience stood and waited until Monique Fremont and her leading man returned four times, each time bringing the other cast members to the front of the stage with them.

Someone handed her a bouquet of flowers. She took them and curtsied.

"Thank you," she told the audience, with the slightest hint of a French accent. "Thank you for making me so welcome and giving me a new home."

The audience erupted again.

"She is a very fine actress," Stanhope said, making it plain he really didn't consider her graciousness anything but an act.

"I hope she visits us again," Pamela said wistfully. Her comment surprised Gabriel. She had been very quiet. In fact the only words he recalled her saying other than the greeting upon his arrival at the Stanhope home was that about Monique Fremont being "a remarkable woman."

"She will," Stanhope said and looked down at his daughter distastefully. "But I will not have you bothering her."

Pamela's face tightened, the fleeting pleasure gone. Her hands in her skirt clenched together.

Gabriel leaned over and whispered into her ear. "I think she liked you," he said in a voice too low for her father's ear. He thought—hoped—it looked more like an endearment.

For a moment Pamela smiled slightly. Then she turned her eyes back to the stage.

So did he.

Monique Fremont's eyes seemed to be gazing in their direction. Gabriel saw a slight tightening of her lips before she once more flashed that brilliant smile and swept off the stage.

"I think I will go backstage and give her my personal congratulations for a magnificent performance," Lord Daven said. He turned to Stanhope. "Would you join me?"

Gabriel looked about with an air of complete indifference. Daven had been invited to accompany them, and he despised the man every bit as much as he despised Stanhope. Greed oozed out of his every pore; so—every time the man looked at Monique—did pure lust.

But taking young Pamela home fit his plans, and he had no doubt now that Monique could take care of herself. He had done everything he could in warning her. She had decided to ignore his warnings.

Now he had to take care of Pamela, and in doing so he would have access to Stanhope's home.

Stanhope said "I must accompany my daughter and Manchester home. I would not like the ton to be talking about them."

"Your consideration toward your daughter is touching,"

Manchester said courteously. "Your coachman can vouch for the fact I will take her straight home."

"I do not believe you would dishonor Pamela," Stanhope said. "It is only appearances. Obviously no one cares about those in the colonies, but . . ."

Gabriel wanted to thrust his fist in the man's face.

The colonies were colonies no longer and yet the British seemed intent not to accept that reality. Stanhope was also very careless with the well-being of his daughter. He obviously was ready to sell her to anyone to profit his own pockets. That filled Gabriel with a ferocity even greater than he had anticipated.

He'd never considered whether Stanhope had a family, much less an innocent daughter.

The sudden need to protect her was a complication. And an opportunity, he admitted to himself.

He wanted to get into the house again. Perhaps tonight. But if not, he would visit a few gambling hells and try his luck. He needed funds. He would need a great deal shortly. He'd hoped to steal what he needed from Stanhope, but then there had always been the other option.

He had to win, though at different places. He did not want anyone to know he had the skill to win large amounts of money, or that he could best an aristocracy that spent so much time gambling away nearly everything they had inherited.

Gabriel tried to keep his contempt from showing. Instead, he summoned a foolish smile. "I would not dishonor a future bride," he said again.

"Make up your mind, Thomas," Lord Daven said. "I am leaving now. I have a slight bauble to give the lovely Miss Fremont in celebration of her great success."

Gabriel looked at Pamela and saw none of the pleasure that had been there just seconds earlier. "I will be safe, Papa," she said.

Stanhope looked at her for a long time. "I will tell Garvey to look after you."

"Oh, yes, Papa. He will."

Stanhope turned to Gabriel. "I trust you as a man of honor."

Man of honor, indeed. Stanhope didn't know the meaning of the word. Well, Gabriel did. At least as far as Lady Pamela Kane was concerned.

Gabriel helped Pamela on with her cloak. Then he ushered her through the crowd to where he knew Stanhope's carriage would be waiting.

He didn't say anything to his young companion until they were inside, and the coach was winding its way down a London street. He watched her visibly relax.

"I am sorry you missed going backstage," she said in a small voice.

"I would rather be with you," he said.

She looked at him with wary blue eyes. "I would have liked to have seen her tonight," she said shyly. "She is everything I would like to be. She is so . . . confident. I do not think she would allow anyone to . . ."

"To what?" Gabriel asked after a moment's silence.

Pamela seemed to back into herself, as if to make herself invisible. Her lips trembled slightly.

*Damn Stanhope. How many lives had he destroyed?*

"You promised to tell me about the ton," he said gently.

"I . . . I only know the gossip from the country. He brought me here only because of you." She swallowed hard. "I led you to believe I could help you. I cannot."

Her voice trembled and her hands shook slightly.

"I still think it is a good bargain," he said. "Yours and mine."

"Why?"

"Because you are a very appealing young lady and I enjoy your company. I do not wish to be pursued by other women. It serves my purposes to allow everyone to believe I am your devoted slave."

"You would be no woman's slave," she said with more insight than he'd expected, but then she had surprised him several times. Still, it was disconcerting. How many times had his mask slipped?

He chose not to answer, and she fell into silence. He wondered whether she would ask him inside. It would be highly improper, particularly with no woman family member in attendance.

Gabriel wondered again why Pamela was being dangled in front of his eyes, like a newly killed goose at Christmastime.

Did Stanhope believe it would blind him to the particulars of a business arrangement or that his influence would keep Gabriel quiet if he'd sought information about that long-ago partnership which ended with a suicide?

"Tell me about your young man," he finally said.

She glanced up toward the bench. The driver couldn't hear their voices over the sound of wheels against cobbled streets, but he sensed the fear in her. She said nothing.

He waited.

"My father would destroy him if he knew," she finally said. "He already . . ." She stopped in midsentence again.

He could not pry further. She was obviously terrified of her father, and he knew she would not tell him of her father's threats. She was too afraid, though she showed signs of spirit long battered.

"If you ever need a friend," he said, "I am available."

"Why? I heard my father talk about you."

"He believes I am a worthless fool."

She was kind enough not to answer, but her silence was just as convincing.

"And what do you think?" he asked.

"I think you like Miss Fremont and you wish to make her jealous."

"And you think that is why I am calling on you?"

"Why else? You suggested the bargain."

"Yes." He wanted to say she looked as if she needed someone. But that would be too far out of his role.

Instead, he sat back and looked out at the homes they passed. Lights flickered through the night.

*London.*

It had been such an adventure for a boy.

His father coming home, his big voice booming. His mother's delighted laughter . . .

He shook off the memories as the coach rolled to a stop.

He recalled the last time he was in a carriage alone with a

woman, and how he had kissed her, thinking that one kiss might tell him Monique Fremont was nothing but the conniving courtesan she appeared to be. But it hadn't.

It had only made him want her more.

He felt nothing but sympathy for the young girl next to him.

When the coachman opened the door, he helped her down and walked her to the door. He knew he should ask to come in. It was an opportunity to reach Stanhope's safe.

She would say yes.

But as he looked into her vulnerable face and eyes, which seemed to search for the truth, he couldn't do it.

Not now. Not tonight.

Instead, he bowed. "It was a delightful evening, Lady Pamela."

He turned around and walked quickly down the street before he could change his mind.

He would spend the rest of the night in a gambling hell. Maybe there he could forget lovely gray eyes.

# Chapter Eleven

Monique felt the usual exhilaration after the performance. It had gone better than she had hoped. Opening night had made the entire cast glitter. They were better—she was better—than they had ever been in rehearsal.

She was enough of a professional to take satisfaction in that, even as her gaze had traveled during the performance to the first box.

She had known they would be there. She had arranged the seats. What she had not been prepared for was seeing Manchester and Pamela, their heads bent together as if they were telling secrets.

As for Stanhope, her plan was working. At least she hoped so. She had received more flowers from him—perfect roses again—and an invitation to supper Saturday night.

Daven and Lord Stammel had also called, each of them bearing gifts. Lord Stammel's had been fine French chocolates, which she gave to Dani. Daven had sent an exquisite fan.

And tonight she had told Lynch about the competition among the three close friends.

She had warned him not to tell anyone, though she knew he would.

A story like that would increase ticket sales and the life of the play. She'd made very sure that she told him she would leave if he said anything to anyone. He would make sure none of it could be traced back to him. And, ultimately, to her.

She should have received satisfaction from the success thus far of her grand plan. It had proceeded exactly as designed. Except, of course, for one unexpected wild card.

*Manchester.*

He had sent everything into a spin.

She just didn't know where he fit. She would have sworn that the unholy attraction that sparked between them would die when she discovered exactly what kind of man he was. Instead, it had grown stronger.

Forbidden fruit, she told herself. That's all it was. Nature was contrary. You always wanted what was unavailable. Like Eve's apple.

But even knowing that, realization of his presence in the box had hit her like a pair of runaway horses.

She sat at her dressing table as Dani carefully removed the rouge from her face. It was the best rouge, from Portugal, but Monique was well aware of the damage powders did to the face. Once it was removed, her eyes appeared larger, highlighted by the dye that darkened her eyebrows and lashes. Only a trace of lip salve remained.

Dani helped her change from the elaborate stage gowns, which required a long corset, to a simple muslin gown that did not. A shorter, much looser corset worked quite well, and the gown was without the many frills and trim that embellished the fashionable lady today. Simplicity flattered her slim form.

Just as Dani removed the jeweled combs from her hair, a knock sounded at the door. Lynch asked permission to enter.

Monique did not move from her seat before the mirror.

"I did not give you permission to enter," she said.

"I do not need permission in my own theater."

"You do, if you wish me to stay."

"We have a contract, you and I."

"And it does not give you the right to invade my privacy," she said. She knew she had leverage she didn't have a week ago, or even last night. In the past several hours, she had become a valuable commodity.

"There is a crowd outside waiting for you. The Earls of Stanhope and Daven have asked for the pleasure of a few moments of your company. I was not sure what to tell them." Lynch's Adam's apple bobbed up and down.

"Did you let them know you knew about the arrangement?"

"Certainly not," he said, obviously offended. "Nor did I tell anyone with the newspapers," he added too quickly.

"But . . ."

"A slight wager. That's all. Just a wager on who might win."

"And who did you wager with?"

He looked away. "A friend. He will not say anything."

She stared at him, then turned back to the mirror and hid a smile. Better and better. Every gambler in the city would be betting on who might win the honor of becoming the protector of Monique Fremont. It would become public very quickly.

Stanhope could not withdraw now, not without losing face. Nor could he harm her. Too many eyes would be on the four of them.

He had gotten away with attempted murder nearly twenty-five years ago. He had probably gotten away with the murder of his wife.

This would be one time he would have an enormous audience.

"I will see them in ten minutes," she said.

After he backed out, she wondered whether Manchester was still with them. And her half sister.

If he was, well, then she would have to endure the wastrel.

If he wasn't, where in Hades was he? What were his intentions toward Pamela?

And why did she care so much?

It was at the second gaming hell that Gabriel heard of the competition. Betting was frantic.

He'd learned that London aristocrats bet on everything. This was a natural.

Tongues wagged.

The odds, of course, were on Stanhope. He was the wealthiest and most powerful of them all. Yet some said that Daven had charm and was not saddled with the suspicion of killing his wife.

Gabriel listened. Apparently, Monique Fremont agreed to take one of three men as her protector within a month.

He was apparently out of the running. Because he was not rich enough? Not powerful enough?

She had not even given him a chance to enter the bidding. Not that he would have accepted if she had. He'd never wanted, or needed, a woman so much he would humiliate himself to become part of a public contest.

He didn't think Stanhope would have, either. Unless he had been maneuvered into the competition.

Even he—a newcomer to London—realized that Stanhope couldn't retire from the field now.

He'd been neatly trapped.

To what purpose? He had not suspected that Monique Fremont would so blatantly play men against each other. Still, he couldn't help but appreciate how well she had manipulated Stanhope.

If that was her purpose?

But Stanhope's romantic problems were none of Gabriel's concerns this night. He needed funds and he needed them quickly.

He needed to get Monique Fremont out of his mind.

Gabriel turned his attention to the cards. He won steadily. Amounts small enough not to attract attention. First one hell, then another.

He emerged with nearly a thousand pounds. A fortune for some. Not nearly enough for him.

He knew Stanhope had money. He had jewels as well. Since Gabriel had recklessly let his conscience keep him from using Pamela, he would have to indulge in a bit of burglary.

It was dawn before he reached his lodgings. Sydney was

patiently waiting for him, giving nothing away as he took Gabriel's cloak.

"Have a good night, sir?"

"Yes. How is your sister?"

"She is happier than anytime I can remember. She lives in your library."

"I wish there was more there."

"There is plenty. Do you require anything, sir?"

"Have you been awake all night waiting for me?"

"You pay me to do that."

"No," Gabriel said. "I pay you to take care of my clothes and to serve meals and to help your sister, and occasionally tie my cravat, though neither of us is very good at that. I do not pay you to stay awake all night."

"I thought you might wish a bath, or some food."

"I wish only bed, Sydney. But my thanks for your efforts."

Sydney looked disappointed. "Yes sir."

Gabriel almost relented and asked for some food. But he had taken food at the gaming establishments and he needed rest more than he needed sustenance.

He suspected he would get very little sleep in the next few days.

Stanhope could barely control his rage when he read the London newspapers the next morning.

He didn't know whether a servant had overheard something, or whether either Robert or Henry had mentioned something they should not. It might have even been Monique Fremont herself.

In any case, the damage was done. He was as trapped now as some of his victims had been. He did not appreciate the irony.

If he did not continue with the challenge, he would be laughed out of London. That was one consequence he could ill afford. He had too many enemies. Only his reputation for power and ruthlessness held them at bay.

The prime minister's people were awaiting their chance to ruin him. He had enough on them to send them to Australia or some other dismal godforsaken place. But if they suspected a weakness . . .

"Where's my daughter?" he demanded of a maid who had, unfortunately, stepped into the dining room to replenish the chafing dishes. It mattered little that there was only one master to eat, and a daughter who seldom appeared for breakfast.

"I do not know, milord," the maid said.

"Fetch her. Tell her I expect her here in no more than ten minutes."

She curtsied. "Yes, milord."

She sped away as if the devil were after her. He was slightly mollified by the idea. He *was* the devil. He had worked hard at cultivating that image.

He looked at his pocket watch, then set it down next to his plate and listened to it tick.

His daughter appeared in nine minutes. Her hair was combed into a single long braid, and she was dressed in a morning gown. Her gaze wandered around the room, avoiding him.

"Sit down, Pamela," he said.

She sat.

"Tell me about last night."

"There is nothing to tell, Papa. Lord Manchester brought me home and left after seeing me to the door. Did not Garvey tell you?"

"What did you talk about in the carriage?"

"Just the play."

"Nothing else? Nothing about his background, or his family?"

"No."

"Did he ask to see you again?"

"No," she said again.

He frowned. "I want you to be pleasant to him."

"Why?"

"That is of no concern of yours. Just do as I tell you."

"Yes, Papa."

"You look pale," he said, glaring at her.

"I did not get much sleep."

He continued to look at her. Something was different. Perhaps her eyes. The fear wasn't as evident. Her back was straighter. There was the slightest hint of defiance. She had never asked him why before.

He didn't like that one bit.

"Are you lying to me?"

"About what, Papa?" Her eyes were wide and innocent.

"Your ride home last night. You are positive he said nothing about his family or me?"

"Just that he admires you."

"Did he say why?"

"You are successful at business."

"Do you want to continue to see him?"

Surprise flitted across her face. Then something like dismay. He didn't like that, either.

"Answer me, gel."

"No," she said. "I do not. He is not . . . sophisticated."

Stanhope relaxed. "You will do as you are told."

"Yes, Papa."

"You may go. I do not want you to spoil my meal."

She backed away and disappeared quickly out the door.

He started to eat again. . . .

He would ask Ames to watch Pamela. For a moment tonight he had sensed something between—but no—Manchester was a fool. Not even his naive daughter could be interested in him.

Today he would get together with old Pickwick and a friend of his who was trying to sell an old ship. It was barely floating, but that would suit his purposes well.

He would purchase it, give it the name of another more respectable ship and send it out to sea. With just a little help, it would sink, along with the cargo. He could claim the insurance.

And his new partner? Well, he would be aboard. One way or another. He would be lulled by a new relationship with Pamela and with the Stanhope family. He would never suspect he was a sheep to be sheared.

He smiled as he took another piece of ham. It would be a fine day.

*       *       *

Gabriel slept for several hours, then rang for Smythe and ordered a bath, then breakfast.

He had many things to do today.

He finished both, then looked at his wardrobe. Most of his clothes were brightly colored. And expensive looking, even if they were not tasteful. He needed a disguise, and the problem was coming and going from his lodgings without the other occupants of the area taking notice of changes in his appearance.

Gabriel felt he could probably trust Smythe, yet their acquaintance was too short for him to be really sure, and much depended on maintaining what everyone thought he was. And then there was the child.

The only solution was another room. Somewhere he wouldn't be noticed going in and out. He did not want any gossip that could lead to the new marquess.

He'd looked at the two papers that Smythe had brought with his meal of fresh-baked rolls, ham, and eggs. He made a mental list of available lodgings, several of which were in the waterfront area. He would purchase some additional items of clothing he would need along with the theatrical kit that his friend in Boston had provided.

He finished dressing, this time toning down his clothes to a pair of trousers, a plain shirt, and a black cloak. Thank God, it was cold and misting outside. He left his quizzing glass in a drawer and the cane in a corner. He did not want to draw attention to himself.

He nodded to Smythe as he approached the door. A flicker of surprise crossed the man's face at his appearance.

"Shall I call a carriage, sir? 'Tis cold and wet."

Sir was a hell of a lot better than "my lord."

"No," he said. "Thank you. I am just taking a stroll."

Smythe had the discretion not to look surprised at the idea of his master taking a stroll in the rain. He was obviously adapting to his new master's strange habits. "I will see to your clothes while you are gone."

Gabriel nodded. God, he wished he could confide in the man. He needed an ally.

He dismissed the idea as he walked down the steps to the street.

A number of carriages passed and splashed water on him as he walked quickly down the street, then turned onto a less traveled lane. He wanted as few people as possible to notice him.

He increased his pace, ducking his head against the wind. He didn't mind the weather. He was well used to storms at sea, to rain that felt like ice.

Gabriel knew the way. He had a mind that could readily memorize maps and charts. He knew exactly where he was going.

He discarded the idea of taking the first lodging he saw. The neighborhood was too respectable. He would be noticed going in and coming out in different clothes.

The second was not acceptable, either, but for the opposite reason. It was in a neighborhood where nothing would be safe. He suspected everything he left there would disappear in a matter of moments.

The third came closest to meeting his needs.

It was a plain but clean room located over a tavern. Patrons would be going in and out. No one would notice what he wore. There was a back stairway.

The tavern owner lived above the tavern and rented out three rooms. Two of them were to ladies, he announced.

More likely, prostitutes, he thought. Better and better.

"I have some . . . a friend," Gabriel explained without explaining. "Discretion is important."

"Ah, a lady."

He did not say anything, letting his silence confirm it.

The man studied his plain but obviously good clothes. "How long will you be needing it?"

Gabriel grinned. "I am not sure. As long as the lady's husband . . ."

Greed shone in the tavern owner's eyes. "Ten pounds a month."

It was robbery. The landlord might as well be wearing a mask and carrying a gun.

"Seven," he bargained, knowing it was expected.

"In advance?"

"Yes."

"Done," the man said.

"As I said, I want discretion," Gabriel pressed. "It will be worth an extra five pounds at the end of two weeks."

The man brightened. "Yes, Mr.—?"

"Mr. Brown," Gabriel said.

"Mr. Brown, it is. I am John Bailey. When can you pay?"

Gabriel took out a small pouch of coins and counted out fifteen pounds.

"When do you want to use it?"

"I will be bringing some of my belongings over later today," he said.

Bailey nodded.

It was done.


Monique looked at the cards collecting in the bowl on the front table, along with a growing collection of gifts and flowers.

Poor Mrs. Miller. She was harried. Monique had her returning gifts as quickly as they came, particularly to Stanhope, Stammel, and Daven.

She wanted to make it clear to all of them that she did not care for money. Then when the thefts began, no one would look in her direction. Hopefully, they would look at each other.

Back went a silver comb and a pearl necklace and a silk shawl. Flowers were refused as the number threatened to overtake the small town house. Candy was given to the poor and a note sent to givers thanking them for a donation to the unfortunate.

In the meantime she dined with Stammel at London's most fashionable restaurant. Every head turned as they entered. In hours, the odds would change in the contest.

She knew how to win his heart. Let him talk.

So she listened as he bragged on his business prowess.

"I understand you and Daven are partners with Lord Stanhope," she said, widening her eyes with admiration. "I believe you must be the one with the ideas."

He visibly preened. "I would not say that, although my advice is always heeded," he said.

"I hear that you have the largest shipping company in London."

"Not quite, mademoiselle, but we are getting there. Of course, most gentlemen do not dabble in business, but when you have talent . . ."

"You should use it," she finished. "I admire people who lead useful lives."

"And your family?" she asked after a short pause.

His face flushed. "A wife, mademoiselle, but she stays in the country."

She gave him a Gallic shrug. "Most men have wives. It is of no matter. What of Lord Stanhope?"

He frowned at the conversation turning to another man. "His wife died," he said shortly.

"Hmm," she said.

"He has vowed to never marry again," he added, as if afraid she might think a widower a better prospect. It was not unheard of for a member of the nobility to marry an actress. "And there is . . ." He stopped himself.

"Ah," she said, "you cannot stop there. What did you intend to say?"

"Only that he is not . . . interested in serious alliances."

*He is already thinking of betraying his partner by saying too much.*

She was well aware of what he had started to say. There were rumors.

She smiled. "Are you saying you are?"

"I would make a contract. You would be a wealthy woman," he rushed on, obviously feeling he had an opportunity.

"I do not care about wealth," she said.

"What do you care about?"

"I will be clear," she said. "I enjoy the company of men. But I am not a loose woman. I do not want or need an entourage of admirers."

"Then what . . . ?"

"I want a companion whom I can trust and who trusts me, who is willing to talk to me about important matters. I want a friend as well as a lover."

He looked startled. Not quite sure what to say. It was quite obvious he had never considered a woman in that way. He squinted his eyes as he tried to understand.

"But of course," he said, obviously intent upon doing or saying anything that might win him this challenge.

"I have never done this before," she said, "but the three of you are all so charming."

He looked confused.

She starting eating again. The fowl was quite exceptional.

Gabriel walked down the street outside of Stanhope's town house and collapsed on a corner like the beggar he pretended to be. He buried his head in his arms. He had been here for the last three evenings. No one paid any attention to him now.

He wore the same ragged clothes he'd been wearing these past few days after a visit to his tavern room, and a cap that came down over the dark wig he wore. The clothes were loose enough to conceal a pistol. And a knife. He was proficient in the use of both.

It was late evening. Lights shone from five rooms of the Stanhope home. He saw other figures in the library.

Excellent. He hoped it was Stammel and Daven. The fact that the three business partners were now pitted against each other in seeking the favor of an actress made the contest all the more interesting.

For Gabriel's plan to succeed, he needed to visit Stanhope's safe after the other two men had been at the residence. They had to be the only two to have had access to the safe.

So, as he had the past few nights, he hunched down inside his coat and waited.

Pamela sat on a window seat and stared out of the window at the park across the way. The streetlamps shone down on the green lawn beneath, and she was reminded of the green lawns at home.

Her gaze was drawn to a beggar sitting on the grass down the street. He'd been there several days, but he was always gone in the morning. One afternoon she'd started out to take him a farthing, but her father had stopped her.

"We do not want him here," he said. "I forbid you from encouraging him. If he is not gone soon, I'll call the runners on him."

She'd not tried again, because she was afraid the servants would tell her father, and he would have the beggar hurt. But it wounded her heart to see such misery.

She counted the minutes until her father left on his usual nightly rounds. Tonight it was later than usual, but he had those terrible friends with him. She hated the way they looked at her, as if she were a filly to be sold.

After they were gone, she could visit the library and find something to read. There would not be the romances she loved or the poetry, but at this moment she would read anything she could find.

Anything to keep her mind off the current disaster. She yearned to be back in the countryside, sitting beside a stream with Robert Bard, the son of the local physician. He would be leaving soon for Edinburgh to resume his study of medicine.

Her father would not consent to the marriage.

She had often asked her aunt why her father would even care, since he had not presented her at court nor given her a season. Her aunt would get a tight look on her face and introduce another subject. It wasn't until she heard two servants talking just before she left that she really understood.

"Surprised I am he sent for Lady Pamela," she heard the housekeeper say. "I thought he feared her appearance would stir up all that talk about—"

"Hush," said the butler. "He will discharge us all if he knew we were gossiping."

"Everyone knows he killed the poor thing's mother," the housekeeper said defiantly. "The poor lady. I worry about the young miss with 'im."

Pamela's heart froze. She'd always known something dark and secretive pervaded her father's house. He'd always been cold to her, cold and even cruel. She'd been grateful to be sent to her aunt's home.

And now she knew why she had been sent away. In the few days she'd been here, she had seen his eyes. He hated her.

Because of her mother? Because he had hated the woman who had given her birth?

Pamela didn't remember much about her mother. She had died when Pamela was only six. She remembered sadness. And the smell of roses. She remembered kind touches.

Her journey to London had been full of fear and her meeting with her father so dreadful that she'd visibly trembled. She'd tried to keep her legs from failing her when he'd said he wanted her to attract a marquess.

Her apprehension had doubled when she'd chanced upon a newspaper discarded by her father. She glanced to the fold and noticed the mention of the Marquess of Manchester. A gambler, the story had said, and a poor one at that. An ungraceful upstart from America.

She'd shuddered.

Oddly enough, he had been the only one who had been even a little kind to her. Everyone else at her father's soiree had looked at her as if she had two heads. She was an earl's daughter who had never been presented at court. Apparently, that was enough to keep tongues wagging. Had she disgraced the family? Was she weak of mind? Had her father really killed her mother?

She'd heard the whispers and they'd cut to the quick.

Then she'd been forced to take the odd marquess to the garden despite the questionable nature of an unchaperoned outing.

Surprisingly, he had proved to be kind. Or if not kind, disinterested in her as a marriage prospect and ready to make a bargain that would help them both. She hadn't believed it at first. If he was a friend of her father's, he had an ulterior motive.

And he did. He obviously wanted to stay in her father's good graces. And yet she believed there was more to it than that. Perhaps he really was sympathetic.

She wanted to believe. She wasn't sure she should believe.

She had no choice.

She thought of Robert again, wishing she could run off and join him in Edinburgh. He had even proposed that. But she knew that her father would destroy Robert and his father. She could not let that happen.

She watched as a carriage rolled up and her father entered it. She exhaled, not aware that she had bottled up her breath as he walked from the house.

The very room seemed to express relief.

He would not be back until dawn, if his pattern held true.

She looked out again. The beggar appeared asleep. Maybe he would still be there in the morning. She would take him a few coins then, or maybe some pastries. Cook always made more than they could eat.

She put on her night robe, lit a candle from the oil lamp, and padded down the stairs. No Ames. He must be upstairs attending to her father's wardrobe. The other servants had retired to their quarters in the basement or up on the third floor.

She used the candle to guide her way into the darkened library and set it on a table. The dark curtains were drawn and she placed the candle where it was hidden from the window so not even a flicker of light could be seen.

She skimmed the titles on the shelves, pulling down one book, then another. Some of the books had never been opened. She loved the smell of leather and paper.

She chose one volume, a history of China, then rearranged the books so that it didn't look as if one was missing.

Clutching the book to her side, she retrieved her candle and padded back up the stairs.

# Chapter Twelve

Gabriel waited until all but one light in the hallway was quenched. Grateful for the fog creeping in from the river, he waited until it enveloped the street, making even the outline of Stanhope's town house difficult to see.

Under a gaslight he looked at his pocket watch. Past one. He probably had an hour to get in and out.

The street was quiet with the exception of an occasional lone carriage. Stanhope and his friends had left the house an hour ago. Long enough for the servants to have retired.

He moved along the street until he reached the gate into Stanhope's property. As before, it wasn't locked. He opened it and entered. He didn't even need to slink into the shadows thanks to the fog enveloping him. At the back door, he took out his picks. In seconds he had the lock picked, and he slid inside the house.

He closed the door and waited until his eyes adjusted to the darkness. Only the slightest glow from the oil lamp in the hall gave a hint of light. But he knew the house. He had memorized every hall, every turn.

Still, he listened for several seconds for the laugh or grumble of a servant, for a valet preparing for his master's return. Nothing. His heart beat loudly. It was one thing to invade an empty house, another to invade one occupied by living humans.

He made out vague forms. A table. An umbrella stand. The stairs. He walked on the outside edge of each step in shoes designed for such nefarious purposes. Still, he heard a creak and stopped. Listened again. Then he took another step.

He reached the landing of the second floor and went down the hall to Stanhope's suite, looking for a trace of light. What if the valet was preparing the next day's clothes . . . ?

Nothing. He opened the door and slipped inside, then headed for the safe. He knelt beside it, placed his ear against the lock, then let his fingers find the tumblers. He knew the numbers now, and it took less time than before.

He needed a light, but he didn't want to take the time to use tinder and flint, and he didn't want any light to filter through the drawn curtains. Instead, he had to remember the contents he'd seen before. The banknotes were toward the back.

He reached in and found them. He took a stack of them, tucked them inside his coat, and closed the safe.

He heard someone ascending the stairs, saw a light moving upward in the hall. He crouched behind a large chest and waited.

The light and footsteps faded. Whoever it was had turned in the opposite direction. He peered out and saw young Pamela enter a room down the hall. She closed the door, and he was encased in darkness again.

He allowed himself to breathe. God help him if she'd turned around.

Remembering the creak of the steps, he remained still for another few minutes. Hopefully, she had gone to bed and would not venture outside her room again. Hopefully she had not asked a maid for something to be brought to her.

His plan could tumble down from a foundation he already knew was weak.

He took his first few steps, paused, then continued. Down the stairs, down the hall. Out the door.

He quickly sped out of the garden and down the street, pulling off the wig and tucking it inside the coat. He walked swiftly toward the waterfront.

The tavern would still be open. He would go through the back entrance, up to his room and change clothes, then share a brandy downstairs. He needed to smell like liquor.

Smythe would be waiting for him. His valet would wonder if he returned home without the smell of brandy about him.

*Poor Smythe.* He must really be wondering about a master who was in residence only a few hours of the day. The poor man's frustration mounted daily in his inability to better serve the man who employed him.

He reached the tavern and his room, removed the notes from his clothes, and counted.

Twenty thousand pounds.

Enough for a partial payment on a partnership. Enough to send Stanhope into a rage and make him wonder about the honesty of his partners.

He changed clothes quickly. Back into the too tight breeches of a gentleman. The cravat was askew. After all, he had indulged in a night of debauchery.

The tavern was full. The owner served as barkeep and welcomed his new resident. Without asking, he poured a cup of what Gabriel had ordered before.

No one else paid him any attention, apparently considering him no more than a nuisance.

He pretended drunkenness and listened to the waterfront gossip around him. Most of the patrons were sailors looking for and talking about possible berths. The *Bristol Star* was looking for a cook. The *Mary Ann* needed a second mate. Five ships had anchored today. There would be available berths after they were unloaded, then provisioned.

He knew every ship owned by The Group.

Three of them were anchored in the Thames. Five were at sea. There were rumors of another purchase.

*His ship.* His intended investment.

It was—in every one's estimation—a ship lucky not to be at the bottom of the ocean.

He rose and staggered drunkenly to the door.

It had been a profitable evening.

\*          \*          \*

This was Stanhope's night.

Monique did not look forward to it. Yet she had no excuse to refuse his invitation to a private ball. The theater was closed this evening.

She had taken great care with her appearance. She'd visited a modiste days ago and offered a large sum to have a gown readied in three days. The modiste had also read about the wager. She was obviously hopeful that her name would be mentioned.

The dress was a deep violet muslin in contrast to the pastel colors she knew the other ladies would be wearing. Pastel was in fashion.

But she was not a lady.

Dani dressed her hair. "I do not like that you go alone with this man," she said.

"It is a ball, and everyone will know that Stanhope brought me. His daughter is coming with us. I will be perfectly safe."

Dani looked skeptical.

"Everything goes according to plan."

"I understand, but . . . I fear him."

"I do, too." She stared at herself in the mirror. What part of Stanhope had passed on to her? Was she wrong for doing this? She'd always considered it a matter of justice, but . . .

He was her father. Everything dark and evil. Did evil lurk in her as well?

That terrified her more than anything else. Was that why she was endangering Dani? Playing God herself? But if she didn't, who would?

Her purpose was fueled by the lack of even a glimmer of recognition on his part. But, of course not. Her mother had meant nothing to him. The seduction of a young girl. An attempted murder when there was a child. And the terror that had always followed her, broken her.

Stanhope would never do that again.

So now she would go to a ball with a man who had no idea he was escorting his daughter. A daughter who hated him.

She applied a bit of rouge to her cheeks, then coloring on her lips.

Monique Fremont stared back at herself in the mirror. She

didn't recognize herself. Merry Anders was lurking in there someplace, needing to be free again.

Someone who wanted to love rather than hate.

She wondered whether it was too late, whether the decent part of her had been consumed by the other.

She heard the authoritative rap on the door downstairs and her housekeeper opening the door.

Then she gave Dani a forced smile and went to the door. She was not going to be fashionably late.


Pamela looked impossibly young as she entered the ballroom of one of London's most fashionable residences, accompanied by the Earl of Stanhope and Monique Fremont.

Their names were loudly announced by a butler, just as his had been announced moments earlier upon his arrival. Since this was Gabriel's first formal ball in England, he'd been somewhat bemused by having his name announced and everyone turning to stare.

He'd been invited four days earlier. Conspicuously tardy for such an invitation. Then he'd received a personal note from Stanhope, asking him to attend.

Since Gabriel had not been welcomed by the ton, he wondered what Stanhope held over the head of his host. Upon his arrival in the glittering ballroom of one of the finest homes in London, he'd been regarded curiously by the other guests.

It was, Gabriel knew, part of the courtship ritual of English society.

He had appeared as ordered, dressed in his best formal clothes. His cravat was a little too grand. He felt his neck was being stretched several inches, and he wondered if that was how a condemned man felt. His pantaloons were of the newest style and covered the full length of his legs. They were as tight as his skin and damned uncomfortable. He felt he couldn't move without them splitting.

Still, he noticed clusters of older women eying him with speculation and whispering excitedly to their daughters.

Apparently even a wastrel American marquess was better than no marquess at all.

Most of the gentlemen, however, gave him the cut direct.

The whole event amused him. The mothers, the daughters, the men, the marriage mart.

And then he'd seen Pamela, dressed in a light blue gown that shimmered in the light of hundreds of candles. Her brown hair had been pulled back and tied, a profusion of curly tendrils tumbling artfully around her face. She turned toward him, her eyes widening as she saw him, then she gave him the slightest tentative smile.

But what made him really straighten was the woman who walked behind her. Dressed in a violet gown that contrasted with creamy shoulders and arms, Monique Fremont made every other woman in the room look inconsequential. Every head turned to stare at her.

Her gaze met his, and he thought he saw a slight shiver move through her. But then she turned to look up at her escort, and he wondered whether he'd imagined it.

In seconds half the men in the room were moving in her direction.

He approached Pamela, instead, and gave her a brief bow.

"I am delighted to see you, Lady Pamela. I hoped you would be here."

She gazed up at him, and he was reminded of the innocence in her eyes, despite being the daughter of Stanhope. There was also apprehension.

"Thank you, my lord."

Then Stanhope turned toward him and nodded. "I am most pleased you could join us this evening."

But even while his words were cordial, Gabriel saw anger glowing in the man's eyes.

Gabriel didn't doubt that he had discovered the theft. And probably recently. Stanhope simmered with barely controlled rage, which made him a very dangerous man.

Gabriel wondered whether either woman sensed it as he did. Or perhaps only he did, because he knew that the earl might well have had a very unpleasant surprise in the last few days.

"How could I possibly miss an opportunity to see your lovely daughter?" He turned toward Monique. "And it is delightful to see Mademoiselle Fremont again." He bowed slightly. "You look"—he searched for the right word—"magnificent."

And she did. The dress made her eyes smokier, deeper, more mysterious. Her face was alive with that vitality that made her more striking than her features. Unwanted desire twisted his stomach.

"My lord," she said courteously, though he detected a slight edge in the words.

His gaze turned to Pamela and he smiled. "I hope you both will honor me with a dance this evening."

Pamela looked downward, and he wondered if she knew how to dance.

Monique's eyes, on the other hand, sparkled as if at a challenge. "I will look forward to it."

Stanhope frowned. "I intend to reserve your time, my dear," he said.

"Oh la, my lord. Surely you need time to speak to your friends." She fluttered her fan. "And Lord Manchester is an acquaintance."

Stanhope was trapped. Gabriel glanced quickly at Monique. Was she really that expert a manipulator or was it, as her guileless smile would indicate, merely graciousness trapping the graceless?

He would wager his captaincy on the former.

She was manipulating a manipulator. For riches? If so, it was a damned dangerous way of doing it.

They were interrupted by the host, who expressed pleasure at the arrival of the earl and his guests. Gabriel exchanged extravagant greetings with the host, then watched as the man's wife escorted Pamela to a chair where she sat with other young ladies.

Stanhope looked at him steadily. "I would like to talk to you later about what we discussed at my home. Perhaps in the game room?"

"My pleasure," he said. "Are your friends here tonight?"

Stanhope's face darkened. "No."

"I had hoped to talk with them again," Gabriel persisted.

"I imagine you will find them in the clubs," Stanhope

replied shortly. "And now I would like this dance with Miss Fremont."

Gabriel bowed. "If you do not object—I will ask your lovely daughter to dance with me."

A brief, curt nod answered him, and Gabriel went over to Pamela. "Do you have room on your dance card for me?"

A look of gratitude crossed her face. "Yes, my lord."

He leaned down and whispered in her ear. "I am an oaf of a dancer."

Her eyes lit. "I have had little practice," she confided in a whisper.

"Then may I accompany you for food and drink?"

"Oh yes, my lord."

He offered her his arm, and they walked to the large central table in the dining room, where guests were selecting tidbits from the lavish board. He picked up two plates. "What do you like, Lady Pamela?"

"Anything," she said as the crowd at the table stared at them with curious glances. He could feel her discomfort.

"Would you like me to choose?"

"Please," she said.

"Why do you not find us two seats," he said, "while I fill our plates?"

He watched as she retreated to an out-of-the-way corner and claimed one of two seats. He quickly filled the two plates, his brimming, hers not quite so full, and joined her. A servant offered champagne and punch. Pamela took the punch, he took the champagne.

"Thank you," she said shyly.

"You are welcome. I am not fond of dancing, myself," he said. "But did you not have lessons?"

"My aunt taught me," she said, "but I have never attended a dance before. And all these people . . ."

She ate small bites, casting quick glances around the room. He, too, was aware of all the stares. He even heard some of the comments. He knew she did, too.

"It's the American imposter."

"Stanhope's daughter. Never even been presented at court."

"She's been hidden away. There must be a scandal."

"And Manchester. An imposter. A buffoon."

All the words drifted back to them and her face grew paler. "They are looking at us because you are lovely," he said, refusing to acknowledge the group cruelty.

She put her fork down and looked at him. "You are a kind man, my lord."

He couldn't remember when anyone had called him kind. He'd been a hard taskmaster both as a sailor and as an American naval officer. He'd plotted a long laborious path of revenge. He'd never been kind.

"Please do not convey that sentiment," he said.

"Why?"

"I am a businessman, Lady Pamela. I am also a gambler. Weaknesses are deadly."

"Is being kind a weakness?"

"In some eyes."

"Then I shall keep that observation to myself," she said. "But I do not understand how Miss Fremont can prefer my . . ." She cut herself off and looked down at her plate. Her face was flushed.

"Thank you," he said.

She ate slowly, and he realized she did not want to go back to the chair where she'd first been seated. He'd understood immediately the social etiquette that had placed young, unmarried women in chairs to wait for the young lords to request a dance. It must be excruciating for someone like Pamela, who was already terrified of her father and obviously in love with someone she couldn't—or shouldn't—be in love with, to have to sit in the midst of a crowd and yet be so very alone.

But they could linger no longer or she would be ostracized.

A quadrille was being announced. "Will you give me this dance?" he asked. "I warn you though that I will require *your* help," he said.

That was quite untrue. The shipbuilder who had hired him as a lad and promoted him had also insisted he learn the niceties of society. *"It will be important if you wish to progress,"* he'd told a much younger man.

However, he could fake being awkward easily enough. She

nodded and accompanied him to the floor. Her face was stiff, her smile false.

He bowed and whispered, "Look in the corner. Doesn't he look like a turnip?"

Her glance went to a gentleman dressed in a purple waistcoat. He was nearly as round as he was tall.

She giggled, and then the music began. He made a point of watching other dancers, even stumbled a step or two, and allowed an embarrassed smile. He leaned down. "I warned you," he said, and he saw her visibly relax as she coached him. She was the teacher, and he saw that she warmed to the role.

Through a sideward glance he saw Stanhope and Monique dancing, and he admired their grace together. He would not have suspected Stanhope of being a fine dancer, but he should have. Stanhope was a man to whom mastery meant everything. He watched as Stanhope leaned over and said something to her. She responded with a quick smile that made his heart sink.

He turned back to Pamela. She too had seen her father, and he could feel the tension returning.

"Do not look at him," he said. "Look at me."

She gave him a fleeting smile, and then the music stopped.

He knew the rules. Pickwick had informed him when Gabriel had mentioned he had been invited to the ball. He could not dance twice with the same young lady without declaring his intentions. And Pamela was new to the ton, new to society. Even if she cared nothing about it now, she might someday.

He reluctantly took her back to the chair.

Then he saw Monique detach herself from a group of men and make her way to the ladies' retiring room. Minutes later he watched her slip out unobserved by the group of men who were arguing as to who had the next dance with her. She slipped behind the backs of guests, then made her way out the French doors to the veranda.

Damning himself for recklessness and stupidity, he followed her. She stood alone, obviously lost in her own world. He saw her take a deep breath, then gaze upward at the cloud-filled sky. A cool wind and a slight mist evidently kept every-one else inside, but it seemed not to bother her. Instead she seemed to welcome it.

He moved toward her, reached out, and touched her shoul-der. "Your dress will get wet."

She spun around. "You appear at the oddest times, my lord."

"I might say the same of you," he replied.

"I see that you find Lady Pamela quite attractive."

"She's a very pleasant young lady. You seem to find her fa-ther so."

She tossed him a challenging glance. "Do you really be-lieve so?"

He could easily lose himself in those eyes. He would sell his soul to know what she was thinking at the moment.

From inside came the first strains of a waltz. Her body swayed in motion to the music.

"May I have the pleasure?" he asked, knowing full well that she might refuse.

"Yes," she said simply, taking his arm.

She was as graceful and light as he had imagined. Her smoky gray eyes were barely visible through the light that fil-tered outside from the room's candles. He could see them in his mind's eye—sultry and mysterious—as he whirled her around the veranda.

His gloved hand felt the tight clutch of her corset but even then he thought he could feel the flesh beneath it.

She moved with him in perfect synchrony, as if they were made to dance together, the actress and the rogue marquess. As if they were the only two people in the world as they spun and whirled.

Then the music stopped and so did the enchantment.

He looked down at her flushed face. Bloody hell, but she was lovely.

"Thank you," she said breathlessly. "You dance well," she added in a low voice.

"For an American?"

"For the man I just saw stumbling in the ballroom."

"You inspire me."

Her eyes widened as she looked beyond him. He turned and saw Stanhope coming out the door. "I will tell Lord Stanhope that I was giving you a lesson in the dance, and you are an apt pupil."

He grinned. "You are an exceptional teacher." She gave him a sideways glance just as Stanhope reached them. His eyes looked even angrier, if that was possible, and Gabriel wondered whether he'd noticed the energy that hummed between Monique Fremont and himself.

He had. His glance swept both of them. "Mademoiselle," he said in a stiff voice. "I believe it is time to go."

She nodded.

Stanhope turned to him. "Do not play with my daughter, Manchester. I am warning you."

But Gabriel knew he didn't give a damn about his daughter. He was warning him about Monique.

"Rest assured, Lord Stanhope," he said. "I think your daughter is charming. I was simply keeping Miss Fremont safe for you, and in turn she offered me a dance lesson." He stopped. "Oh, and I thought you would like to know that the funds are on the way."

He bowed and turned away.

Monique could feel Stanhope's fury. It was taking every bit of his willpower not to show it. But it did show in the carriage—in the way his hand clutched the handle of his cane.

She wasn't sure where it was aimed. Possibly at her and Manchester, but she had felt it earlier as well. He'd been a powder keg ever since he arrived at her town house. Something had happened today.

She knew her half sister felt it, too. Her face was carved in stone, her eyes were full of apprehension.

Stanhope had originally planned to take them to two balls. The second, he indicated, was at the home of an important investor who had wanted to meet the acclaimed Miss Fremont.

"I think we should take your daughter home," she said.

She saw him evaluate that proposal.

"Yes, Father," Pamela said. "I am tired."

He turned on her. "I do not care what you are. I asked you to keep Manchester interested and you . . ."

Pamela bit her lips. "Lord Manchester danced with me and escorted me to supper. You know any more would be . . ."

Stanhope turned on Monique, his face twisted with fury. "And you, madam, you made a spectacle of yourself with Manchester."

Monique lifted her chin to do battle. "You do not own me, my lord. You left me to go off to your friends."

"You had no right to . . ."

"To what?"

"What exactly is he to you?"

"He is nothing," she replied. And that was what he was. Nothing. She remembered the way he had leaned over and whispered something in Pamela's ear, the way she had looked back at him with something akin to worship. Moments later he'd done the same blasted thing to her.

He was a scoundrel and a womanizer, and she couldn't understand why she still felt warm inside whenever his image invaded her mind.

Stanhope rapped his cane on the back of the carriage. It came to a stop and a small door opened. "Your lordship?"

"Stop at my house," he said.

In minutes the carriage rolled up to the Stanhope residence. He stayed in his seat as the driver stepped down, opened the carriage door, and helped Pamela alight.

Pamela soundlessly thanked Monique with her eyes.

Then the carriage moved again.

She looked at Stanhope. "Where do we go now?"

"The Lancaster ball," he said.

She watched his face. "Something is disturbing you. Surely it can't be that one dance?"

"No . . ."

She waited for him to continue. She'd discovered long ago that a wide-eyed glance was more effective than spoken questions. Patience had its rewards.

But not tonight. Not with Stanhope. "It has nothing to do with you, mademoiselle." His lips turned into what she supposed was to be a charming smile. "I am sorry I was abrupt. Some business matters."

"I understand," she said.

"We shall enjoy the rest of the evening," he said. "It should be a sad crush."

"Sad crush?"

"A crowded affair," he explained. "Your English is so exceptional I tend to forget that you are French."

"*Merci,* my lord. It is my training as an actress."

"Of course." He was all charm now, though she still felt the tension in him. "Now let me tell you about our host and hostess. The marquess is so looking forward to meeting you."

"Will the Earl of Daven or Lord Stammell be present?"

He frowned. "They do not often attend such functions. I imagine they are gambling at White's or some other establishment."

She fanned herself.

"I understand you had supper with Stammell."

"He is an interesting man."

"Strange. I never thought so."

"I thought he was your friend."

"He is my business associate."

"Tell me about your businesses."

"It's much too complicated and boring for you, my dear. Why don't you tell me instead about your impressions of London? How does it compare to Paris?"

Gabriel left the ball. He had other plans tonight.

Even at one in the morning the city was humming. Boston went to bed at night. London was coming alive.

He wondered how anyone accomplished anything when a night of revelry ended at dawn.

Gabriel had caught a few hours of sleep earlier, knowing it would be a late evening.

His objective tonight was to find Stammel or Daven and relieve them of their money. He wanted Stanhope to believe they had reason to steal from him. A few large losses would suit his plan just fine.

He realized it was a balancing act. He had made a reputation as a bumbler, and now he intended to be a card shark. It had to be dumb luck.

*He could do that.*

He made his way from one club to another. He missed Daven by a matter of minutes at one establishment. Then he found Stammel.

The man looked up at him through squinting eyes as Gabriel reached his table. "Room for another?"

"Ah, Manchester, is it?" Stammel said with a gleam in his eyes. The other men at the Stable looked at him curiously. "Marsh is just leaving."

One man looked surprised at the news, then nodded. He swept up some notes and obediently stood.

Gabriel sat down. "What are we playing?"

"Whist."

"Cannot say I know the game well, but . . ."

Several hours later he leaned back, a cigar in his hand. A pile of notes and paper lay in front of him.

"A bloody good game," he said with satisfaction. "Never won so much before. Hardly won at all, in fact. Fancy that!"

"You have to give us the opportunity to win it back," Stammel said.

"I jolly will, but not tonight, gentlemen. I can barely see the cards for the champagne."

"Tomorrow night?" Stammel persisted.

Gabriel shifted positions and gave him a shrug and eyed one of the pieces of paper in front of him. "Perhaps. In the meantime, when can I expect you to settle with me?"

Stammel's face reddened. "A gentleman would . . ."

Gabriel stood. "I have other affairs," he said. "Other business." His glance returned to Stammel. "One does not gamble what one does not have. I will expect your funds at my lodgings tomorrow." He gave the address, turned, and bowed to the others. "A fine pleasure, gentlemen."

He found his cane, stuck his quizzing glass in his eye, and made his departure. Once outside, he looked for a carriage. He had several hundred pounds in his pocket and a five-thousand-pound note from Stammel.

# Chapter Thirteen

Monique dreamed she was dancing a waltz. Around and around, faster and faster until her feet no longer touched the floor. The whirling became feverish. She wanted to stop but her partner would not release her.

She knew she could not continue, that she could no longer breathe, but he would not let go. He went faster and faster . . .

Then she glanced up and saw he wore a mask. It seemed expressionless at first, then painted lips turned into a sneering smile.

She woke. She was bathed with moisture and felt racked by a terrible anxiety. She tried to recall every detail of the dream but with every passing second it faded as though she were trying to grasp a piece of fog.

Monique hadn't dreamed since childhood. She'd lived in fear as a child. Her mother's own terror had transferred to her. She had vowed she would not allow fear to rule her life, and the only way to do that was to eliminate the source.

She rose and went over to the window. Dawn was breaking. She'd been asleep less than two hours.

Dani must still be asleep in the adjoining room. She had stayed awake until Monique had arrived home, her face drawn with worry.

They had shared a glass of sherry while discussing the evening with Stanhope. Monique did not mention the waltz with the American marquess.

Stanhope had been the perfect gentleman the remainder of the night, after leaving Pamela at his home. They had gone to the second ball, and she'd been grudgingly dazzled by a home that was more a palace.

She recalled the distaste with which she viewed the elaborate buffets, which would probably feed a good portion of London. Even though the host was an older man with a very young wife, he'd made more than a few ribald suggestions every time Stanhope had left her side.

The evening had given her a glimpse of why Stanhope was as powerful as he was. He could be charming. But even under that charm, an undertone of violence lingered, a subtle reminder that he would do whatever necessary to get his way.

People respected his power, feared his ruthlessness. She could see it in their expressions.

She had gone to bed with Stanhope's dark image mixed with the blond hair and green eyes of Manchester prying on her mind. She hadn't been able to banish the feelings she'd had when waltzing with the American marquess. She remembered the possessive feel of his hand on her, the mischief in eyes that were usually expressionless. He'd been a superb dancer despite the stumbling attempts she'd glimpsed earlier when he'd danced with Pamela.

As much as he'd tried to convince her it was all her magnificent instruction, she knew better. He had both confidence and grace that couldn't be taught. Not in minutes. Especially with a dance so new.

Manchester was a chameleon. He was hiding his true self, and there could not be an honest reason for doing so.

Of course, honesty was not one of her better qualities at the moment, either. Was it a simple matter of like recognizing like?

Or did the attraction between them run much deeper? And at what point did their interests clash?

She'd spent a long time pondering those questions before slipping off into sleep. And then the nightmare.

Was something telling her to be even more wary of Manchester than she already was?

Was he even more dangerous to her aims than Stanhope?

She only knew she had to avoid him.

The waltz was a mistake in every possible way. She still remembered the intense look in his green eyes, the slightly amused smile on his lips, the confident feel of his hands.

Maybe she should learn a little more about the Marquess of Manchester.

With that decision made, she turned away from the window. She would find a solicitor to make queries. Unfortunately most of the answers probably remained on the other side of the Atlantic Ocean but for now . . .

She wanted to know where he went, what his habits were, and what complications he might cost her.

Nothing more. Nothing personal.

Lynch would know someone. He was a careful man. He probably investigated potential investors.

She would go to the theater early tonight. Perhaps she would even have supper with the theater manager.

"I heard you had substantial losses two nights ago," Stanhope told Stammel.

"Fool's luck," Stammel said. "I will win it back."

"I was unaware you had that much blunt to throw away on gaming."

Stammel flushed. Of the three, he was the one always in financial difficulty. Mostly because of gambling debts.

Stanhope played with his watch fob. He was not ready to accuse Stammel of stealing from him. He did mean to watch him.

"You will need funds for our new venture."

"I thought Manchester was your source of funds. That was the plan."

"He will not participate if we do not put our money in as well."

Stammel shrugged. "Just tell him you have it."

"He is not that big a fool. He will want proof."

"I will win it back. I always do."

He did not, but Stanhope knew it was useless to mention that. Stammel had been useful in the past. He had family money, and because of his title he had influence. He'd always been a gambler, but in recent years he had been drinking excessively, and that made him lazy and reckless.

He didn't doubt for a moment that anything but fear would hold back his partner. Any scruples Stammel once had disappeared years ago, long before he had participated in the ruination of Manchester's father and the theft of his company.

And that thought brought him back to Manchester. There were inconsistencies in the man he didn't like. Or was it simply the way Monique Fremont's eyes were drawn to him when he was in the room?

Stanhope didn't fool himself. He knew the actress was not seeing him because he was the most handsome man in a room. Or the most charming.

She was obviously trying to make the most advantageous financial arrangement she could.

He did wonder why she'd included Daven and Stammel in her little game. Because she knew they were business partners? Did she think they might be of equal stature?

If so, she was the fool. If not, he wondered exactly what her game was.

She did interest him. Any woman who tried to play him for a fool interested him.

No one used Thomas Kane. Not a woman. Not the man who had been his associate for more than twenty years.

"No more gambling," he told Stammel.

Stammel's face twisted. "I have to recoup my losses."

"Has it not occurred to you that he might be considerably better than he wants you to believe?"

"No, Thomas. I would swear upon my mother's grave. He was drunk but the demmed cards just kept turning up for him. He has already lost big sums."

"I will require ten thousand pounds from you," Stanhope said.

"I do not have it. Not . . . now. One more game," he insisted.

Stanhope looked at him for a long time. "Only under the right circumstances," he said.

Stammel gave him a questioning look.

"I will have a house party and hunt at my estate," he said. "You can play him there where I can be present. I will know if he is cheating."

"And our wager? It is still on?"

"You mean the beautiful Miss Fremont?"

Stammel nodded.

"You are more foolish than I thought if you think I will lose that contest. But I will give you an opportunity. I will invite her, too."

"Her play?"

"She has an understudy. I will make it worth Lynch's while."

"What if she does not wish to come?"

"I think she will. You and Daven will be there. She can continue to play her game."

"And you?"

"I can play mine."


Monique visited the solicitor recommended by the theater manager and was introduced to a man who hired out for investigations of a personal nature.

Robert Grimes was a former Bow Street Runner, a thick man with untidy hair and sharp eyes.

"I need discretion," she said.

"All my clients do," he said. "That is why I am often recommended."

"I want to know everything about the Marquess of Manchester. Where he goes. Who he sees."

Grimes didn't flinch. "He has been in the London newspapers lately."

"Yes."

"He is a lord, an important man. I will have to be cautious."

"I *want* you to be cautious. I do not want him—or anyone else—to know of my interest."

"It will be expensive, mademoiselle."

"It does not matter."

Perhaps it was because he had already seen much as a Bow Street Runner, but nothing flickered in his eyes as she told him what little she knew about the new Marquess of Manchester.

The *Morning Post* reported that the celebrated actress, Monique Fremont, had been seen in the company of the Earl of Stanhope.

While the *Post* discreetly did not mention the wagers for the lady's company, it apparently thought it necessary at least to indicate it knew what was common knowledge in every gaming hell and sporting establishment.

Gabriel read the rest of the *Morning Post*, then *The Gazette*. Nothing about him, which was well.

He went back to the article. It had been three days since the ball, and the French actress still dominated his thoughts, taking his concentration from the matter at hand.

She'd been like a feather in his arms. Light. Quick. Graceful. And for some reason she had lied for him.

She was so infernally clever. She was an accomplished liar.

She had caused him to be careless.

Hell, he had done it to himself.

He had never been attracted to liars. He preferred an honest courtesan. He had known what they were, and what they wanted, and what he wanted. It had always been that simple and straightforward.

He did not know what Mademoiselle Fremont was, what she wanted, or, more vexing, what he wanted from her.

She was like a siren's song, and he had to remember what happened to the sailors who succumbed to it.

*Don't be a fool. She has made it clear she cares only about the highest bidder.*

He put the newspaper aside and finished his tea.

Smythe hovered nearby. "Are you finished, my lord?"

His mouth tightened at the form of address that Smythe couldn't quite relinquish. He hated the bloody thing. He blamed the entire English aristocracy for allowing The Group to destroy people. The nobility didn't have to pay debts, the nobility didn't work, the nobility lived for its own pleasure.

"What is your pleasure?"

"You can help me dress," he said, realizing how much Smythe craved being of assistance. "There are clothes to be fetched from my tailor, and your mother will need some supplies. I also have a list of books that I wish you to purchase." He had spent an hour this morning trying to find ways to employ Smythe's time. "You might also look into the purchase of a horse for me. I want a settled mount."

"But, sir, I know nothing about horses."

"Then find out," he said. That should keep Smythe busy awhile at least, busy enough not to worry about his master's whereabouts. "I will require a mount for tomorrow."

"But . . ."

"Thank you, Smythe," he said. "And now you may prepare my bath."

Smythe permitted as much of a smile as he ever had. "It will be ready shortly."

Gabriel looked outside. The sun was not quite overhead. Not noon yet.

His first order of business would be to leave a card at Stanhope's, asking to meet with him about the proposed investment.

He would time his visit to find the man asleep. He didn't want to talk to him, did not want to be probed, but he did want to prod him into action.

In the meantime he had to get together funds of his own. He had the banknotes he had taken from Stanhope's residence, more from gaming. He had another ten thousand remaining from what he'd saved from his share of prizes during the war.

He required twenty thousand more.

He also had an estate he had not yet seen. It was, according to his solicitor, fifty miles from London. A day-and-a-half ride at best.

Perhaps it was time to visit his inheritance and see what he might use from it. And determine for himself whether or not it was worthless and should just be abandoned to the Crown. Pickwick said it was entailed and bankrupt, but he knew for a fact that Pickwick was a liar.

Part of him had been reluctant to make the journey. He'd never actually felt it belonged to him. His grandfather had disowned Gabriel's father, had abandoned him when he'd been disgraced. He'd never asked whether the charges were true.

And he had made no effort to help Gabriel's mother.

Gabriel had never forgiven him for that.

He remembered his grandfather from several visits when he was a boy. He'd thought his grandfather a singularly joyless man. Neither had he cared for his oldest uncle.

*Spares.* That's what the English called all but the first-born son. Every good Englishwoman was bound to give her husband an heir and spares.

Hadn't worked well in his family. The two older sons were dead without issue. And the third and last son— Gabriel's father—had disgraced the name and committed suicide.

Even before the scandal his grandfather had disapproved of his father, who was in "business." Better that he had taken a commission or even been a rakehell. He'd disgraced the family with his independence and insistence on earning his own way.

If it weren't for England's inheritance laws, Gabriel would not have received so much as a pence. Disowned or not, he was the direct heir.

Bitterness was like bile inside. If his mother had received any help at all, any kindness, then perhaps . . .

But that was wishful thinking. He could not change the past.

He had asked whether there were tenants at the Manchester estates. Only a few, he'd been told, and they maintained the grounds in turn for farming some plots of land.

He hoped there might be jewels or valuables that were not entailed, which could be sold until he had the time to steal more from Stanhope and his pack of thieves.

Before he left London he would have to make provisions for the family seat and those employed to maintain it, since he had no intention of staying in England. He wanted to return to sea. At least the elements were honest.

That reminder brought the unwelcome image of a woman with dark hair and smoldering eyes.

She was as complex as a storm at sea.

And obviously just as treacherous.

He left the house, confident that the efficient Smythe would have located a horse by day's end. And a good one at that.

But now he had other business. He hoped to have his copy of Stanhope's seal today.

Monique sank down in the oversized bathtub and thought about the growing number of cards delivered to her town house. Only two had really interested her. One was for a weekend party at the country home of the Earl of Stanhope. Another came from a famous London hostess, a widow whose salon attracted the cream of London's nobility. A third for a costume ball at the home of an earl.

The reason for the two latter invitations, she realized, was curiosity. Her presence at an affair would probably guarantee the presence of others. She knew that all of London was talking about the competition between three business partners.

The invitation from Stanhope was intriguing. Of course, she could not attend. She had performances.

Mrs. Miller's eyes had lit as she saw the seals on the envelopes. Servants—including housekeepers—were judged by the social acceptability of their employers.

Her prestige had just increased several notches.

Monique had been amused at the reaction. She was nothing but a curiosity and an obsession. Her acceptance in London society was based entirely on that, quickly gained and just as quickly withdrawn. And if the ton discovered she was a thief as well . . .

Her thoughts went to Stanhope, then to Manchester. Two self-indulgent men. She knew what Stanhope was. Murderer. Defiler of women. She did not know exactly what Manchester was. A womanizer, certainly. A thief and cheat, probably.

Why did she care?

She hoped the runner would give her some answers.

In the meantime she would accept the invitation to Lady Isolde's salon. She would send her regrets for Lord Stanhope's weekend. His reaction would be interesting. She doubted he took refusals well.

She sank deeper into the bathtub.


Gabriel wasn't sure of the moment he became aware that someone was following him.

He had reached the waterfront when the hackles on his neck rose. It had happened before in ports throughout the world. He had learned to heed their warning.

He ducked into a seamen's tavern. As he usually did when going to this part of town, he wore more casual clothes. Breeches. Plain boots. A linen shirt and a cloak that hid the fact he wore no waistcoat or cravat. He could always claim he knew the dangers of being too obviously the dandy in a dangerous part of London.

He chose a table in the back and a chair that had a full view of the door and the interior of the tavern and ordered an ale.

Patience, he told himself.

He sat there for a long time, watching as sailors and workmen came in for their one pleasure. He drank one glass of ale, then another.

A heavy man dressed differently than the others finally entered. Sharp eyes darted around the interior, obviously trying to determine whether there was another way out.

Then his gaze swept over the tavern, lazily, as if looking for a friend. They did not hesitate on Gabriel.

He took a seat, facing the opposite direction, but Gabriel knew the man would be aware if he stood and left.

He was being watched, followed. He'd expected no less, though he had expected it to take more time for suspicions about him to be raised.

So much for meeting with the forger for the next few hours.

He sat back in his chair. He would spend the afternoon here, then walk around London. Perhaps he would even visit Hyde Park and enjoy the spectacle of the bulky man trying to follow him on the paths. He would be as obvious as a donkey among horses.

He ordered a meat pie and another ale. He ate slowly. Not very appreciatively. Mrs. Smythe's cooking was far better.

Gabriel paid the bill, rose, and made for the door. He walked unsteadily, as if befuddled by drink. He paused once and leaned against a fence, which gave him the opportunity to glance behind him.

No one. His imagination perhaps.

Still he intended to be careful. He flagged down a hackney and gave directions to the town house he had rented. If the man was following him, he might have an interesting time catching up with him. But today demonstrated how much he needed a mount.

A gentleman simply did not walk everywhere, though Gabriel was well used to doing just that. There were few carriages for hire.

The coach halted in front of his residence and he stepped down. He looked around. No sign of the person he believed to be following him. He had an impulse to take the carriage back to where he had originally been headed, but a small bribe to the driver would undoubtedly reveal where he had been taken. He wanted no connection between himself and the small print shop.

He took the steps quickly and used the door knocker. Mrs. Smythe answered. Her eyes narrowed at the whiff of the bad ale he'd been drinking. She stepped aside to allow him to pass her.

"Sydney has compiled a list of some likely mounts for

you, my lord," she said, taking his cloak. "He could not make appointments because he did not know when you would be back."

"I am ready now," he said.

She nodded. "There was one offered just two lanes away," she said. "He went to inspect it."

As if the very words had summoned him, Smythe appeared from the back. "Sir."

His face had more life than Gabriel had ever seen before. "I found a horse," he said. "A very fine horse."

"You said you do not know anything about horses," Gabriel reminded him.

Smythe's face fell slightly. "I believe it to be a fine horse," he corrected himself. "It is gray. Tall. The owner said he was well mannered."

"Did he say why he was selling him?"

"It was his son's horse. The son died in France."

So that was why it was a very fine horse. Gabriel had discovered his valet had sympathy for everyone who fought for Britain.

"And how much is this fine horse?"

"Three hundred pounds," Smythe said. "I know that is a large sum, my . . . sir . . . but it did look like a . . ."

"Fine horse," Gabriel finished for him. "Well we shall go and inspect this paragon before someone snatches him from under our very noses."

"I also found a mews," Smythe said with an eagerness that Gabriel thought was part pride in fulfilling his master's desires and at the same time joy in helping the family of a fallen comrade.

Gabriel reached for his cloak again. Three hundred pounds was more than he wanted to spend, but he did need an adequate—even flashy—mount.

Tomorrow would be a good day to inspect his estates. He could foil the man hired to follow him without raising suspicions. Visiting one's estate would be expected of anyone.

"Smythe, I am in your hands."

Smythe looked a bit uncertain about that. But he opened the door for Gabriel and followed him down the five steps to the street. Gabriel saw his shadow at the end of the street, reading a newspaper.

Gabriel ignored him, and ten minutes later he was running his hands over a large gray gelding. He was a handsome fellow, and obviously well treated. He eyed Gabriel inquisitively, as if he knew he might be looking at his new master. He playfully reached out and muzzled Gabriel's hand.

"I would like to ride him," he told the groom, who had been sent out to assist them.

The groom quickly saddled the horse, and Gabriel mounted. He was a good horseman, not a superb one. After his mother's death, the sea had been his life. Though the sea gave him a natural balance, he had not been riding all his life as had many Englishmen.

The horse was more than mannerly. The gelding took several prancing steps, obviously eager for an outing and exercise. He responded well to the slightest touch on the reins.

"His name?" he asked the groom.

"Specter."

"Specter." Gabriel liked that. He left the stable and urged the horse into an easy canter. He didn't need more. He returned to the stable and dismounted, looking at his valet. "You are right. He is a fine horse." He turned to the groom. "I would like to purchase him."

The groom shuffled his feet. "The baron will wish to talk to ye. He . . . the 'orse, 'e means a lot to 'im."

Gabriel was amused at the idea of being approved, but he liked the owner the better for it.

"Lead on," he said.

The groom stabled the horse, then looked down at the ground. "I will miss 'im, I will."

Gabriel looked around the small stable as they exited. The groom suggested he go to the front of the house while the groom went through the servant's entrance with Smythe.

Gabriel was admitted to a library. A man of approximately sixty years sat in a chair and rose with obvious effort. His feet were in loose footwear and Gabriel realized he suffered from painful gout.

"Lord Tolvery," Gabriel said, bowing slightly.

"And you are the famous Marquess of Manchester," his host said.

"I am flattered you have heard of me."

"Do not be," the baron said in blunt tones. "The notices were not favorable and I am particular regarding Specter's new master. He was my son's horse for eight years. I do not want to part with him, but he needs riding. As you can see, I can no longer ride."

He sat back down in the chair with great weariness.

Gabriel wanted Specter.

"I have no place to stable him," he said. "You seem reluctant to part with him, and my residence has no stables. Your groom said perhaps I can stable him here until I find more suitable lodgings. I will, of course, pay you and your groom to care for the horse, and in the meantime you can assure yourself that I am the right owner for Specter."

The baron's eyes rested on him.

"You are a military man," he said unexpectedly. "You have the bearing, the look about you."

Gabriel did not want to lie to him. He said nothing.

"You are not the fool the newspapers say."

Again he simply stood there.

"Do not be concerned," the baron continued. "Not many others would see it, but I was in the navy for twenty years and the admiralty office five. I have been with military men all my life. You have the rolling, balanced look of a naval officer." His eyes narrowed. "Did you fight in the last war?"

"Yes," Gabriel said simply.

"Against England?"

"Yes." Gabriel wasn't sure why he was answering the questions. The answers could destroy everything he worked for. Yet there was something about this man—perhaps a memory—that told him he could be an ally. But not if he lied.

"I knew your father," the baron said. "He was a friend. I met you once. A bright lad. I hardly think you would have changed so much despite what you would have others believe."

Gabriel summoned up the images from his childhood, trying to remember the man who sat before him.

"I was younger and slimmer then. My own lad was your age. He came late to us in life and he was a blessing."

He looked away and his eyes filled with tears. "I should have done more to help you and your mother then. It will be to my everlasting shame that I did not, but I had a commission in the navy, and the scandal threatened it. I knew your father was innocent. I couldn't prove it, but I knew him . . . and I knew Stanhope."

His hand shook in his lap. "I had my own family to protect, you see." Gabriel maintained his silence.

"And now I do not. My wife died, and Reggie was killed last year. I have nothing left but memories and regrets. I did not honor my name."

His gaze met Gabriel's. "I saw in the news sheets that you had returned. I had thought about contacting you and offering my apologies. But then . . ."

"You thought I did not care."

"A possibility."

Gabriel was reluctant to continue the conversation. He'd already revealed too much to a man he did not know and whose backbone was admittedly less than Gabriel thought acceptable. "The horse?" he said.

But the baron was not going to let go. "You are going after Stanhope and his friends." A statement, not a query.

"How could I do that? It was a long time ago."

"Things like that brand a boy. And a man." Tolvery leaned forward. "I will not ask any more questions, but I have a debt to pay. Specter is yours, and if I can help in any way . . ."

"No," Gabriel said, his voice hardening. "I will not accept a gift in lieu of loyalty. My mother needed friends."

"Yes," Tolvery whispered. "Then ask what you will."

"The same as when I entered. I will pay for the horse. I would like to board him here. And I would like to occasionally use the phaeton and carriages, but only if I pay for them."

The baron nodded. "It is done. Just let young Jock know

when you need him. He is a reliable lad, and he loves Specter, as he loved my son." His gaze moved to a portrait. "Everyone did, you see. He was everything I was not. He lived for honor."

Gabriel nodded. He could not do more.

How many other friends of his father had betrayed him?

# Chapter Fourteen

Monique put off her suitors for several days. Rejection, she found, increased desirability.

She had sent her regrets to Stanhope and he had not yet answered. Daven called at her home daily and attended the play yet another time. Stammel had sent imported chocolates and said he hoped she would go riding with him soon.

She finally accepted when he appeared at noon and begged her to go riding that afternoon. She started to refuse. It was, after all, deplorably late notice, and she truly needed a respite from her masquerade.

But the day was glorious, and she had heard much about Hyde Park. A ritual for the nobility in London. A place to see and be seen. She liked the idea. It was bound to raise the betting to a feverish pitch.

And Stammel had been the least forceful of the three. Perhaps she needed to charm him into being more of a competitor.

"Thank you, Lord Stammel," she said. "You may pick me up at three, and I must be at the theater in time for my performance."

Stammel beamed. Whether it was because he really cared for her company or the fact he would be seen as successful in the contest, she didn't know. She didn't care as long as it incensed Stanhope.

She had thought that the two men—Stammel and Daven—would fear Stanhope enough to back away. But all three seemed intent on seeing the wager to its end.

She selected a gown carefully. She would not be outrageous this afternoon as she met more of the ton. The dress was of a light blue muslin with a minimal amount of decoration, unlike the many flourishes on so many gowns today. It did have long sleeves and a high neck and was eminently respectable. Dani helped her into it, and perched a hat on top of gathered curls.

Monique looked in a box of jewelry and selected a simple bead bracelet, the only piece of jewelry her mother had. She had been given other pieces by protectors in France, but those had been sold off as her mother grew older and protectors became more stingy.

Monique had collected other pieces since then, mostly good replicas. But today she wanted something that connected her with her mother, and this particular bracelet was all she had. She had not worn it when she thought she might meet Stanhope. He might have recognized it, since her mother had always worn it.

She waited for Stammel's arrival in the downstairs sitting room. She had a distaste for being even fashionably late, even for the likes of Stammel and his companions.

He arrived exactly at three with an armful of flowers and imported candy. His face was wreathed in an eager smile.

"It is a lovely day," he announced, and for a moment she wondered how he could breathe. His poor valet had probably spent hours stuffing him into clothes meant for a leaner man.

"At your request?" she said with a smile.

He looked puzzled, as if wondering what she meant. Then realization flooded his face. "Why . . . yes," he replied. "I ordered it just for you. Are you ready to go?"

"*Oui*. I have been looking forward to it. I have heard that Hyde Park is quite lovely."

"It is. All the beau monde turns out on a day such as today."

"Do you not have business?"

"Nothing is more important than you, mademoiselle," he said gallantly.

"That is very kind," she replied. "I do have one reservation, though. I have heard that there are sometimes ruffians in the park."

"Be assured I can protect you," he said.

"I will feel very safe then," she said.

He was a bore. Insufferable. But she preferred his company to that of her father's. Stanhope was evil. This man was corrupt. There was a difference.

She pasted her smile back on her face as he led her to the curricle. Two very fine bay horses were being held by Stammel's tiger.

He helped her step up on the seat and took the reins.

She made several admiring comments about the horses and carriage, and the way he drove, which he did very well. Then she settled back in the seat and enjoyed the drive. It was a warm day for London.

Heads turned to stare at the stylish carriage, the matched horses, and the occupants. Stammel obviously enjoyed the curiosity.

He turned into Hyde Park, and she was greeted by the sight of a multitude of phaetons and other types of carriages as well as walkers and horsemen.

They passed several carriages, and she saw a certain pattern that amused her. Stammel nodded courteously as they passed other carriages, stopping twice to introduce her.

She tried to remember names. If these were friends of Stammel, no doubt they were also friends of Stanhope's. There were the Viscount Thayer and his Viscountess; Lord and Lady Russell. If they did not stop, he might well identify the occupants of the passing conveyance.

As a ritual it was fascinating, and she could not disguise her interest. Hyde Park had the air of unreality. People driving along paths in endless procession.

"Have you seen Lord Daven recently?" she asked innocently.

"No," Stammel said abruptly.

"Are you not in business together?"

"We have some interests in common," he said, obviously reluctant to talk about another man. "But I have others of my own. Daven is not the most cautious of men, and he owes most of the merchants in London."

"I thought he was a very wealthy gentleman."

Stammel raised an eyebrow, as if questioning that statement.

Monique did not say anything, just allowed Stammel to feel that he had gotten his point across. Daven had money problems and would not be the best protector for her.

She would have to find a way to tell Daven that.

They were turning back to the main path leading out of the park when a man on a gray horse approached them. Her heart tripped and stumbled over itself. The dratted man. Was he everywhere?

He headed straight for her.


Gabriel enjoyed the first outing with his new mount, though it was a bittersweet journey. He rode to the Manchester estate, making it there and back in three days.

He arrived in late afternoon, riding hard and stopping only long enough to rest his mount.

His grandfather's—now his—estate was much as described by Pickwick. It was in drastic need of repairs. He walked through drafty halls stained by rainwater leaking through a roof. A few paintings remained. His ancestors, he supposed.

Everything of value had been stripped away, most likely by his grandfather and father's brothers. The furniture was even more worn than the overused fields. Carpets had rotted, the roof leaked, and decay was everywhere. Having neither the interest nor funds even to try to restore it, he would do as Pickwick suggested; allow it to revert to the Crown. He made himself a promise that he would provide funds for the few elderly retainers who remained.

He felt not the slightest jolt of regret at releasing the property, no connection to it. Only relief that nothing here drew him to it. His life was in America.

However, no one else was to know that yet.

He hadn't seen his shadow upon returning home late on the third day, but there was a man in a wagon sitting not far down the road. Changed tactics? He was too tired to care. Tomorrow he would take up the game again.

He had accomplished one thing. He had seen the estate and it had no emotional power over him. No sense of obligation or heritage. Now he could concentrate on the reason that had drawn him to London.

The wagon was gone when he woke the next day. He did not see his follower, but he suspected the man—or someone else—was lurking around. Gabriel intended to lose whoever it might be. He wanted to see Stammel's residence, and he wanted privacy to accomplish it.

He arrived at the baron's home in the afternoon and watched as the groom saddled Specter. He'd given the lad a few shillings last night, and the lad grinned at him. "He is like 'is old self. Frisky, he is."

"Because he has a fine groom," Gabriel observed.

The lad beamed as Gabriel mounted and settled into the saddle. Leaving the stable, he looked around the street. No one. But then if the man was any good at his calling, he wouldn't be easily seen, especially if he thought he had once been sighted.

Gabriel had always enjoyed walking, but Specter gave him the freedom he needed. He wished he had considered obtaining a horse earlier, and not just as a way to keep Smythe occupied. But he hadn't planned on staying in London that long, and he hadn't wanted a responsibility. The arrangement he had now with Baron Tolvery was perfect.

He nudged the horse into a fast walk, wanting to look behind to see if he was still being followed but, heeding his better sense, he did not. Instead he walked the horse for several blocks, finding himself going in the direction of Monique Fremont's rooms. He was turning a corner as he saw a carriage pull away. A very fashionable carriage. Lord Stammel and Monique.

Gabriel decided to follow at a distance.

Mademoiselle Fremont was certainly doing very well for herself.

When it was obvious that they were going to Hyde Park, he pulled away and turned down a different lane. He wanted his meeting with Stammel and Monique Fremont to appear accidental.

As he reached the park, he saw a young girl selling flowers and on a whim purchased a bouquet of rather motley blooms, tossed her two shillings, and earned a brilliant smile as she looked at the coins with disbelieving eyes.

"Thank ye, milord," she said.

He nodded and continued.

He felt the fool with the bouquet tucked on the saddle, but he moved on, watching curiously as the lords and ladies drove around in handsome carriages. He inclined his head now and then when he recognized someone. Not many. His acquaintances had been limited to the gaming hells, Stanhope's soiree, and the ball.

Specter drew appreciative glances. He drew curious ones.

Then he saw Stammel's carriage in front of him. He urged his mount forward as it approached. Stammel had no choice but to stop and acknowledge him.

Gabriel bowed slightly from his position on the horse. "I understand we might soon be business partners."

"I look forward to it," Stammel said. "Stanhope says you are an astute businessman."

"I have done quite well in Boston," Gabriel admitted. "But I would not like to bore Mademoiselle Fremont." He offered the flowers to Monique. "A young girl was selling these and she was quite charming. I could not resist and now I am delighted I could not. They are not as lovely as you, but I hope you will accept them."

"And if I had not come into your path, my lord?"

"I would have found them another home, but none, I think, as suitable as yours."

"Charmingly said," she returned. "I would not like to see them orphaned."

He grinned at her quip as Stammel glared.

"Ah," she said. "A flower girl, you say."

"She had only a few left and she looked weary." He immediately knew he shouldn't have added the last.

"Ah," she said. "The American marquess has a heart?"

"A whim," he insisted again.

She reached out to take the flowers, and Gabriel saw the flash of resentment in Stammel's eyes.

As she took them in her arms, he saw something fall from her wrist onto the ground. He knew he should mention it to her, but instead he backed the horse slightly and gave a bow of his head. "Good afternoon, my lord. Mademoiselle."

She gave him a smile that lit her eyes this time. "*Merci, monsieur.*"

"Lord Manchester," Stammel said and flicked the reins. The horses moved forward.

Gabriel waited several moments, then saw another carriage coming. He quickly dismounted and took up a single bead bracelet, then mounted again.

Now he had a very good reason to visit Monique Fremont. He hadn't thought a personal visit from him would have been accepted now that he was calling on Lady Pamela.

He looked forward to a few private moments with Monique. Perhaps he could discover more about her and why she had focused on the three men who had also drawn his attention.

He looked at the simple bracelet. It did not look like something she would wear. Her clothes were all expensive, elegant in their simplicity. They were designed to compliment her, not to take attention away from her. There were no bows, little lace, few flounces. No ribbons.

Gabriel had expected her jewels to be just as well chosen. Elegant pearls. A cameo. Sapphires. Yes, the latter would best suit her.

But the bracelet looked valueless. Unless she wore it for sentimental reasons.

And what would those be?

He tucked the bracelet in his riding jacket, then took a look around. He saw no one who looked in the least bit as if he was following him.

The sun was descending. The breeze was increasing. The

skies were clouding. There would be fog tonight, and that suited his purposes.

He left the park, seeing that young girl was gone. Another girl selling flowers had taken her place.

Thinking he would impoverish himself, as well as destroy the image he'd worked so hard to cultivate, he purchased more flowers, this time for Lady Pamela. A trip to Stanhope's to see his daughter was necessary to keep up the charade of a man eager for her hand. Perhaps Stanhope would be there. Perhaps he could bait him.

Then he would disappear into the fog and the dock area.

And tomorrow . . . tomorrow, Miss Fremont. That thought lightened his heart, even though he feared she might be every bit as treacherous as his foes.


The bracelet was gone!

Monique had returned home and managed to rid herself of Stammel, who obviously hoped to stay longer.

"It would not be fair to the others," she had explained, and he'd left with poor grace.

Then she took off her gloves and found the bracelet missing. Could she have lost it in Stammel's curricle?

He was gone, and she did not want to make him wonder why she was worried by a simple bracelet, and he might even mention it to Stanhope, who might well remember it.

She wanted to weep. The bracelet was all she had left of her mother. It wasn't much but she treasured it.

Perhaps she could suggest they go riding again, and she could search the floor of the carriage.

Dani noticed her concern. "Where could it be?"

"Perhaps on the floor of Lord Stammel's carriage," she said.

"I can search it while you are on stage," Dani offered. "He usually comes to the theater."

"He would have servants."

"I can say you sent a message for him earlier and I was late in delivering it."

Monique considered it. "We shall see," she said, though she realized she would do almost anything to retrieve that bracelet.

"You might go outside," she said, "and look along the lane. I might have dropped it getting in or out of the carriage."

Dani's face lit, and she quickly left the room and went out the door. In minutes she was back, shaking her head.

Disappointment ran through her. "Paul Lynch's carriage will be here any moment."

She chewed on her lower lip for a moment, then nodded her head. "As soon as you finish with my hair at the theater, go to Stammel's home. If you can find the curricle, you might look inside, but if you see anyone, leave. I cannot lose you, too."

"You will never lose me," Dani said.

Just then she heard the carriage that came for her each night. She had not had time to change clothes, but she took her cloak from Dani. It promised to be a cold night. "Take my gray cloak," she instructed Dani. "It will fit in well with shadows."

Monique wasn't sure she was doing the right thing. She might be putting Dani in jeopardy. But she would have a reason for going and if worse came to worse she would explain about the bracelet and hope the man didn't wonder to Stanhope why she hadn't just asked him. And Dani had been an accomplished thief. She knew how to be invisible.

The carriage rocked through the streets and delivered her to the backstage entrance of the theater. It was a full house tonight, just as it had been since the play first opened. Mr. Lynch was a very happy man and was ready to do almost anything she asked.

As she went through the door, she sensed a new level of excitement. Members of the cast were whispering excitedly.

"The Prince of Wales is here tonight," someone told her.

Lynch hurried up to her. "Prinny is here. I gave him my box. He will most certainly want to meet you afterward. If he likes the performance, perhaps the theater will be licensed for dramas."

There was a plea in his voice, as well as excitement. He almost tittered with it.

"I will do my best, as I always do, monsieur," she said.

"You will meet with him after the play."

"If he requests."

Lynch beamed.

When she went on stage, the magic wrapped around her as it always did. All her personal concerns disappeared, and she became the betrayed wife. Richard Taylor, her leading man, was always competent, but now he had an extra dash about him.

They took more curtain calls than ever before. She looked up and saw that Prinny was standing, a vast smile on his face.

When she returned to her dressing room, Dani was not there. She should be back by now. Stammel's town house was not that far away. Monique's pulse speeded and she said a small prayer. She should never had made so much of the bracelet. If anything happened to Dani because of her—

A knock came at the door, and she knew instinctively it was the Prince of Wales, a large man with a face that reflected dissipation.

"I wish to offer my compliments for a splendid performance," he said as his eyes slowly undressed her.

She curtsied. "Thank you, Your Grace," she said.

"You shall join us for supper," he said with royal command.

"Thank you for the honor, but I have a previous engagement."

He eyed her speculatively. "I have heard about the competition, Miss Fremont. And I have placed my own wager, knowing the three men involved. Is one of them the lucky man tonight?"

"I should not say," she said coquettishly. "I would not like to influence the wagers."

"A discreet woman," he said. "But I do not give up easily."

And then he was gone, and Lynch stood there with his mouth open. "You refused Prinny," he said with dismay. "I will never receive a license."

"He said he does not give up," she reassured him.

"Then . . ."

"Then nothing," she said. "But anything attained easily is not valued."

The answer seemed to mollify him. He backed out.

She gave a deep sigh. She felt like a juggler, balancing far too many balls at one time.

And where was Dani?

*     *     *

Gabriel had the forged seal in his pocket. He'd gone by the printer's, then the inn, where he changed clothes and emerged with them well hidden under a cloak.

The fog had settled over London by midnight. He rode Specter to a respectable part of the city, a section quite close, in truth, to Stammel's home. It was time to pay the man a visit.

If Stammel stayed to pattern, he would either be at the theater pressing his attentions on Monique Fremont or in one of the men's clubs.

Gabriel wanted to get inside, to see whether Stammel had any documents that Gabriel could use. The more he knew about The Group's business affairs, the more he could do damage to them.

He had decided not to use the foil of a beggar, but rather a drunken gentleman who couldn't find his own house.

As he had done with Stanhope's home earlier, he took note of the oil lamps flickering inside. One by one they flickered off until only what must be the hallway appeared visible. Most of the servants were likely abed and any others in the servants' room awaiting the arrival of their master.

The fog was similar to that of the other night. Forms turned into little more than shadows.

The streets were empty except for the rare clattering of a carriage.

As he approached, he saw a figure slipping out of a path next to the house. The form was short, graceful, and wore a gray cloak he thought he recognized.

It could not be Monique. She would be acting.

Then he heard a shout and a wiry figure running after the first. The woman started running toward him, and the hood of the cloak slipped and he saw a profusion of red curls. She didn't see him until she passed just feet away. She shied away and continued to run. The man behind her was gaining.

Gabriel stepped behind a streetlamp and watched her pass, then staggered into her pursuer. Both of them went down.

The pursuer tried to untangle himself, but Gabriel couldn't quite gain his feet and kept landing on him.

He heard a curse.

"You should watch where you are going," Gabriel said rudely. "Running in the streets, striking gentlemen. I could have been hurt. Who is your master?"

"That person is a thief," the man said.

Under the light, Gabriel saw that the man was small and wiry. He probably served as groom.

"What did she take that was so important that you assault decent folk to retrieve it?" Gabriel asked in a slurred voice.

"She were in the stable. Tryin' to steal my master's horse."

"But she did not, did she?" Gabriel said. "Or she would be on it, rather than running for her life. Most likely, she was seeking a warm place to sleep tonight."

The man was not ready to give up. He was looking toward the trees. There was no sign of the intruder.

"I think I should call the constable," Gabriel said with haughty indignation. "We cannot have assaults in the streets."

The servant brushed himself, obviously surrendering. "Please no, yer lordship. I was doin' me duty."

"Well then, we shall forget it for tonight," Gabriel said, "but I would be careful, my good man, about accosting gentlemen and knocking them down." He turned and lurched back down the street.

The household would be roused now. He would search some other time. But now he had an intriguing piece of information. He would have sworn the figure was Monique Fremont's maid.

Was she looking for the bracelet? And, if so, why?

Another facet to the very fascinating Monique Fremont.

# Chapter Fifteen

Monique found an assistant to help her change clothes. She said that Dani had been taken ill and left.

She prayed that Dani would be at their lodgings.

She arrived there in the carriage and hurried inside.

Only Mrs. Miller greeted her.

"Is not Danielle with you?" she asked after peering out the door.

"No. She had some errands. She should be home soon."

*A lie. A prayer.*

But Mrs. Miller accepted it. "Would you like me to prepare a bath?"

It was the first time the housekeeper had offered to do anything outside of the usual duties.

"Thank you," Monique said, accepting the offering.

The housekeeper smiled. "It will be ready soon. Can I help you with the dress?"

Monique needed help indeed, but to admit it was to say that Dani would not be there to do it.

"I can manage, thank you," she said.

Mrs. Miller left the room to heat water for the bath. But water was not what she needed. It was Dani. Perhaps she should summon a hackney and look for her. Just as she decided to do exactly that, Dani appeared in the doorway, still enveloped in Monique's cloak. Her face was nearly white.

"Dani?"

"I could not find it," Dani said. "The groom saw me. He would have caught me if not for a gentleman who tripped him."

"A gentleman?"

"I think it was the Marquess of Manchester."

"What was he doing there?"

"I can not know for certain. There was a fog and he wore a cloak, but this man . . . I think it was him."

But why would he have been there? Why would he be spying on Stammel? Because she had been with him? But she was not that important to him. Even the bouquet had been a whim. He'd never shown more than a fleeting interest in her.

Then she remembered what he'd said in jest about the flower girl. Could he have truly meant it? And Dani? Had he truly set out to help someone being chased?

"Do you think Manchester recognized you?" she asked. She had no doubt that the Samaritan was Manchester. He seemed to turn up everywhere. It made her even more curious about him. There was such a thing as too many coincidences.

Dani looked stunned. "I do not know. Perhaps. The hood of the cloak fell open but the fog was thick."

"We need to keep you away from Stammel's residence," Monique said. "Perhaps the man who chased you is Stammel's tiger. If so, you must keep out of sight when Stammel pays another visit."

Monique reached over and gave Dani a hug. "Thank you for trying."

"I know how much it meant to you."

"Your safety is much more important. I should never have allowed you to go."

"Allowed?"

Monique laughed. Dani had always been far more than a maid but even if she had been only that, she would have gone her own way. Dani had a spirit that Monique had always admired.

"Requested," she corrected herself.

"But what if Lord Stammel has already found it?"

"I think he would have been here to return it. Or at the theater," Monique said. "He would use any opportunity to visit."

"Then where could it be?"

"The park," Monique said. "I must have lost it in the park."

"Do you know where?"

"No. The marquess . . ." She stopped, remembering the way she reached out to take the flowers. It was the only time her arm was extended outside the carriage.

Another coincidence?

She would talk to the marquess tomorrow. She would learn what she wanted to know. She was no longer going to play his puppet, and at the moment she felt as if she was doing exactly that.


Gabriel realized he was allowing a woman to come between himself and the vow he'd made years ago.

It was still alive in his heart, that vow, but so was a woman who mystified him.

He'd already allowed both her and her maid to interfere with what he had to do. He had assisted them several times, and yet he sensed she was a woman who seldom needed assistance. Why him? Why had he always been in place to be the protector?

He damn well didn't want to be a protector. He wanted to complete something twenty-three years in the making.

He looked at the bracelet in his hand.

He and Monique Fremont had engaged in some kind of sensuous dance ever since the day they had met. He had tried to deny it. He knew she had done the same. All their encounters screamed that one truth.

He kept remembering that dance. The waltz. They had melded together then, lost in the passion of music and rhythm and the enchantment that always wrapped around them. He wondered whether she knew that she was dancing with a rogue.

Somewhere deep inside he thought she did. They were of a kind, he and she.

But he could not trust her. It came down to that. He did not know what she wanted, what she was after, and, most of all, how it would affect what he had to do.

His father's face. He would never forget the despair in it. The only way it would fade from his memory was when justice was done, when the Earl of Stanhope suffered as his father had.

Monique sent a note with Dani to the detective she'd hired and arranged to meet him at one of the parks that dotted London.

He was apologetic as he greeted her.

"I don't have much for you," he said. "I lost him several times, but I cannot tell you whether he knew he was being followed and tried to evade me on purpose. One time, he caught a hackney and I couldn't find one. He purchased a horse and I cannot keep up with him." He paused, then added, "He has been down to the dock area several times and I am asking people about him."

"Can you learn more? About the Manchester family?"

He brightened. "I can do that, miss. I have friends at the newspapers."

"Good, then proceed. Follow him when you can."

He looked relieved. He obviously thought he would be dismissed. "I will do as you say."

"Meet me back here in two days at the same time," she said.

He touched his cap. "I will have something for you."

"Please do," she said.

He hesitated. "Can you tell me anything that might help me? Why you are interested in him?"

"No," she replied. "It is not necessary for you to know."

"Then I will be on my way," he said.

She wondered whether she was making a mistake in not telling him more, but then what did she know? Nothing. It was instinct, instinct and the fact that Manchester appeared everywhere she happened to be. And why would he visit the dock area? It was not a place that she thought would attract such a man.

But then he had surprised her over and over again.

She was not surprised that the detective had been unable to follow him, or find out much about him. He'd made obfuscation an art. She had run into one blocked door after another with him.

But then he might have discovered the same thing about her.

Monique had a light tea and was preparing for the night's performance when Lynch appeared at her door.

She led him into the small drawing room, then sat, knowing that his presence was probably not good news.

He perched uncomfortably on a chair. "My lord Stanhope has asked me to give you several days off."

"You have never liked him," she countered. "You told me so that first evening in London."

"I warned you about him, but he still is influential and has many friends in high places. He can help me get a license for the company or he can prevent it."

"And you are willing to bet me on the outcome?"

"No," he said. "I did not see you repelled by the Earl of Stanhope even after my warning. Thus I can only think you know best. Therefore I readily consented to letting your understudy take your place for two performances."

"How much did he pay you?"

Lynch's face reddened. "He can help the company obtain a license from the Crown."

"And for that you sell me?"

"It is your decision, mademoiselle. I am merely giving you the opportunity. Take it or not." He turned to leave.

Monique relented. She *had* pushed him to introduce her to Stanhope and his friends.

But she did wonder what he had been offered to give her permission to miss several performances. It was not due to ego but realism that she knew she had been responsible for the steady crowds. He would have some disappointed patrons. So Stanhope must have dangled a substantial plum in front of his eyes, the prospect that the theater would be licensed by the Crown. She wondered just how Stanhope would do that, since it was very rare indeed.

Did he really have that kind of power? Did his influence reach into the royal family and Parliament?

"Thank you," she said. "I will accept your offer." In truth, it was what she had wanted. It was dangerous, yes. But it might well end the game sooner.

He nodded, looking relieved.

Just as he left someone else rapped at the door.

Lynch again, probably.

She went to the door herself and opened it, only to find the Marquess of Manchester lounging outside, overdressed and wearing that foolish quizzing glass. But by now she knew he did it only to deceive.

He gave her an exaggerated bow. "Mademoiselle Fremont."

Her heart speeded, even at the travesty he made of himself. She told herself it was only because of last night. She wanted to know whether he had recognized Dani or not. Apparently he had or he would not have been here.

Despite the intimacy of the waltz, the kiss they had exchanged, he had made no effort whatsoever to pursue any romantic course with her. He had not called on her. He had not even asked her to have supper with him. Despite the heat in his eyes and the amused smile on his lips, he'd never gone beyond a seductive look and a kiss that apparently meant nothing to him.

And yet she could not help but feel they were locked in some complex dance that neither of them understood. At least, she did not. She wondered whether he did.

"My lord," she acknowledged. "I must leave for the theater shortly."

"I will not stay long then," he said. "I believe I might have found something that belongs to you."

He reached in his pocket and pulled out the bead bracelet. "A pretty trifle," he added.

She stared up at him. "But how . . ."

"I saw it after your carriage had pulled away. I thought about catching up with it, but then I was not entirely sure it belonged to you."

But he was. She saw it in his eyes. So why hadn't he approached her then?

Did he sense she didn't want Stammel to see it? Or did he just want an excuse of a visit? But he didn't need an excuse. Other men had paid visits without one.

She reached for it. "*Merci,* my lord, but the visit wasn't necessary. It means little to me."

"Oh, in that case, I will keep it as a token." His eyes held that infernal amusement, as if everything was a game.

"*Non,*" she said sharply. "As meaningless as it is, it is mine." Her hand was still stretched forward.

He hesitated, then dropped it into her hand. "To the contrary, mademoiselle, it must mean a great deal to you if you sent out your maid like a thief in the night to retrieve it."

"I am not sure what you mean."

"An excellent attempt, but I recognized your Danielle trying to escape a groom who was chasing her." He paused. "It does mean something to you?"

"Why do you care? It is none of your affair."

"Because we continue to see each other in somewhat . . . odd circumstances."

She stared at him, waiting for him to continue as her fingers closed around her bracelet.

"You have an interest in three gentlemen who also interest me. I wonder why?"

"Is it so strange? I can tell you my interest. They are powerful and wealthy. I would be delighted to hear yours, if I but had the time. As it is, I can discuss nothing at the moment. I will be late for tonight's performance."

"A midnight supper?" he asked.

It was obvious he was not going to let her go without a commitment. It was blackmail plain and simple. He was holding Dani's life hostage.

"Where?" she asked.

"Here," he said. "It would be more . . . private that way. If, that is, you have discreet servants."

"Dani is completely trustworthy. I believe my cook also to be reliable."

"I am being followed," he said with an indifferent shrug of his shoulders. "You should probably know that."

She hoped her eyes did not reveal anything. "Why should I care?"

"It could be a jealous admirer."

"I cannot imagine why. I have not accepted anyone as a protector."

His eyes were hypnotic. For a second she thought he might suspect her, but how?

"I wondered whether you might have heard something," he said. "I cannot imagine why anyone would be interested in my movements."

"No, my lord. I have heard nothing."

Amusement flickered in his eyes again, as if he knew she was lying.

"Then tonight," he said.

"After the performance."

"Yes."

He reached out and took her hand and leaned down with exaggerated politeness and kissed it. She wore no gloves and the sensation shot through her body.

She nodded, then stepped back and shut the door on him.

She leaned against the door—and said a small prayer. How did he anger her, amuse her, challenge her, attract her all at the same time?

More importantly, what did he want from her? What would he do with the knowledge that Dani had been on Stammel's property?

The bracelet had been far more important to her than Gabriel had thought.

She'd tried to school her face, but he'd seen the flash of relief and even joy when she saw it.

It was—as she said—a trifle. Probably not worth more than a pound. But it was more than a decoration to her. A gift from a lover? A family member?

Who was she?

She spoke perfect English. He had seen few people who could speak both French and English flawlessly, without even a hint of an accent. She was an actress. She studied voices and accents, but even then . . . he would have sworn that she had an English background.

He would find out later this evening.

He also saw the slightest flicker in her eyes when he mentioned he was being followed. Or was it the absence of surprise? Either way, he believed she knew something about it.

But in the event he was mistaken, he would lead his shadow on another merry chase tomorrow. Or maybe he would even stop him and demand an answer. But if he was wrong, then he would be exposing a part of him. The man he was pretending to be would not notice such a thing.

He put his beaver hat back on his head and walked down the steps and down the street. He would retrieve Specter, take care of a few errands, including a visit to Pickwick, the solicitor. And then he would lose Mr. Black, the name he had given his shadow because he dressed in that somber color.

He would pay a visit to Lady Pamela to soothe her father, then be at Monique's door again.

He could barely wait to hear her story this time.

How much to tell him?

Monique's mind wondered through that problem as she performed a role she knew so very well.

What if their interests merged? What if they did not?

He could be an ally. He could also be an enemy.

Dani was the only person on earth she had trusted with her secrets.

Yet something in her felt an odd connection to him. They shot lightning off each other. Which meant nothing, of course. It did not mean she could trust him with even the smallest bit of information.

Especially the fact she was Stanhope's daughter. His bastard daughter.

That information could be fatal to them both. She had no illusions that the man who fathered her would hesitate to kill her or anyone else who got in his way. Especially if he thought they had any information that would further harm his reputation, information that he had tried to have her mother and herself killed.

She had a few hours to invent a story the marquess would believe.

*He had the same.*

Now why did she think that?

Despite her personal distractions, the applause was as strong as it had been every night. If she was not as luminous as in past performances, no one seemed to notice.

Or maybe they had noticed a sparkle of battle in her eyes. Perhaps the very light that he seemed to awaken in her.

Several times her eyes had swept the audience. He—the marquess—was not there. Neither was Stanhope or Stammel.

After the play she and Dani took the carriage home, her heart racing as she did so. She had prepared some lies. She had prepared part of the truth. She wasn't sure which she would use. Manchester would demand answers, and so would she. She could only hope that she would be better at controlling the unwanted reactions he usually ignited in her than in previous meetings.

"What are you going to tell him?" Dani asked.

"I do not know. But I want you to stay out of sight."

Dani nodded. "I do not feel he wants to do you harm," she said. "I like him. Even for a lord. He does not give much away, but I feel there is something good about him."

Monique was not convinced about the "good" part. He was a gambler. He was paying court to a young woman he obviously did not care about, and the only reason could be her fortune. He made it his business to seek the company of scoundrels and cheats and killers.

He was obviously ruthless if not the fool he sometimes played.

He was most definitely not a fool.

Nor a bumbler.

Could he be an imposter? She'd considered several explanations to his chameleonlike shell. Could he have taken on the identity of the real marquess who had been in America for so many years?

And why were his efforts directed toward Stanhope? Because he was wealthy and powerful and looked like a good target?

She hoped she would know in the next few hours.

She truly hoped she would know more about him than he learned about her.

They arrived at her lodgings, and the driver put down the steps and helped them alight, then waited until they were inside.

Mrs. Miller met them there. "You have a visitor, miss," she said.

So he was here already. She turned to Dani. "You might want to leave."

"Too late," came a voice from the direction of the small sitting room to her right.

She whirled around. "You are early, Lord Manchester. Are you not aware it is poor manners?"

"I am not particularly known for my manners, Miss Fremont." He smiled. "And why not include . . . Danielle, is it? . . . in our discussion about last night?"

Dani looked startled, a little like a trapped rabbit.

"Because she is tired and deserves some consideration," Monique said as smoothly as her racing heart allowed. "She was indeed up late last night trying to retrieve something that was mine."

"Such loyalty," he noted.

It could have been mockery, but Monique considered it more praise. "Dani has been with me a long time."

"You should not send her on dangerous errands."

"She did not send me, sir," Dani said. "I went on my own because I knew she was worried about—" She stopped abruptly.

"The bracelet, I know. Is that worth Newgate Prison?"

"I would have explained," Dani said. "I did not need your assistance."

"I don't think Stammel is the type of man who listens to servants," he said. "Much could have happened between the time she was taken until the time you could find her."

A warning. And it struck at her like a hammer. He was

right. She had tacitly approved Dani's mission. It had been a mistake.

She nodded. "You are right, monsieur."

"My name is Gabriel," he said. "It is friendlier."

"You are not my friend."

"No?"

"Neither is it proper."

"I didn't think you were overly concerned with what is proper."

Of course, he didn't. He had seen her first at a gaming hell, then in the company of a notorious man. And he was right. She had never cared about proprieties. They were for people who could afford them.

"There are good reasons for proprieties," she said stiffly.

"To keep people at a distance, you mean," he replied with amusement. "But you and I have gone beyond that, have we not?"

"I do not know what you mean."

"Oh, I think you do," he said. "There is something between us, something that neither of us wants." He turned to Dani. "And I will keep your nighttime activities to myself."

Monique felt the heat rising in the room, just as it always did when he was near. She wanted Dani here, and yet . . .

"Dani, will you tell Mrs. Miller to prepare a meal for us?"

"Yes, mademoiselle, " she said, using the formality she usually did with outsiders present and escaped from the tension in the room. Dani couldn't help but have felt it.

"What do you want from me?" she asked.

"You are an attractive woman. Why should I want anything but your company?"

"You have the company of Pamela Kane."

"A mutual agreement between the two of us," he said. "She has a young man back home. An unsuitable one, I think. If I act the suitor, then her father will not push her off on someone else."

"An act of kindness, my lord?"

"It benefits both of us," he said.

"Because it brings you closer to the Earl of Stanhope?"

"He is a wealthy man. I am in need of funds. He is some-one who can help me invest."

"You would not be in need of funds, if you did not gamble."

He raised an eyebrow. "Really?"

"I read the newspapers."

"Every member of the nobility gambles," he said.

"Is that why you do it?"

"I must admit I also enjoy a wager."

"You talk in riddles, my lord. Or are you really the Marquess of Manchester?"

He looked at her closely. "You doubt that?"

"I think something is not as it seems."

"Not that, Miss Fremont. I am truly the Marquess of Manchester through some macabre progression of circumstances. I did not ask for it. I did not particularly want it. But here I am. Nobility. From poverty to estates, even if it is bankrupt." His voice was filled with irony and amusement.

It was an oddly attractive combination, but then everything about him attracted her. Everything except that infernal quizzing glass that was gratefully absent at the moment.

His green eyes attracted her. The emerald-green gaze seemed to see everything, to peer inside the heart she'd always kept guarded. The unruly sandy hair that could never quite be tamed. The lean hard body that did not belong to a fool or gambler. He had the kind of muscles that came from activity, from hard work. He radiated confidence, at least when he wasn't acting the fool.

He wasn't doing that now.

"What do you really want?" she said in a low voice.

"What do *you* want? What game are you playing?"

They were dancing again. Whirling around and around and never getting anywhere.

"I only want security," she lied. She wanted to tell him everything. How she wanted to tell him. But she still was not sure of his character. Still not sure he would not use it for some ploy of his own. She also worried that it would put him in danger.

"You can have security. You can probably have any man

you want. Why Stanhope? Why someone who might have murdered his wife?"

She went still. "You apparently still want to do business with him."

"And you still want to play games with him." He shot the words back at her. "He is a dangerous man to cross."

"How do you know?"

He hesitated too long. Now she knew that it was not only wealth he wanted from Stanhope.

Just then Dani returned. "Mrs. Miller wants to know whether to serve supper in the dining room or here."

"In the dining room," Monique said hurriedly. She was too close to him now. The slightly musky scent of him was intoxicating. His closeness raised the heat in the room.

She backed away a few steps, then turned. "My lord, the supper I promised you is ready."

"You promised something else as well."

"Supper will have to do for now. I am always hungry after a performance. I seldom eat dinner beforehand."

He bowed. "Then I will wait." He started to follow her. "But not for long," he added in a low voice.

She tried to ignore his words as she led the way to the small, much too intimate dining room. Strange she had never realized how small it was until now. Probably because she had seldom dined here. She usually ate in her bedroom with Dani.

The table gleamed with china and crystal glasses. Mrs. Miller seemed very pleased with herself as she satisfied herself that all was prepared. There was chicken. Bread. Cheese. Grapes and other fruits. A bottle of wine was uncorked.

Because of a marquess? Or had he worked magic while he had waited for her?

She started to give him a sideways glance and saw that he had no such reservations. His perusal of her was bold and open and intense.

She took a piece of chicken and nibbled. Her usual appetite had faded.

He watched her even more intently.

"Are you not hungry?" she asked. She immediately regretted the statement. Hunger was in his eyes but it was not the kind of hunger she meant.

She hoped her own desire did not show as obviously. She was using food to disguise it when really her stomach churned inside. Or was it just that deep, internal ache that occurred every time she was in his presence, and never so much as at this very moment?

She'd wondered from the beginning what about this loutish American marquess attracted her. Now she knew. The façade cloaked a very complex and obviously intelligent man. What she did not know was his intent. And what he would do to accomplish whatever it was he was after.

But now she did not care. She felt lost in eyes no longer guarded, in the heat that warmed her beyond bearing, with the ache that reached to the core of her.

She longed to reach out and push a lock of hair off his forehead, to touch the face that fascinated her.

Instead, she forced herself to take another bite. Her tongue licked her lips. She tried to keep her attention on the leg of chicken but her gaze kept wandering over to Manchester, who had given up any pretense of eating and instead continued to watch her as a muscle flexed in his throat.

"It is very good," she said.

"Is it now?" he said in a low hoarse voice.

"Mrs. Miller worked very hard on this meal," she tried again. "I think . . ."

He raised an eyebrow. "Yes?"

"I believe she misses cooking for a man. Her feelings will be hurt if she doesn't think you enjoyed it."

"I will tell her I enjoyed it intensely." His mouth crooked up at the side in a half smile.

"She will think you lied if the food is still there."

"I will hide a piece in my coat."

"It will ruin your coat."

"Ah, a small price to pay for making a woman happy."

"Lying, you mean."

"If necessary."

"You lie a lot," she observed.

"And you do too, I think," he said. "It appears we are birds of a feather."

She had nothing to reply to that, so she took another piece of chicken and played with it.

"You look charming when you do that," he said.

"Do what?"

"Lick your lips."

She was accustomed to flattery, to wild extravagant compliments, but his observation was somehow far more seductive. Her blood seemed to slow and thicken like warm honey.

"What do you want?" she finally managed.

"At the moment?"

She found herself smiling. "I think I know what you want at this moment."

"And you?"

She knew what she wanted, too. Unfortunately it was a very dangerous and unfortunate want.

"I want to know why you are pretending to be a foolish man."

"I think all men are foolish around you."

She sat straight. "Words," she said. "Words designed to hide the truth. Why are you here? In London? Why do you want a business arrangement with a man known to be less than honest?"

The lazy, sensuous eyes didn't blink.

"I do not know him to be less than honest."

"It is common rumor."

"It is also common rumor that I am a disgrace to a long and noble title." His voice was full of irony.

She wiped her mouth with the napkin.

"And now my turn," he said. "Why did the bracelet mean so much to you?"

"You told me nothing. It is not your turn at all." The level of heat and electricity had risen to astounding levels. She felt her every nerve reacting to him. Only words kept them apart. Only words constituted armor. Without them . . .

Without them, she would succumb to him. Even now, she was tempted to reach out to him.

*You cannot trust any man.*

How many times had her mother told her that? How many times had she watched the truth of the words?

Then why . . . ?

"I think you should go," she said.

He rose. "As the lady wishes," he said. "I wish you luck with the good earl."

His voice was light. It didn't hold any of the passion his eyes had just held. Instead, both his eyes and voice were well masked.

"Good night," she said, standing. She wondered whether she had been the only one to feel the magic.

He leaned over. His fingers touched her cheek, and then he kissed her. It was not the kiss of a foolish man. Or an indolent one.

Nor was hers the response of a loose woman after another man.

It was pure volcanic. Layers upon layers of molten heat.

He stepped back. So did she. Her legs trembled slightly. She'd never wanted anything as badly in her life.

Except her father's downfall.

She swallowed hard.

Neither of them moved beyond that one step. Neither of them ran for safety.

Strange that she would think of it in that way. And include him in the thought.

Yet despite the mystery—even danger—whirling around him, she did not want him to go. The room would become colorless without him. The air would become stale. The day would become just another day.

Color lay in holding out her hand. She knew it. Felt it.

Color.

Life.

She had acted life. She had not felt it.

She was a woman, and yet she had never felt a man's tenderness. She had never allowed herself intimacy. She had not even been curious about it. Her mother had loved, and it had destroyed her.

She'd never wanted to be naive.

He stepped closer again. Despite his words, he seemed no more able to leave than she was to insist that he do so.

His fingers touched her chin, then the hollow of her throat. She knew he must feel the sudden speed of her pulse.

"I should go," he whispered.

"Yes."

"You want me to?"

"Yes." But she heard no certainty in her voice and neither, apparently, did he.

He leaned over and his lips brushed hers.

The volcano exploded.

# Chapter Sixteen

Gabriel had been ready to leave. He'd had enough of games. She was not going to tell him anything, and he certainly didn't intend to tell her anything she could reveal to the man he'd dreamed about ruining these many years.

Yet he had lingered a moment too long. He had allowed himself to indulge those very compelling feelings. He had wanted to touch her again, to see whether her skin was really as soft as he remembered, whether her hair still smelled of roses. Whether those eyes could ignite fires within him.

Surely not.

Not if he used the discipline that had brought him to where he was. As brittle as her explanations were, as wily as her answers, he saw a vulnerability that touched him. He kept trying to tell himself that it, too, was only a pose, an actress's trick.

Yet he really didn't believe that. She did not trust him. He couldn't complain about that because he didn't trust her, either. Yet he could not rid himself of a feeling that there might be common cause here.

A feeling that was all too dangerous. If she really was the courtesan she seemed to be, she could destroy him with a word.

Yet the temptation was overpowering. Instead, he kissed her lightly on the cheek, then found himself unable to leave it at that. Her skin was as soft as he remembered, her hair like silk, her breath like the light breeze of a spring day.

She was intoxicating, and he understood why and how she had half of London panting after her.

He wondered whether part of it was because she was so different from other women he had known. Of course, he had taken little time in the past few years to cultivate a woman. Instead, he'd favored women who'd wanted no more than a momentary affair.

He'd never been tempted to linger.

This woman could make him linger for a very long time.

That terrified him, even as it intrigued him.

But he also knew her eyes were on a bigger prize, a wealthier prize.

That thought spurred him. She had no interest in an extended affair. Perhaps a brief interlude would dull the aching need inside him.

All those thoughts flitted through his mind as he hesitated, knowing that he might well not retreat easily from this bed as he had others. Her eyes, now a stormy gray as expressive as a squall at sea, appeared to reflect the same confusion that he had. Doubt mixed with desire.

Desire won. His lips pressed down on hers. He tasted her lips, then his tongue explored her mouth, tentatively at first, then with a sense of growing urgency.

Her arms went around his neck, and his arms tightened around her, drawing her near. Her gown was muslin and feather light and he could feel her body through it. Soft and supple but with strength. No girl's body, but a woman's.

He felt it change as his hands stroked her back, then moved to her breasts as his lips continued their seduction of her mouth. He felt her tremble as his fingers played with her nipples, erotically, intimately, feeling every response: the swelling, the hardening of the nipple. His lips moved down toward the throbbing pulse of her throat and nuzzled it, feeling her quiver, almost vibrating under his touch. He knew exactly what those tremors were, because they were rippling through him, too. His body was no longer his own to rule.

His lips drew away from her, and he looked at her face.

Her body was reacting to his, and reacting in a seductive, instinctive way, but the look in her eyes . . .

*Startled.* And her lips . . . they had engaged his but in a curiously inexperienced way. As if every sensation was new.

She was an experienced woman who played wealthy men against one another, but some of her reactions made him wonder if . . .

He was wrong. He knew he was wrong. It was just a coquettish game that she played.

His loins were rigid and heated, and he felt as if he were on fire. He couldn't stop now. He crushed her to him again, his mouth insatiable as it tasted again and wanted even more.

"Your bedroom?"

Her expressive gray eyes looked enormous. Desire burned in them. But so did something else he could not fathom.

She hesitated, and he realized she was struggling with something he did not understand. Then a slight, almost imperceptible nod.

He put an arm around her shoulder, guiding her toward the stairs. "Up the stairs?"

"Yes," she said. Not *oui,* he noticed. Her accent sometimes disappeared. It was obvious she was as comfortable with English as with French, and she used French to portray a certain image.

But he would mull over that tomorrow. His curiosity was overshadowed by a more urgent need now.

She led the way to a bedroom. She stopped there, turned, looked at him with questions in her eyes.

He touched her face, tracing her elegant cheekbones with feather-light movements. So soft. So incredibly soft.

He heard a movement behind him. He was loath to turn, to take his attention away from her.

She jerked away, as if burned, then looked beyond him. "It is all right, Dani," she said. "You can go to bed."

"Is there anything . . ." He heard the doubt in the maid's

voice but he did not turn. Instead, he watched emotions cross Monique's face.

A touch of hesitation. Then, "No," she said.

He heard footsteps move away. "She is protective of you," he said softly.

"We have been together a long time." Her words were little more than a whisper.

"Am I safe?" he asked lightly.

"I do not know whether either one of us is safe."

He knew she meant herself and him. He didn't know, either. There had been something from the very first time they saw each other. He'd believed in love. He had seen it between his parents. He also knew how destructive it could be, how it had ultimately destroyed his mother.

But this wasn't love. It was lust, he told himself. Like recognizing like. They were both after something and didn't mind using any means available to achieve it. He just wasn't sure whether their goals were in direct conflict.

If so, this . . . interlude . . . was extraordinarily foolish.

And yet his heart quaked as he put his arms back around her and she moved into them and she looked up at him with a kind of wonderment in her eyes, the same fascination he felt. Her lips were already swollen by their last kiss and now with the slightest tremor, they were beguiling.

*She is an actress.* But despite the mental warning, he saw an odd innocence in her.

Beguiling . . . and dangerous.

He almost believed she felt the same aching attraction, the same electricity that made his body react in ways not altogether familiar. He nibbled at her earlobe, and her body responded with shivers of what he thought was anticipation. The same anticipation that was enveloping his body in heat.

He'd never before felt this raw, naked, physical appetite. He'd never felt this drumming in his heart, or the intense white hot heat that ran through his body when he touched her, looked at her, and especially when he saw that same flame in her eyes.

His hands undid her buttons on the back of her dress, slowly and sensuously, his fingers lingering possessively on her skin. Heat flooded him, and he had to force himself to go slowly, to give her as much pleasure as he himself intended to take. He tried not to think of Stanhope's hands on her skin.

He shifted the gown off her shoulders, and she stepped out of it. Dressed only in a sheer shift. No corset over it now. But then with her body she needed none.

Her breasts were taut against the sheer cloth. His hands went inside the shift, fondling her rounded breasts, then the nipples. He heard her swift intake of breath. His hands lifted the shift from her body and she stood naked except for the silk stockings held up by pieces of cloth.

Saints in heaven but she was lovely. He saw the astonished look of pleasure on her face as his hands continued their seduction of her body, hesitating at the back of her neck, running downward, then touching her breasts again, gathering the left one with his hand and leaning down to kiss it. Her expression of wonder and surprise startled him. She seemed to be experiencing these things for the first time.

He took his hands from her and unbuttoned his waistcoat, then his shirt, until he stood in only his tight breeches and boots. She looked at him, the lashes sheltering her eyes, giving her a half-sleepy, sensuous look. Her right hand went to his shoulder, touched and explored, then moved up to his hair.

Now it was his turn to slow, to try to control the spasms her touch created. He tried to warn himself again, but each one of her touches pulled down another stone of his defenses.

Her hand moved again, trailing fire every inch as it moved over his chest and downward, along the skin that stretched taut over the ridged muscles of his body.

His body paid no attention to his mind, not to the scruples or reservations. It had only want now. And it was exercising that in the most blatant way.

His arms went around her, and he pulled her to him. Her body melded into his, kindling a flame he knew would have to burn itself out. Lightning leaped between them, jagged and violent yet blinding them with its intensity. Need took over, a need so great it threatened to consume him. His mouth savaged hers, insatiable as it tasted and wanted more.

He felt the whisper of her breath, then heard the soft groan and he could wait no longer. He lifted her and took her to the bed, his lips still locked on hers. He released them as he lowered her body. He sat on the bed, pulled off his boots, then quickly stripped off his breeches.

For a moment he paused. Something in her eyes again stopped him. But then she held out her hand, and he fell to the bed beside her.

He stroked her body, watching the reactions as his fingers touched the soft hair at the triangle between her thighs. He touched and seduced until she gave a small cry, and he positioned himself above her, moving slowly, teasing, then started to enter. Her arms went around him, holding him tight, and she whimpered as he penetrated deeper till he encountered a fragile barrier.

He had never bedded a virgin, but he knew instantly, and with certainty, that Monique Fremont was exactly that.

It was too late to stop, though. He felt the barrier give, heard her smothered cry.

Damn it to hell. He started to withdraw, but her arms kept him close.

"No," she whispered.

The word was an aphrodisiac. Very slowly, very cautiously, he moved deeper inside her, feeling a growing response to him. It was instinctive and primitive, and ever so enticing. Sensations built. Need flamed. Shimmering waves of heat pounded through him. He moved with a rhythm that grew more and more frantic, a whirlwind of power.

Their bodies seemed made for each other, their responses feeding upon the other.

He sought to prolong her pleasure, to savor the infinitely precious moments of unity combined with rushes of pleasure. Then that moment of magnificent explosion . . .

She cried out, and he knew she too had reached the pinnacle of sensations. He was too aware that he had never made love like this before, nor had he felt the exultation that accompanied the climax.

But as he fell back to earth, his body still shuddering with the aftermath of splendor, one fact kept ringing in his mind.

*She had been a virgin.*

*    *    *

Monique had never realized that the act of intimacy could be
so shattering. She'd never realized it paled the fireworks
she'd seen only days ago. Or was it an eon ago?

Even as she had granted him her bedroom, she knew it was
a mistake. Inviting him tonight had been a mistake. Suc-
cumbing to her runaway emotions was a greater mistake.

But now she had no regrets. She lay in his arms, her body
sated but still reacting to sensations that lingered deep inside.
There was soreness, yes, but it was nothing compared to the
marvelous journey she'd just taken.

He was still inside her, not as he had been seconds before
but still warm and throbbing.

He felt as if he belonged there. She had never thought,
never believed, the act could be like this. She'd always
thought of it as something distasteful. But then she had heard,
as a child, the grunts of men from inside a closed door and
later saw the tears of her mother, the discoloration of her skin.

But tonight . . . had been gentleness as well as passion.

His hand caught hers and his fingers tightened around it.
He sighed heavily, then moved off her. He rose and went to
the water pitcher and found a towel, dampening it.

He returned and gently washed her, his movements slow
and tender and even those excited her again. When he'd finished he lay next to her, propping himself up on one elbow
and gazing at her.

She knew he had questions. He knew she had been a virgin despite her pose as a worldly woman.

He leaned over and kissed her softly. "Why did you not tell
me?"

"I did not think this would happen."

"Did you not?" he asked wryly.

Perhaps deep inside, she secretly acknowledged. He had
intrigued her from the moment she had spied him on the ship.
She had been drawn to him in ways she'd never expected.
And tonight she'd received some answers that had been
plaguing her.

He was no fool. He was no libertine. He was no user. He
had thought she was what she had wanted everyone to think:

a courtesan as well as an actress. When he'd discovered she was a virgin, he'd been prepared to stop despite the heat that had drawn them together.

"Do you want to tell me why?" he asked in a lazy, sensuous voice.

She did not have to ask what he meant.

"No," she said.

"You are not French, are you?"

She moved her head to look into those green eyes that seemed to look straight through her soul. "Why . . . ?"

"You are too at ease with the language, even for an actress," he said. "You grew up with English."

"I grew up in France," she corrected him.

"But of English parents?"

"I had an English mother," she admitted even as she wondered why she was giving him that information. But she seemed as powerless now as she had been an hour ago when she brought him to her bed.

"Tell me about your mother."

She thought it a curious question, but then she realized that it was an opening into her life, into her mind.

"There is nothing to tell," she said. "She died several years ago."

"And your father?"

She stiffened. "My mother had many lovers."

"Is that how you play the . . ."

"Whore so well?" she finished for him.

"Never that," he said, his hand tightening around hers.

"I am an actress," she said, again avoiding a direct answer.

"But to what end?"

"I might ask the same," she said.

"I am but a poor American trying to make my way in the wilds of English aristocracy," he replied with amusement.

"You want something from Stanhope."

"I want a successful business arrangement. I need funds to rebuild an indebted estate."

"Have you been there?"

"Yes," he admitted. "It's in dismal condition."

"But you care deeply about it?"

"It's my heritage."

"Why do I not believe you?"

"I have no idea, Miss Fremont," he said. "Perhaps because we are both accomplished liars."

"Then you admit . . ."

"Admit what?"

"That you are a fraud."

"On the contrary. I am indeed the Marquess of Manchester, impoverished long-lost heir."

"I have heard tales of a scandal."

"Have you, now?"

"Your father . . ."

"My father was accused of selling shoddy goods to the army," he said. "He was disowned by my grandfather. Quite fortunately, though, the estate was entailed, and he could not keep me from getting it. He did bankrupt it, though, possibly to make it useless to the heir of the son who disgraced him. There is little but debt and land that produces little in income."

"And you need income."

"Any way I can get it," he said. "Stanhope made me an offer that can triple my funds. Quickly."

"And you trust him?"

"Do you?"

She hesitated. Should she warn him? "I have heard he is not entirely honest in his dealings."

"And that is the kind of man you want as a protector? Or," he said, "you have a different game in mind?"

She wanted to tell him. Dear Mother in Heaven, she wanted to tell him. But he had made it clear that he intended to press his business with Stanhope, and she would be giving him a means to win Stanhope's confidence.

*He wouldn't use it.*

She knew that in her bones.

Yet part of her could not give him that knowledge. Only one other person in the world knew. And that was Dani.

She didn't know this man. She only knew that she was terribly susceptible to him, and that he clouded her mind and judgment. She needed to think before telling him any more.

Her hand touched the small blond tendrils on his chest, then went to his neck. She snuggled into his arms and her lips found his as their bodies came together again.

This time she knew what to expect. She was sore, but the craving inside her was even more compelling. He entered slowly, carefully, at first, then thrust deeper with the same urgency she felt.

She'd *thought* she knew what to expect, but . . .

This time they whirled together in a feverish dance toward a destination she now wanted above all, only to find it more spectacular, more magnificent than before. Bursts of wonder and thunderous waves of pleasure swept through her like a great tidal wave until she could bear no more. Exquisite quivers filled her as together they drifted back to earth.

And she rested in his arms. Contented now.

She closed her eyes.

No more questions tonight. Perhaps tomorrow. Perhaps tomorrow she could force answers. And perhaps . . . she could offer some.

*Perhaps.*

Stanhope prepared for the weekend at his estate with the same meticulous attention he paid to everything.

He had paid Lynch enough to secure his releasing Monique that weekend. He had not yet received her reply, but she would come. He knew it. She wanted what he could offer.

Manchester had already accepted.

Both Stammel and Daven would be there, as would twenty other gentlemen of the ton, along with eight of their wives. He'd had regrets from others, but he would overlook the slights. For the moment.

He planned a hunt and entertainments, including dancing. He would dazzle Monique with the estate and its fine gardens, with his guests, with his wealth. And he would claim the bet. He intended to take her to bed. He also planned to spring the trap on the new marquess who irritated him for no particular reason. He would make it clear that he needed a substantial deposit on the shipping contract.

And after he had the man's signature and funds, he would

see that Manchester disappeared. Stanhope didn't see the
marquess as a threat. But he did not like loose ends, and Manchester was exactly that. He could rewrite events long since
forgotten.

And something about the marquess nagged at him. He did
not care for that kind of nagging.

Monique Fremont also was a puzzle. A much more attractive one to be sure, but a puzzle all the same. There was something familiar about her, and he kept thinking that he should
know her.

At the same time he was quite sure he would have remembered a woman with her charm and talent. He just wasn't sure
of her motives, though. She did not even pretend an attraction
to him, even as she had coldly set out her terms for an
arrangement. Why the three of them? Why three men known
to be business partners?

There were no rumors of other men, although Manchester,
again, was an irritant. He seemed to be around her entirely too
often.

Yet he was paying court to Pamela, and his daughter, surprisingly, had few objections. That made him suspicious as
well. Pamela had always been compliant, but he did not like
the docility with which she approached the prospect of Manchester as a husband.

And lastly, money was missing from his safe. The only
people who had access to his home—other than servants—
were his business partners. There had been the soiree, of
course, but he had checked his safe the next morning and
everything had been in place.

Stammel? Daven?

Would either dare?

Only if one were desperate.

For one of the few times in his life, he thought events
might be spiraling out of control. He could remember only
two other times. One was when sailors survived a ship that
was meant to sink. They lived to tell of shoddy construction
and a cargo of stones rather than muskets.

Fortunately, he seldom took chances. In case of just such
an eventuality, he had forged one of his partners' names to all

the documents. Stanhope had been properly contrite, regretful that he had any part in such a despicable action.

Manchester's father received the blame, and conveniently killed himself before suspicion could be turned elsewhere.

Stanhope had planned that the son follow the father's footsteps.

But now he was beginning to wonder whether the course was the wisest one. It might be best if the bloody man died on the road, victim of a bandit. And sooner rather than later.

Monique rose lazily and reached out for him.

Her body was sore, and yet she felt quite grand.

She had reached out earlier, found him lying next to her, his eyes on her. She couldn't see what was in them, but his hands were gentle as they touched her.

He did not try to make love again, but she relished the feel of his body next to hers, and she drifted back into the sleep.

Now she searched and he wasn't in bed, nor in the room.

She rose. The sun was high in the sky. She wondered how late it was. Where had he gone? She rang the bell.

Dani was there almost immediately, a gleam in her eyes. Her lips were in a rare smile.

"You look different," she said.

"Do I?"

"*Oui.* So did my lord." The smile spread.

"Where is he?"

"He said he had business. He left you a note." Dani handed it to Monique. "He is a handsome man, *non?*"

Monique knew she was reddening. Her face felt warm. Just as the rest of her. And yet she also felt deserted. No farewell. No parting kiss.

She took the piece of parchment and read it.

> *Monique—*
> *Thank you for a memorable evening. I regret I had to leave early, but I had unavoidable business and I did not want to wake you. If I can ever come to your assistance, please contact me.*
> *Gabriel*

She felt her face grow even warmer as the full impact of the message struck her. Curt. Indifferent. *Please contact me,* indeed. When it snowed in hell.

"What is it?" Dani said, looking alarmed.

Monique passed the note over to her, watched her face as she read it. "This does not sound like him," Dani said. "He is not a cruel man."

"Well, we misjudged him," Monique said. "I knew . . ." her voice trailed off, and she fought back rare tears. Of rage, she told herself.

She had given herself to him because . . .

Because he had appeared gentle and tender and . . . drat it, she had wanted him. She had never known that lust came to women as well as to men. Lust. That was all it had been. On both their parts. She had just justified her lapse as something else, something . . .

She would know better in the future.

She had almost, for a moment, forgotten why she had come to London.

Monique turned to Dani. "It is time to accept Lord Stanhope's invitation."

# Chapter Seventeen

Gabriel took his frustration out on Henry Worth, the Earl of Daven.

He would have rather visited Stammel, but Dani's intrusion might well have made the baron more careful.

Daven did not gamble as recklessly as Stammel did, but he did have his weaknesses. One that probably drew both him and Stanhope together. They apparently were quite fond of establishments said to cater to rather bizarre interests of their patrons.

Gabriel spent part of the day with the forger, making certain changes in documents he had taken from Stanhope's safe along with the money. Contracts with various shippers. He had gone over each of them carefully.

The contracts would be rewritten, amounts altered to make it appear that Stanhope had cheated his partners. He probably had, but Stanhope was a careful man.

Gabriel would then replace them in the safe and hope that Stanhope wouldn't look too closely. When an investigation opened, they would be found in Stanhope's possession. Another rope around his neck.

Part of his plan depended on a falling out between thieves. He wanted them all scampering for safety. He wanted them to know the despair that his father felt before he pulled the trigger of a pistol.

Monique Fremont and her challenge to the three partners had assisted him in that. Perhaps not immediately, but he'd seen tempers shorten. It wasn't Monique, he knew. To the three men, a woman was mostly something to be used and discarded. No, it wasn't Monique. It was the challenge itself.

Gabriel prayed that Monique knew exactly what she was doing.

He was tempted to act like Don Quixote and tilt at windmills. How could you save someone who did not want to be saved?

Instead, he tried to get her out of his mind by tending to his own business . . .

That business was finding out more about Stanhope's business dealings and enlarging his meager stake. He had far less than the sum Stanhope had required as his investment. Still, he thought Stanhope would accept a lower amount if necessary.

The earl was a man who would take something rather than nothing, particularly if he wished to rid himself of what could become an embarrassment.

Gabriel attended his tailor and ordered a riding coat for Stanhope's country party. He stopped in at a fashionable restaurant and made an ass of himself by trying to join a party which obviously did not want his presence.

Finally, he ended the evening at a gambling hell where he appeared to indulge in a great many glasses of brandy. He lurched home, not trying to avoid anyone who might be following him. He noticed, though, that rather than the bulky man, a young lad shadowed his progress.

The lad was good. Careful. But Gabriel was aware now. Probably no one else would have noticed, particularly the careless heir everyone thought him to be.

He returned to his lodgings. For once Smythe was not waiting for him. He had suggested that the man take a rare night off, perhaps to see old army friends. He'd also told Mrs. Smythe he would not need her this night.

Gabriel quickly changed into serviceable black clothes that

would be worn by a servant. He rubbed coal in his sandy hair and tucked it under a dark cap. In a pocket was a black silk scarf. Then he added a dark gray cloak.

It had started misting, and he knew fortune was with him. He took an umbrella, left through the servants' entrance, then hurried down an alley as if he were on an errand.

He walked three blocks, then found an alcove in which to wait. No footsteps sounded nearby. He stepped out. Mist had turned into fog. This city was made, he thought, for intrigue.

Gabriel walked to Daven's residence. Most of the lights had been quenched.

At the servants' entrance in the back, he tried the door. It was unlocked. Apparently Daven did not hold to the same standards as did his business partner.

He entered, keeping to the dark corners, listening for any footstep. He had more risky work to do here than at Stanhope's. He had explored that residence when no one was inside. He had no idea how many lived here, but he knew there was at least one groom. There would also be a housekeeper, maid, and valet. That was the minimum of servants for a home like this.

The hall was silent, as it should be in the pre-dawn hours. Servants were usually up and busy at dawn, lighting fires, preparing the morning meals. The valet might well be preparing Daven's clothes for the next day.

He quickly traversed through the lower level of the town house. It was not nearly as splendid as Stanhope's. It was, in truth, fairly threadbare. Perhaps he had overestimated the number of servants.

One reception room had little furniture.

He found the study. He didn't light the oil lamp but relied on dim light filtering in from the hall. The desk was piled high with papers and bills, totally unlike Stanhope's. Gabriel glanced through them. Many of the bills were overdue.

He smiled to himself. Daven might not be the gambler Stammel was, but he certainly must have other vices. It appeared he owed practically every merchant in London.

The desk wasn't locked. Inside were more bills. Then an envelope filled with banknotes.

He wondered why so many banknotes when a mountain of bills remained unpaid.

But then Gabriel's tailor, who had demanded his fees in advance, had explained that some peers were notoriously lax in paying bills. The law protected them in matters of debt, and they could defraud creditors with impunity. The merchant's only recourse was to decline to provide services or goods to that particular individual. Staring at the pile of bills, Gabriel wondered how Daven obtained any services at all.

But at least Gabriel had found what he wanted. He pocketed the banknotes, then closed the desk. One thing about Daven's desk: he would not know if someone had prowled through it. He would realize soon enough, however, that his banknotes were missing.

Gabriel moved swiftly out the door, down the hall, and out the back. He moved around the side of the house and ducked when he saw a carriage pull up. Daven alighted.

Breathing again, Gabriel waited until the door opened, then left the property.

He hummed a sailor's tune as he strolled down the street.

Unfortunately, now that the danger was gone, his thoughts returned to Monique. He never would have tried to seduce her if he had known she was a virgin, God help him. He never would have gone up to her bedroom.

The fact that she had been a virgin complicated things. He needed time to evaluate exactly what had happened.

Why was she acting the courtesan when at twenty-five she'd never been bedded before? What he'd thought to be coquettishness was inexperience. But she had been as eager as he. She had not wanted him to stop. She had been as much the aggressor as he.

Why? She had made it very plain she was after a fortune, that she did not object to pitting three men against each other for her favors.

What if Stanhope won? The thought sent a sharp pain through him. Then why had she given herself to him last night? Perhaps she'd just wanted to use him to prepare for whoever won her game.

He could not quite believe that.

Bloody hell. She tied him up in knots.

He knew he could not draw her into his own intrigue. It was too dangerous. He had intended a brief liaison with her, something that would mean little to either of them, and perhaps even put another thorn into Stanhope's hide.

What he'd found instead was something he'd never expected. She made inroads into his heart. That was dangerous.

He assuaged his conscience with the knowledge that she had used him as much as he'd used her. She had never expressed any deeper emotion than their mutual attraction.

He tried to forget the wonder in her eyes, the way her fingers had loved him. He'd lost himself in both of them, but in the gray glimmers of dawn, he'd realized Monique traveled a path different from his.

Gabriel wanted to make it easier for both of them. Hell, nothing would make it easier. Not now. He wanted her. God how he wanted her. He knew he was failing miserably in avoiding thoughts of a woman with dark hair and an enchanting smile.

At least she wouldn't be at Stanhope's weekend. She had the play. She had a contract.

He could suffer through the weekend. He would appear to court Pamela, and he would finalize the business opportunity with Stanhope. He only hoped it was the same kind of opportunity Stanhope offered his father. The switching of a few signatures and it would be Stanhope who stood accused.

Monique Fremont. He only wished . . .

Several days after her unfortunate lapse in control and judgement Monique and Dani rode in Stanhope's coach, alone except for the driver above and a groom.

She'd been told the journey would take most of the day but would not require an overnight stay at an inn.

Dani was drably dressed as usual. Monique had selected a midnight-blue dress with a low neck. She wore a cloak against the chill that permeated the morning.

Monique had second thoughts about taking Dani with her, but her friend had no intention of staying behind. "If you have trouble with the safe, then I can help," she said. Months ear-

lier she had introduced Monique to a thief who had taught her
some useful skills.

But Dani had been far more adept than Monique. She had
been a pickpocket, and her fingers were more facile than
Monique's. "I can also help secret whatever you find. No one
sees a servant."

"A very attractive servant," Monique said, "if you would
but let people notice."

Dani humphed. "And why should I do that, only to have
someone leave me a note the next morning?"

Dani had become more and more angry on Monique's be-
half in the last few days. She felt responsible because she'd
thought Manchester kind and decent. Now she vocally wished
him to hell more than a few times.

"He knows I am after Stanhope," Monique said, excusing
him, though the ache of rejection ran deep. "He knows I have
promised myself to one of three men. How could he ever
think well of me?" She paused. "It does not matter, in any
event. I have other more important things to accomplish."

Dani gave her a skeptical stare. She had been as angry as
Monique. For some reason she had raised Manchester to
heroic proportions.

"No man is trustworthy," she said. "When this is done, you
and I will return to France."

"You should have told him about Lord Stanhope," Dani
said unexpectedly.

"Told him what? That Stanhope is my father? And what if
he decided to use that information?"

"If he knew everything . . ." Dani tried again.

"That my father is a completely ruthless man. Manchester
is aware of all that. He said as much. But he is still willing to
deal with the man."

"I think he has some honor," Dani persisted.

"You would make a good advocate, Dani," Monique observed with a sigh. "But he is obviously faithless. While paying court to my half sister, he seeks out my bed. Then he
leaves without so much as a farewell. What kind of honor is
that?" She paused, then added sadly, "And what kind of
woman does that make me?"

Dani fell into silence. Monique stared out at the passing countryside. Everything was impossibly green, sparkling with the dew of early morning. Peaceful. Deceptive.

She prayed Manchester would not be attending this weekend. She did not know how she would face him again. Nor did she need interference with what she had to do.

She only wished that her detective had discovered more about Manchester.

Why did she care? He obviously did not care about her, other than for a night's pleasure. That stung. More than stung. The pain went deeper than she wanted to admit, even to herself.

She should avoid him from now on, and concentrate on the task to date.

And yet he was paying suit to her sister. How could she ignore him? Should she warn Pamela that he was a bounder? How could she explain her interference?

Everything had become far more complicated than she had ever imagined.

And it had started from the first moment she had seen Manchester on that dratted ship. She wished with all her heart he had never come to London.

They stopped at an inn to rest the horses and for her and Dani to dine. After the first glance at the Stanhope coach with its elaborate crest, the innkeeper and grooms could not do enough for them. It was obvious that Stanhope was a frequent and valued—or feared—patron. She and Dani were served in a private room, although the innkeeper had asked whether the maid should dine in the kitchen.

"Of course not," she had replied.

The food was plain, but tasty. Slices of beef with potatoes, cheese, and fruit. A good wine accompanied the meal.

Following supper, they were told by the coachman it would be another few moments before they could leave.

Thankful for the respite of the jolting of the coach, Monique tried to relax. She expected the next few days were going to be more than a bit complicated.

It had been less than a day since she had seen Manchester, and her body still pulsed with her newfound knowledge of lovemaking. It pulsed even stronger when she thought of him, though she despised herself for it.

Restlessly, Monique rose and went to the window, watching as another coach rolled into the courtyard. There was no crest and it appeared to be a hired coach. A fine gray horse was tied to the back of it.

Her blood went cold, then hot, as she recognized the gelding. It was the same one Manchester had ridden in the park. She couldn't take her gaze from the door as Manchester stepped down, followed by a large man in somber clothes.

Manchester said something to him, then they disappeared inside the tavern.

She wondered whether he had noticed Stanhope's coach, which was to the side of his, whether he thought Stanhope was inside.

Then the door to the private room opened, and the coachman appeared. "We are ready to go."

She had no choice but to follow him out the door to the main room. Manchester stood just inside the main door of the tavern. He wore skintight tan pantaloons, a white linen shirt, and a dark brown riding coat. He had not bothered with a cravat. Behind him was the man she had seen alight from the coach with him.

Manchester looked stunned, then frowned deeply as his gaze met hers. "The innkeeper said other members of the earl's party were here. I did not realize you had been . . ." His brows snapped together in an expression of utter consternation.

"Invited?" Monique asked. She wanted to throw a tankard of wine at him.

Silence.

"I truly did not intend to intrude," he added, "but the horses needed rest."

"It is of no matter. We are ready to depart, in any case," Monique said with as much dignity as she could muster.

Some emotion flicked across his face. It disappeared so quickly she wasn't sure she'd even seen it.

"I do not want to . . ."

"I do not care what you want, my lord," she said sharply.

"I did not realize you had been invited to Lord Stanhope's home."

"Nor I you," he said. "But I am . . ."

"Delighted? I think not."

Their eyes met and, to her dismay, whatever existed between them—passion, need, lust—still radiated between them. Heat puddled in her stomach. She detested him. He was everything she had always avoided: a man who used women, then left them.

But fate—or the devil—seemed determined to throw them together. She wanted to rail against whichever it was.

She looked at Dani, who stared at the tall man who stood silently at Manchester's side.

"Come, Dani," Monique said. She walked to the door, waited for Dani to go before her, then turned back and tossed Manchester a gaze of contempt before retreating.

Her legs did not want to carry her as she walked through the door. She forced herself not to look back as she climbed in, followed by Dani. Against her judgement, she glanced up at the window of the small private dining room. She saw his face looking down. Watching.

Dear God. She wanted to tell the coachman to turn around and return to London. Yet she had come too far to allow such a mistake to cancel all her plans. She should have known Manchester would be invited. Perhaps she had. She just had not expected that her reactions to him would still be so strong.

*Three days.*

She had only three days to turn Stanhope against the others. Three days to avoid the Marquess of Manchester.

She wondered how she would endure it.

Stanhope's estate was magnificent.

Gabriel regarded the country manor with grudging admiration, especially in comparison to his own poor property. Then he reminded himself that it did not matter. He wanted a deck beneath him, and the sky above. He wanted to return to America as soon as possible.

He was finding himself very uncomfortable with the trap-

pings of the English aristocracy. He longed for the sea and the
honest companionship of fellow sailors.

The manor in front of him was glaring evidence of the ex-
cess that had killed his father.

He alighted from the coach. A footman opened the door as
he approached. Several other servants—grooms—emerged
from the stable to take care of the horses.

Smythe had tied his cravat in the coach and replaced his
riding coat with a waistcoat, one that was not in the best of
taste. He added a beaver hat and put his quizzing glass in
place.

He had lost his amusement in his role. He had seen the
shock and disdain in Monique's face. Because she was re-
pulsed by what had passed between them? He had not wanted
to wake her that morning, and he'd had business . . .

Hell, he hadn't only been confused. He'd been befuddled.
He'd needed to gather his wits about him, and he couldn't do
that with her in the room. In the same residence.

She had never said anything about love, or affection. She'd
never hid the fact that she was pursuing a wealthy protector.
She was obviously an opportunist. A woman on the make.

*And a virgin, damn it.*

It simply did not make sense.

He should have contacted her, but he'd had business . . .

Bloody hell, he had thought . . . to hell what he had
thought.

In that moment at the inn he'd suddenly seen himself
through her eyes and did not like what he saw there. He'd always thought of himself an honorable man with women. He
had never led one to believe a liaison was anything more than
that.

He had not planned to seduce Monique Fremont. He'd
wanted information, but then . . . that bloody attraction between them got in the way and one thing led to another. He'd
even hoped that it might get her out of his bloody mind.

Instead, she had insinuated herself in his heart. He'd been
trying to deny it for the last two days. He'd been telling himself she had been using him, that the only thing she cared
about was money and power. Why else would she instigate

such a contest between three wealthy and even dangerous men? Why would she sell herself?

And yet he had seen flickers of hurt in her eyes despite the haughty cut.

That led him back to the question as to why she was doing what she was doing. She must do well as an actress. Her clothes were expensive, her home respectable and pleasant. She had a maid.

He had never seen her wear expensive jewelry, though. That had surprised him, since she had so many admirers.

What if she had reasons of her own to go after the same three men he sought? He knew his father hadn't been Stanhope's only victim. Rumors abounded in London's gambling hells about his ruthlessness in business.

All those questions haunted him on the drive from the inn to Stanhope's estate.

*She would already be there.*

He followed a footman inside and was met by the butler, who requested his name, then instructed the servant to take him and Smythe to the blue room.

Gabriel noted the magnificent hall on the right, the marble flooring, the grand staircase leading to the next floor. He'd started to mount the steps behind the servant when he saw Pamela.

Her solemn face lit when she saw him, and he felt like a fraud. She trusted him.

"Lady Pamela," he said.

"My lord, I am so glad you came." She leaned over and whispered in his ear. "I do not like many of these people."

"Miss Fremont?" he asked. "I saw her at the inn about midway."

"Oh, she arrived an hour ago, and yes, she is very pleasant, but I do not care for my father's business friends. One is always looking at me in a . . . greedy way. He will not dare to do so with you here."

So much faith. Faith he didn't deserve. He had offered to act her suitor for his own selfish reasons. A rational part of his mind reminded him that it suited her purposes as well, that there were no illusions for either of them. That had not been the case with Monique. She had deceived him by implication, if not actual words. She played the role of experienced woman well.

"I will be delighted to be your protector," he said.

She gave him the shy smile that was so appealing to him. "I will see you at supper then," she said.

He bowed. "I look forward to it."

He followed the footman up the stairs, then down a long hall to a room on the left. He wondered where Monique had been placed.

*Get her out of your head.* He could not appear to have an interest in her, not if he had declared his intention to form an alliance with Pamela. He had done enough damage already.

Smythe efficiently unpacked his clothes, then followed the footman to his quarters. He would return immediately to see to Gabriel's needs, he said.

Gabriel went to the window and looked out. Manicured gardens stretched out directly beneath the window. He looked beyond the flower beds and saw well-tended green hedges that looked impenetrable.

A maze? He had heard of them but had never actually seen one.

He pulled on a waistcoat of questionable cut and taste. His cravat was looking a little worse for wear, but that didn't matter. In fact, he liked that small touch.

Unwillingly, he thought of Monique and wondered whether she was with Stanhope or Stammel.

Damn, the thought curdled his blood.

He decided to do a little reconnaissance. He walked the full length of the hall and wondered which room was occupied by Monique if, indeed, she was on the floor at all. Then he went to the next floor. More rooms. He saw what was obviously a woman's maid back out of one, and disappointment struck him as he saw it was not Dani.

An older well-dressed couple left a room down the corridor and nodded to him as they passed. They did not introduce themselves. It was definitely what he'd heard termed as the cut indirect. He thought it an amusing term.

He finished his walk on that floor, then descended the

staircase. Others were coming down from the second floor. Some he recognized, others he did not.

The women were all in magnificent dresses, the men far more formally dressed than he.

One man with whom he'd played whist stopped to exchange a word. "Manchester. Did not know I would see you here." His puzzlement was only too obvious.

"I hope to press my suit for Lady Pamela," he explained.

The gentleman—a baron, Gabriel thought—arched an eyebrow. "You do say?"

"Yes. And it has Lord Stanhope's approval."

"Humph," the man said. "We all thought you would be returning to America when you saw the state of . . ."

Gabriel shrugged. "My ancestral home? I visited briefly but I find London more entertaining."

"One should take care of one's business," the baron said. His name was Blackshear or something of that nature.

"I am doing that," Gabriel boasted. "Lord Stanhope is bringing me on as a partner in one of his businesses."

The eyebrow arched even higher. Amusement seemed to play in his eyes, then he bowed slightly. "I must join my wife," he said.

"Indeed," Gabriel said. "I hope to have one of my own soon."

"Pamela is a sweet girl."

"Yes," he said. "She is."

"Well then maybe we could enjoy a game of whist later. Or billiards. You will have to tell me more about this business with Stanhope."

Gabriel bowed slightly in return. "It will be my pleasure."

The baron turned and continued his descent down the stairs.

Gabriel watched him, wondering what he knew about Stanhope's business dealings. Perhaps over that game of billiards . . .

A large group of gentlemen were gathered in a library on the left. Cigar smoke filled the room. He went past it and investigated the rest of the main floor, finding a smaller dining room and what appeared to be a withdrawing room or parlor that was more feminine in appearance.

Like Stanhope's town house, the walls were lined with portraits, apparently more of his ancestors. They too wore grim expressions, but then many of the portraits from earlier years bore that same appearance, including those of his own ancestors. Apparently frivolity had been frowned upon.

He paused at the sound of a loud voice. "Are you accusing me?"

He recognized Stammel's drink-blurred voice coming from a room. The door was open.

Then he heard a lower reply. "I am not accusing anyone. I am merely saying that money is missing from my safe and Daven has also lost a large sum. You seem to be the only . . ."

"Damn you, Stanhope, you have no right. We have been partners for more than twenty years. I would never . . ."

Stanhope faced the door with a cue stick in his hand, giving Stammel a look that stopped his words in midsentence.

Satisfaction coursed through Gabriel. He stepped inside what was obviously a game room. His gaze wandered about the room as if he had heard nothing. A huge mahogany billiard table dominated the room. Other tables, including one with a magnificent chess set, were artfully scattered around.

"I am sorry," he said. "I did not mean to interrupt. I hope you do not mind my wandering about, but I was looking for Lady Pamela. I thought perhaps a stroll . . ."

Stanhope immediately dropped his cue and approached Gabriel, his hand outstretched. "So good of you to come to our little weekend," he said heartily. "Have you seen my daughter yet?"

"Very briefly as I arrived," Gabriel said. "She looked charming." He looked around the room. "Your home is magnificent."

"Thank you," Stanhope said with pride. "I have restored it since my father died. As for my daughter, I hope you will see much of her this weekend."

"It will be my great delight," Gabriel replied extravagantly.

"Would you like to join us for a game of billiards?"

Stammel shot Gabriel a baleful glance.

"I have little experience with billiards," Gabriel said.

"I will teach you," Stanhope said. "Every gentleman should know the game."

"Then I am your pupil," Gabriel agreed.

"And perhaps, a game of cards after. I understand you enjoy a game of chance."

"I do not have much coin with me."

"Your note is good," Stanhope said.

Gabriel nodded, allowing a pleased smile to spread across his face.

Stanhope handed him a cue.

# Chapter Eighteen

Monique desired a bath. It had been a long, bumpy ride, and she felt dusty and stale. Mother in Heaven but she needed to relax after the long journey and particularly after seeing the detestable Manchester again.

After a parade of footmen filled the small tub with hot water, she slid into it. It was, unfortunately, not of the size and convenience of the one in her rooms.

But the hot water felt good. She wanted to wash away Manchester's scent, which she imagined still clung to her. And she had business to do tonight.

The water cooled only too quickly, and she accepted the wrap Dani offered her.

She had to prepare for supper. It would be difficult with Manchester there. She would ignore him as he deserved to be ignored. Tonight she would be charming for Stanhope and his friends.

Dani helped her dress. Her gown was a deep red velvet with a low neck and long sleeves. It was a heavy garment, and not one of her favorites to wear, but it could hardly be missed.

A bell rang throughout the manor. Thirty minutes before supper. The maid who'd shown her to the rooms had explained that a bell would precede the actual call to supper.

Dani worked with her hair, pulling it to the back with combs and pins and allowing tendrils to fall to the left of her face. Then a touch of rouge made from red sandalwood. "You will put all the other women to shame," Dani said.

"Rubbish," Monique said. "I will look like the courtesan, the fashionably unpure." And, she reminded herself, she was exactly that now, thanks to Manchester.

Minutes later, she was ready.

"Why do you not go downstairs and talk to the servants? We must know which room is Stanhope's," she said.

Dani nodded.

Monique took her hand. "Be very careful."

"I always am," Dani replied.

Monique opened the door, took a deep breath. Hopefully, this would be one of her last performances.

Dani waited until she left, then started down to the servant's quarters, where she had been told she could fetch something to eat. She also wanted to pick up any gossip she could.

She left the room only to find herself grabbed by a well-dressed portly gentleman. "Well, what do we have here?" he asked. His breath was foul with whiskey.

She wrenched herself free and fled down the hall toward the back stairs. She ran straight into a body.

She looked up and saw a large man with red hair. His hands caught her and kept her from falling. He wore a plain dark suit, obviously a valet to one of the guests.

She backed away. "I am sorry, mon . . . sir."

A spare smile broke a plain, honest face and she remembered him from the inn. He had been with Manchester.

"No need, miss," he said, "I had something on my mind."

There was something about the earnest smile on the man's face. "I did also. An errand for my mistress."

He paused and then said in a tone that seemed almost painfully delivered, "And I am looking for my lord."

Dani knew she should hurry on, but there was something about the man's steady brown eyes that kept her from moving. He was very tall. She was smaller than most women. His hands were big, his shoulders very wide.

His face was serious, his eyes concerned. His hands had been gentle when they had righted her. Yet there was nothing weak about him. She realized that immediately.

"The Marquess of Manchester?" she asked.

He looked at her curiously, then recognition lit them. "You were at the inn."

She nodded. "He has called on my mistress."

"I know little about his acquaintances," the man said. "I was employed by him a few weeks ago." He shifted awkwardly on his feet.

"You do not look like a valet," she said.

"I was a soldier, but there is little need for them today. Lord Manchester hired me though I had little experience."

"You miss the army?"

"I miss doing something I knew," he said. "I make a poor valet. My lord had to teach me how to tie a cravat. I know I irritate him because I am always there. But I need the position and I am not sure how to please him."

She smiled up at his earnestness and the way he seemed to be surprised at his own words, that he was even uttering them. She told herself she only wanted more information for Monique, but there was something about him that made her feel comfortable. "You are happy with him?"

"Yes," he said simply. "He has been kind to my family. He gave my mother a position and allowed my young sister to move in. But he is not used to having a servant and I am not used to being one. We both struggle with that problem."

Dani was fascinated with him. "You fought in France?"

"Yes," he said simply, obviously realizing that she was French.

She smiled to let him know she understood. Then she moved away. "I have an errand for my mistress."

"And who might that be?"

"Monique Fremont. She is an actress."

"And you like your employment?"

"*Oui,*" she said, suddenly almost speechless. Dani knew she should hurry on. She had never dithered like this before. She had never even been tempted to stay a moment in a man's company.

"I must go," she said.

"I hope we will meet again."

Dani was surprised by the fact that she hoped the same thing. Not only that, she wished she had combed her hair more neatly, that she wore something other than the black-and-white maid's dress that she wore by her own choosing.

She could only nod and dart around him, heading for the stairs.

She forced herself not to look back. She didn't have to. How could she forget his shy smile, which oddly complimented the large, formidable body.

Gabriel lost badly at billiards, but recouped at several games of whist prior to supper. Guests had trickled into the room, one by one, and by supper time money flowed at the gaming tables.

Stanhope had been the consistent winner at the tables, and Gabriel suspected he was cheating. Gabriel's gaze would catch the earl running his fingers over the cards as he dealt. At the call for supper Stanhope had won several thousand pounds. As they parted, his host offered to keep the winnings in his safe upstairs. Games would resume later, he announced.

Gabriel followed his host up the stairs to dress for supper, noting that Stanhope continued to the end of the hall. He watched until Stanhope entered a room, then went to his own room.

Smythe was waiting for him. He looked odd, almost as if he were in a trance, but Gabriel had no time to question him. It took all their efforts to get him into snug-fitting pantaloons and a waistcoat that was so tight he thought he would choke.

When he returned to the great hall, where the guests were congregating, Stanhope was already there, Pamela by his side.

"Manchester," Stanhope said. "You will sit next to my daughter."

Gabriel bowed to Pamela, who was dressed simply in a white muslin dress with a high waist. Her hair was dressed only with a ribbon holding back curls. "Enchanted," he said.

She gave him a shy, grateful smile.

He heard a loud gasp and turned around to see Monique enter the room. Everyone in the room had turned with him.

She was magnificent. Her head was held high and she walked in like a queen. The dress fell in simple elegant folds around her, and its color contrasted with the pale colors the other women wore. Her eyes flashed and her lips parted in a smile both seductive and secretive.

Several women waved their fans in disapproval, but the gaze of every man was fixed on her. Gabriel felt heat rise in his groin. Damn but his pants were tight enough already; he wondered if the sudden arousal showed. Then he noticed other men were having the same problem.

But only he had held her, had touched her intimately. Only he had heard her sigh with wonder.

He forced himself to turn his gaze back to his companion.

"She is beautiful, isn't she?" Pamela said in a small voice.

"Yes," he said honestly. "But you too are quite lovely."

Her eyes held his, seeking the truth of it.

"There is a fortunate young man, somewhere," he said.

She smiled and it truly did take his breath away.

The rest of the meal was lost in trying to conquer the unruly emotions he felt. Desire coursed through him every time he glanced at Monique. So did anger. Despite all his warnings, she did not appear to realize she was clutching the tale of a tiger. He wanted to shake her. Hell, he wanted to put her on a horse and ride away.

She certainly wouldn't listen to him now. She despised him. And with reason. If only he had realized . . .

He tried to make conversation with Pamela, but she was shy even now. "Your manor is exceptional," he said.

"It is not mine," she said. "I live with my aunt some miles from here. Papa says he is gone too much and that I needed a woman's influence. But I know he doesn't like me."

He could not force himself to disagree, to lie. Stanhope did not care for another living thing. That was obvious. And he suspected she knew it and would detect a lie.

"What do you enjoy in the country?"

"I enjoy riding," she said. "And read—" She stopped suddenly.

"Do not stop," he said.

"Papa said everyone will consider me a bluestocking. He disapproves."

"I consider reading an asset," he said. "I admire intelligence."

"So does Ro—" She stopped again.

"So his name is Robert?" he said in a low enough voice that their neighbors could not hear.

Her cheeks reddened. "You will not say anything . . ."

"No," he reassured her.

Still, her hand trembled slightly.

"I swear it," he said.

They were like a small island at the table. The gentleman next to him totally ignored him, and the guests across the table glanced at him as one would look at a zoo animal and then glanced at Pamela with sympathy. Monique had not once looked his way, and he noticed her deep in conversation with Stanhope. Too frequently her light laughter drifted down to him, and he wanted to . . .

Hell, he wanted her in bed again. He wanted her hands running over his back. He wanted . . .

"She is so vivacious," Pamela said softly.

"Aye," he said.

"I wish I could be like her."

He looked down at her again, her earnestness was reflected in blue eyes that were not quite as dark as Monique's. Once again, he was struck by vague resemblances in their faces.

"I like you the way you are," he said.

"You are nothing like they . . ." Again, she stopped.

"And what do they say?"

Her face flushed, and she went silent.

He turned back to his food. There were innumerable offerings of beef and quail, venison and salmon. The sight of so much food killed what appetite he had.

But he ate as his mind turned to more important matters, mainly the safe Stanhope mentioned. He wondered whether it had the same combination as the one in his town home. He had to find a way to get to it. The only time, he knew, would be at supper tomorrow night.

Gabriel had one day to find it. He and the others would be leaving the day after tomorrow. That meant he had to find a way to miss supper tomorrow night. He needed an excuse that would eliminate him as a suspect.

"Manchester," Stanhope said loudly from the front of the table. "How do you find the English countryside?"

"I find your part of it very amiable," he replied.

"You have not been to your holdings yet?"

"I have," he said, realizing everyone at the table was listening. Stanhope was deliberately baiting him. He had to know, as everyone had to know, that his holdings were poor.

His eyes met Monique's. Her expression was masked.

Stammel spoke up. "Of course, your father's name is a problem. Everyone remembers—"

Gabriel bit back what he wanted to say. Instead, he said mildly, "That is history, my lord, and has nothing to do with me."

"We have just been at war with America," said another. "Where were your sympathies?"

"I have made my choice," he said.

"Oh, posh," Monique said with a soft laughter. "Such dull conversation. I prefer to hear more about the prince and the ball that has all London talking."

In seconds everyone was talking about the upcoming ball that the Prince of Wales had announced. He was surprised at Monique's assistance and, indeed, how neatly she had accomplished turning attention away from him.

The rest of the supper was interminable. He engaged Pamela as much as he could, drawing out the fact that she also painted. Her eyes lit as she talked about it and her mare. She was obviously a gentle and sensitive soul, and he liked her tremendously. He hoped that the demise of Stanhope would make it possible for her to have her own life. He certainly did not want her hurt by his actions.

*Did she love her father as well as fear him?*

The meal finally drew to an end after plates of various desserts were offered to the guests.

They stood, and Pamela said, "Thank you, my lord. I will join the ladies."

"Perhaps you will show me the gardens tomorrow."

"Perhaps," she said, then added mischievously, "Or perhaps Miss Fremont will."

"I think she is occupied," he replied.

"I think not," she said, then turned and left before he could say anything more.

"Join us for brandy and cigars," Stanhope said, appearing at his side.

"Of course," Gabriel said. "And perhaps another game of whist."

As Monique had left the table, Stanhope bent over and kissed her hand.

"I must entertain my guests," he said. "But perhaps we can have a word later."

"I have had a long day, my lord," she said. "I plan to retire shortly."

She saw anger in his eyes, and the effort he made to conceal it. He held her hand possessively. "It is time to make your choice, Miss Fremont."

"Two more weeks," she reminded him. "You promised . . ."

"I promised nothing. I thought only to humor you for a while."

She looked up at him with an expression that usually won whatever she wanted.

He would have none of it. "Do not play with me, Monique."

She felt a chill run through her, even terror. She forced herself to look up at him. "I made a bargain with the other two. I cannot break it."

"We will see about that," he said in a low voice.

Then he turned around with a smile and accepted a compliment over the supper.

She recalled Manchester's warning.

"Miss Fremont."

She turned around. One of the wives was standing there. "We are retiring to the music room. Will you join us?"

It was the last thing she wanted, but she had no choice. She wanted to retire to her room. She wanted to sort out impressions. She wanted to wash away the memory of Manchester smiling so easily at Pamela.

*"Merci.* That would be very pleasant," she said.

Aware that she was asked only out of politeness to the host and most certainly not for herself, she obediently followed the other ladies into a room dominated by a pianoforte. A young woman was asked to play and sat down at the pianoforte. She played well enough and had a pleasant voice, but the song had little appeal for Monique.

She wanted to leave and would have were it not for the presence of Pamela Kane. Monique found it hard to keep her eyes from her half sister, from the unhappiness in her eyes.

Just moments ago, Pamela had conversed with Manchester with lively interest. She had smiled.

Was her sister falling in love with a man Monique knew to be a rogue?

And what could she do about it? What should she do?

Manchester was only using Pamela to get to her father.

Just, she feared, as he had used her.

His leaving that morning remained a festering wound, but she had no intention of letting him know it. That was one reason she'd stepped in tonight when he'd obviously been a baited bear. She did not want to see anyone humiliated that way, particularly when she remembered the pain in his voice when he had spoken of his father.

Or was that too only an act?

Pamela rose, declared she had a headache. It was all that Monique needed. She too, stood. "I am feeling a bit ill," she said.

Pamela's declaration drew sympathy. Hers obviously did not. She was an outsider, a curiosity, an oddity, and not particularly a welcomed one after the way all male eyes had followed her tonight.

Pamela waited for her at the door and they left together.

Monique wanted to say something. In truth, she wanted to put her arms around Pamela and tell her someone cared about her. She wanted to warn her sister against Manchester, but how could she do that when she herself had made the same error?

Was it protectiveness or jealousy? If the latter, why?

Manchester was despicable.

"Thank you for what you did," Pamela said shyly as they reached the second floor. "What Papa and his friend did was . . . unfair."

Monique stopped. Her chance. "Be cautious of them all," she said.

"But Lord Manchester is kind," Pamela said.

Manchester was many things, but kind was not a term Monique would apply. A chameleon was a more apt description. A man who changed constantly, according to his environment and his purposes.

"He wants something from your father."

"I know that," Pamela said.

Monique was surprised at the confidence in her tone.

Pamela drew her over to the side of the hall and looked around, obviously assuring herself that no one was listening. "Can I tell you a secret? Will you keep it for me?"

Monique was startled. "You would trust me?"

"I saw the looks between you and Lord Manchester," Pamela said. "I do not want you to believe he is faithless."

Pamela was not the shy unworldly girl everyone thought. And now she was searching Monique's face for confirmation of trust.

"I will keep your confidence," she replied simply.

"I . . . care about a man back home. My father will not even consider him. Lord Manchester sensed that. He offered me a bargain. I will accept his suit and he will give me his protection. As long as he appears interested, my father will not try to marry me to someone . . . I do not like. I know he does not care about me in a romantic way and I can be at ease with him."

"And if it comes to marriage?"

"He will back out. I will be discarded. My reputation ruined. No other man will want me. Perhaps then I will be free . . ."

Monique was stunned. She suspected Manchester did not

care about Pamela. Yet to spell out his intentions to Pamela was so foreign to what she had expected of him. He was a man who kept explanations to a minimum, who guarded his secrets as well as she guarded hers.

What other secrets did he have?

She tried again. "You looked as if you enjoyed each other."

"Because we do not need to pretend with each other," Pamela said. "He seems interested in me simply because of me." It was said with such humble surprise in her voice that Monique's heart went out to her.

"Do you know your father well?"

"No. I cannot remember ever seeing him much as a child. It has just been lately that he has shown any interest in me, and I think that is to advance some plans he has." Pamela reached out. "Be careful, Miss Fremont. I have heard . . . stories."

Monique was touched. Pamela was risking much to warn her. She wanted to tell Pamela everything, but she feared she might be putting her sister in danger. If Pamela told Stanhope who she was, or let anything slip, they both would be at risk.

"Thank you," she said instead, "I will heed your warning."

"You and Lord Manchester . . . you are in love."

"No," Monique said, sharper than she should.

Pamela shook her head. "It was in your eyes, Miss Fremont, and in his."

"Nonsense," Monique said. "I care nothing for him. He is impertinent and a rogue."

"Some women like rogues."

"I am not among them."

Pamela shifted uncomfortably. "I just want you to know. You are so pretty and Lord Manchester is handsome . . ."

"I appreciate your advice more than you will ever know, Lady Pamela," she said.

Pamela blushed. "You will not tell my father?" she asked again anxiously.

"Of course not." Monique hesitated a moment, then added, "I should like us to be friends."

Pamela's face lit.

"And I would like to hear about the man who has stolen your heart."

"I would like that, too," Pamela said, her eyes sparkling.

"Perhaps we may have lunch together."

"I can ask the cook to prepare a picnic," Pamela said. "There are ruins not far away, and we can take horses. You do ride?" she added.

"Yes, but not well."

"Then we will choose a mannered horse."

"And you? Do you ride well?"

"Yes," Pamela said. "I like riding. And painting. I would like to sketch you if I may."

"I would be honored," Monique said, eager to spend time with her sister. Thievery could wait.

"Then I shall see you at noon?"

"Yes."

"You may have breakfast in your room, you know," Pamela said. "I asked. I do not care for most of the guests. They are rude."

"Except for Lord Manchester," Monique said.

"Yes, except for him. He is different." She frowned. "Most of the men are going hunting tomorrow. I am afraid . . ."

"Do not be afraid for Manchester," she said. "He is a superb rider."

Relief spread over her face. "That is good. I do not trust Lord Stammel. He does not like Manchester. He owes him money. I heard him complaining to my father about it."

Monique didn't know if she concealed her surprise. She knew, of course, that Manchester gambled. That much was in the London sheets. But she was under the impression he lost, not won.

Different sides of the complicated Manchester continued emerging.

But now at least she knew he was not serious about marrying her sister.

She was relieved for Pamela's sake, and that was all.

"Tomorrow then," Pamela said.

"Yes. I would not miss it."

Pamela continued up another flight of steps.

Monique watched her go up, a lightness to her steps. For the first time she seemed a girl of twenty. A happy girl.

Monique was five years older. She felt eons older.

In just a few days there had been a change in her, at least partially because of Manchester.

Monique looked around the hall. No one there, not even servants. The men were smoking, drinking, gambling, the women listening to their younger members playing the pianoforte. She'd been such a misfit.

She did not want to be one of them. She never wanted to be one of them. Yet she'd felt such an odd sense of loneliness, of belonging nowhere. For the first time she wondered what it would be like to feel secure like those women did, to know exactly one's place.

Monique opened the door, hoping Dani would be there with the information she needed.

Dani was there, curled up in a chair, reading a book by an oil lamp. She put it down on the floor as Monique came in. "I discovered where Lord Stanhope's rooms are."

"Where?"

"At the end of the hall," she said.

Monique saw an odd expression on her face, something like wistfulness. She knew Dani well and had never seen it there before.

"Did something happen?"

Dani shrugged her shoulders. "I met a valet. He works for Manchester. He claims that the marquess is a kind employer, that he took in his mother and sister."

Dani had always been sympathetic to Manchester, ever since that first ride in the carriage. Her attitude had changed after his desertion of her the other night, but now . . .

Monique pieced that together with what Pamela had said.

Manchester most certainly was an extraordinarily complicated man. She was also bemused by what Dani was not saying. There was a look on her face that told Monique she was holding something back.

"Tell me about the valet."

"He kept me from falling when I was rushing down the hall," she said. "Then I saw him later in the servants' hall. He is a former soldier, not a valet by trade. He needed employment to feed his mother and sister, and Manchester selected him over a large number of more qualified applicants. He did not even know how to tie a cravat, he said. Then when Lord Manchester discovered he had a young sister, he employed the mother and allowed the child to move in with him."

The tumble of words was far more than Monique had ever heard from Dani before. Amused but still a bit wary, she asked, "What does this ex-soldier look like?"

"He was a sergeant and he is very large. But shy. His hands are huge but they were . . . gentle."

Monique stared at her friend. Dani had never, ever used the word *gentle* before. Nor had she ever expressed the slightest interest in a man.

She did not know whether to be delighted or afraid for Dani.

Just as she did not know whether she should be afraid for herself.

She no longer knew what was true and right.

And of what to be most afraid.

# Chapter Nineteen

As he always did, Gabriel woke at the first glimmer of dawn. He had slept restlessly after a late evening of gaming. He'd lost on purpose, but not badly.

Memories haunted his sleep . . . his father's face when he had handed him the envelope, the desperate plea in his voice minutes before he killed himself. Monique's clear, sharp voice when she had defended him earlier tonight when he could not defend himself. Pamela's face as she smiled.

If he ruined Stanhope, would she be as devastated as he had been? Stanhope was still her father, and scandal could haunt her as it had haunted Gabriel's mother.

But could he allow Stanhope to continue to plunder?

Or was that only an excuse for revenge? Was he his brother's keeper, or an obsessed man out for vengeance, regardless of who was hurt?

He'd never been plagued before by doubts.

He would have to decide soon. Stanhope had asked him to join a hunt at eleven, then wanted to see him at five this afternoon. He did not look forward to the hunt. He had never enjoyed hunting for sport. He'd seen too much death to consider it as entertainment.

He decided to clear his head by a ride this morning before

the other guests rose. It would not be as fine as dawn at sea,
but it would do.

He pulled on a pair of riding breeches and shaved himself
as he always did. Smythe would be at his door in minutes.

As predicted, his light knock came just as Gabriel was
wiping his face. His face was, as usual, anxious to be of service. "May I help you with your clothes? Or a bath?" he asked
hopefully, though he obviously had been perplexed by
Gabriel's frequent bathing habits.

"I think you sleep with your ears open to the moment I
wake," Gabriel said.

"I try, my lord."

"There you go with the 'my lord' nonsense again."

"It is best to do so here."

Gabriel considered that for a moment. Then he looked at
Smythe closely. He wondered if Smythe knew—or suspected—far more than he'd thought.

"Did you see Dani last night?" It was none of his business.
He realized that, but he wanted to know more about Monique
and wondered whether Dani had confided in Smythe in any
way.

Smythe looked uncomfortable and yet there was a slight
smile on his face. "Yes, sir."

He wanted to continue but found he could not use Smythe
in that way. It would not be fair to ask.

"I am taking Specter for a ride this morning," he said.
"Then there is a hunt and a meeting with my host. I will not
need you hovering around until just before five. Perhaps you
can find something to do with Miss Fremont's Dani."

He watched as a smile played on Smythe's lips. By God,
but his man was smitten.

•    "I will be here to help you prepare for supper," Smythe
said.

"That will be more than adequate. And now you can help
find my riding coat and a clean shirt. Since you've become so
adept at cravats, I can use your help there."

In minutes he had dressed in a riding coat and breeches and
struggled with pulling on his boots. Even with boot hooks, it
took longer than he liked. The damn things came to his knee.

But they were fashionable, and the Marquess of Manchester needed to be fashionable.

He stopped by the dining room. Plates already covered the sideboard. He took ham, eggs, and cold fowl from the offerings and sat alone. Apparently few rose at this hour.

Halfway through the meal, Lady Pamela entered. She gave him the usual shy smile, then busied herself at the table. She was dressed in a riding costume.

She looked at him, at his clothing.

"You are going riding?" she asked.

"Aye. I hate to waste a good morning."

"So do I," she said with a grin. "May I accompany you?"

"It would be my pleasure."

"My father does not like me to ride. He does not like me to do anything alone, so I leave long before he rises," she confided. She stole a quick glance at him. "I plan to ride with Miss Freemont later. I don't think my father will object to that."

She had changed in the past few days. She was still obviously afraid of her father but more willing to defy him. Perhaps because she felt she had an ally now.

They both finished their meal quickly, then went out to the stable.

He'd been surprised at her announcement that she planned to ride with Miss Fremont later in the day. He had noted Monique's quick glances toward Pamela, but he had not thought she would try to befriend the girl. Was Lady Pamela part of whatever plan she had?

He would not have thought that of her. And yet what common interest could there be between a young country-bred aristocrat and an actress?

He planned to ask that question. He did not want Lady Pamela hurt.

Yet he was planning to destroy Pamela's father. Hypocrisy? Bloody hell, he hated questioning himself.

They reached the stables and a sleepy lad saddled two horses, his Specter and a pretty mare for Pamela.

He helped Pamela mount, then mounted himself. He noted immediately that she was a fine horsewoman. She led the way, moving from a walk into a trot, then a canter. "There are ruins nearby," she called to him.

Gabriel followed, enjoying the bite of the morning chill. He did not have to act with Pamela. She accepted everything he said he was, and liked him anyway.

They rode for thirty minutes or so, then drew up at old stone ruins.

"This was the first Stanhope hold," she said. "I was told about it two days ago when I first arrived, and rode to see it. There is such an air of desolation here. Sadness." Her lips pursed in concentration. "I believe two lovers died here."

She slid down from the sidesaddle and tied the reins to a tree. He did the same and followed her into the ruins. Then she stood there.

"I can almost hear them," she said.

"You are a romantic, Lady Pamela."

"Yes, I am," she said. "For years I had little to do but read, and I loved romantic stories. Then a neighbor taught me to ride, and I found something I was good at."

"And painting," he said.

"I said I liked it," she said. "I did not say I was good at it."

"I imagine you are very good at it."

"I am going to sketch Miss Fremont when we come here this afternoon," Pamela said. "She said I could." A gleam danced in her eyes.

"Are you trying to tell me something, Lady Pamela?"

"Whatever would that be, my lord?"

"You are a minx," he said. "And you look so . . ."

"Malleable?" she said disdainfully.

He stared at her for a long time. "I thought that at first, but now I think there is a great deal more strength than you believe."

The wistful look returned. "I have always wanted to be strong. I always dreamed myself as brave and independent. But then my father comes, and I . . . all that courage leaves me."

He remembered what Pamela had said about her young man. Her father would destroy his father. How could they have any happiness based on misery and destruction?

She looked into his eyes. "But you and Miss Fremont do not have that problem."

"I believe we have many problems, Lady Pamela."

"Call me Pamela," she said. "Why? I saw the way you looked at her, and the way she looked at you. She called you impertinent and a rogue."

He raised an eyebrow. "And you believe that means she is interested in me?"

"It was the way she said it."

"And you decided to try to unite us," he concluded.

"I thought you might like to know she will be here this afternoon. We will have a picnic, and I . . . we would very much like to have you join us."

"How could I resist such a charming invitation?"

"You are laughing at me."

"Never, my lady."

"Then you will come?"

"I will try," he said, once more wondering why she was so much Monique's champion. Because of the faint resemblance? But that meant nothing.

"Tell me more about the ruins," he said, changing the subject.

"They date back to the tenth century," she said. "They are said to be haunted and no one comes here."

"Except you?"

"I think they are kind ghosts who are looking for each other."

He was beginning to understand a little. She did not think she and her love would ever be together. So she was trying to unite two other people.

He felt the terrible fraud. "I think we should go," he said.

"I wish to stay."

"Then what kind of gentleman would I be to leave you alone to fend for yourself? Your father would horsewhip me."

"I think not," she said with a small sigh.

He stood there waiting. He would not leave her here alone. In a moment she surrendered with a small sigh. "All right."

He helped her mount. "You see," he said. "It is a good thing I stayed to help you mount."

She gave him a heartbreaking twist of the lips that was meant to be a smile.

"Do not give up your dreams, Lady Pamela," he said softly.

"You really care about them?" she said with that vulnerability that always struck a chord in him.

"Yes," he said.

"You are a very nice man, my lord."

He wondered whether she would keep that thought after he ruined her father.

They laughed together as if they were sisters.

Monique sat amidst the ruins while Pamela sketched. She found herself repeatedly looking into her sister's face and had to force herself to look up at the cloudless sky. It was a true blue. The same color as her sister's eyes.

She wondered how someone so untouched had survived Stanhope. Only, she thought, because Stanhope had not wanted anything to do with her, just as he'd wanted a child five years older than Pamela to disappear.

"May I see?" she asked.

She watched emotion flit across Pamela's face. Embarrassment. A little pride. "It is not very good," Pamela said.

Monique rose and went over and looked at it.

She had never seen herself in the mirror with that expression.

A slight smile crossed her face in the sketch. She looked younger. Wistful. Yet there was a quality of movement in the sketch. Of vitality. It was as if there were two people in the sketch. Two personalities.

It was very good indeed.

"How long have you been sketching?" she asked.

Pamela shrugged. "I used to draw as a child, but it was my secret. I was afraid . . ."

Afraid that pleasure would be taken from her. "Did you have an education?"

"Oh, yes. The vicar in the village came to our home twice a week. He would bring me books."

"No other children?"

Pamela shook her head. "But I used to visit the stables, and the grooms were kind. Just like Adam here."

How could anyone be unkind to her? Except their father. "Did you see your father much?"

Pamela's expression did not change. "Rarely. He would come and stare at me, then look away. Sometimes he would ask a question but I was always too frightened of him to answer."

"But you are no longer so afraid?"

Pamela said nothing for a moment. "He does not love me. He only wishes to use me. I know that. But I am braver. Lord Manchester says I should seek my own dream. I wish that I could, but how can you take happiness at the expense of someone else?"

"Who is someone else?"

"I have already said too much," she said.

"I will never repeat a word," Monique promised.

"Robert. His father is a doctor. My father would never approve of the match. My aunt found us together and said my father would ruin his family. My father had other plans for me, she said."

"Lord Manchester."

"Yes," Pamela said.

"You can always come to me," Monique said.

Pamela looked up at her. "Why?"

Monique took a deep breath. "I do not have a sister," she said. "I would like one."

"I have a duty to my family."

*No.* Monique wanted to scream the word. No one had a duty to a monster like Stanhope. But then many people would not have defended Monique's mother, either. She had been a whore.

Not even fashionably unpure, as some courtesans in London were called. No such exalted term for her mother.

"You are very good at sketching. Have you ever tried oils?"

"I have no money."

Monique wanted to kill Stanhope with her own two hands. Everything in his two homes announced the fact that he was a very wealthy man. Yet, he could not spare a pound or two for paints and canvas.

"You look happier than before," she said.

"I think Lord Manchester has given me courage."

"How?" she asked.

"He talks to me as though I am someone he truly likes, as if I am truly worth knowing."

Pain drove through Monique. She had felt that way. Worthless. Helpless. Then she was introduced to the theater. That had given dignity back to her, a sense of worth. Still, if it were not for Dani, she would be very lonely indeed.

"Do you have friends?"

"Only Robert. My father did not want me 'tainted,' but I met Robert one day in the town, and I was able to meet him occasionally. He bought me the sketching pad. I knew, though, that my father intended a prestigious marriage for me. I was . . . surprised when it was Lord Manchester."

"Why?"

"He is not like the other men around my father," she said simply.

He was not, Monique admitted.

Pamela was sketching again, her fingers moving quickly over the pad. Monique saw her eyes on a bird perched on a limb. Her face was creased in concentration.

Monique closed her eyes, pledging to herself that regardless of what happened she would make sure Pamela had some safety. Monique had funds she had saved these past few years. They were meant to be used to destroy Stanhope, but Pamela's salvation was more important.

Monique decided she would see a solicitor as soon as they returned. If anything happened to her, she wanted Pamela to have the resources necessary to move beyond Stanhope's reach.

Gabriel trailed along with the pack of hunters, purposely staying toward the rear. He planned to angle away later and ride to the ruins.

He knew he shouldn't.

Yet he was as drawn to them as surely as a magnet to a

lodestone. He told himself he wanted to know why Monique had interjected a defense for him last night to the displeasure of men she was trying to attract.

Specter was rested after the morning ride, but he was unusually skittish. Gabriel concentrated on maintaining control. Stammel approached him once and raised an eyebrow. "Problems?"

"None I cannot handle."

"I suppose Americans are not as accomplished as we in England."

"I suppose it depends on what accomplishments you mean," Gabriel said in a steady voice. "Gaming for instance. You still have not yet honored your debt."

Stammel glared at him, then cantered away.

Specter started to follow, then bucked slightly. It was so unexpected, Gabriel almost lost his seat. He allowed the others to go ahead, then when they were out of sight, he dismounted and checked the blanket and saddle. Spots of blood stained the underneath of the blanket.

He ran his hand over the blanket and found a small burr there. He dislodged it. If he had been less accomplished, he could well be lying on the ground somewhere.

Stammel? Daven? Stanhope? Which one wanted him injured?

He doubted it was Stanhope. The earl still hoped to drain him of what funds he might have. Daven had no reason.

Stammel actively and publicly disliked him. Besides he owed him money.

He would have to be more careful than he'd thought. Until now, he'd considered Stanhope the main threat. He doubted now whether Stanhope had any idea of what Stammel—if it was Stammel—had intended.

Another little wedge between the partners. Perhaps tonight he could make a deeper one.

With those thoughts in mind, he took the reins and started the long walk back.

So much for temptation. He would not have time to find a new horse and ride to the ruins. He was no longer surprised that he felt a jolt of loss. He told himself it was for the best.

For both of them.

He only wished he did not regret it so.

The meeting with Stanhope was short.

Stanhope had arrived just prior to the arranged meeting.

"We lost you," he said. "The groom said you came walking back."

"Oddly enough, I found a burr under the blanket of my horse."

Stanhope stared at him. "The groom didn't say anything."

"I didn't tell him what had happened. Only that he had some kind of irritation."

"Why?"

"I thought it should be your business," Gabriel said.

"You obviously believe it was intentional."

"I cannot understand how else a burr would get under a saddle," Gabriel remarked dryly.

"And whom do you suspect?"

Gabriel shrugged. "Stammel owes me money," he said simply.

He saw Stanhope's eyes glint. "I will approach him about it," he said. "You can be sure that nothing like that will happen again."

"I hope not. I should hate to go to the authorities," Gabriel said.

A silence.

"Be assured that I will have a long discussion with Robert," Stanhope said.

He leaned back in his chair. "Now do you plan to make an offer for my daughter?" he said.

"I do not wish to rush her, but I believe she favors my suit."

"Several people saw you return together this morning," Stanhope stated in an accusing voice. "That is not done in England, not with young people who are not engaged."

So he did know more about Pamela's movements than she suspected. "It was an accidental meeting," he said.

"Nonetheless . . ."

"Society would question such a quick engagement," Gabriel said. "I would not wish to harm her reputation."

"I did not think you concerned yourself about such things."

"I hope to stay in England and take my rightful place as well as title," Gabriel said pompously. "I cannot do that if more scandal haunts me or my intended bride."

"Just do not wait too long," Stanhope warned. "Or I shall look elsewhere."

"I would hope for a little more security first," Gabriel continued. "Our business arrangement . . ."

"Do you have your share?"

"I should have it next week. I would like to know the particulars."

"I will show you the contracts on Tuesday upon my return." He stood, as if dismissing Gabriel.

Gabriel also stood. "And now I believe I will explore your maze. I have been intrigued by it since I arrived."

Stanhope looked pleased. "Yes. It is quite intricate. Guests have been lost there for hours."

*Only Stanhope would think that amusing.*

"If we do not see you by supper's end, I will send a servant for you," Stanhope said. "We plan to have games of chance again tonight. I am sure you will want to join us."

It was a challenge again. The man seemed to love them. It didn't call for an answer.

Gabriel bowed slightly and left the room.

He stood outside for a moment, then went out the front door, telling the butler he was going to the maze.

"My lord, perhaps you would like to take a footman with you," he said anxiously. "Supper is in an hour."

Gabriel gave him every bit the haughty look that the gentleman earlier had bestowed upon him.

"No," he said. "I wish to discover its secrets on my own."

The man looked dubious but stepped back. "If you do not return . . ."

"You are not to bother yourself," Gabriel said arrogantly.

The butler backed away.

Gabriel walked briskly to the maze. No one else appeared interested at the moment. Few guests were outside; those that were apparently were returning from calling on neighbors. The grooms were busy with incoming carriages, but he made sure they saw him.

He reached the entrance of the maze and entered, immediately enveloped by the tall manicured shrubs. Instead of exploring further, he very carefully sat down. He had no intention of becoming lost. He planned to wait until an hour passed and supper started. Most of the servants would be busy.

He would then visit Stanhope's rooms and perhaps a few others.

Perhaps he could find enough to pay his share of the partnership.

He closed his eyes.

And started counting minutes.

Monique went to the window. She looked below and saw Manchester walk toward the maze. She had heard servants talk about it, how difficult it was. People had been trapped for hours.

Yet Manchester walked into it alone.

He truly was a fool.

She still was stung from the fact he had not appeared at the ruins as Pamela had expected him to do. She shook the thought from her head and turned to Dani. "Tonight," she said. "We will strike tonight. Have you found someplace to hide whatever we find?"

"*Oui,*" Dani said. "The best place is in the earl's own coach. It will take us back, will it not?"

"But how?"

"I will find a way," Dani said.

And Dani would. They had both assumed that there would be an intense search after items turned missing.

Items from Stanhope. From Stammel. Perhaps a few other guests. She wanted Stanhope's country party to end in disaster. The more she could throw him off balance the better. "You can tell Lord Stanhope's butler that I am ill. I would appreciate a bowl of soup."

"Then tonight . . ."

"Tonight I will see how well you have taught me."

*    *    *

Gabriel waited until he thought the guests would be sitting at the table. As he'd thought, no one came looking for him. Stanhope would find it a great joke to leave him here all night.

He went to the entrance of the maze and looked out. He saw no one, not even grooms.

He strode from the maze, not hurriedly or stealthily. He did not want anyone to think that he was hiding something. At the same time he hoped no one saw him. He went to the servants' entrance, not to the front one. If discovered, he would merely claim embarrassment at being late. But he saw no one; most, if not all, of the servants would be assisting with the elaborate supper.

He made it to his room without seeing anyone. Smythe was sitting there waiting for him.

Smythe rose quickly from a chair. "My lord, the Earl of Stanhope was looking for you."

"I became lost in his maze," Gabriel said. "And now I fear it is too late to join them for supper without looking the fool." He met Smythe's gaze. "I do not want you to tell anyone what time I arrived," he said.

Smythe nodded.

"You may go down and eat," Gabriel said.

"But can I not . . . ?"

"No," Gabriel said sharper than he intended. "I would like some time alone."

Smythe hesitated, then his face lit in a way Gabriel had never seen before. "Yes, sir."

Gabriel looked at him with curiosity. There was something a shade different about Smythe. "Has something happened?"

"No, my lord. I mean . . . sir. I was just with Miss Dani. Miss Fremont's maid. She is a very . . . fetching. She is French but . . ."

He was prattling. Smythe was actually prattling. And about Dani, of all women. Dani who never wore color, who seldom lifted her eyes to anyone except in defense of her mistress.

Gabriel found himself smiling.

"She seems a very nice woman," he said. He didn't add that she might be a thief as well. Well, so was he.

Smythe straightened. "I will probably not see her again."

"Why do you not go down to the kitchen and see about a meal?" Gabriel said helpfully.

"But what about you, my lord?"

"I am not hungry," Gabriel said. "I will get something later. Go. I order it."

Smythe did not object this time. Instead, the touching eagerness in his face affected Gabriel in an odd way. Perhaps because he too was feeling some discomforting signs of the same affliction.

He waited until Smythe had been gone several moments, then sipped some brandy. He spilled a little on his waistcoat. If he were found in someone's room, well, he could say that he had wandered into the wrong one after taking a glass or two. He'd been distraught about missing supper.

Gabriel started at the end of the hall. He wondered again which room had been given to Monique and whether she was in the great hall, seated next to Stanhope.

He knocked on one door, just in the event a servant was awaiting the arrival of a mistress or master, then quietly opened it.

Swiftly he went through the drawers of the clothespress. He found a box of jewelry. He picked through it and found a pair of diamond earrings. He pocketed those.

Enough here. He did not want to be too greedy, and the earrings were easily concealed.

He opened the door and left the room. Four more quick visits. Several additional items, including a jeweled pin for a cravat, more earrings, and two bracelets. Then he made his way down the hall. He had earlier asked a servant for the location of Stanhope's room. He would try that next. He wanted to inspect Stanhope's safe.

Gabriel walked swiftly to the room and knocked. No sound. He turned the knob on the door and opened it.

He stepped inside. The skin on his neck prickled. The curtains moved ever so slightly.

Leave, he told himself. Someone did not want to be seen by him and he sure as hell did not want to be seen by him.

"Stanhope?" he asked, as if he was really seeking the man. No answer.

He stepped outside, walked several steps down the hall, then leaned against a wall and waited.

No one exited immediately. Five, perhaps ten minutes went by, then the door of Stanhope's room opened.

Monique Fremont stepped out. She immediately saw him, and her face paled. Her hands were free but he saw a bulge in her dress. It should not be there.

Damn it. They could not linger here. Nor could they be found with valuables that did not belong to them.

"Come with me," he said, taking her wrist and giving her no choice.

They walked down the hall, she walking beside him. No protests. No pulling away.

He reached his room and drew her inside, then closed the door.

"What in the hell are you doing?" he said, recognizing the hypocrisy in his outrage. He was a thief. Why should he care if she were one also?

*Because it was so damned dangerous.* She had no idea of what Stanhope was capable. Now everything was clear. She had taunted all three men in order to be in a position where she could steal enough to make her very, very comfortable.

He reached out and put his fingers down into the front of her dress. It emerged with a large number of banknotes. And an exquisite diamond necklace.

"Not the ordinary place to wear one."

"Give it back," she said.

"I don't think so," he drawled slowly.

"It is none of your business."

He fingered the necklace. "This belong to Stanhope?"

"He gave it to me."

"A pretty piece. I wonder what a widower is doing with it," he mused. "A family heirloom perhaps." He paused. "If he gave it to you, then you can go downstairs with me and display it."

"No."

"If he found it in your possession, you could hang," he said softly.

"He won't find it," she said defiantly.

"So you admit you stole it."

"I admit to nothing." Her eyes narrowed. "What were you doing opening the door when he is at supper?"

"Looking for you?" he suggested with a hint of a smile.

But her eyes were looking at a small, almost unnoticeable bulge in his coat. Before he could move, her hand had touched it, then retrieved the earrings he had lifted a few moments earlier.

"They should look charming on you," she said.

"I thought so." He permitted himself a small smile before explaining, "It is meant as a gift."

"Then I look forward to seeing them on Pamela's ears." She hesitated. "Why are you not at supper?"

"I could ask the same thing, but now is not the time. As far as our host knows, I am in the maze. Lost."

"And if someone sees you?"

"I just emerged and was too embarrassed to appear for supper."

She gazed at him with suspicious admiration.

No pretense now, he noticed. But then there was no reason. They had caught each other.

"Do you know what Stanhope is?" he asked with exasperation.

"I know exactly what he is. I do not know who *you* are."

"A thief," he said. "Just as you are."

His hand cupped her chin.

She stared defiantly up at him, her eyes flashing.

He knew it. So help him, he knew better.

He leaned down and his lips brushed hers, then he crushed her against him.

He felt the reluctance in her body, then surrender.

# Chapter Twenty

His lips pressed into hers, and she responded with a desperation he had not expected.

Nor had he expected his equally frantic need.

Damn, but he wanted her. He wanted her in his arms. He wanted her under him again. But what really astonished him, the need went beyond the physical. His heart wanted her. Blazes but his soul needed her like a ship needed the sea.

He hadn't realized how much until this afternoon when he'd missed seeing her at the ruins. He hadn't realized how much until he saw her leaving Stanhope's room. His heart had dropped.

If anyone else had seen her . . .

The kiss deepened, her body melting into his in a way he well remembered. He remembered how she'd reacted to his every touch. He remembered the proud tilt of her head, her slow sensuous smile.

He released her lips but kept her hand imprisoned in his.

"You know what it would mean if he caught you with something of his?"

"Yes."

"You were willing to pay that price?"

"I would have found a way . . ."

"Not with Stanhope, damn it."

"Why do you care?" she asked. "You left . . ."

"I left because I thought you wanted something more than I could give you," he said. "I did not want to complicate things for you."

"Or yourself," she accused.

"Or me," he agreed softly. "You had no place in my plans."

"And now?"

"I want you safe." He avoided her gaze. He had not answered her question.

"But you want something else as well," she said.

"I want Stanhope in a prison colony," he said. No more games between them. She obviously had no love for Stanhope, if she was stealing from him. She would not trust him if he did not trust her. "I want his friends Stammel and Daven to keep him company."

"Why?" she said in a soft voice.

"You have heard some of the rumors about my father," he said. "He was no traitor. He was merely foolish. He trusted Stanhope."

"Then you . . ." Her voice was incredulous.

"I want to prove Stanhope and his friends are guilty of numerous crimes. I want to rub the faces of the ton in it. None of them stepped forward to help my father. Not one, even though I suspect they knew the truth."

"And Pamela? Is she part of your scheme?"

"I will do nothing to hurt Pamela." He paused, searching her face. "You care for her?"

She looked at him for a very long moment, then shrugged. "I feel sorry for any daughter of Stanhope's."

He considered that. But something in her eyes told him it was not the complete truth. He decided to push her. "Now," he said, "it is your turn at some explanations."

She looked at him without guile. "He hurt someone I care about."

"Who?"

She didn't reply.

"How were you going to explain the missing money? You were the only person missing from supper."

"Except for you?"

"But you did not know that."

"I saw you go into the maze."

He stared at her. "You were willing to lay the blame on me?"

"I truly thought you would return in time for supper."

"It seems we have a bit of a problem now. We have both taken belongings that do not belong to us. You know my reasons. I want to know more about yours."

"It is none of your affair."

"If I am to be partly blamed for your misdeeds, it is. Stanhope will tear this place apart to find that money, and we are the only two people missing from supper. The jewelry that I took, well, that could have been taken at any time. The money in the safe, no."

His hand cupped her chin, forcing her to look directly into his eyes, then ran his fingers lightly along her cheekbones. "We will be the first suspects."

"Not if we both lost valuables, too," she said.

"That might be a little too convenient."

"You are protected. The staff believes you are still in the maze."

"But you are not, and Stanhope's no fool. The gaming will begin tonight after supper. He will be checking his safe."

"Perhaps not," she said with a small smile. "Dani put laudanum in the wine to be served to him tonight. Apparently he saves the best for himself. He will be very sleepy."

He stared at her, trying to cloak his admiration for her daring. And his fear for her recklessness.

She returned his gaze.

"Who did he hurt?" he asked suddenly.

"What do you mean?"

"You said he hurt someone you cared about. Whoever it was must be very important to take the risks you are taking."

She shrugged. "What difference does it make? He hurts people. You said he kills people."

"I did not realize you were listening."

"I was," she said.

"How did you get those banknotes? Stanhope said he was putting them into a safe."

She did not say anything.

"Ah, the estimable Miss Fremont can crack safes."

"And how did *you* plan to get into it?"

"I do not think we have time to trade secrets at the moment," he said. "I was only going to investigate his room, perhaps pay a visit later when Stammel might also be wandering around."

Her eyes widened. "Stammel?"

"He needs money. Stanhope also lost a bit of money from a safe in his London home recently," he added. "No one had been inside except Daven and Stammel, and Stammel seems to be more in need of money. In fact, he owes me a sizeable gambling debt, and, oddly enough, I had a slight accident today. A burr underneath the saddle of my horse."

Concern flashed across her face. "Your horse threw you?"

"He tried. I found the burr before much damage was done."

"Does anyone know?"

"I told our host. I thought he should know. I think Stammel did it on his own. Stanhope still hopes to take a sizeable amount of money from me. He will strike then."

She studied his face.

"Give me the money," he said.

"No."

"I can get it back before he knows it's gone. You obviously know the combination to the safe now. You can reclaim it after tonight's gaming."

"How?"

"Oh, I think I can lure him out by claiming that a diamond pin is missing and accuse him of harboring a thief. I will throw suspicion on Stammel. It will not be difficult after the incident with the horse. I will make such a scene that guests will be pouring out of their rooms. A few other guests will find a few items missing. They will also be found in Stammel's rooms. He would have had opportunities today to steal them. He would not have had an opportunity to rifle Stanhope's safe."

"And?"

"If Stanhope turns on Stammel, Stammel might well turn on him."

"And I should trust you?"

"Yes."

"Why?" she asked defiantly.

"Because we have the same goals, perhaps even similar reasons. But most of all, you could get caught and that might inconvenience me."

"Inconvenience you?"

"I would have to rescue you."

"No one rescues me. I've been taking care of myself since—" She stopped suddenly.

"Since when?"

She shrugged. Then seemed to surrender. "I will take it back."

"No,"

"How can I be sure you . . ."

"Trust, Monique. A little trust."

"I am not good at trusting."

He wasn't sure he trusted her that much either. "It is late," he said. "If Stanhope returns earlier than we think, I would rather that I be discovered in his room." He thrust the jewels he'd stolen into her hands. "You can put these in Stammel's room. If he comes in, you can say that you were waiting to see him and tell him you'd decided in Daven's favor."

She did not argue. Instead, she took one long look at him, gave him the combination to the safe, then left the room.

He watched as she walked down the hall. Before long, servants would be streaming back to prepare for the needs of their lords and ladies. He and Monique did not have much time.

Gabriel made it into Stanhope's room and quickly found the safe. In seconds he had it open and placed the banknotes inside. Then he closed it.

As he rose from where he'd knelt, he heard a noise outside the room, the turn of a knob, the creak of a door opening. Then he heard a familiar feminine voice.

"My lord. "Monique's voice came drifting through the

crack in the door. "I am feeling so much better. I understand you have musicians downstairs. I would so . . . like to hear them with you."

"My dear, a delightful offer, but I am holding some funds, and I seem to be . . . more tired than . . . I thought."

"Just for a few moments," she pleaded. "I do not think the other ladies like me and I do not want to sit alone. A few moments only."

"I must get money from my safe first," he said. "My guests . . . are waiting."

Gabriel glanced around. His gaze caught the huge bed that dominated the room. He hurried around and sank to the floor, praying he was out of sight of the door.

He flattened himself even farther as it opened.

"May I come inside, too," Monique said in a flirtatious voice.

"Of course," Stanhope said. "I will be only a moment."

Gabriel heard the rustle of skirts as she moved between Stanhope and the bed. In seconds that seemed like minutes and minutes that seemed like hours, he heard Stanhope's voice. It was slurred. He wondered exactly how much laudanum Dani had applied.

"Your manor is exquisite," Monique said.

"You could stay here with me," Stanhope said, his voice even more slurred than before.

Then he heard a sudden gasp and a grunt. He knew without seeing that Stanhope was embracing Monique. His skin crawled. He wanted to stand and throw Stanhope across the floor. He almost did.

He heard nothing else for several moments. Then the sound of a body falling on the bed. A soft snoring. He looked up to see Monique approach him, a finger of one hand to her mouth. He watched as she moved to the door and looked out, then summoned him with the other hand. He rose silently, glanced at the sleeping Stanhope.

He longed to kill him with his bare hands. Not only for his father but for touching Monique.

Then he turned to the door and went out. She was standing outside.

"The jewels?" he asked.

"In Stammel's trunk."

He nodded. Her face was flushed, her lips swollen. Her hair was mussed. "The bastard," he said as he tucked a curl behind her ear.

"I will fetch his valet," she said. "Did you replace the notes?"

"Aye."

She looked in his face. "And now?"

"I will go down and play a game of whist or two. I will be most embarrassed about being lost in the maze. And then I will retire for the night, only to find my most prized cravat pin missing."

Sheepishly, she looked up at him. "I still have the necklace."

He grinned at her. "I still have the earrings."

"Give them to me," she said. "Dani has found a place in the Stanhope's coach to hide them."

He looked at her for a very long moment. She was so bloody damned beautiful. He handed her the earrings, then touched her cheek with tenderness. "You are a very intriguing woman, Monique Fremont."

He leaned over and kissed her. Before he completely lost his senses, he turned and hurried down the stairs, where he heard loud voices of guests moving around.

He missed Monique already.


Once in her room Monique leaned against the closed door and drew a long breath.

Dani was there, looking anxious. "You went without me?"

Monique handed over the pieces of purloined jewelry to her. "Hide them for us," she said. "I believe there will be some kind of outcry before dawn."

Dani looked at her curiously.

"Lord Manchester found me leaving Stanhope's room."

Dani was silent. Waiting.

"He was about a bit of thievery himself. I had taken banknotes from Stanhope's safe. He pointed out, rightly enough, that only a few guests or servants would have had access during supper. Those guests were Manchester and myself, and we did not want the servants blamed. "

"On the other hand, jewelry could have been taken at any time." She swallowed hard. She really disliked the idea that Manchester had been right. "He suggested that I plant them in Stammel's room. He returned the banknotes."

Dani smiled. "Sydney said his master is smarter than most people believe."

Now it was Monique's turn to look questioning.

"Sydney is Manchester's valet. I told you . . ."

"Yes you did. I did not know his name was Sydney."

Dani shrugged as if it were a matter of indifference. But Monique knew it was much more. Had Dani finally found someone who could make her forget a childhood that still haunted her?

"Take the jewels," she said. "Hide them. There could well be a search any moment."

Dani nodded and left the room.

Monique went over to the window. She couldn't see Dani from there, but she was restless. Manchester was taking risks. So was she. And she knew that after tonight, she could no longer play this game. The feel of her father's hands on her was worse than she had even imagined. She could not have tolerated even that much of a touch had it not been for Gabriel Manning, the Marquess of Manchester, who lay so silently on the other side of the bed.

She knew now she was not alone in this once-seemingly hopeless quest against such a powerful man.

Manchester had been right. She should have waited to take the banknotes. Despite the laudanum, Stanhope had been awake as he had fumbled with the combination and opened the safe. If the notes had not been there, he would have ordered a search. She did not know whether she could have gotten them to Dani in time, and whether Dani would have had time to secret them in the coach.

She had been foolish not to wait on Dani, but she had not wanted to involve her friend more than she already had.

Her encounter with Manchester outside Stanhope's room had stunned her. So had the fact that they apparently had the same goal, that he was every bit the thief she had learned to be.

She would laugh if the situation were not so fraught with emotional complications.

She'd learned a little more about him, that he felt deeply the disaster that had befallen his father. Still, that one piece did not complete the puzzle. She still did not know who and what he was. He wanted Stanhope convicted, but she did not have a better sense of what kind of man he was.

Monique told herself it did not matter. She did not need Manchester. She did not want him. She wanted nothing to do with him. Yet her heart had crumbled as she and Pamela had waited earlier in the ruins, expecting him to appear even as they had pretended not to wait.

And then she had run into him after committing a crime that could mean a death sentence. Instead of fear, she'd felt excitement.

What was wrong with her?

She went in search of a footman and told him that Lord Stanhope had collapsed in weariness on his bed and might need his valet. Then she returned to her room.

When she returned, Dani was there, a satisfied look on her face. "It is done," she said.

"Then I think it is time for both of us to go to bed. Stay here with me tonight. We will be leaving early in the morning, I believe."

Dani nodded. She helped Monique off with her gown and corset and into a nightdress. Then she brushed her hair and braided it.

When she finished, Monique took the brush. She wouldn't sleep this night, and she needed to do something. "I will brush yours," she said.

They changed places and Monique brushed Dani's red hair. It was curlier than her own and Dani usually pulled it straight back in the most unflattering style.

But as it curled around her face, Dani looked quite pretty. Her blue eyes sparkled. Her cheeks were flushed, and, Monique suspected, not just from the journey to the carriage.

Monique finished. She hoped with all her heart that Dani's

Sydney was a loyal and trustworthy man and not like his master, who apparently wanted nothing more than one night's pleasure. Manchester was more like a comet than a man. A brilliant star that would destroy anyone in his path. He had no interest in staying in Britain, and he had no scruples.

Monique shivered slightly as she remembered Manchester's arms around her. "He said he intended to come to the ruins today," she said, "but someone hurt his horse. He thinks it may have been Lord Stammel."

"Sydney did not say anything about it."

"I wonder how much he knows about the marquess."

"He says very little about him. Only that he is grateful to him."

"Pamela is smitten with him, too," Monique said. "And you. Even when he plays the buffoon, he seems to draw people to him."

"Except for Lord Stammel, and Stanhope, both of whom seem to want something from him."

"Money, Manchester believes. But I think it might go beyond that. Stanhope was a business partner with Manchester's father. The father was accused of treason. Manchester believes Stanhope is responsible. Perhaps Stanhope feels he could be a threat to him."

"*He* is after Stanhope, too?" Dani asked.

"So he says."

"But how?"

"Apparently the same way I planned. Turn the three—Stanhope, Daven, and Stammel—against one another. They must know all of each other's secrets."

"But if any one of them said anything—"

"I know," Monique said. "They would be convicting themselves. But angry people are usually careless people."

Dani was silent for a moment, as she often was. Then, "Are you, perhaps, getting in one another's way? We could leave London and leave it to him."

"And forget about destroying Stanhope?" She could not do that. She had lived for that one purpose for more years than she wanted to remember. Until Stanhope was dead, she could not free herself of memories. He was a detested part of her. She was a part of him.

She suspected Manchester felt the same.

What did that make both of them?

Gabriel went to the gaming room. Still in his riding clothes, from which leaves clung, he apologized for not being present for supper. He had become lost in the maze, he said, and did not discover his way out until a short time ago.

"Mazes are quite simple," Stammel said, baiting him. "But perhaps not for a man who cannot stay in the saddle. A stable lad said you walked the horse in."

Gabriel smiled at him. "I had a discussion with our host about the care our horses are given. It appears there was a wound on my mount's back. As for the maze, we do not have such amusements in America. I wanted to explore it. As Lord Stanhope said, it is intricate and presented a challenge. And I am here, as you see."

Stammel glared at him, and Gabriel wondered if he hadn't been a little too clever. Cleverness was not one of the Marquess of Manchester's attributes.

"I wondered whether you would not like to recoup some of your losses," he said, then added, "Where is Lord Stanhope?"

"He went up to get some funds," one of the guests said. "He did say he was tired."

"He will probably be here soon," Gabriel said. "I saw him with Miss Fremont. She might well be a distraction."

Stammel's frown deepened. Still, he sat at the table. He was obviously one of those gamblers who did not understand his own limitations.

"May I join you?" Gabriel asked.

The room exploded into conversation that had momentarily quieted during the exchange between Stammel and Gabriel.

"If you wish," Stammel said curtly.

Gabriel found himself a chair, loosened his cravat, and was soon engaged in a game of whist. As the betting increased, he fixed his gaze on Stammel. "I hope you can pay this time," he said quietly.

The table went still. "Are you impugning my integrity?"

"I would never do that," Gabriel replied easily. "I just want to understand the British rules. I am, as you so often point out, a simple man from America."

"You will have the money when Lord Stanhope returns," Stammel said.

Gabriel nodded. "Let us begin then."

An hour later Gabriel had consumed several glasses of brandy and lost fifty pounds to one man at the table. Stammel had lost only twenty-five. His luck was so good that it overtook his lack of skill.

"Another game?" asked David Morgan. Gabriel had memorized the guest list and knew Morgan was one of the few men present without a title. He was Welsh but apparently influential with the government.

"You might ask him to show his blunt," Stammel said meanly.

It was exactly what Gabriel wanted.

"Not necessary," Morgan said. "Manchester is a guest, and a friend of Stanhope."

"Ah, but if Stammel has a question, I have banknotes in my room and Stanhope has some of my funds in his safe." Gabriel put his quizzing glass in his left eye and rose. "I wonder what is keeping him," he said.

Gabriel wove on his way to the door. In truth, he'd had more brandy than he wanted; for appearances' sake he'd kept pace with his companions.

Once out the door he maintained his pose, went to his room, and rummaged through several drawers in his wardrobe, then went to Stanhope's room. He knocked. When no one answered, he opened the door.

Still dressed, Stanhope was snoring on the bed.

Whatever Dani had managed to put in his wine had worked well. He smiled at her audacity.

He left, gently closing the door behind him.

He made his way down the grand staircase and burst into the game room. "My money is gone," he said. "There is a thief here."

*       *       *

The manor was in an uproar. At his words the men in the gaming room dispersed, some seeking their wives in the music room, some retiring immediately to check their rooms.

In minutes he heard several cries of outrage and demands to have property returned. One well-dressed woman was in tears.

Everyone wanted to know where Stanhope was.

The butler and valet knocked at his door as five or six men stood outside his bedroom. Hearing nothing, they went inside, then returned, spreading out their hands helplessly.

Stammel had disappeared with the rest but had not reappeared. Gabriel wondered whether he had looked to see whether any of his own valuables were missing. And found that cache of jewels planted in his room?

Gabriel went inside Stanhope's bedroom. He lay across the bed. Gabriel took the pitcher of water from a table and poured a little on Stanhope's face. No movement. He shook him. The man worked slowly, his eyes opening slightly, then fluttering closed again. Gabriel shook him again, and Stanhope moaned, opened his eyes again, and tried to focus.

"Wha' is . . ." His words were slurred.

Gabriel looked toward the door, where the valet and butler stood like pieces of marble. "Get some hot tea," he said.

"My lord," Gabriel said. "There have been some thefts."

"My head . . ."

"You must have drank too much wine, my lord," Gabriel said, lacing his words with concern. "Is there anything I can get you?"

"To—morrow . . ."

"Money is missing, my lord, along with jewels. You must act or someone will go to the constable. I do not think you would want that."

Stanhope tried to rise, obviously tried to comprehend what Gabriel was saying. "A . . . thief?"

"Five people have been robbed, including myself," Gabriel said. "You should check your own . . . possessions. You said there was a safe."

The latter words made an impact at last.

Stanhope struggled to sit up. His coat was wrinkled, his

cravat awry. He looked nothing like the usually well-groomed earl.

He blinked in the light from the oil lamp. "What in the hell are you talking about, Manchester?"

"I have been robbed of a hundred pounds and a diamond cravat pin. Surely you have seen it on me. Others say they are missing items as well."

Stanhope shook his head, then stood. "My head. I did not drink that . . . much wine."

Gabriel arched an eyebrow. "Should I send someone for a constable?"

"No, no. I will see to it. I will compensate any . . . losses. It must be a servant. I will ask George, my butler, to conduct a search. I . . . we will find the culprit."

Gabriel looked around, then leaned toward Stanhope. "Perhaps if you called the constable, we should tell him about the burr planted under my saddle." He feigned sudden enlightenment. "Perhaps the two incidents are connected."

Stanhope stiffened. "Are you accusing Lord Stammel?"

"Oh, no," Gabriel said hurriedly. "I was just remarking on the coincidence."

Stanhope's dark eyes glittered with anger. Gabriel was not sure whether it was aimed at him or at someone else.

Gabriel stood. "Perhaps the butler can reassure the guests," he said. "I will ride for the constable if you wish."

"No!" The word was like a crack of a whip. The man was becoming fully awake now.

"Tell everyone to go to bed. I will have James conduct a search of all the servants' quarters and question them. I am sure that we will find the culprit there."

Gabriel shrugged. "But if . . ."

"I will make sure everything missing is replaced. There is no reason to spread gossip about," Stanhope interrupted sharply. "I hope you will respect my wishes. Tell James and my valet to attend me."

"As you wish," he said and backed out, informing the butler and valet to enter.

The gathered guests looked at him.

He shrugged. "Lord Stanhope says he will discover the

thief. He recommended that we all retire for the night. I, for one, plan to do just that. But first I will need some brandy."

Just as he turned, a shriek broke the tense silence.

And it came from Monique's room.

# Chapter Twenty-one

"My bracelet is gone."

Monique's cry was followed by the door to her room being thrown open.

She emerged in a night robe, her hair braided, her gray eyes sleepy and sooty looking, and her expression outraged.

She had never looked so appealing to him. She was the essence of righteous indignation.

"Someone," she continued in a low, moderated but very passionate voice, "has been in my room ruffling through my personal belongings. I want to see Lord Stanhope."

It was all he could do to keep from smiling. He had seen her on stage. He had watched her beguile men who usually couldn't be beguiled. He had seen her anger and her passion and even her vulnerability.

Now her eyes flashed, and her face was flushed as she confronted a hall filled with men in what some would call dishabille. Their attention was certainly diverted.

"Lord Stanhope," she said again. "Where is he? This is an outrage."

Stanhope unfortunately chose that moment to emerge from his room. It was the first time he was not impeccably dressed.

His cravat was in disarray. His shirt was not completely buttoned. His eyes were red, and lines of strain creased his face.

Control and appearances had always been Stanhope's weapons. This weekend had obviously had several purposes, one of which was to win the wager. Another, Gabriel suspected, was to lure him even deeper into a web and possibly show important friends that Gabriel was a weak and incompetent man desperate for money.

Thanks to Monique, Stanhope's house party was in complete chaos, his closest business associate accused of intending to harm, even kill a guest, and Monique, whom he had wanted to impress with his wealth, had been robbed.

Gabriel almost felt sorry for him. *Almost.*

Monique ignored him, turning her rage on Stanhope. "I want to return to London tonight. Myself and my maid. I would not feel safe one more moment in this . . . place. And I expect you to find the villain who robs helpless women."

"Hear, hear," said a man who Gabriel remembered was a baron and a member of the Parliament. "I also will take my leave immediately. My wife is distraught from all this business."

Stanhope shook his head. "My butler will search all the servants."

The baron drew himself up. "My servants have been with me for years. They are above reproach, Stanhope. I resent your implication. My wife and I are leaving immediately."

"I will also be leaving as soon as our coach is ready and my lady and I are packed," said the man who had met Gabriel on the staircase when he'd first arrived. The man who'd barely managed to be civil to Gabriel earlier turned to him. "Are you going, too, Manchester?"

"Abominable situation," Gabriel agreed. "But I am sure that Lord Stanhope will find the culprit. Or make good our losses."

Stanhope looked at him with narrowed eyes.

"I am still leaving, my lord. I trust you will have the coach ready within the next hour," Monique said. She turned away and stalked down the hall.

Gabriel was filled with admiration. She would be gone with the jewels—

Stanhope started to go after her. "It is dangerous on the road at night," he said. "You should wait until tomorrow."

"My maid is hysterical," Monique said. "For her sake alone, we must go. She is a timid soul and fears for her life." She turned and walked into her room, closing the door behind her.

Gabriel swallowed a smile. He had never seen anyone less timid than Dani.

"Perhaps my man can ride inside and I will ride alongside the coach," he said to Stanhope. "Smythe is an ex-soldier and very capable of protecting the ladies."

"I will go myself," Stanhope said.

Gabriel shrugged. "If you wish, but you have guests. I have none."

He watched as Stanhope obviously weighed his alternatives.

"Stanhope," Gabriel said, "you can make amends later. I will make her understand this is not your fault."

Stanhope whirled on him, rage in his eyes. If there had not been others present, Gabriel knew the man would have struck him in pure fury over carefully laid plans destroyed.

Stanhope was a man who needed to control. He evidently knew little about failure.

*He was going to learn.*

After a moment Stanhope seemed to gain control.

"How long has your man been with you?" Stanhope demanded.

"He was a soldier of the Crown," Gabriel said. "He has impeccable references." Really, Smythe had no references at all. Gabriel hadn't felt he needed them, but he was not going to say that to Stanhope. He did not want Smythe implicated in any way.

"When did you get back to the house?" Stanhope then asked.

"After supper," Gabriel said carelessly, ignoring the obvious implication. "You were right, the maze is difficult. I thought you might send someone when I did not appear at supper, especially after the mishap on the hunt. Perhaps you really do not wish a partnership. I will look elsewhere," he added with indignation.

"My butler was told specifically that you did not want any assistance," Stanhope replied with a shrug. "If I had thought for a moment that you were afraid . . ."

Gabriel had baited Stanhope as much as he could about the maze. Now he had something else to worry the man. "I am grateful for being invited to your home, Stanhope, but I would feel safer in my own lodgings in London. I thought England to be a safe place and America a wild, undisciplined land. Now I know I was mistaken."

"You will leave England?"

"Eventually. I do want to talk to some people who knew my father," Gabriel said. "Just before coming here, I met someone who claimed my father should not have killed himself, that the charge of treason had been false."

"Who could that have been? The Crown prosecutors were very sure," Stanhope said sharply. "It is common knowledge . . ."

Gabriel shrugged. "Someone disputes the common belief."

"And who would that be? Why would he not have come forward earlier and saved your father?"

"I understand he was afraid," Gabriel said. "I do not know whether I should believe it or not, but I feel I should hear him out."

"Who is it?" Stanhope asked again, this time with a trace of fear.

"I would rather not say until I know his tale is true," Gabriel said. "I am to meet with him next week."

He watched as Stanhope's usually emotionless eyes blinked. "Maybe you can remember something . . ."

Several other guests were still hesitant and standing around.

Stanhope broke away and approached them. "If you will feel safer, I will place footmen outside your rooms. You will be safer here tonight than on the roads. I beg of you to give us an opportunity to find the culprit."

One by one, mumbling as they moved along the hall, the

guests dispersed. As the last one departed to his room, Monique and Dani reappeared at their door. Gabriel had never thought that women could dress so quickly. Monique's hair was no longer in a braid but dressed neatly in a bun and framed by a hat. She wore a cloak that covered whatever she wore beneath.

"You cannot leave without escort," Stanhope said. "There are thieves and highwaymen on the road at night. Manchester has offered to escort you, or I can send men of my own."

"Lord Manchester will be suitable," Monique said. "He has come to my assistance before." Then she seemed to soften. "I will see you in London."

Stanhope bowed. "It will be my honor," he said. "And I assure you that I will recompense you for your loss. If you could tell me something about the bracelet . . ."

"It is but a trifle but meaningful to me. It is the only thing I have left of my mother's." Tears appeared at the edges of her eyes. "I truly do not know why someone would take it. It had only a few gems of poor quality."

"I will attempt to find something that will be equally as memorable."

"There is no need, my lord."

"There is every need. Your mother . . . she is still alive?"

"No. She died several years ago. She was very beautiful."

"I would expect nothing else," Stanhope said. "I am very sorry."

"I must go," she said. "Lord Stanhope, can you help us with our trunks?"

Stanhope had no choice now. "As you wish. I will have a man ride ahead and make sure you will be accommodated at the inn."

He looked at Monique, then at Manchester. For a split second Gabriel thought he saw suspicion in the man's eyes, but if so it disappeared quickly.

"I am in your debt," Stanhope said stiffly. "And I plead with you not to open old wounds. Most likely, someone believes they can take money from you."

"I will remember that caution," Manchester said. "You

have been a friend to me, and I will not forget it. Now if you would send someone for my valet . . ."

He bowed to Monique. "It will not take us long."

He would make bloody damn sure it would not take long. He wanted Monique out of the house before Stanhope had second thoughts.

Monique watched the interplay between Dani and Manchester's valet as Stanhope's coach bounced over rough roads.

She kept listening for other riders, for a resultant search of her and Dani or perhaps of Manchester's man. She heard none.

Dani and the big soldier named Sydney Smythe said little, but their eyes had barely left one another.

"Do you miss being a soldier?" Dani asked after several moments in the coach.

"No, miss. Being a soldier means freezing nights and broiling days, and poor food, months of waiting, then . . . "

"Then?" Dani had prompted.

"It is not a good thing to kill other men just because they live in a different place or have a ruler that tells them they must fight," he said with sudden intensity even as he darted a look at Monique.

Smythe was obviously awkward in her presence. He'd said little, when they left, but he had helped Dani into the coach, leaving Monique to his employer. The man was impeccably correct, though he looked rougher and certainly much larger than any of the other valets she'd seen. She'd wondered whether men did not want to seem overshadowed by their servants.

Manchester certainly had no such fear. When they were alone, he showed a natural confidence that no one could feign. He could try to hide it and had been successful with people who did not see those few private moments she had seen. They had not expected anything more than what he'd pretended to be, mainly because of their own arrogance and feeling of superiority.

She thought of him riding outside the coach. He had assured her that his horse was well enough to carry him, that he had padded the wound. He would ride with them in the coach during the daylight, but he too had heard that bandits haunted this road at night. He told her quietly that he had brought a brace of pistols with him.

She felt safer than she had ever felt in her life. She had no reason other than that sense of capability. And now Smythe. There was something about him as well, a protectiveness that warmed.

He certainly was no ordinary valet.

She thought with gentle amusement of the way Dani and Smythe alternated between trying not to look at each other and being unable to keep their eyes from one another. Had she and Manchester been that obvious?

Monique would have thought that Smythe's sheer size would have intimidated Dani, but her friend had not hesitated for a second before taking his hand. It still amazed her, and yet she had seen Smythe's gentleness when he'd held out his hand to Dani and held it a moment too long. She was happy for Dani. The two had no obstacles in the way of romance, not like she and Manchester.

It was extremely irritating that nothing had cooled the fire between them. It had taken every bit of her acting experience not to show any reaction to him, especially in the hall outside Stanhope's room. He'd looked uncommonly attractive as he had offered her his protection, much to Stanhope's chagrin.

But there could be no future for them. He was still a lord of the realm. He was a marquess, and even if that were not true he was obviously a man of substance. Those men did not marry actresses who pitted men against one another. And she had no intentions of becoming a man's mistress. She had seen what it did to her mother. She would never put herself in that position.

After taking care of Stanhope, she planned to concentrate on her career, make enough money to retire comfortably somewhere where no one knew her. She would never allow herself to be a victim, to make herself subservient to another person.

She closed her eyes, tried not to think of Manchester rid-

ing outside. But she smiled inwardly. She and Manchester had
done a good day's work tonight.

And to her astonishment, it felt good she had not had to do
it alone.

The journey to London was long. And yet . . . not long
enough. At its end Gabriel would have to find a way to get
Monique out of London. And out of his life.

Gabriel had made arrangements to have his own rented
coach driven to London by one of Stanhope's coachmen in
order to escort Monique and her maid. He had agreed with
Stanhope that the earl's own coach would be far more comfortable for Monique than his own rented one.

It was, he knew, exactly what Monique had wanted.

He had chosen to ride behind the coach in the event, he
said, that the coach was accosted by highwaymen.

There had been no question of Smythe riding inside. He'd
never been on a horse and eyed them with caution.

But there had been other reasons Gabriel had chosen to
ride his own mount, even though he had to endure thoughts
he'd preferred to go away.

Gabriel had never trusted anyone with his secrets before.
Even Samuel knew only a small part of his background and
nothing of his plan other than the fact that Gabriel wanted to
clear his father's name in some way. It had seemed wise to
keep his own counsel. It was more than a little difficult now
to surrender a part of himself to someone else. And while he
had not told Monique everything, he had told her more than
he'd ever told anyone before.

By doing that, he had placed his life in her hands, and she
had done the same with hers.

It was still difficult to understand exactly how that had
happened.

He did not want to be responsible for her neck.

Apparently, she had the same goal as he did. The question
was how to get her out of the way so he could do what needed
to be done without more interference. He did not want his
own actions to rebound on them.

That meant getting Monique and Dani out of his life, and

that thought was surprisingly painful. The thought of never seeing her again left a huge jagged hole in him. He wouldn't admit it was his heart. But the only way he would rid himself of nightmares was fulfilling his father's charge. He knew his father would never rest until he did.

Neither would—could—he.

He had spent hours on his horse in nearly pitch dark except for the thin light coming from the lanterns on the coach. He could, in truth, have traveled in more comfort inside the coach, but he did not want that proximity to Monique. He'd already made mistakes. He wanted her far too much for both of their sakes.

And so he had shivered in the cold English morning and had welcomed the light of dawn and the sign for the inn used earlier to rest the horses.

A few hours' sleep, some food, and daylight would revive his senses and take his thoughts from a lady who could be nothing but trouble.

When they stopped at the inn where they had rested the horses two days earlier, Monique suggested that she and Dani stay inside the coach while Smythe went in to query whether they could obtain rooms at this unearthly hour in the morning.

Gabriel, she suggested, might want to inquire as to the horses.

It was only too obvious to Gabriel that they wanted to be inside the coach alone.

He agreed and took the coach driver to rouse a stableman while Smythe went into the inn to request a room for Monique and a separate one for Gabriel.

It took them some time to rouse a sleepy lad, then he unsaddled Specter himself, looking carefully at the sore caused by the burr while the driver negotiated for feed for the other horses. Gabriel left orders to give them all the best oats the stable had, then returned to the coach, wondering whether the ladies had had time to extract what they wished to extract from wherever they had hid the valuables.

They apparently had. Monique winked at him. It had been mischievous and approving, and he found his heart pounding a little harder.

Several minutes later Smythe reappeared. He had secured several rooms for the ladies in which to rest, bathe, and dine. Monique and Dani alighted from the coach, a reticule clutched tightly in Dani's hands. She refused Smythe's attempt to take it from her.

Poor Smythe looked crestfallen, but Dani looked up at him with a breathless smile, and he had returned one of those rare shy smiles.

Gabriel and Smythe shared another room, but Gabriel did not take the few hours to sleep. He often returned to the window, thinking at any time that Stanhope would come to the conclusion that only two people could be the thieves.

Having not eaten the night before, he shared a cold chicken and some ale with Smythe. Gabriel wondered how far he could trust Smythe. He was an Englishman and a soldier trained to obey orders and that meant to protect the king and his subjects against such lawbreakers as himself. And Gabriel suspected his valet was far more astute and aware than he ever indicated.

After filling his stomach, Gabriel rose and went to the window.

"I can keep watch," Smythe said as he rose from the table and joined him at the window. "You need some rest. I had some in the coach."

"I do not trust Stanhope," Gabriel said. "He might try to blame either Miss Fremont or myself."

"You need not explain, my lord," Smythe said. In that one second, Gabriel knew that Smythe was far more aware of what was occurring than Gabriel had hoped. He might not know exactly why or what, but he knew that the Marquess of Manchester was not entirely what Gabriel had wanted the world to believe.

Gabriel gave him a searching look. "I will allow nothing to touch you," he said. "I will make sure you and your family have what you need."

Smythe returned his look. "You have already given us much," he said. "I did not even hope to get employment. Neither did my mother. And my sister is happier than I have ever seen her. School. And books. I never thought we could give her those."

"Would you consider leaving London?" Gabriel knew once again he was trusting someone who could betray him.

"But where, sir?" No "my lord" this time. Smythe was learning.

"To America. There are opportunities for a man like you. I know . . . a shipbuilder who is looking for good reliable men. I think it would suit you far better than being a valet."

"You are disappointed with my employment, sir?" His face fell practically to his shoes.

"To the contrary, I have been delighted with you and your family. But I suspect I will be leaving soon, and I would like to know that you all are secure."

"But you are a marquess. Why would you leave?"

"I am afraid my estates are entailed and I am penniless. I would just as soon leave them to the Crown to do with what they may. I have never aspired to being a gentleman."

"You were a soldier. " It was more statement than question and the first personal observation Smythe had ever made, but then neither had Gabriel ever invited confidences before.

"Why would you think that?"

"You are decisive, sir. You have the assurance of an officer, of a man who knows what he is about. And there is a look in your eyes, one that is hard to disguise. You understand more than you let people know."

"And I imagine you were a very good sergeant."

Smythe did not reply. Instead, he waited for an answer or a rebuke.

"I was a sailor, not a soldier," Gabriel finally admitted. "I fought England."

He awaited a reaction. There was none.

"You have the walk of a sailor," Smythe said, as if Gabriel had only confirmed what he already knew.

"That does not bother you? That I fought with the Americans?"

Smythe looked surprised as if the thought had never occurred to him. "You employed me, sir, when no one else would."

Gabriel knew the man had just pledged his full loyalty. "Will you consider the trip?"

Smythe looked stricken and Gabriel realized that he had suggested the impossible. "I will pay for the voyage," he said. "For the three of you."

"I could not . . ." Smythe started.

"I value loyalty above all else," Gabriel said. "It is not a quality easily found. Nor is an excellent cook. I know of a man who has been complaining for years about such a lack. I can guarantee both of you jobs and, if you must, you can repay me for the voyage."

Astonishment spread across Smythe's face. Even disbelief. Then a smile. The broadest smile that Gabriel had seen, even broader than the one that had flashed when he talked about Dani.

That thought apparently struck him at the same time, and the smile dissolved into uncertainty.

"Miss Fremont?"

"I expect Miss Fremont will be leaving London soon, also."

"But they have an engagement."

"They are in danger," Gabriel said.

Smythe looked at him for a very long time, searching his face.

"The jewels," he finally said.

It was not Gabriel's secret to reveal. "No," he lied. "But Miss Fremont is playing a dangerous game with Lord Stanhope and his friends. Stanhope is a ruthless man."

"I have heard rumors about him," Smythe said. "They say he shipped rotten meat to the troops in France. I heard more talk about him at the manor. His servants hate him but they need the work. I would not allow our Elizabeth to be in his employ."

Nor would Gabriel.

"I think it would be best for Miss Fremont and Dani to return to France," he said.

"Perhaps they would like America, too?" Smythe said hopefully.

It was a thought, one that had not entered his mind yet. Or

perhaps it had, and he had dismissed it. Monique was a celebrated actress. While there were theaters in America, they did not have the sophistication of those in Paris and London. Could he ask her to give up the theater when he knew he could not give up the sea?

And that was supposing that she cared at all.

A horseman rode into the courtyard and he stiffened. He did not believe Stanhope would call the authorities on him. He had too much to hide, himself. Gabriel could cause Stammel problems, and therefore his host problems, if anything came out about the burr under the saddle blanket.

But then Gabriel imagined Stanhope's groom could be bribed or threatened into denying the wound on Specter's back, the blood-speckled burr that did not belong where it was found.

How many rumors could Stanhope continue to juggle without damaging his support in the government? How much scandal?

"Perhaps," he finally answered Smythe's hopeful question. "But their home is in Paris."

"Dani does not like Paris," Smythe said.

He was looking at Gabriel as if he could solve that problem, and every other problem in the world. Damn it, he couldn't solve his own problems.

"I will ask Miss Fremont," he said. "And if Dani wishes to go without her, I will pay her voyage as well."

"She would not leave without her mistress," Smythe said with absolute certainty.

Gabriel wondered exactly how much Smythe knew about the two women. But he also knew Smythe's loyalty was not to be bought or traded with another.

"Perhaps I *will* get some rest," he said after the rider dismounted and minutes went by. There was no pounding at his door, no constable demanding entrance. Just another traveler.

"I'll wake you if anyone approaches," Smythe promised.

Most of England was probably at bed. Gabriel was used to a bustling Boston where everyone rose at dawn and the streets were busy early in the morning. London on the other hand seemed to sleep most of the day and awaken at night. At least the English gentry.

He must have been far more tired than he thought for he fell asleep immediately. He was still tired when Smythe wakened him. "The innkeeper said we should leave if we wish to reach London by dusk," Smythe said.

He rose and went over to the mirror in the room. His face looked older, more lined. His eyes were dull, and bristle darkened his cheeks. Smythe, on the other hand, looked clean shaven and fresh, even eager. Damn the man.

"You might see whether the ladies are ready," Gabriel said, "and have the horses hitched. I'll see to Specter myself."

"Yes, my . . . yes sir," Smythe said.

Miraculously there was hot water, fetched no doubt by Smythe. Gabriel appreciated him more and more.

He shaved quickly, then pulled on his boots. Then Smythe was back. "The horses are ready. The ladies are, too," he said.

Gabriel left the room and went down, paid the innkeeper, then hurried to the stable and looked at Specter's wound.

It looked no worse, but he decided there was no reason to ride apart from the coach during daylight. Neither highwaymen nor Stanhope would strike in broad daylight.

And the prospect of hours with Monique was, unfortunately, an irresistible one.

# Chapter Twenty-two

Monique felt a jolt in her heart as Manchester tied his horse behind the coach, then helped her inside and entered behind her.

It was more crowded now with two men. They sat opposite her and Dani, and Manchester's long legs brushed hers.

He had shaved in the last few hours. His hair was damp. He had unbuttoned his waistcoat and his coat was open. He still wore a rumpled cravat.

He was the most unconsciously masculine man she had ever seen, and her heart lurched as he lounged in the seat across from her. Her body tingled where his knee touched hers, even through the cloth.

"Did you rest, mademoiselle?"

"*Oui*, my lord," she said. If he was going to be formal, then so would she be.

"And you accomplished everything you meant to accomplish?"

"I believe so," she said coolly, knowing full well what he meant.

He gave her a lazy grin. "I regret that you lost something dear to you."

"And you, my lord, did you lose something dear to you?"

"There is very little dear to me."

"Not even Lord Stanhope's daughter? Will she not be wounded at your desertion?" The question was unreasonable. Pamela had already explained everything. But for some reason Monique didn't entirely understand, she was spoiling for a fight. Perhaps because his proximity aroused those same aching, hurting, longing feelings inside. They had caused her to do something foolish earlier, and she feared they would do the same again.

She could not bear being deserted again, left like the questionable lady she'd portrayed herself to be.

"It is no desertion to assist a lady in distress," he replied.

"Have you pressed your suit further?" she continued. She knew she was being obvious. She wanted to trust him. She had trusted him earlier.

The fact is she did not trust him with herself. Not again. He was poor, she knew that from what he'd said. Perhaps the greatest revenge would be marrying Pamela. He would certainly inherit enough to put his estates to right.

"No," he said. "I think she is perfectly comfortable with my lack of ambition in that regard."

She lifted her gaze and met his eyes, and she hated the amusement in them, as if he knew exactly what she was doing, and thinking. Why did he have such a rough attractiveness?

Drat him.

He crossed his legs, and one of them brushed her knee again.

"My apologies," he said lazily, but she saw his body stiffen as if he too felt the heat of the flame licking at her from that mere touch.

Dani and Manchester's valet were both looking out the window, isolating themselves from the tension inside the carriage.

She had thought their presence might bring some balance to the interior of the coach, but she was feeling a warmth from that side of the coach as well.

"Since we're sharing the same coach, perhaps you would call me Gabriel."

*Gabriel.* She knew his name, of course, but somehow on his lips it seemed intimate, as enticing and seductive as everything about him.

The air seemed charged. She felt as if a storm were brewing, one over which she had no control.

His green eyes reflected that storm. They were usually clear, unemotional, like pieces of glass. Now they flashed with something like desire. Or perhaps challenge.

But then he had always challenged her.

Challenged and intrigued and fascinated.

He was doing the same now.

She wanted to look away. She wanted to ask questions, but she did not know how much his valet knew.

She felt like a butterfly on a pin, pressed against a very hot board. She hated that feeling of helplessness.

"How is your horse?" she finally asked. It was a foolish question but she needed something to break the explosiveness of the air.

"He is better now that I am off him," he said.

"He is quite handsome. Where did you find him?"

"A baron. The horse belonged to his son, who was killed in France."

"You will keep him."

"Until I leave England."

"And when will that be?" She noticed that Smythe shifted slightly in his seat, and his eyes went to Dani. Dani, she noted, looked prettier than anytime since she had known her. Her checks were flushed and her eyes full of life.

"When my business is completed."

"You do not plan to stay, then?"

He did not answer. "Do you?"

"I am an actress. I go where I can obtain employment."

"I would think you could find employment anywhere."

"But the part is not always right."

"And it is now?"

He did not mean the play, and she knew it.

"Yes," she said.

"Some parts are more . . . perilous than others. It might be wise to find another."

"And how would I do that?"

"Any city would welcome you. You might even travel to America."

She narrowed her eyes. It was the first time he had mentioned his country. Or expressed any interest in her future. Did he just want her out of the way? Or something more? And why did he speak in riddles? "Are there many theaters there?"

"In Boston certainly."

"I could not violate a contract."

"The American climate is healthier than the one in London," he said with sudden intensity.

"I like this climate. It is . . . bracing."

"It is dangerous," he said again. "Think about it."

"I know no one there."

"I can give you names. References."

"And when do you suppose I should go?"

"Now," he said.

"I have not completed my business."

"I will finish it," he said shortly.

So that was what he wanted. A clear field to do what he wanted.

The devil with that.


Stanhope stared at the jewels hidden in a box of cravats in Stammel's trunk. They were not all there, but enough to convict the man. At least in Stanhope's mind.

He'd watched all day as his guests left, some with curt words. The country weekend, designed to impress Manchester, Monique, and several other potential investors and government officials, had ended in disaster.

Now he stood in Stammel's room after one of the footmen, charged with searching while the guests were at breakfast this morning, had found some of the missing jewels in Stammel's belongings.

He recalled the events of these past few weeks. Banknotes missing from his London town house. Daven's missing funds. Stammel's gambling debts, including the note he owed Manchester. The burr under a saddle that could have resulted in Manchester's death.

The marquess's death would be no great blow, but Stanhope wanted his money first. He wanted no questions. He did not want "accidents" at his home. The marquess needed to be caught with his hand in the king's purse as his father had been.

And Stammel had nearly destroyed his plan, casting suspicion on all of them.

The most egregious act had been that damned burr. It had made Manchester suspicious. And causing a mishap on his estate would revive the old scandal concerning Manchester's father.

Stanhope gritted his teeth. There was no question now. He had to get rid of Stammel.

Stammel had been his partner for thirty years. He had done most of the more unsavory work, but now his gambling had made him unreliable. If Stammel were arrested and threatened with a noose, then he would implicate Stanhope.

Stammel had to die, and sooner rather than later.

The question was whether he should tell Daven. After several moments of thought, he decided not. Daven did not particularly care for Stammel, but he might well feel his own future could be in jeopardy.

No, he had to do it himself and in a way it would not be linked to him or his properties.

*The jewels.* He would leave them where they had been discovered in Stammel's belongings. He would suggest some business in London and request that Stammel return to the city late this afternoon. He would be on the road at night.

Stanhope replaced the jewels where they were mixed with the neck cloths. He could retrieve them when Stammel's coach was accosted by highwaymen, then return them to their owners, saying a servant had been apprehended with them.

With those details worked out, he strode into the dining room, greeting the guests who remained. He looked at Stammel, who was sitting to his left, his face red and mottled from drinking. A rare pang of regret struck him.

Until lately, Stammel had been the perfect partner. He did what was asked of him, and usually efficiently. And without qualms of conscience.

But Stanhope could not take chances. Not now. Not with Manchester in London.

He smiled at his partner and saw Stammel's eager recognition. He wouldn't mention his leaving until late this afternoon. A special message from London perhaps. He would have some very competent men waiting for Stammel beyond the inn.

Stanhope went to the sideboard and piled a plate with food. He'd planned another hunt today for those who planned to stay. There were not many. Coaches and riders had been leaving all morning. One who remained was Charles Chase, a high government official who approved government contracts.

"I can promise you a good day of hunting," he said.

"I have been thinking I should be returning to London," said Chase. "My office . . ."

"One more day," Stanhope said. "The hunting will be fine today and we can forget the unpleasantness of last night."

Chase looked dubious. One of the attractions this weekend had been the presence of the famous Monique Fremont. Now she was gone, and he'd had only a brief time with her.

"I was hoping Miss Fremont would change her mind and remain."

"Ah, you know women. They frighten easily. Not like us."

The man straightened in his chair. "Perhaps until tomorrow," he said.

"We will begin the hunt at noon. You can select your mount."

Stanhope sat at the table with a full plate. He did like good food, and his cooks were quite excellent.

Mrs. Miller opened the door as if she had been sitting next to it for days awaiting their return.

The front of the hall was filled with flowers.

"They have been arriving steadily," she said. "A messenger said you had left Lord Stanhope's home and to be ready for your arrival."

"How nice," Monique said with cool indifference.

The housekeeper looked beyond Monique and saw the two

men. "Lord Manchester." She fluttered. She drew back when she saw Smythe's sizeable bulk behind Manchester.

Monique tried to contain her smile. No telling what the worthy Mrs. Miller thought about her male . . . acquaintances.

"We were traveling at night," Monique explained. "Lord Stanhope seemed to believe we needed protection. Lord Manchester and his valet kindly offered to accompany us and will stay for supper."

Mrs. Miller looked ruffled as Dani directed Smythe as to where to take their trunk, and the two disappeared. "I did not expect company."

"Anything will do. Bread, cheese, cold meat if there is any, and ale for the gentlemen."

Mrs. Miller's face relaxed slightly. "I can find something."

"I knew you could, Mrs. Miller. You are a treasure."

The housekeeper gave her a suspicious look, then retreated to the kitchen.

"A gracious invitation," Gabriel said to Monique, apparently choosing to ignore the tension that had continued throughout the ride.

"It is the least I can do. And I have some articles that belong to you."

He gave her an enigmatic smile. "Does that mean you will consider leaving London?"

"Only if you do."

He seemed to search her face, then shrugged. "How did you hide the jewels? The search started immediately."

There was no reason not to tell him. He was as guilty as she. "Dani cut a piece of upholstery on one side of a cushion, then tacked it back. She is a very good seamstress."

"Can Stanhope find it?"

"*Non,*" she said, reverting back to the French that was more familiar to her. "Dani repaired it while we were at the inn."

"How many more talents do you two have?" he asked, his eyes creasing with amusement.

"As many as you have, my lord," she countered. "I am still exploring the extent of them."

"I am a simple marquess."

"You may be many things, but never simple, my lord."

He arched an eyebrow, but she ignored it. "You may wait in the sitting room," she said.

"And you?"

"I plan to get more comfortable," she said. With that she turned away from him and left the room.

Gabriel decided not to ask how "comfortable." He tried not to envision comfortable.

Instead, he turned toward the street and looked out. The gas lamplight cast eerie glows on the cobblestones glazed by a light mist.

He studied the sitting room until the housekeeper reappeared.

"Miss Fremont said that if you would like some spirits, there is brandy and glasses in the cabinet," she said before backing out the door.

He wandered over to the cabinet. Did Monique keep it here for her gentleman callers? For Stanhope?

Gabriel poured himself a full portion.

Why had she wanted him to wait? She had been curt with him during the journey, even angry yesterday, though she had saved his hide in Stanhope's room.

The truth was he did not understand her. He did not know what she wanted. She was unlike any woman he had ever met. She had a daring that scared the bloody wits out of him. He worried about another person, something he'd not done in years.

Not true, some inner voice reminded him. He'd worried about his sailors, the men under his command, but that had been duty. These feelings went beyond duty.

He took a large gulp of brandy even as he knew he needed to retain his senses. She obviously wanted to talk to him. She must want something from him.

Hell, he wanted something from her.

Where in the hell was Smythe? He'd had more than enough time to take up the trunks. Now he needed a diversion. Any kind of diversion. He went to the window and looked outside. The coach was gone. Back to Stanhope's country manor, he expected.

He also noticed that his horse was gone. No doubt Smythe's doing. He had probably taken Specter to the mews that was around the corner. He should have been the one to do that. Specter was his mount.

Bloody hell, but he had lost all his senses, all his well-honed discipline.

He heard a noise at the door and he whirled around. Monique stood there. She wore a simple blue dress. Her dark hair tumbled down her shoulders and back. Her gray eyes were smoky.

God help him, but she was desirable.

And what made it worse, he liked her. Blazes, he liked her. More than liked her.

Lusted after her.

Unfortunately, that was not all. He knew that every time he thought about her leaving London. He thought about it every time he considered returning to America. Returning home, then to sea, was once what he wanted most after Stanhope's fall. Now it seemed a very lonely prospect.

He had never felt lonely before. He had been too fixed on goals. To accumulate enough money to ruin his father's accuser, then to defeat the British, now—with victory in sight—to end the game.

Gabriel had expected to feel triumphant. Instead he felt empty.

"Monsieur?" Her voice was huskier than usual.

He felt his body stiffen, the core of him turning molten. He had to force himself to stand still, not to stride over to her and take her in his arms. Control, he told himself. Control.

"You do look . . . comfortable," he managed in an even tone.

She had a hand behind her. Now she held it out. A necklace and earrings shimmered in her palm.

"Here," she said. "I do not know how to go about selling them. Not here in London."

"And you think I do."

"*Oui.*"

He made no movement to take them. "You trust me?"

Her face did not show any emotion as she gave a slight shrug. "As much as I can trust anyone."

"Should I take that as a compliment?"

"I have never trusted a man before, my lord. It is new to me. Do not ask too much."

He reached out and took the jewelry. "I will find a buyer and return your share."

"I do not want it," she said. "I do not want anything that has his taint about it."

"But you . . ."

"I wanted to know what you would suggest. I said I did not trust easily." She paused, then added, "I have been saving money for years," she said. "I have what I need. For both Dani and myself."

"And you think *I* might need it."

"I want you to leave London," she said.

"Leave?" He was intrigued. That was supposed to be his suggestion. *For her.*

"I can get closer to him without hurting anyone else," she said, lifting that chin again.

"You mean Pamela?"

"*Oui.* She is a young woman who needs help."

"And that is your concern?"

"I have made it so."

"But you hate her father because he did something to someone close to you."

She was silent.

"Pamela and you resemble each other."

"Do we?"

"Aye. I thought it a bit odd."

"A coincidence."

"I wonder," he said.

Her body went rigid. "Will you leave?"

"I have property here in England. You do not."

"Everyone—including you—says it is worthless. And you seem much more interested in the sea. You go to the—"

She stopped suddenly.

He squinted at her. "Where do I go?"

She looked away, then back at him. "I hired someone to follow you."

"So it was you. Not Stanhope." He should have realized it wasn't Stanhope. It had never occurred to him that she might have a reason . . .

"No, not unless there is someone else following you."

"Why?"

"You were not what you appeared to be. You could have been associated with Stanhope. I did not know whether you were a risk to what I intended."

"And what did you intend?"

"I told you. I want to destroy him."

"And then . . ."

She shrugged. "I will continue as an actress."

"If he discovers what you are about?"

"No one knows. No one but Dani. And you."

He was silent for a moment. "Will you tell me who he hurt? And why?"

"No," she said.

He put a hand on her shoulder and touched strands of hair. Blazes, but it was soft. "We are in this together. You can get me hung. I can do the same to you. Or transported. Is it worth it?"

"Yes," she said starkly. "And you? You must feel the same."

He had. He tried to tell himself he still did.

He could not do it. Vengeance might be worth his life. It certainly wasn't worth hers. They were skirting that all-important fact. As for telling her everything about that evening in his father's study, he could not. How could he tell her he had left his father to kill himself? Just as he had not been with his mother when she died. He had failed everyone important to him.

And how could he tell her that the only way he could atone was to fulfill his father's request?

She was watching him as if she had a view into his soul. Compassion was in her eyes. Compassion and empathy. Her eyes were moist.

"Do you have family now?"

"No."

"No . . . lady?"

Gabriel felt a certain satisfaction at the question. "No."

"Was Pamela right? That you really have no intentions toward her?"

"Yes," he said simply. "Do you really think that I could make love to you and court another woman?"

"I do not know. I still know so little of you. And you left so . . . secretly the other night."

"You were not in my plans, Monique. Nor do I believe I was in yours. I had to leave or . . ."

"Or?"

"I would never have left."

"And now?"

"And now . . . I care too much. I am dangerous to you. I want you out of London."

"I want *you* out of London."

They glared at each other. But it was a glare that held far more than competition or challenge. The storm was back with all its wild promises. He felt its intensity as the winds raged between them, sweeping away everything in their path. Reason. Caution. Reservations.

All those considerations left her eyes, as he knew they left his own. He took a step forward. She took one. They were in each other's arms, their lips meeting, their bodies melding into each other, their fingers teasing and caressing.

His tongue plundered her mouth, and she explored his. He drew her closer and knew she felt his arousal. Her body responded to his.

God, how he wanted her. They were the two worst people for each other.

Or were they?

He swore to himself.

He had never been weak. Not since . . .

Her eyes were searching his. Asking. He wasn't sure of the question. He wasn't sure of his own answers. He only knew the draw was irresistible. He had always loved storms, had always been drawn to them despite the peril. His lips tightened against her, then as they remained melded together, he picked her up.

She pulled her lips away. "Mrs. Miller . . ."

"To hell with Mrs. Miller," he said as he started to mount the steps.

Her arms went around his neck, and he sensed more than heard something drop. At that instant he did not care. He only cared about her. Monique. The only woman who had made his heart beat quicker, and warmed his blood and quickened his senses.

She was magic. It did not matter who or what she was, or what the future might hold.

Nothing mattered except her.

# Chapter Twenty-three

Monique felt his strength as he lifted her so easily. His lips played with hers as he ascended the stairs and somehow managed to open the door of her room.

She heard Dani's gasp. Then a giggle as her friend scurried out the door. Dani never giggled. Monique was so startled at the sound she barely heard the words, "I will tell Mrs. Miller to delay supper," and the sound of the door closing behind Dani.

The marquess lowered her so she was standing, his lips still melded to hers. Only very reluctantly did she move away. Very slightly.

She gazed up at him, at the intensity in his face, the fire in those usually cool eyes.

Monique had known she should say farewell at the door of her lodgings. Once inside, she knew that she would succumb.

Still, she'd invited him in. Standing here before him, her legs trembling slightly, she wished she could blame someone else. Perhaps even the devil.

But if nothing else, she was honest with herself.

She had not wanted him to leave. She wanted to know more about him. She wanted to know what he intended to do with the jewels. She wanted to know . . .

Drat, she wanted to know everything about him.

So she had invited him for supper. She thought she could control herself. Now, standing before him, she knew she had been lying to herself.

She had known it when she had changed from the dusty, stained clothes she was wearing. She knew it as Dani took the pins from her hair and brushed it until it shone. She knew it when she'd pinched her cheeks and even added a small bit of color to her lips.

She merely wanted to know more about him, she told herself again. She also needed him to yield this battle to her. They were interfering with each other. She was sure she had the greater grievance, and the greater right to seek justice.

*Stanhope was her father.*

She knew she could not tell him that.

What would he do with that knowledge?

She did not know. How much did he want his own revenge?

He stood silent, cravat wrinkled and pulled apart by impatient hands, eyes weary.

Her pulse quickened as his eyes turned emerald with desire. An unconquerable aching inside smothered all her arguments. Her words had been armor. His had been the same.

They parried, both knowing that neither would win.

She had never considered herself a weak person. But the moment they were alone it was as if some sorcerer had taken away her will. She'd relished his arms. His confidence. His strength.

Their gazes met as she stood there. Too near. Yet too far. She swallowed hard, then fixed her eyes on his neckwear.

"You can rid yourself of that silly cravat." His imperious dandy cravat that he had worn since they had left Stanhope's home in the middle of the night was now stained and wilted.

"Surely not silly," he said, drawing himself up in fake indignation. And yet there was a huskiness to his voice, a catch in it that told her he was feeling all the emotions that she felt.

Drat but she was drawn to him. From that sandy hair and those clear green eyes that seemed to see right through her, to the lean hard body, he was irresistible.

So was that bit of larceny she'd seen in him.

She would be hard-pressed to say why she had been drawn to the popinjay from the moment he'd rescued her at the theater.

Perhaps . . .

There was no such thing as two souls intended for one another. 'Twas nothing but an accident of fate, and they both had futures that precluded the other.

Still . . .

Still, she could not step away from him. She heard a noise coming from deep inside his throat, a groan of private protest, but like her he seemed unable to heed it. She understood then that he had some of the same demons as she.

He bent his head again and their lids met, and she was lost in a flood of sensations that had no reason. They were like gluttons, soaking up the essence of each other, and she realized they had been starving for each other during those wretched hours in the coach. All that time, they had been reaching out for each other, stopped only by their companions and their competing goals.

Monique felt his mouth drive hard against hers and his arms went back around her again, one of his hands burying itself in her hair.

He drew her body closer to his, as close as they could come with clothes separating them. She trembled as one shock wave after another jolted through her. Heat licked around the core of her as he pulled her tighter against him.

All thoughts disappeared, swamped with an overwhelming longing even stronger than those on the first night he had taken her to bed. She knew now what to expect, the glorious sensations . . .

She had no will when he was around, when he touched her. And now he was doing just that. Every place. His mouth was hard against hers, his tongue seductive as it teased her lips into opening, then explored, hungrily at first and finally incredibly gentle.

His fingers ran around the back of her neck, massaging her tired muscles until the tension faded from them, and her body relaxed against his. He unbuttoned her dress, and his mouth moved from hers and feathered her neck with kisses as his hands tugged her dress off.

She stood in her chemise, her body shivering with reaction from the seductive gentleness of his touch. Hot searing need was building in her, sending tingling sensations through every nerve ending.

Every resolve, every defense she thought she'd constructed tumbled away like sand carried away by seawater.

He guided her to the bed, then took off his cravat, followed by his shirt. He sat down and pulled at his boots while she watched.

He cursed under his breath, but she got the sense of it and couldn't help but smile. He was usually very efficient when no one but her was around to observe.

She left the bed and found a chair, moving it toward him. Then she took the heel of the boot and pulled.

She went over backward as the boot pulled loose.

Startled and chagrined to realize her chemise had flown up to reveal two stockinged legs, she scrambled up, knowing she looked like an awkward child.

But he was there, one boot on, one boot off, looking concerned and amused. He leaned down and offered her his hand and with one gentle tug she was up on her feet.

"You would not make a very good valet, " he observed.

"You are an ungrateful wretch."

His finger touched her cheek. "Are you hurt?"

"Only my pride."

"You looked lovely."

"With my legs over my head."

"Fetching," he corrected.

"And you look a bit odd with one boot on."

"I hate the bloody things," he confided. "But they seem to be all the fashion in London."

"What do you usually wear?"

*Mundane things.* They were talking about mundane things. And yet their words were breathless, underlaid with unsaid suggestion.

She looked up at him, and his green eyes were intense, even brooding.

"Not these bloody things," he said, avoiding her question as he had avoided so many others.

Her hand went up to his face. There was the slightest bristle now.

"You still have a boot on." She knew her voice was little more than a whisper.

"Do you want to try again?"

"I think I will watch you," she said.

He obviously had more incentive. His boot came off swiftly.

Then he stood. She untied the laces of his breeches, slowly, awkwardly, distracted as she was by lips that trailed kisses from her cheek to the nape of her neck.

When she finished the ties, her hands went to his chest, exploring the hard ridges, the muscles that flexed slightly under her touch. His body was rigid, her own alive with shots of electricity.

He released her, stepped out of the tight breeches, then pulled her chemise over her body. There was no corset. She had taken it off earlier when she had first arrived, and now there was nothing between them.

He held out his hand and guided her down on the bed and lowered his own body until he hovered over her. He kissed her hard, demanding, seeking. The kiss—and the touch of his body—ignited an explosion inside her, a series of detonations that exposed a raw craving so strong she knew it must be satisfied or she might well explode.

She put her arms around him, slowly pulling him down to her, feeling his need, the throbbing that teased, then entered her. Slowly. Carefully. There was no pain now, only expectation, only an overwhelming need to know whether this new journey would be as powerful, as exquisite . . .

He moved in and out with a slow seductiveness that drove her to near insanity. Her body strained against him, and she felt him fill her, move inside with a rhythmic dance that made her body come alive with wonderful, exquisite feelings too complex to ever define. Her body reacted instinctively, joining a primitive dance that evoked exotic reactions that built and built . . .

Her legs went around him, drawing him even deeper inside as sensations cascaded through her, even as she knew that this was but a prelude, that together they were rushing toward some paradise.

A cry escaped her and his mouth came down on hers, his kiss snatching the sound from her even as he made one last thrust and erupted inside her, sending waves of shuddering warmth through her, then explosions that rocked her body and cast a rich, mellow glow in its wake.

He collapsed on her for a moment, then rolled over on his side, carrying her with him. He held her tightly, and she heard the beat of his heart, the sound of withheld breath.

Her body still quaked with aftershocks of pleasure as she felt him move and withdraw from her. She felt him shudder as he held her for a long time, his hands moving possessively but gently over her. She, in turn, explored his back with her hands, her fingers catching in crinkly sandy tendrils at the back of his neck.

"I never knew it could be like this," she whispered.

"It is usually not," he said. "This is rare."

She was pleased at that. "Truly?" she asked.

"Truly," he confirmed with that deep, husky drawl.

"Are you going to leave again?" she asked, hating the question but having to know the answer.

"No, not now."

"Then later?"

He wrapped his arm tighter around her and pulled her closer. He leaned over and feathered kisses across her cheek. "You know we might have a child."

She stiffened slightly. She knew. She had known nights ago when he had first taken her to bed. She of all people knew the dangers of such a liaison. Yet, she had closed her mind to the possibility.

She did not answer, only opened her eyes to look at him. "You must have . . . made love before," she said. "Did you not worry about it then?"

"I was careful," he said, his fingers drawing hair from her face. "The women knew what to do.'"

"And you do not think I do?"

His lips crooked at one side in a half smile. *"Non,"* he said, mimicking her in an oddly warm way. "I did not know you were a virgin the other night. Had I but known . . ."

"Is that why you left? You did not want responsibility?" She forced the words out.

"No, pretty lady. That is not why. I take responsibility for what I do. But I realized then . . ."

She waited for him to continue.

"That I felt far stronger than I wanted to feel," he finally continued, his eyes intent on hers. It was one of the few times he'd allowed any emotion to show. "What I am doing is dangerous, Monique. I did not want you involved in it." He took her fingers, catching them in his hands, which only now she noticed were hard with calluses.

"Perhaps you did not notice I was already involved," she said.

"I did not know that you could also break into a safe."

"I did not know you were a thief."

He watched her carefully. "Perhaps it is time for more honesty between us."

She stiffened.

"Why?" he said. "Why are you risking your life to steal something Stanhope would give you? Especially if you did not intend to keep it."

She looked at him straight in the eyes. "The same reason I started the contest between the three men. I wanted them to turn on one another."

"Why was that so important?"

"I told you Stanhope hurt someone I cared about."

"Who?"

"My mother. Stanhope ruined her, then tried to have her killed. She had to flee England but had no funds, no talents, no references. She was English in a French city. She ended up going from man to man, each a little poorer, each a little more brutal. From what you said, he had done that before."

His eyes never left her, but his fingers touched her chin. "And you . . . how did you escape the same fate?"

"One of my mother's friends was an actress. She saw me mimic someone in the streets and took me to her theater company. I helped with makeup and costumes and studied. There was one small part and then another."

"And your mother?"

"She died of pneumonia. Not enough food. Not enough heat. Not any hope. She just . . . faded away."

"She was English?"

Monique nodded.

His hand tightened around hers. "You cannot let it go?"

"Can *you*?" she asked.

"I am not sure what you mean?"

Disappointment, even anger, filled her, making the sense of euphoria fade. She had told him her secrets—at least part of them and he was still playing the fool.

She withdrew her hand and moved away. "I do not think you stole those jewels, or even came to England, to save an impoverished estate."

He caught her hand again and pulled her to him. "My father," he said in a voice ragged with emotion. "Stanhope and his friends framed him. He was to be charged with treason. He shot himself minutes after asking me to clear his name someday. He wrote down the three names of the men responsible."

The smile was gone now. Agony was in his eyes. She wondered whether the same grief had shone in her own eyes minutes earlier.

"I heard the shot," he said in a cold hard voice. All the warmth was gone. "I saw him lying in a pool of his blood. It killed my mother as well but it took her several more years to take her final breath."

She slowly exhaled. She hadn't realized the breath was caught in her throat. "How old were you?"

"Ten."

"He asked that of a ten-year-old boy?" Horror edged her voice.

"There was no one else," he said. "My mother . . ." He stopped. "But that is something else . . ."

He worked his fingers between hers, then clutched them tightly.

"I had the same idea as you did," he said, changing the subject away from his own pain. "Turn them against each other. But I have something else in mind as well. I need his confidence first. I have to be his partner in a venture, then there will be papers . . . I do not want to kill him. I want the government to do that for me. I want him disgraced. Then I want his government to punish him. They have ways . . . that I think would be worse than death for him."

She was silent, shifting through the words. Bitter words. As bitter as her own had been. They were both here for the same reason. It astounded her. And it broke her heart.

And the past few hours she realized she loved him. She loved the gentleness that was counterpart to the hardness she also saw in him. She loved his quiet competence and grace.

"What are you really?" she asked.

The severity of his face eased slightly. "When I am not an impoverished lord?"

*"Oui."*

"A sailor," he said simply.

"More than that, I think. A captain, perhaps?"

He hesitated, and she knew that he wondered whether he was saying too much. He must have some secrets left of his own. Just as she did. And if she pried into his, he might well pry into hers. What would he think if he knew she was Stanhope's daughter? The daughter of a whore and a murderer?

She shuddered and he pulled her back down next to her, holding her tightly in his arms.

Despite his warmth, though, she felt a chill. She loved him. But she did not altogether trust his ability to accept her. They had made love, but they had been brought together by hatred. What kind of future could that possibly bring?

*I can forget about my mother.*

But she could not. She had started something that had taken on a life of its own. She had worked toward justice since her mother died years ago. And then there was Pamela. What would happen to her if she left?

Manchester's hand turned her face so he could see it. "Will you leave? Go to Boston and wait for me there? I can make the arrangements."

"And you?"

"I will take care of Stanhope."

"No," she said. "It is my battle. You can leave and I will join you later."

"Do you really believe I will leave you to finish what I started? Leave you in danger?"

"Then we are at a stalemate," she said.

"What if we left together, leave Stanhope to his own fate?"

"What about Pamela?"

"We can take her with us."

Her eyes glowed for a moment, then the brightness faded. "I do not think she will come. Her young man . . ."

"As long as Stanhope lives, she will never have him. Not if she stays here," he said. "And what would you say to her? Run off to America with us. She does not really know either of us. We can offer her little."

She bit her lip. "We can . . . work together here, you and I. We did well at Stanhope's manor." She had summoned all her courage to make that offer.

"There is too much risk." There was no give in his statement. It was a denial plain and simple.

"Then I will do what I have been doing," she said defiantly. "With you or without you."

His finger traced the bones in her cheek, then went her neck and rested there. "It is a lovely neck," he said. "I do not want to see it hurt."

"You cannot frighten me. I have considered all the consequences."

"Has Dani? If she had been caught the other night, neither of us could have saved her."

He had found the one consequence that concerned her the most. "I did not want her to come."

"My Smythe is quite taken with her," he said.

She wondered why he was changing the subject.

"She likes him," she replied cautiously.

"They could get a new start in America."

"And his family?"

"They, too. I am associated with a shipping company. I can arrange passage for them all. There are many opportunities there for willing hands. He would do well."

She shivered slightly and his right arm went back around her. "Think about it," he said. "Think about leaving with them. I will be there soon after."

He pulled her to him and his lips met hers and reason fled. Tomorrow. There would be time tomorrow to make decisions.

That was her last rational thought before their bodies met again, and his lips rained kisses on the nape of her neck. Her body started tingling again, and she felt the complete wanton as she wrapped her arms around him and brought him even closer to her.

Her fingers ran around the back of his neck, and she heard the soft groan. "Ah, Monique," he said.

"Merry," she corrected softly.

His lips left hers, and he nuzzled her earlobes a moment. She wondered whether he had even heard her.

Then he looked at her, a half smile on his lips. "Merry." It was as if he were rolling it on his tongue. "A pretty name."

"A whimsical name," she said. "My mother always yearned for things she could not have, but she had high hopes for me." She heard the sadness in her own voice. For a moment she was back in the dark, cold room where her mother had died.

Then Gabriel ran his tongue along the back of her neck and the momentary melancholy faded. She needed his warmth, his comfort, his strength. She'd never realized how lonely she'd been until these past few days.

But so many words were still impossible between them. Her secret had been held so deeply all these years that it was locked inside. Her mother had told her over and over again that revelation and discovery would mean death. She had lived with a fear that had been so locked into her soul that she did not think she could ever share it.

She had told Dani, only to make her understand how dangerous this journey was, and why she'd needed certain skills that Dani and her acquaintances had.

And now Manchester had asked her to go to America. But he'd said nothing of love, or marriage. He had kept a part of him detached from her just as she had done.

For a moment an iciness in her soul counteracted the heat

kindled by his body. Then his lips captured her mouth again in a long, smothering kiss, and she felt the same tormenting need that had racked her body earlier. It was painful, yet so exquisitely new and compelling and wonderful that she felt she couldn't breathe.

"Merry?" She noticed he was still tasting the name on his lips.

She raised her eyes to meet his. They were intense and brooding.

She had never seen them like that before. In the past they had been clear, revealing little, or amused.

He was asking her a question. Should he continue? She wondered why he was asking now.

But then she felt desperation of her own. Uncertainty. Would she—could she—forgive herself if she left undone a goal she'd had nearly all her life? Could she ever live in peace knowing Stanhope was alive and probably seeking new victims?

He was waiting for an answer to the unspoken question. It hovered in the air.

She swallowed hard, then touched his face with her hand. This might be one of the last times she saw him. He would not like what she was considering.

"Do not leave me," she said. "Not now."

He leaned toward her and kissed her with a tender violence. Every movement of his body made hers hum with feelings. His breathing was ragged against her hair, and her body moved toward his, hungry, so very hungry.

This time their bodies merged with a violence and need that eclipsed everything else.

"Gabriel," she cried out.

His lips quieted her but she felt the fierce hunger in both of them, the need that neither could control. He drove deeper inside her as if claiming her for his very own. Her body pulsed with his, danced in his, each giving in a way they had not before.

And then there was a shattering burst of ecstasy, a pleasure so strong she wanted to remain in his arms forever. They lay there together, their hearts beating in rapid tandem, their bodies damp with sweat.

Her body shuddered with the marvels of aftermath, ripples of sensation continuing to flow through her as she relaxed in his arms, trying not to think it could be the last time.

# Chapter Twenty-four

They had a late supper. A very late supper.

Gabriel had quietly risen after he thought she was asleep. He had no intention of leaving her this time. He would never leave her the way he had before. Not without a word, without explanation.

But he was hungry and wondered about poor Smythe.

Gabriel pulled on his shirt, which came to his thighs, and got as far as opening the door. Outside was a tray laden with a platter of fruit and bread, cheese and chicken, a bottle of wine, and two glasses.

The very capable Smythe, he thought with a smile. He wondered where his valet was at the moment but deduced that he was well looked after.

He lifted the tray and took it to the bed.

Monique was lying still, her eyes closed, yet there was a stiffness that told him she was not sleeping.

He leaned down and kissed her. "I am not leaving, love," he said.

She opened her eyes slowly, fluttering them as if she had just awakened. The actress in her again.

"I *was* sleeping," she protested.

"You look beautiful," he said. "Too beautiful. I was afraid I would ravish you all over again."

"I like being ravished," she replied lazily.

"I hope you do not tell all the gentlemen that," he said.

*"Non,"* she said. "I do not tell any *gentlemen* that."

"That was a cruel blow," he said.

"I do not care for gentlemen," she said.

"Good." He handed her a grape and watched as she daintily ate around the seeds and the juice colored her lips. Her tongue reached out and licked them.

She was more delectable than any tidbit of food. But now he had to keep his senses about him. He had to find a way to get her safely out of London.

She pulled off a piece of cheese and popped it in his mouth.

He ate the cheese, pulled off a piece of chicken, and offered it to her. She took it in her teeth and watched as he did the same. There was something erotically sensual about feeding each other. He fought against the desire rising in him again.

He poured a glass of wine and took a sip. She leaned over and took a sip of her own.

"You have good taste," he said even as he knew his eyes were probably saying something else altogether.

"I truly do not know where that wine came from," she said.

"Smythe. He has turned out to be a rather inventive valet."

"I think Dani believes so," she replied, nibbling on another grape.

He had to force himself not to take her again, then and there.

Instead he rose, well aware of his near nakedness, and went to the pitcher and bowl on the dressing table. He poured water into the bowl and rinsed himself. Then he returned to the side of the bed where his breeches lay crumpled in a pile. He pulled them on and fastened them. Then turned back to her.

She watched him as she sipped the glass of wine. Damn, but he wanted her. But every time he succumbed to the want inside him, he feared he might be endangering both of them.

They both needed their wits to leave this game with their lives.

He had to think, and the simple truth was he could not think with her in the room. Hell, in the same city. He had to find a way to get her out of it.

She sat up, the sheet covering most of her body. Her gray eyes looked sleepy but questioning.

He leaned over and kissed her. "I must get back to my lodgings, love, I will get no sleep with you next to me and I have business in the morning." He paused. "I will be back later today," he said.

Her eyes darkened slightly but she only said mildly, "That is just as well. I have to be back to the theater."

Gabriel did not want to go. Everything in him wanted to lie next to her, but he knew neither of them would get much sleep. They were like gunpowder and fire together.

"Will you have supper with me after the play?"

*"Oui,"* she said simply.

He touched her cheek, caressing it with a longing that would not go away. "Later then?"

She had burrowed back deeper in the bed. He took the tray and put it on a table. He hesitated again, then pulled on his shirt and coat. He paused at the door, then forced himself to open it.

He didn't look back as he walked swiftly down the hall.

Monique couldn't quell a feeling of abandonment again, even as she understood his reasons. She also needed some time of her own. She could not reason with him in proximity. There was too much attraction, too much emotion, too much desire.

And she did have to be back to the theater tonight.

*The jewelry. The few pieces they had kept.* She suddenly remembered them. Had Manchester taken them with him? She had offered them to him, but then the two of them had been swept away into madness. Had he remembered them? She did not want Mrs. Miller to find them.

She reluctantly rose. Her body still felt warm inside. She found her nightdress, then the night robe, and put them on. She went to the window and saw him walk down the street with his valet. They looked more like two friends than master and servant.

Carrying the oil lamp, she went down the steps to the drawing room, to where he had picked her up, to where she thought she might have dropped the jewelry.

The floor was empty.

Smythe was uncanny. He'd appeared as Gabriel had found his cloak laid neatly on a table.

"Bloody hell, how do you do that?"

"Do what?"

"Know my every move?" Gabriel asked. "I thought you might well have gone to our lodgings."

"And miss a few hours with Miss Dani?" Smythe asked.

It was another confidence.

"My lord?" he said then, his tone suddenly uncertain, "Sir?"

Gabriel raised an eyebrow.

"I . . . I found some jewelry in the living room."

Gabriel felt as if the air had just been sucked from the room. Damn but now he remembered . . .

"Where is it?" he asked.

Smythe held out his hand and emptied its contents into Gabriel's. "I feared someone . . . might find it."

Gabriel took it. "Does Dani know you found it?"

"I did not wish to involve her," he said. "I heard one piece of jewelry described before we left." His voice was agonized. "I did not know what to do."

"Come," Gabriel said. "We will find a hackney to return to our lodgings. I will get Specter later."

Gabriel knew he would discover how right he had been about Smythe's loyalty.

Once they had found a hackney, they climbed inside.

There was no lantern inside, and Smythe's face was hidden in the shadows.

"I stole them," Gabriel said in response to the unspoken question that had hovered between them.

Silence. A kind of agonized silence, and Gabriel sensed

that Smythe was feeling betrayed. He had given his loyalty and, even more than that, to someone who was a thief.

"I want you to know why," he continued. Smythe held his life in his hands now.

Smythe's silence continued.

"Lord Stanhope was in business with my father twenty years ago. My father owned a shipping company. Stanhope provided government contracts. A ship carrying supplies sank. Only a few men survived. They returned with a story of rotten food and empty boxes that should contain muskets. The ship was unseaworthy and apparently meant to sink. My father was accused of treason."

Smythe was listening intently.

"My father was innocent. He knew it was his word against Stanhope's, and Stanhope had influence, even then. My father did not want to see my mother and myself subjected to a long trial. He killed himself just as he was to be arrested.

"Seconds before he shot himself he gave me the names of three men he realized were responsible. He asked me to obtain justice."

"Forgive me, my lord, but how do you know he told the truth?" Smythe's voice was steady. The fact that he said "my lord" was very telling.

"You would have to know my father," Gabriel said slowly. "He lived for honor. He never would have charged me to seek justice if he had been guilty. There would be no reason once he had died. When I was old enough, I had Stanhope and his friends investigated. They leave a wake of ruined partners and unexpected deaths. The only way to expose them is to turn them against one another. Taking the jewels is one part of that plan." He consciously avoided any mention of Monique and Dani.

Smythe was silent for several moments, then said, "His servants fear him. Dani trusts you." Another silence. He was obviously considering his mother and sister.

Then he nodded, the movement visible in the dark interior. "If I can help you . . . ?"

It was the ultimate in trust. "My thanks," Gabriel said simply. "But I will not let you or yours be involved."

"Is that why you would pay our way to America?"

"I did not want any . . . actions to affect you."

"Is it true about opportunities there . . . ?"

"Yes. It is a big land, much of it unsettled. There is much room to grow and land for the taking."

"My sister can go to school?"

"Aye."

Smythe stood straighter. "Then I say yes."

"Your mother?"

"She will go."

"I will make arrangements later today."

"May I give you some assistance now? I . . . that is the reason I picked up the jewels. I thought you might be in some difficulty."

"I knew there was a reason I selected you that day," Gabriel said. "But no, I think not. I would rather . . ."

"No one has helped us before. You have been kind to Elizabeth. I want to help now."

Touched, Gabriel did not say anything for several moments. He had come to England to steal, to cheat, to betray, to do anything necessary to fulfill an oath he'd once made. He had not expected to fall victim to emotions.

He had. He truly liked Pamela. He admired Smythe. *And Monique—or Merry—well, he . . . he—drat it—he loved her.*

The hard shell that he'd constructed that day outside his father's office was slowly crumbling. Which could make him careless.

Maybe he *should* leave. Kidnap Monique if necessary. Take her to America. He suspected she would like the vibrant, exciting country that was building a new society. America would love her.

He smiled at that prospect. He was not sure America was ready for Monique Fremont. Or Merry . . .

Merry what? She had not mentioned her last name.

*Merry.* He tasted the name. It did not resonate. Monique did. Monique was sophisticated, worldly, even a little exotic. Merry belonged to a happy child. But he suspected Monique had never been a happy child. The thought saddened him.

He found himself wanting to give her everything she'd

never had. He wanted to hear her laugh. Wanted to see mischief dance in her eyes. He realized now that except for the moments they had made love, she had been reserved, even cautious. Almost waiting for him to leave, to desert her.

The carriage reached his lodgings. Smythe stepped out first and started to pull down the steps, but Gabriel ignored them and alighted, taking the big step easily. He started for the entrance, suddenly realizing that his small trunk was back at Monique's. He would have to stop by there tomorrow.

But first he had business that must be transacted.

And there was the matter of rest. He needed a little of that, too.

The waterfront was bustling as Gabriel approached it on foot.

Under his dark cloak, he wore plain clothes.

No one followed him today, or at least no one he noticed. He had taken several precautions, slipping in one tavern and leaving by the back door, then wandering down some backstreets. Satisfied he was alone, he found his way to the printing shop and entered.

The printer was perched on a tall stool, sitting exactly as he had before. He looked up and scowled. "Thought I had seen the last of you."

"Why?"

"You got one of them, did ye? I thought that might cool your blood."

Gabriel arched an eyebrow. "One of them?"

"Lord Robert Stammel was overtaken by brigands last night and murdered. Jack Pryor just heard the news. There will be hell to pay for this one. A lord dead on the road."

"It was not me. I was in Stanhope's own coach with a coachman as a witness, along with a lady, her maid, and my valet." Even as he uttered the words, however, he was digesting the information. Maybe he *had* been responsible.

The thought stunned him. He had wanted to turn the members of The Group against one another. He had not thought Stanhope would rid himself of a problem by murdering someone everyone considered his best friend. It was a reminder of

how ruthless his opponent was. How dangerous the game
Monique was playing.

Or maybe it had not been Stanhope at all. Maybe it had
been Daven.

Winsley was watching him carefully. He finally shrugged.
"None of my affair as to what happens to 'im. But I did not
think ye the kind to waylay a man."

"But you approve of thieves?"

"Good ones," Winsley replied with a crack of a smile. It
quickly faded. "It was Stanhope then?"

"Most likely. He might have believed Stammel was stealing from him."

"And was he?"

"Probably," Gabriel said. He had meant to ask Winsley to
find a buyer for the jewelry. That was out of the question now.
If it was ever traced back . . . With a silent curse he knew the
jewels would be in the Thames later tonight.

"What brought you here?" Winsley asked.

"I might have some contracts that need a few changes."

"How long will I have?"

"A day."

"Do you have samples of the handwriting?"

"I will get them for you."

Winsley turned and bent back down to the table in front,
where agile fingers sorted type so quickly it made Gabriel
blink. He had been dismissed.

Gabriel left the small, cramped print shop and moved
quickly through the backstreets until he reached the docks. He
looked to see whether any of his company's ships had anchored. The *Cynthia* was gone as expected.

No familiar names. He went to the shipmaster's office.
Several men sat inside a small room. A haze of smoke rose
from the pipes two of them smoked.

They looked up at him.

"Are there any ships leaving for America in the next two
days? Taking passengers?"

"Aye," said the stoutest of the men. "The *Amelia* will be
leaving in two days. You might want to talk to the captain. For

a pence, Billy will row you out there." He nodded toward a thin man in tattered clothes.

The thin man stood. "Aye, Gov'nor. I know the ship."

"American?" Gabriel asked.

"Aye, it is that."

Gabriel nodded. "Can we go now?"

"Aye."

In minutes Billy was rowing a rickety boat toward one of many ships anchored off the dock. As they approached one, he saw the name.

The ship looked sleek and well maintained. A rope ladder was lowered as they approached and he quickly climbed it. The decks were clean and the visible sailors looked busy and efficient. Gabriel was impressed.

While waiting to see the captain, he glanced over the furled sails. The sheets looked to be in good repair.

The seaman who had gone to alert the captain returned. "He'll see you now."

Gabriel followed him down the companionway to a door. The seaman rapped, then opened it.

Gabriel entered and saw a short, powerfully built man standing behind the desk. He held out a hand. "I am Captain Jeremiah Morris."

Gabriel took it and liked the feel of it. Strong. Confident. "Gabriel Manning," he said.

The captain's eyebrows arched. "Manning? You are not the Manning that captained the *Liberty*."

Gabriel's heart skipped a beat. He had not expected anyone to connect him with the privateer captain that caused the British to lose more than a few ships. He did not want to lie, particularly since he planned to request a very unorthodox favor from this man.

He nodded. "But I wish you would not let anyone else know."

"You fear reprisal here?"

"I have delicate business."

Morris nodded, evidently thinking it must have something to do with the government. "My ship was one of those stopped by the British navy before the war, and my sailors taken. I have little liking for them." He shrugged. "Unfortunately my cargo brought me here."

"When are you leaving?"

"Day after tomorrow. We are loading tomorrow at the docks."

"Do you carry passengers?"

"We have a few cabins."

This was the difficult part. "There is a lady, and another family. I would like to buy passage for us."

"Three cabins?"

"Aye," Gabriel said.

"I think I can accommodate you."

"How much for the passage?"

Morris named a sum far below what Gabriel knew was common. He did not argue.

"Is this your ship?"

"It belongs to Mallard Shipping, but I have an interest," Morris said proudly.

"It is a fine-looking ship."

"Aye, it is that. Only two years old and New England built. Would you like to see the cabins?"

Gabriel nodded, then said cautiously, "I ask you to say nothing to the port authorities about this. The lady in question is being terrorized by an English lord. If he knew she was leaving England, he might use any means to prevent it."

"I know your reputation, Captain," Morris said. "I will say nothing. But be aboard by midnight tomorrow night. We will sail at dawn."

"I will bring payment tomorrow," Gabriel said.

"It will be my honor to have you aboard," Morris said. "Perhaps you would share some of your experiences with me."

Gabriel nodded, though he would not be there to do so. That conscience that continued to get in the way nudged him. It was becoming very annoying.

It was for her own good, he told himself.

A seaman took him by the cabins. They were small and plain, but clean. There were some belongings there, and he suspected the first and second mates occupied them when there were no passengers. "They will do very well," he said.

Then he was back on deck. Billy's unseaworthy boat rocked back and forth against the side of the ship. Gabriel quickly climbed down, timing his jump to the roll of the boat.

It was done.

Monique sent for her detective. Mrs. Miller found a boy to deliver the message.

In two hours he was at the door. She ushered him into the small parlor. "I am ending the investigation of Lord Manchester," she said.

He had a sheaf of papers in his hand. "But . . . I have learned about his background. His father was accused of treason."

Monique started to stop him, then allowed him to continue. Perhaps he had discovered something Gabriel did not know.

*Gabriel.* How easily the name now came to her mind. She had pushed him away by trying to think of him as Manchester. Now he was most definitely . . . Gabriel.

"He shot himself, according to the official report," the detective continued, "but he had protested his innocence. He had claimed that the signature on a contract was not his. A magistrate ruled that it was."

"Does it mention any other names?"

"Aye. His partners were the Earls of Stanhope and Daven. But they were cleared of any misconduct."

"Anything else?" she asked.

He hesitated.

"Do not hesitate," she insisted. "I want to know."

"Some people thought the offense was not Mr. Manning's but the two earls," he said. "One who voiced such an opinion disappeared. No one else dared speak out."

She mused over that piece of information. "Is there more?"

"Aye, the marquess has engaged a room in a waterfront inn. Apparently he meets a lady there."

Monique went still. "I thought you lost him."

"I was afraid he might see me. I placed a young lad here and a lady on a street where I once saw him. She followed

him to a tavern. The young lady paid the tavern keeper for information. The gentleman took the rooms two weeks ago to
meet with a lady. He implied she was married."

"Has anyone seen her?"

"No. They are very discrete."

"Thank you," she said. Her heart pounded. How much was
true? He had said nothing about rooms on the waterfront.
How much else had he not told her?

"Anything else, miss?" the detective said.

She hesitated.

He shifted from foot to foot, then said, "Did you hear the
news about Lord Stammel?"

"What news?"

"He was found dead on the road to London. Highwaymen,
they say."

*Gabriel had planted jewels in his room.*

*Stanhope!* Apparently, the plan had worked only too well.

It struck her, then. She had known how dangerous he was.
She had heard it for years. But this was here and now. A chill
ran down her back.

And Gabriel? His life was certainly threatened as well.

If he left . . .

She had been picking at an idea all day, ever since their
conversation last night. She had been debating herself.

Now she knew.

"Can you do something else for me?" she asked.

"I am at your service, miss."

"See if there is a ship that is bound for America in the next
few days."

He nodded.

"And I will need the services of two men. Trustworthy but
not beyond breaking a law."

He stiffened.

"I know that you told me you will not break the law," she
said soothingly, "but perhaps you might know someone without your . . . scruples. I assure you that no one will be hurt."

"Then . . . ?"

"There is someone in danger. The same kind of danger I

believe Lord Stammel found. I wish to get him out of the country. He does not wish to go."

"The Marquess of Manchester," he said.

"I mentioned no names."

His gaze did not leave hers. Then he looked away. "I will ask two gentlemen to call. After that, it is none of my affair."

"Thank you," she said. "Do you have your bill?"

He handed her a sheet of rough paper with figures jotted on it. The sum was more than reasonable. She paid him.

"If you need anything else, miss . . ."

"I will call on you," she assured him.

"The two men are Mickey Kelley and Sam Barr. They look rough, but they are intelligent enough, and loyal."

He left, and she sat down in a chair. She would have to leave for the theater soon. But a thousand thoughts rushed through her mind. Stammel dead. And Manchester—Gabriel—had a room in the dock area. Why? He'd not mentioned it to her.

But then she had not mentioned some things to him, either.

And if she proceeded with her plan, how would he feel then? It would end every possibility of a future with him.

But his life was more important.

He had mentioned going to America together. Had he meant it? Could either of them just leave Stanhope to continue killing?

She honestly believed she had the best opportunity to safely bring him to justice.

She finally stood. It was time to get ready for theater.

# Chapter Twenty-five

Gabriel told Smythe when he arrived back at the town house he was renting that he had arranged for passage for him and his family.

"You are going too, sir?"

"Not now," he said. "Miss Fremont and her maid will be going."

Smythe looked startled. "Danielle said nothing about that."

*So it was Danielle now.*

"She might take some convincing," Gabriel admitted. "But I heard today that Lord Stammel was killed last night. I fear that both Miss Fremont and Dani are in danger."

Smythe's brows knitted together. "Lord Stammel?"

Gabriel nodded. "I suspect Lord Stanhope is responsible."

"But why? He was a guest there."

"He owed me money. He drank too much. I think Stanhope believed he stole from him."

Realization dawned across Smythe's face. "The jewels?"

"And money."

Smythe looked stricken.

"Others have conveniently died around Lord Stanhope," Gabriel continued. "That's why I want you and your family to leave. And I am trusting you to look after Dani and Miss Fremont."

"You may need help."

"Your family cannot go alone," Gabriel said. "Neither can Miss Fremont and your Dani."

"She is not my Dani, sir," Smythe said with dignity.

"She looks at you as if she was," Gabriel observed.

Smythe looked pleased. "Is that true, sir?"

"Aye, it is."

"May I say that Miss Fremont looks at you with regard?"

"You may say so, Smythe, but I doubt if she will in the next few days."

Smythe waited for him to continue.

"It is for her own good," Gabriel said. "And Dani's. I will have letters for you to give to the owner of the shipping company that employs me. He will find a place for you to live. And employment.

"Hopefully, Miss Fremont will choose to go," Gabriel continued. "But if she doesn't, I will need your help. Now that Stanhope has killed his partner, he will be even more dangerous, especially if he believes Monique has anything to do with it."

Smythe nodded. "I'll do what is necessary."

"Good. Did you get my trunk from her residence?"

"I brought it back today. The horse is still at the stable."

"I will fetch him," Gabriel said. "I hope I can take him to America."

Smythe smiled. "I did well, then?"

"You did very well. You do well in every task I give you. I hope in America you will work for me. Or the shipping company."

"I am not good at reading and writing," Smythe said haltingly. "I hope my sister . . ."

"You can do anything, Smythe. I am quite confident of that."

Smythe's face turned a ruddy color.

"I am going to call on Lord Stanhope's home and see whether he is expected," Gabriel said.

"Should I go with you?"

"I think not. I might make a visit inside if he has not yet arrived. If anything happens to me, I want you to take Miss Fremont, her maid, and your family to America. There is a letter and funds in the top drawer of my desk. The ship is the *Amelia*. The captain is Morris."

Smythe's face fell.

"I do not want you anywhere near Stanhope's home. If something happens to both of us, your family, Monique, and Dani will not have any protection."

Smythe nodded reluctantly.

"Is there anything I can do?"

"The cravat. I want to look distinguished."

Smythe permitted the slightest smile as he produced a ruffled linen shirt, a pair of breeches, and boots. "Which waistcoat?"

"The most obnoxious one," Gabriel said.

Smythe reached into the wardrobe and found one of a purplish hue, a color that Gabriel himself had selected after being repelled by it. He thought if he was, then so would others.

He waited patiently as Smythe tied his cravat. "How did you ever learn to do it so quickly?" he asked.

Smythe cleared his throat. "I paid a valet down the street to teach me," he said.

"How much?"

"A half pound."

It was considerable for a servant.

"He also taught me how to clean your clothes, sir, and what you might expect from me."

"And have I met your expectations?"

"No sir. I have decided you are a most unusual lord."

"Comes of being an American," he said.

"But you were born here."

"Aye, I was, but I am American in heart and soul. And I suspect you will be, too."

The first doubt crossed Smythe's face, and Gabriel suddenly realized what he had proposed to Smythe. He was taking him away from everything he knew. Smythe had agreed readily enough, but was he playing God with other lives?

He'd told himself it was for Smythe's protection, but

Smythe needed protection only because of Gabriel's own actions.

And now he was planning to whisk Monique away from her career and her own needs without giving her a chance to say yea or nay.

"Are you sure you and your family wish to go?" Gabriel asked. "No doubts?"

Smythe nodded after the briefest of hesitation. "Employment is difficult to find here. Elizabeth has few chances."

Gabriel nodded. He looked in the mirror. The cravat was quite extraordinary.

Indeed, Smythe could do anything.

Yet the thought of playing God plagued him. He had no right to take Monique away even if he thought it necessary.

He would just have to be more persuasive.

Monique reached the theater long before the performance.

She already knew that Lynch was a gossip and had friends at the various newspapers in London.

He looked delighted at seeing her. "My dear. I was not sure you would return today. The understudy . . . well, she is not *you*. The audiences have not been happy."

"You heard about Lord Stammel's death?" she said solemnly.

"All of London is talking about it. Dastardly footpads. They will be caught, though. The Crown cannot ignore the murder of one of its distinguished peers."

*Hardly distinguished.* Monique had shed few tears for the man. If half of what she had heard was true, Stammel deserved his fate. Instead, she concentrated on giving the performance of her life. Her hand shook and she managed the slightest warble in her voice. "I am not entirely sure it was footpads, monsieur."

Lynch's brows knitted together. "What do you mean?"

"I heard a dreadful row between Lord Stammel and the Earl of Stanhope. Some jewelry was stolen during the house party and it was found in Lord Stammel's room." She hesitated. "And then there is that . . . competition."

Lynch's mouth dropped as she continued. "If—if anyone

knew I said anything . . . you must not say anything to anyone," she said in a quaking voice. "I did not realize Lord Stanhope was a violent man or I never would have . . ."

She wrung her hands together. "That contest was a terrible idea. To think I might have been responsible . . . and then I overheard—" She stopped suddenly.

"You are not saying . . ."

"I am not saying anything. *You* cannot say anything. Unless you wish to be responsible for my—" She stopped suddenly. She knew her face was pale, her eyes frantic.

"Promise me you will say nothing. Nothing."

He continued to stare at her. "I have heard rumors about him," he said, conveniently forgetting that Stanhope's bribe to him allowed her to attend Stanhope's party.

"You swear you will not say anything?"

"I swear," he said. "Do you . . . need someone to protect you?"

"Against an earl? I am but an actress. If he knew or suspected I had heard anything . . ."

His face went white. Prinny had been singing her praise and had even suggested he might help obtain a license for legitimate drama. She was his chance at success.

The question was what he would do with the information. She had a fairly good guess. She only hoped she was right.

She tried not to think about what Manchester would think. He would disapprove. She knew that in her heart. But it had occurred to her after he had left.

If her plan worked, it could be a matter of hours before Stanhope struck. Not days.

Lynch would be unable to keep the news to himself, even though it might endanger his prize attraction.

And Stanhope could not afford to let her live.


Stanhope was in residence.

Gabriel knew that as he arrived. Light blazed throughout the house.

Before he could rap the knocker, the door opened and he was admitted. He presented his card.

The butler bowed. "Lord Stanhope has just suffered a terrible loss," he said. "He may not be seeing anyone."

"I understand," Gabriel said.

But seconds later the butler had returned. "Lord Stanhope will see you, my lord."

He followed the butler into the library he now knew well. Stanhope had obviously regained his composure since that evening at his manor when he had looked so disheveled. His hair was neatly combed, his dress the height of fashion.

"I am pleased you called," Stanhope said. "I have an urgent matter to discuss with you."

Gabriel bowed. "I came to express my condolences. I will understand if our business arrangement has been canceled."

"Why would you believe that?" Stanhope said.

"Stammel was your friend and partner. I thought perhaps his role would be necessary in the transaction."

"It was important, but not crucial," Stanhope said. "In truth it will give you a larger percentage if you wish it. I did have something else in mind, but now Stammel's death has created a void. I have a contract for muskets destined for British troops in Ireland. All our ships are at sea, and delivery is essential. There is a ship that is available, but my resources are stretched at the moment."

"And Lord Daven?"

"His also, I fear." Stanhope paused. "There is something else. Stammel was going to travel with the arms. We have been cheated before by customs officials. Someone from the company must accompany the cargo."

"But I know little of this kind of business," Gabriel protested.

"It does not matter," Stanhope said. "As long as they think you do. It is simply to deter theft." He paused, then added, "But I need to put the shipment on the seas in the next few days."

"I do not have all the money yet. It will be two more weeks at most."

"How much do you have?"

"Thirty-five thousand pounds. Lord Stammel owed me another five thousand."

Stanhope picked a cigar.

"Stammel was my friend. I will assume that debt. I have no time to delay," he said. "There is another investor interested, but if you will undertake the voyage and protect our interests, I will make you a quarter owner."

Gabriel grinned foolishly. "That is kind of you."

"Then perhaps when your funds arrive, we can find another small investment."

"What kind of return can I expect? I intend to bring honor back to the Manchester name."

"You will double your money on this shipment. On the next, perhaps we can do better."

"The papers?"

"I will have Pickwick draw them. I understand he is also your solicitor. But I consider this a gentleman's agreement."

"Indeed," Gabriel replied. "And Pickwick is a happy coincidence."

"You agree, then?"

"Aye. Double my money? A fine investment."

"There will be others, my boy. Many others—now that you may be my daughter's husband."

"Did Pamela return with you?"

"No," Stanhope said regretfully. "This business with Stammel is ugly. I did not want her involved." He hesitated, then said, "I would like to announce the betrothal between the two of you."

"If she gives her consent."

"She will," Stanhope said. "I will have Pickwick draw up a marriage agreement."

*Because no one would suspect Stanhope of murdering the betrothed of his daughter?*

"I will send for her tonight. She should arrive tomorrow night. Perhaps you can call on her the next morning. I will arrange for you to be alone. We can make a formal announcement in the *Morning Post*."

"And when does the ship leave?"

"The next morning."

Gabriel nodded.

Stanhope cleared his throat. "Miss Fremont? She arrived home with no more difficulty?"

"She is naturally concerned about her bracelet. Apparently it meant much to her. But there were no highwaymen; of course, she had my protection." He said the last boastfully.

"Unfortunately Stammel was not so fortunate," Stanhope said drily.

"Have they caught the villain yet?"

"No, but the road will be patrolled in the future."

"Please accept my sympathy."

"It was very kind for you to call," Stanhope said.

Gabriel nodded. "If you need anything . . ."

"You can bring your payment when you see Pamela. I will have the papers ready for your signature. Please do not tell anyone else the sum you invested. I will have some angry friends. Including Lord Daven."

Gabriel started to leave, then stopped and turned back to his host. "May I have a copy of the cargo manifest? And the name of the ship."

Stanhope raised an eyebrow.

"If I am to supervise the shipment, I do not wish to look totally ignorant of its contents and the procedures. I probably will not understand it, but some familiarity might be helpful."

Stanhope gave him a searching glance. He hesitated, obviously reluctant. "You do not trust me?"

"Of course I do. It is only to familiarize myself so I will not look the fool."

"It will not make much sense to you."

"Then I can ask you questions."

Stanhope shrugged. "If it is that important to you."

Gabriel shrugged. "If I am to be in business, I suppose I should learn a little about it."

Stanhope stood. "A glass of brandy while you wait?"

"Thank you, yes. I never turn down good brandy, and I have tasted yours."

He watched as Stanhope poured a glass from a bottle on a table, then handed it to him before leaving the room.

Left on his own, Gabriel itched to look through the desk to see whether there was anything there he had not seen in his previous foraging. But he did not want to lose this one victory. Not only would he see the supposed cargo manifest, but he should have Stanhope's handwriting for the forger.

He resisted temptation. He could ruin everything by being greedy. Stanhope was getting careless. For some reason he wanted Gabriel on that ship.

Which was a damn good reason for not getting on it.

Had Stammel really been intended to sail with the ship? Had his death been an opportunity for Stanhope? A plausible reason to rid himself of the troublesome Manning family? The last link to the past gone, probably drowned?

But what if the manifest did not contain Stanhope's signature?

He sipped on the brandy and went to the window, then brushed by the desk. Several papers on the desk, but they might be missed. Blazes. He tried to open the top desk drawer. Locked.

Then another drawer. To his surprise, it opened. He knew Stanhope's writing from the papers on his desk. What he needed most was a signature. Then he saw a sheaf of bills.

Voices outside. The butler announcing another sympathy visit.

Gabriel grabbed several of the papers, shut the drawer, and fitted the papers into his trousers, straightening his tight waistcoat as he did so, but it did not look smooth. He remembered Monique's trick and spilled brandy on the garment.

When Stanhope stepped back in the room with papers in his hand, Gabriel was frantically swabbing at his coat, undoing several buttons. "My lord, my apologies. Some brandy. So clumsy. I spilled some on your fine carpet as well."

Anger darted across Stanhope's face before he smoothed it out, hiding the fury behind a courteous mask. Stanhope was obviously a man who did not like imperfections. In anything.

"My butler will see to your waistcoat," he said in a tightly controlled voice.

"No need. It is not one of my favorites." He reached out. "The manifest?"

Stanhope stubbornly held on to the papers.

"My lord?"

Slowly, Stanhope gave them to him, contempt barely visible in his eyes. "You will bring your investment tomorrow."

"Yes."

A knock came at the door.

Stanhope strode to the door and opened it. The butler handed him two cards.

Stanhope turned back to him. "I must see these gentlemen. They came to express their condolences."

"You did not tell me the name of the ship."

Stanhope looked harried. "The *Peregrine*."

"A fine name. I will be here at four. Again, my apologies for the spill, Stanhope."

Stanhope's face darkened at the familiarity, then as before it cleared so quickly that it was difficult to be certain he had seen any emotion other than goodwill.

Gabriel turned and left, his left arm holding the stained waistcoat together.

Once outside the room, and the residence, he straightened. He had picked up Specter earlier, and now swung up into the saddle. He had done good work this day.

Stanhope tolerated the stream of callers, who expressed surprise, sympathy, and curiosity.

He felt that something was wrong, off balance. He usually had utter confidence in his decisions but now . . .

Stammel had been a problem for the last few years. He drank and gambled too much. Year by year, his love of drink and chance had grown to dangerous proportions.

Stanhope hated to admit any weakness, but he had liked Stammel. And Daven. They had been the only friends he'd ever had. Part of the friendship had been built on self-interest, and yet they were the only people who knew him for what he was, and still accepted him.

Regret for a necessity annoyed him.

So had the nagging feeling that he was missing something. Matters were not going as expected with Monique Fremont, and he feared becoming a laughingstock. His power was his apparent invincibility. If he could not obtain a piece of baggage like Fremont, then his fortress would begin to wear away.

And Manchester? The man appeared to be a gullible fool. He was as obviously besotted with Monique as everyone else, despite the fact he was courting Pamela. That alone enraged him, not for his daughter's sake, but that he thought he could compete with Stanhope.

Stanhope wanted the engagement. He wanted it public so he could grieve openly when his son-in-law-to-be was lost at sea. In the meantime he would have Manchester's money. He needed it. His funds had dwindled these past few years; too many rumors had curbed his activities. But Manchester presented an opportunity. The man had no support, no friends in London. His connection to Stanhope's daughter would be another advantage, as was his father's reputation as a traitor.

He had hoped for more than thirty-five thousand pounds, but he would take it. And rid himself of a possible embarrassment as well.

He only wished he had more information about Manchester, and who and what he had been before the solicitor found him. He had tried to discourage Pickwick from notifying Manchester that he was the last legal heir. But Pickwick was a timid man, who feared an investigation. He had claimed that he would phrase the letter in such a way that Manchester would stay in America. Unfortunately, he had been wrong.

Hang it all, his troubles had deepened since Manchester arrived, but he couldn't blame it on him. Stammel's gaming had worsened, and he had obviously become desperate for money. The theft at his residence. The theft at Daven's home. It could have been no one but Stammel. No one else could have gotten inside his safe.

And now Stammel was dead.

He was surprised at how much regret that caused.

It was after dark.

Nonetheless, Gabriel decided to visit his forger. Time was of the essence now. He had to finish this before Monique and others were hurt.

Perhaps if she knew it would be just a few days, she would leave with the Smythes.

The thought of her waiting for him in America was a sweet one.

And most likely, he admitted to himself, highly unlikely knowing the lady's determination.

Specter was obviously eager for the outing, and Gabriel did not have time to return him to the baron's stable before finding the printer. Gabriel went through a park and several backstreets to insure he was not being followed. By the time he reached the dock area, most of the shops were closed and most of the taverns were noisy.

Still cautious, he found a public stable and left Specter there. He did not intend to have the horse stolen, something altogether likely in this part of London. Then he walked by foot through the area, his cloak concealing the fine clothes he wore to see Stanhope.

To his surprise, and gratification, a light shone through the window of the printing shop. The door was locked but soon opened at his knock.

Winsley had his glasses perched on his nose as he opened the door for him.

"You are late tonight," he said.

"I have what you requested," Gabriel said. He pulled out the list of items to be shipped along with the personal correspondence he'd purloined. "I have his signature, a sample of his handwriting, and a copy of a manifest of goods supposedly to be delivered to the army in Ireland."

"Come to the back," Winsley said, leading the way to the back room. He perched on his stool, pulled an oil lamp closer, and studied the documents.

"What do you want me to say?"

"This is a manifest for five-thousand muskets and a thousand uniforms along with other equipment. I am sure the boxes will be filled with weights and the ship sabotaged in some way. He is quite insistent that I accompany the cargo to prevent any pilfering in Ireland."

"And Lord Stanhope can claim the insurance without paying for the cargo?"

Gabriel nodded.

"What do you want me to do?"

"Create a bill of sale to show that Stanhope purchased only a thousand muskets to be delivered to the ship."

"And the uniforms?"

"We might need some help with that. Do you know someone who sells shoddy materials?"

"Aye."

"Then create a bill of sale showing the purchase of uniforms to Stanhope at a price well below that shown on this list."

Winsley smiled for the first time since Gabriel had met him. "When do you need them?"

"Tomorrow at noon. No longer."

"You will have them."

"And the price?"

"Stanhope's ruin is price enough," Winsley said.

"Nonetheless, there will be two hundred pounds for you."

Winsley's smile broadened. "Can't say that would be refused."

"Wednesday night, then?"

"It will be ready."


How long would it be before word reached Stanhope that she had heard something she should not have heard?

The question hammered at Monique prior to her performance. But once she went on stage, she turned that part of her mind off and became the wronged wife. The audience was even more boisterous and approving than usual, perhaps because she had returned to the stage tonight. She instinctively reacted to its approval and knew the performance was one of her best.

She felt the usual glow of pleasure as flowers rather than fruit were thrown on the stage.

Lynch beamed as he met her when she and her leading man left the stage. "Magnificent, mademoiselle."

"*Merci,*" she replied. Then, "Have you seen Lord Stanhope?"

"No," he said.

"And you have said nothing, of course?"

Red started to creep into his cheeks. She knew at that moment that he had told someone. "I . . . of course not. . . . You told me not to say anything, but I did ask a gentleman to keep an eye on you. You are very important to me, and . . ."

"What gentleman?"

"A patron of the theater. A man in the government. He was here tonight, his third time. He does not care for Lord Stanhope, and I thought—"

"You might well have signed my death warrant," Monique said.

"No, no. He said he would be very discreet. He said he will investigate Stammel's death. Lord Stanhope would not dare to harm you if people suspect . . . I am only looking out for you."

He was stumbling over his words now. Whether it was his sincere desire to help her, to get his license for serious drama, or his love of gossip, it made no difference. The rumor was out now.

She looked at him with approbation. "What is done is done. If anything happens to me, or if I must leave London, it lies at your door."

He wrung his hands together. "I . . . I . . ."

"I will never confide in you again, Monsieur Lynch," she said righteously. She turned away from him and marched to her dressing room.

The third and final act was about to begin.

# Chapter Twenty-six

Monique knew Manchester would return to her rooms tonight despite the fact it was already near midnight.

She knew it as well as she knew she would be waiting.

They were like thunder and lightning together.

She wanted to see him. More than she knew it was possible to want to see someone.

At the same time she hoped *not* to see him. Because every time she did, he became more essential to her.

She also knew that if she did what she was contemplating, Manchester would be lost to her. It would end any hope of a future with him.

But *his* life was more important than *her* future. She kept telling herself that perhaps she could have both. But she couldn't. All those years of fear would not go away. As long as Stanhope was free, she could never be free.

And the more she saw of what Stanhope was doing with Pamela the more she realized that running would be an act of cowardice. Perhaps if it had just been herself, she could forget it. But it wasn't. She had a half sister, and Pamela would never be free if her father had the power to manipulate and use her. Stanhope's disgrace might well be her sister's only deliverance. Only then could she go with her young man without destroying his family.

She had to bring it about. And she had to do it without Manchester. She had to protect both him and her sister. And that meant making sure he was on a ship to America. He would be where he belonged, where he had people who cared about him, and whom he cared about.

A sea captain. That image was far more attractive to her than that of a marquess. It required little character to become the latter. It was an accident of birth. She supposed it required a great deal of character and competence to captain a ship.

At the time he'd admitted to being a sailor, his eyes had lit and his lips had had a slight wistful smile. She realized he missed the sea, and she instinctively felt he *loved* it. She, on the other hand, responded to the approval of an audience. She lived fictional lives and became those people during the length of her contract. It had been a matter of escape years ago. Then it had become a way of life. Who was Merry Anders? Who was Monique Fremont? Once upon a time, it had been very clear. Now she no longer knew.

She was nothing but a shadow. Someone who took the forms of her parts.

And, dear Mother in Heaven, she loved him. He filled the empty places in her heart, places she kept hidden since she was a child. She hadn't admitted that void to anyone. Not even to Dani. She had never acknowledged those barren landscapes before.

She had never expected them to be filled. Her distrust of men had been too strong. She had lived most of her life shadowed by her mother's fear and the succession of her mother's "protectors." None of them had proved themselves to be that. Monique had, in truth, barely escaped their advances more times than she wanted to count.

Now Manchester was like a hurricane sweeping through her life, washing away all the fears, the loneliness. Washing away everything but determination to put an evil to rest.

She looked outside. No fog tonight, and the gas lamps lit the street. A carriage passed but did not stop. Then she saw a lone horseman.

The rider passed her lodgings and she realized he must be taking the animal to a mews around the corner. He would unsaddle his horse and water and feed him before arriving at her door.

Dani had already gone to bed. Monique brushed her hair for several moments, then sat at the window waiting. She saw the figure, dressed in a cloak and a beaver hat pulled down over his head, walk toward her residence. She sped downstairs to open the door as he reached the top step.

He took off his hat and stood there with a smile on his lips. "I've missed you," he said.

"It has not been that long."

"You are supposed to say you missed me also."

"Am I?"

"It is only polite."

"I have never been polite."

"Perhaps that is why I like you so much."

She realized she was standing in the open door in only her night robe. She moved inside, and he followed.

"Would you like a brandy?"

"Yes."

He followed her to the sitting room, where a bottle of fine brandy was kept. She was very aware of his eyes on her as she poured two glasses of brandy. She made his much larger.

"Are you trying to get me intoxicated?" he asked as he took it. "You do not have to, you know. I am already intoxicated. You are much too beautiful."

She'd been told that many times, but it had never meant anything to her. Beauty could be a curse as much as a boon. But now she felt a catch in her throat.

"Somehow I do not think you are a man to overindulge."

He took a sip of brandy. "Have you heard the news?"

"About Lord Stammel?"

"Aye."

She nodded.

"It had to be Stanhope."

She was silent. Waiting.

"I talked to him today. He is willing to take me on as a partner despite the fact I do not have the funds he demanded.

He plans a shipment of arms and supplies to Ireland. He wants me to accompany them aboard the ship. To make sure he is not cheated."

"His trust in you is touching," she said.

"Except I believe we are all meant to go to the bottom of the sea."

"Why?"

"He would receive insurance on goods that do not exist. And the added bonus of my money. That, I believe, is what happened with my father. Stanhope substituted empty crates for good and planned for the ship to sink, whereby he could claim insurance for the goods that did not exist. But some seamen unexpectedly escaped, and they had noticed the boxes were lighter than they should be. It was then Stanhope reluctantly said he had left all purchases to my father and produced documents to prove it. Unfortunately they had been forged."

"And do you plan to go to the bottom of the sea?"

"I have a little surprise. A little reverse process."

"And if you miscalculate?"

"I've stayed alive by not miscalculating."

"So has Stanhope."

"True enough," he said. "But he has no idea of what I am about. And I know exactly what he is about."

"He killed Lord Stammel."

"We do not know that."

"Do we not?"

He was silent this time.

"If he would kill his friend for stealing from him, what would he do to you?" she continued. She looked up at his face, pleading with him. "I think Lord Daven might turn on him without your risking your life. I plan to see him tomorrow night. Plant a few seeds in his mind. If he believes Stanhope killed Stammel, he might think he is next."

"He is no match for Stanhope."

"I am not so sure of that," she said softly.

"I want you out of this," he said. "I have bought passage for Smythe and his family to America. And for you and Dani."

"When?"

"It is after midnight now. The ship leaves in about thirty hours."

"And the one that is to carry you?"

"Another day."

Apprehension ran down her spine. "Go with us," she said suddenly.

"He will be suspicious if I disappear suddenly. All this will be for naught. I will make sure Pamela is all right. Then I will follow you."

"Pamela is my responsibility."

"Why?"

She almost told him, then stopped herself. She was the daughter of his father's betrayer.

"She's my friend."

"She's *my* almost betrothed."

Monique sipped her own brandy. "You have already told me that was only a pretense."

"Still . . . as a marquess I can protect her. She will not suffer as much when the truth is revealed."

He was right. He had a weapon she did not. His title. Though most of London did not like the man, they could do nothing about the title. That gave him power and influence, regardless of the state of his properties.

She on the other hand had little with which to protect Pamela.

Still, it did not sit well with her that he was taking on something that was her responsibility.

She thought about the bottle of laudanum she had upstairs.

"I will think about it," she said. "Will you go to the ship, too, to see everyone off?"

"I expect so." His gaze pierced through her as if he knew exactly what she was thinking. "How did the play go tonight?" he asked.

"Well."

"No sign of Stanhope or Daven?"

"No, but Mr. Lynch had news. He believes he will receive a license to perform serious drama."

He looked puzzled.

She laughed. "Only a few theaters can perform Shakespeare and other serious drama. They are licensed by the Crown. Other theaters are limited to farces and lighter entertainment. It is an honor to be licensed. Mr. Lynch has craved such an honor for years."

"And this is because of you?"

"He believes so."

"And if you leave?"

"I do not know."

"There are theaters in America. They do not have to be licensed by a king."

"Is it as wild as I have heard? Full of bandits and savages?"

"At the moment I believe London has more of both," he said. "The cities are safe. So is most of the countryside."

She filled his glass again. "Are you hungry? I believe there is bread and cheeses and some fruit."

He put the glass down and his fingers touched her shoulder, then a ringlet of hair. "I must go, Monique. But I wanted to tell you about Stammel's death. And the ship." He cupped her chin in his hand. "Will you consider the journey to America?"

"I will think about it."

"I can have an answer later this morning?"

"I have errands. Perhaps at four?"

"I will look forward to it."

She wanted to ask him to stay, but she was not going to beg him. It was best, anyway. They had already risked the possibility of a child.

Suddenly the thought was attractive. Compelling. A small version of Gabriel Manning. She was charmed by the thought.

She took a step closer, until their bodies nearly touched. She felt his control in the rigid posture of his body. She lifted her face, inviting a kiss.

His lips touched hers and the world rumbled, shook.

Her hand touched his cheek, where she felt a roughness.

His scent was enticing. Soap and leather and the hint of the sea.

She thought about standing next to him on the deck of a ship as a setting sun traced gold across the sea and a clean breeze brushed their bodies. No more loneliness. No more ugliness. All swept clean.

His lips lingered a moment, then released hers. He stepped away as if burned, a muscle playing in his cheek. His hand touched her face as if memorizing it. "I must go, love."

She gave him a long, steady stare, then nodded. "Tomorrow."

"Think about what I said."

"I will," she agreed.

Without another word, he turned and strode to the door, never looking back.

She hadn't even had the chance to tell him of the rumor she had started.


Leaving her had been the most difficult thing Gabriel had ever done.

He did not want to leave her with child, though. He might well die in the next week. And he was no longer sure he could control himself. She was intoxicating to him, making him forget everything he'd learned, ignore the discipline of years.

Nor did he want to lie in her arms and her in his when he planned to betray her tonight. She would never understand it as anything else.

He needed the rest of tonight to firm his plans.

He had to make payment today for her passage as well as finish preparations to make sure she would be aboard. She *had* to be on the ship tomorrow. She had to be safe.

Gabriel also planned to visit the *Peregrine*. A survey would demonstrate his loyalty to the project. No one need know he was a hell of a lot more familiar with ships than anyone expected. Then there were the documents at the forger's and a visit to the baron who had sold him Specter.

He had to make some kind of provisions for Pamela, or

Monique would never stay away from London. He had seen the intensity of her expression.

Why? He'd asked that question over and over again.

Then something in his brain clicked. It should have earlier, but the idea was absurd. Impossible. Mentally, he pictured both women. Although Monique was probably seven years older, their faces bore more than a passing resemblance. Monique's eyes were gray, not blue; she stood taller, and her hair was darker. But he had seen siblings with dark and blond hair.

What had Monique said about Stanhope? He had hurt her mother.

Could Monique and Pamela possibly be related?

Impossible. Stanhope would know.

But the thought would not leave him as he fetched his horse.

Pamela reached her father's town house at dusk. She and her maid had left his country home just after dawn.

She'd been surprised at the note summoning her to London.

She had not expected to return there for another several days. Her father had left abruptly. No explanation. She'd heard later from the servants that his friend—Lord Stammel—had been attacked and killed on the road.

She regretted any man's death, but she had not liked Lord Stammel. He drank too much and had always stared at her in a way that had made her uncomfortable.

Surprisingly enough, she did want to return to London, despite the presence of her father there. She had a friend now. Two of them.

Manchester and Monique made her think of Robert, the afternoons they had spent discussing books, then the kiss they had shared. Promises made. Until one of the servants told her aunt, who had warned her what would happen

Fear had clouded her life since then. Not for herself but for the pain he could bring to Robert and his family. But in the last few days Lord Manchester and Monique Fremont had given her unexpected courage. Perhaps they could help her be more than a pawn.

The footman—Boothe—welcomed her with a smile. "I will take your trunks to your room," he said. "Would you care for some refreshment?"

"Yes," she said. "Thank you. Is my father here?"

"No, Lady Pamela."

"Do you know when he is to return?"

"He did not say," Boothe said regretfully.

"I would like you to send a note, to Lord Manchester," she said. "He asked me to do so when I arrived in London." She paused. "Do you know his address?"

"Yes, my lady. He lives on New Bridge Street. Your father has had us deliver several invitations to his residence."

She looked at him for a moment. "It is a private note." The inference was obviously that her father was not to learn of it. But Boothe was one of the servants she'd come to trust in the past week, and her maid also liked him.

"I understand," the footman said simply.

She went upstairs to the room. Her father was not someone to defy. She knew she was taking a risk. Yet she felt she had to take it. If punishment came, then so be it.

She quickly wrote the note, then placed it on the table. Tish helped her change from the traveling gown to a more comfortable one, then Pamela dismissed her.

Though she wasn't hungry, she forced herself to eat. She'd had little to eat today, and she needed her strength and wits about her. Manchester had land. He had influence. Perhaps he could find another position for Robert's father and provide some protection.

Although Manchester was apparently involved in a business proposition, there was something about him that told her he was not just another lackey for her father. She sensed strength in him. And integrity.

He was, in truth, her only hope. Because of that, perhaps she was giving him qualities he didn't have. It was worth the risk, however.

She sipped the tea that accompanied fruit and pastries, then looked out the window. Her father's carriage stopped, and he stepped out. That meant he would be here for supper. It was not something she looked forward to.

She was right. In moments Boothe was at her door. "Lord Stanhope has asked for you."

"You did not . . ."

"No, my lady. It is on the way. A boy in the street. It cost me a shilling."

She went to her small pouch of coins and gave him two shillings. "My thanks."

He bowed his way out, a smile on his face.

She glanced in the mirror. Her hair was unkempt from the trip, her face was pale, her dress plain. She decided not to call Tish.

Instead she smoothed her hair, then went down the stairs. She knocked, and he bade her enter.

He was pacing the floor, his face tight and angry. She wondered whether she had done something to offend him or whether it was someone else. He gave her a piercing look that was obviously meant to quell her.

She refused to be quelled. "You called me?"

"You look like a servant," he said. "Or a farm girl."

She met his gaze directly. "I see nothing wrong with that."

He slapped her. "You are a Stanhope. Remember that."

Her face stung with the blow. She felt tears gathering behind her eyes. Not from his action, but the humiliation. She swore to herself he would never do it again.

She lifted her chin and saw his mouth tightening, his fingers twitching. She knew he wanted to hit her again.

She suspected he would have if there was not a knock on the door. The butler announced Lord Daven.

"We will continue this discussion after supper," he said. "Along with your impertinence. We can dispense with your presence at the table."

She left with her head held high as Lord Daven entered. He greeted her, then turned away. She closed the door behind her as she exited the room but not quite all the way.

The butler disappeared, apparently going after refreshments. She hovered at the door, listening to the voices.

"Have you heard the rumors?" Daven asked.

"Just an hour ago. That I had a terrible row with Stammel. I did not. Someone is lying."

"Nonetheless the rumor is spreading through London that Stammel stole from you and you threatened him."

"Only a few people left early enough to spread such a tale. Mademoiselle Fremont and Manchester among them."

"Why would Manchester say anything when he is courting your daughter and joining you in our little venture?"

"He is not to know you are in it," Stanhope said.

"Why?"

"He is taking the voyage to 'look' after our cargo. If you were involved he might wonder why you weren't taking that role, since you would know our business far better."

"Ah," Daven said. "And where will the ship go down?"

"Somewhere off the coast of Ireland."

"With no survivors, of course."

"Well, no known survivors."

"Then if he's the one who has been spreading rumors—"

"We will be shed of him."

"And your daughter?" Daven asked.

"I will find someone else for her. Manchester is nothing but a fool. And so is my daughter."

"What about Monique?"

"I have people looking into the source of the rumor. If she is involved, well I will decide then. I do not want too many accidents, but neither can I allow . . ."

Pamela could delay no longer. The butler was her father's man. He must not find her listening at the door.

She could barely breathe as she sped for the steps, mounting them just as the butler entered the room beneath her. She could see him but doubted whether he had seen her.

Pamela made for her room. Her heart was beating so rapidly she could barely breathe. She knew about her mother. Other rumors. And now she had heard her father plotting murder.

*Manchester. Possibly Monique.* And now she felt certain that he had arranged for Stammel's murder. *Too many accidents.* The words kept repeating themselves in her head.

She had to warn them.

Did Manchester get the note she had sent him? Would he come?

Or would she have to find him?

Before it was too late.

# Chapter Twenty-seven

Gabriel had a fruitful morning, and now he had two more stops to make.

He had picked up the forged papers, and he could not tell the difference from Stanhope's signature on the original and on the forgery. He also visited the *Peregrine*, which was being loaded. Crates were being stored in the hold.

He badly wanted to look into one of them, but that might alarm the captain, who might warn Stanhope.

The captain was an older man of hefty girth. The ship looked sloppy, the crew more like brigands than sailors, and they eyed him suspiciously. He was shown the cabin he would have, and it was no more than a mate's closet. The captain was obviously not pleased to have one of the owners aboard, and Stanhope had not told him to pretend otherwise.

But he dutifully showed him around the ship, and Gabriel inspected the timbers that lined the bottom of the hold. They were rotting, but not enough to make it unseaworthy.

He thanked the captain profusely despite the man's lack of hospitality. He had also visited the *Amelia*. The difference between the two ships was like day and night. He was comforted. Monique, Dani, and the Smythes would be safe aboard the latter.

He had one last stop before going back to his lodgings, sending the Smythes to the ship, and finally making sure Monique was aboard.

He rode Specter to Baron Tolvery's home, gave the horse over to the care of the groom, and asked if the baron was inside.

"Yes, my lord. 'E seldom leaves these days. 'E will be pleased to see ye an' hear about the 'orse."

Gabriel climbed the steps leading to the front door and used the door knocker.

A moment, then two, passed before a footman opened the door. Recognition flashed across his face. "My lord," he acknowledged.

"Is the baron in?"

The footman stood aside. "If you will wait, I will inquire if he can see you."

Gabriel nodded and allowed himself to be led into a small drawing room. In a matter of seconds the servant was back. "He will see you, my lord. If you would follow me."

Gabriel followed him into the room where he had met the baron before.

The man struggled to his feet, grabbing a desk as he did so.

"Please do not rise," Gabriel said.

The man sank back into his chair, a grateful smile on his face. "There is no problem with the horse?" he asked.

"He is everything the groom and you told me he was. And more. I think I received the best of that arrangement."

"Then sit and tell me to what do I owe the pleasure of this visit."

"I am not sure it will be a pleasure," Gabriel said slowly. "I have some information about the Earl of Stanhope, and I do not know where to take it."

Tolvery's eyes narrowed. "What kind of information?"

"I am involved with a business arrangement with him, a shipment of muskets and other supplies to troops in Ireland."

"Is that wise?"

Gabriel stood. "You once asked if there was anything you could do to help."

"Aye, and you refused."

"I have changed my mind."

"Why?" the baron asked bluntly.

"Because you said you had been with the admiralty. You might know people I cannot reach. I do not know who to trust. You might."

Tolvery's eyes narrowed.

"I believe Stanhope has sold faulty goods to the army and plans to sink a ship to hide the corruption and receive the insurance on poor or nonexistent goods. I am intended to be on that ship when it goes down."

"A very serious charge, young Manning."

"I know that."

"Can you prove it?"

"Probably only after I am dead. I wanted someone to know what is happening in the event . . . I am right."

Tolvery's eyes gleamed. "Then how . . ."

"I overheard a conversation between him and Lord Stammel . . ."

"Stammel is dead. I heard about it today."

"After an argument with Stanhope."

"How do you know that?"

"I was there. I overhead everything."

"What do you want me to do?"

"Have someone inspect the crates on the *Peregrine*. It is the ship contracted by Stanhope to ship supplies to troops. And," he added, "you might inspect the ship itself."

"When does it sail?"

"Day after tomorrow."

"And it is being loaded now?"

"Aye."

Gabriel watched as the man considered all the information. A gleam enlivened dull blue eyes.

Gabriel reached in the pocket of the cloak he was wearing. "This is what the ship should be carrying. It is the manifest Stanhope gave me. I doubt whether it matches the cargo."

"And you are sure the ship is not carrying these items."

"I am betting my life on it. I am also risking it just talking to you about this."

"You are sure he killed Stammel?"

"They quarreled. Items were missing from rooms and found in Stammel's. He died hours later."

Tolvery's eyes, earlier dulled with pain and age, glinted with new life. "Convenient for you."

Gabriel permitted himself a small smile. "Thieves cannot help being what they are." He paused, then added, "I saw Stanhope after it happened. There was no regret. Only a certain eagerness to ensnare a new and obviously temporary business partner."

"You are playing a dangerous game."

"Perhaps. You will help?"

"I told you before I owed your father."

"As you warned me, it could be dangerous. A whisper in the wrong ears."

"I am an old man with few pleasures and many regrets, young Manning. Perhaps a new battle is what I need."

"There is someone you can trust?"

"I think so. I cannot guarantee it. Stanhope has information on many ministers who fear him. But there is one man I believe I can trust. I will send a note to an old friend tonight and invite him to join me in the morning."

"My thanks. Time is of the essence."

"Should I mention your name?"

"I think it wise not to. Just that someone—perhaps a sailor who once served with you—noted something strange."

Gabriel wondered how much more he could say. He had the forged documents tucked on the inside of his cloak. He planned to get them inside Stanhope's home tonight. That was essential. They would show that Stanhope purchased far fewer goods than showed on the ship's manifest.

"There is a safe in his home where he keeps all his private papers," Gabriel finally said. "I have seen them there. If there is anything . . . that invites suspicion on the ship, then you might well find something in that safe."

"You, of course, would have no idea of what someone might find?"

"Stanhope is arrogant. He believes he is smarter than anyone else. He would not think to destroy papers."

"Let us hope you are right, Manning. Or is it Manchester?"

"It is Manning," Gabriel said. "I detest the title."

"You are a rarity then," Tolvery said.

Gabriel shrugged. "You will let me know what happens?"

"I will have Jock, my groom, find you as soon as I know."

Gabriel stood. "My thanks."

"It is little enough to compensate for what I should have done years ago."

"Nonetheless, it is dangerous to cross Stanhope."

Tolvery started to stand as well.

"It is not necessary," Gabriel said.

"Yes, it is," Tolvery said as he struggled to his feet, reached for a cane, and balanced himself on it. "I wish you and my son had been friends. I think you would have liked each other."

"One thing more," Gabriel said.

Tolvery waited.

"Stanhope has a daughter. Her name is Pamela. She is an innocent. Wise and kind. She has a young man, a medical student. If anything happens to me, will you look after her? Make sure she can get to her young man, that his family is not harmed."

The baron nodded. "I will do that for the lad I did not assist so many years ago."

"It is over," Gabriel said. "Any debt has been paid."

There was nothing more to say. Tolvery limped to the door. He offered his hand, and Gabriel took it, then took his leave.

He retrieved his horse and looked at his pocket watch. Three. He was to see Monique at four and get his answer. He had never been a religious man, but now he prayed she had decided to go to America with the Smythes, even though his brain told him the woman he knew would not surrender so easily.

Despite the complications, his heart quickened at the thought of seeing her. He mounted Specter, and the horse seemed to capture his anticipation.

He wondered what she had been doing this day, whether she planned to go to the theater tonight. A last performance, one way or another. Either by her choice or by his. The thought saddened him. He was asking her to give up something she loved, something at which she excelled. As he excelled at the sea. Could he give up the sea for her?

He did not know. His stomach churned at the decisions they both would be making this night.

The two bulky men sent by the detective were exactly what Monique wanted. They were polite. Their eyes were intelligent, not cruel, and they listened intently.

She was not sure she would use them, but she wanted them available.

She'd given them instructions earlier. They were to wait across from her home this evening. She wanted them there when she returned from the theater.

When she needed them, she would place a light in the window. Then they were to come to the back door. The door would be open. She gave them ten pounds each, and told them there would be another ten pounds later. She emphasized that she wanted no one hurt, just carried to a ship.

One looked shocked. "You ain't wanting us to have 'im impressed?"

"No," she said. "Nothing like that. He has booked passage for friends. I am afraid he might be in danger here, but he is like every other man. He believes he can conquer anything and everyone." She gave them a soulful look. "I plan to meet him in America. I love him. You understand, do you not? I only wish him to be safe."

They looked at each other, then seemed to exchange some unsaid message. "We will be waiting."

That was several hours ago, and she had faith they would be in position tonight.

She checked the small bottle of laudanum she had tucked inside a drawer in her bedroom. It should be easy to pour a few drops into his wine. All she had to do was convince him to share that wine tonight, and to linger awhile.

She looked at the clock in the room. She said she would give him an answer this afternoon at four. She would lie and tell him yes, she would go with him. That was the one way she could bring him back tonight.

The prospect was agonizing. She had become quite proficient at lying. In truth, they had been lying to each other since they'd first met. But now they had shared truths. Not all of them to be sure, but some. She understood much about him, but she knew he did not—could not—share all her truths.

Which was the greatest lie? That to make him safe, or that to make herself safe from his contempt? For how could he not have contempt for the blood of the man who had destroyed his father? She wondered even now whether that was another reason for tonight's act.

He would never know that he had made love to the daughter of his enemy.

She looked in the mirror, felt the hot pull of tears behind her eyes. She did not cry. She had not cried since her mother's death. She had been stoic most of her life, accepting what had to be accepted and making the best of what came.

But then she had a goal. What would she do when her goal had been reached? When Stanhope was dead or in prison? When the need to avenge her mother no longer crowded away every other emotion?

How very empty she would be without Manchester, with his amused eyes and slow smile and gentle yet very passionate touch.

A solitary tear fell.

Gabriel paused at Monique's residence. He had not had time to return to his own.

He could only hope that the Smythes were prepared to leave for the voyage to America.

He knew he was cutting everything too close. But the murder of Stammel—and Stanhope's offer—had speeded everything. He was simply running out of time.

If only Monique—Merry—had decided to leave with the Smythes.

The door opened before he used the door knocker, and Monique stood in front of him.

Her gray eyes were smoky, her lips curved in a tentative smile. She wore a simple gown that he'd learned she preferred when at home. Her hair was pulled back with a ribbon. She looked delectable.

He stepped inside, closed the door behind them, then lowered his head until his lips met hers. They courted, teased, demanded. His blood quickened and he felt her leaning against him. He wrapped his arms around her, and she snuggled into them.

Gabriel felt as if he had just returned after a lonely and endless journey. With sudden realization, he knew that Stanhope's destruction was no longer landfall. Monique was.

How to make her safe? And keep her?

Give up something less important now. Convince her to give it up as well.

Her arms tightened around him, her fingers tangling in his hair. His heart was racing and he thought hers must be, too. His lips left hers and trailed along her cheek to her neck. His blood turned into lava flow.

Her hands played with the back of his neck, and he felt the same urgency in them that he had.

*Move away.*

His legs had other instructions, perhaps from his heart rather than his brain.

"Gabriel," she whispered in a broken voice.

He knew by the hurting edge in her voice that she would not leave.

He wanted to wipe away the desolation. He wanted to be convincing. He wanted her to trust him enough to leave London. They had each set certain things in motion. He needed to visit Stanhope's home tonight and find a way to place the forged documents in his safe. Or even his desk.

They reached her room and once inside a touch led to an embrace, the embrace to raw desperate hunger. He wanted her. He wanted her to want him enough to give up her plan.

They made love. Frantically and passionately and as if it were the last time they would see each other. He barely managed to withdraw before spilling his seed.

He held her in his arms. He memorized the feel of her, the taste of her. He treasured the slight aroma of flowers and the way her dark hair framed her face.

"Will you come with me tonight?" he said.

"*Can* you leave now?"

"Yes. I did not think I could," he said. "But you are more important to me than Stanhope."

The day was fading, but he saw the question in her eyes. "And in years to come, will you hate me for it?"

"I could never hate you."

"You do not know very much about me."

"I know everything I need to know," he said.

"No."

He stopped her protest with a kiss. His hands reassured her. He pulled her against him.

"I love you, Monique Fremont, or Merry. . . ." He stopped. "Merry what?"

"Anders," she said in a low voice.

"Merry Anders. I like that. But then I like everything about you."

"I have the contract," she said. "I have never broken one before. It is one of the things you do not do in the theater." She paused, then pleaded, "Will you go without me if I swear I will not see Stanhope, that I will end my part in this. I will meet you in Boston when I finish the play. I swear it."

He understood commitments. He'd known when he accepted a command of a ship he could not just walk away.

But this was something else. He saw it in her face. In her eyes.

Did she intend to go after Stanhope? Or was it something else holding her back? Like Pamela.

"I gave some information to a man who knew my father," he said slowly. "He will see that it gets to someone untainted by Stanhope. I also asked him to look after Pamela. To see that she reached that young man of hers."

"That was very kind," she said.

"I trust him to do what he said. He feels an obligation to this matter."

"Thank you," she said, but now there was a reserve in her eyes that had not been there before. She was holding something back. "I cannot break the contract," she said again, stubbornly.

He released her and stood, unaware of the chill in the room.

"Please go tonight," she said. "My contract is complete in another month, and Mr. Lynch will have his license. I will have fulfilled my end of the bargain." Her face was pinched; her eyes, however, were unfathomable.

She still did not trust him. She did not trust him with whatever truth she was withholding. She did not trust him with Pamela's safety. Stanhope was still more important to her than him.

Disappointment was like a sword in his gut. He had been ready to let go for her. His boyish vow. His honor.

*She was not.*

He found his breeches in the dimming light and pulled them on, tucking his shirt inside them. Then he located his waistcoat on the floor. It was in sad shape, but then so was he. He put it on, tied the cravat loosely around his neck.

He looked back at her. She sat on the bed, legs tucked under her. Her face looked anguished.

But not anguished enough to leave with him. To make the choice between hate and love, between the past and the future.

She said nothing.

"I will be back tonight to see whether you've changed your mind," he said.

"You are going then?"

Only God knew at that moment what he would do. He shrugged.

*Would they ever be honest with each other?* He'd tried. God knew he had tried.

She was silent, but he felt her eyes on him even as he avoided them.

He wanted to lean over and kiss her. Pride and pain stopped him. He wanted her above all things, and he wanted her to want him that much. But she did not. His declaration of love, so difficult to make, had gone unanswered and unacknowledged.

Perhaps he had been wrong all along.

Still he had to take her out of harm's way. If she hated him all her days, then so be it. Her life was more important than his future.

He gave her a long, piercing look, then left without another word.

Monique's heart crumbled as he left. She had to force herself to ring for Dani.

She still had to ready herself for the performance tonight. Perhaps the routine of doing so would diminish the pain she still felt at seeing the disillusionment in his eyes. Pain. Disappointment.

*I love you.*

She wanted to say the words back to him. She wanted to tell him everything. She wanted to tell him that she was the daughter of his bitterest enemy and that Pamela was her sister. But the words wouldn't come.

*They just wouldn't come.* How do you say you are the daughter of a monster?

How could she leave now without knowing his fate? Or Pamela's. She had started something that could not be stopped. Stanhope had already killed once because of her actions. What if he tried again? What if she was responsible for her sister's death?

Then she would be as bad as her father.

A knock at the door. Dani entered. Her face looked more alive than ever.

"Are we going to America?"

Monique's stomach tightened. Dani was obviously in love, and her face radiated happiness for the first time since Monique had met her. Monique vowed then that Dani would have her chance at happiness. Even if she had to drug her wine as well.

"I told Lord Manchester I would meet him there when I finished my engagement. I want you to go and find us lodgings," Monique said.

"I will stay with you," Dani said. "A few weeks . . ."

"No," Monique said sharply. Too sharply. She saw the hurt in Dani's face. Even shock. "Please," she said in a softer voice.

"Is it because Lord Stanhope is . . ."

Monique shuddered. "He is responsible for Manchester's

father's death." She had not told Dani that before, though she knew Dani realized Manchester had some reason for joining with them.

"Tell him," Dani urged. "He will understand."

"How can he when I do not?" Monique said. "I am plotting a man's ruin. I am responsible for a man's death. I am a liar and a thief. How am I that different from my father? I have his blood."

"You also have your mother's blood," Dani said. "You are fine and decent and good."

Monique shook her head. "I can never be Merry again. Or my mother's daughter."

Dani's eyes were filled with empathy. "I don't think Lord Manchester wants Merry or someone else. He wants who you are today just as Sydney wants me." She took a deep breath. "I told him what I used to be. He says it doesn't matter. And he believes you are quite wonderful. Because of you, I will not die in prison or on a rope or beaten to death."

"But you are not the daughter of his worst enemy."

"Neither are you. He was never your father. You may have his blood but you also have kindness."

Monique stared at her maid. Could she possibly be right?

Perhaps she would tell Manchester about Stanhope tonight. Then, at least, he could make a choice. Would that not be preferable to living out a lonely life without ever knowing?

*He said he would be back.*

"Help me get ready for tonight," she said with new courage. "It could be my last performance."

*"Oui,"* Dani said. "I will make you *très belle.*"

# Chapter Twenty-eight

Stanhope looked at his watch. Three hours before the theater, and he was to meet with Daven at his club prior to attending the play. He'd had the devil's own time securing tickets. Apparently all of London wanted them. He was determined, however, to see her home tonight.

Manchester had said he would call on Pamela this afternoon. Stanhope wanted the betrothal announced before his son-in-law-to-be went to sea. Especially now that the damnable rumors were circulating through London. Manchester's death *must* be considered an accident.

Which evoked another vexing problem. Stanhope had called on several acquaintances today. None were in.

He had left his card. There had been no answers. For the first time he feared that the new rumors could be ruinous. His first instinct had been to ignore them. He had survived rumors for years. Without proof, he'd been able to counteract them with charges of jealousy. Every successful man had enemies who wanted to bring him down.

And he'd had protection in high places. Some high government officials had invested in his business ventures and reaped high profits. Others had personal eccentricities they'd rather not come to light. They had always stopped queries before, but he'd had no word from them today.

Had he been too confident about explaining away Stammel's death?

Or perhaps everyone was too busy to see him?

Daven had said he would try to discover where the rumors started. A guest at his country home? The actress? Even Manchester. The thought continued to haunt him. Had he underestimated the man?

He considered Monique Fremont. She was a woman. An actress. French. She had no reason to hurt him and every reason to please him. She had been teasing him to up the stakes. Nothing more.

Still there was something about her, something that tickled at his memory. Perhaps that was why he had been more patient with her than he usually was with a woman. It had not only been the contest with Stammel and Daven. She intrigued him.

He'd dismissed those odd flashes of familiarity. He'd not allowed a woman to affect him since he was not more than a lad, not since . . .

He saw her then in his mind's eye. A brown haired girl with blue eyes that had made his heart beat fast. But she had died before giving birth. His father had said . . .

It must have been that resemblance that had weakened him momentarily. But then everyone had doubles. He forced his thoughts away from her to the next potential source of trouble.

*Manchester.* The oaf had reason to hate him. Blazes, but he wished he had some kind of report back on the man's activities in America. His mind returned to the times he had seen Manchester with Monique Fremont. Had he seduced the woman under Stanhope's own nose and used her?

Could he really be that wily?

He wished now that he had hired a man to watch Manchester. He had grown careless during these last fat years. He had lived on proceeds from earlier illegal transactions and some more recent legal ones.

Perhaps he should not have targeted Manchester. Yet he

had every appearance of being a fool. And his father certainly was gullible. There had been no reason to think the son was any more. Pickwick had confirmed his opinion, and certainly so had Stammel.

Yet he always appeared at the side of Monique.

Stanhope cursed himself for not exercising his usual caution.

Perhaps he could discover something more about the man today. Bait him a bit. Stanhope prized himself at being a judge of character, particularly avarice and greed. Manchester had certainly displayed those characteristics.

Too obviously?

He was beginning to get a very sick feeling at the pit of his stomach.

He made a trip up to his room and unlocked the safe. It was as it had been after he discovered the missing money. Nothing else had been moved.

His desk. Manchester had been alone there.

But he kept nothing important in his desk. He had given Manchester the manifest he intended to give the authorities. Nothing dangerous there.

But Manchester had been insistent.

He was doubting himself now. That solved nothing.

He had to know.

Pamela had been with Manchester. His daughter was not very smart, but perhaps she had picked up something along the way.

He called Ames, his valet. "Tell Pamela I want to see her immediately."

"Yes, my lord."

He bowed his way out, and Stanhope waited impatiently. Seconds later Ames returned. "She is not in her room, my lord."

"Search the house, damn it."

Ames left hastily as Stanhope paced the room, his anger and frustration growing. His daughter had been told to stay in the house. Where would she have gone?

Ames returned. "We cannot find her, my lord. No one saw her leave. She did not request the carriage."

Stanhope swore.

Now even his daughter was out of control. At least that was one complication he could fix. The moment the betrothal was announced, she would return to the country under the sharp eyes of someone he hired. He would make sure she never disobeyed him again.

He heard someone at the door but stayed where he was. He heard the butler open the door. Heard the cautious words. "Lady Pamela is out visiting. I will see if my lord is receiving."

*Manchester.* And his daughter had slipped away.

He nodded to his butler, who showed Manchester in.

The marquess bowed. "I was hoping to see Lady Pamela."

"She is visiting friends. I had not informed her about your earlier visit."

"Would you suggest I wait for her?"

Stanhope had few choices. He wanted to meet Daven. Perhaps the man had learned something. He wanted the betrothal, but leaving Manchester alone in his home after all that had happened was not a prospect he liked either.

Damn Pamela.

Perhaps she would soon return. He could afford another twenty minutes, long enough to probe Manchester.

"Yes. In the meantime, did you bring your investment?" Stanhope tried to keep the eagerness out of his voice.

"I had it, but I wanted to go by the ship before coming here and thought better of bringing that kind of money on the waterfront," he said. "You said the agreement will be ready tomorrow. I can meet you at Pickwick's office and give it to you then."

Stanhope shrugged, disguising his sudden discomfort. "What did you think of the ship?"

"Looked like every other ship. Can't say I liked the accommodations."

"It is not a long trip."

"Still, I am accustomed to better. I expect you to explain that to the master."

"I will see what I can do," Stanhope said. "I will meet you at Pickwick's office at noon tomorrow. Time is getting short.

He will not sail without payment." He took two cigars from a box on his desk. "Would you care for a cigar?"

"I would, with thanks," Manchester said.

Stanhope took the top from the oil lamp to light his, then passed it to Manchester. He watched the man's movements.

Awkward, he thought with satisfaction.

"Did you look over the manifest?" he asked.

"Did not make a lot of sense to me," Manchester said.

"Some of the abbreviations might be strange to someone unfamiliar with them," Stanhope explained. Puzzlement was clear in the man's eyes; so was indifference.

"If you have it with you, I can explain them."

Manchester shrugged. "Left 'em in the room."

"You have not talked about your life in America. Do you plan to go back?"

"I like being a lord," Gabriel said. "There is respect with a title."

"That's fine. I would not like to see my daughter go to America," Stanhope said.

"Of course," Gabriel Manchester said, "we have not yet discussed a dowry. I understand that any marriage arrangement includes one."

Strangely enough, the request made Stanhope feel far better. Manchester was a greedy opportunist. "We will discuss that when she accepts your proposal."

"Perhaps a glass of brandy to seal the bargain?" Manchester said. "You will have to tell me where to buy it. It is very fine."

It was not fine at all. Stanhope had his own supply from which he drank. But what could you expect of a fool?

He looked at his watch. Daven would be waiting for him, hopefully with answers.

Stanhope rang for the butler and took one last look around. Nothing here to be concerned about. And he would make sure his servants kept an eye on Manchester.

He lingered to share a few sips of brandy, then he put his down.

"You may wait here for Pamela. I hope you will have happy news for me later this evening."

"You can be assured of it," Gabriel smirked.

Deciding Manchester was not the man who started the rumors, Stanhope left for White's. Daven would have learned something by now.

Pamela had waited until noon, hoping Manchester would answer her message. Then she knew her father would rise shortly. She could wait no longer. She had to reach Manchester.

She looked at her hands. They were trembling. They had been since she'd heard her father plotting with Lord Daven. She'd prayed Manchester would present himself, but he had not. Either he had not received her note or he'd had more important things to do than see her.

She waited as long as she could, even as the overheard conversation continued running through her mind. When the front hall was empty, she slipped out the door, hoping no one had seen her.

Apparently they did not, for no footsteps or calls followed her. She was not sure what direction to take. All she knew was New Bridge Street, and she had to stop several times to ask a Charlie, one of the watchmen employed to guard the streets, for directions. The hem of her gown quickly became soiled, and her soft slippers afforded little protection. She had no coat despite the chill in the air; she'd feared that would give her intention away.

She looked enviously at several sedan chairs, but she had no coin, and she'd continued until she saw the street name and a row of houses. A few more questions took her to Manchester's lodgings.

"His lordship is out," she was told by the middle-age woman who opened the door.

"I . . . I am Lord Stanhope's daughter," Pamela finally found the courage to say. "I . . . Lord Manchester . . ."

"Oh yes, my son has mentioned you."

She must have looked confused because the woman continued quickly. "My son, Sydney, is valet to the marquess."

Pamela had seen the large valet several times. She had been awed by his size. "I have seen him." She hesitated, then asked, "Do you know when Lord Manchester will return? I have some urgent business with him."

The woman looked shocked for a moment, and Pamela realized young unmarried women did not go to the residences of gentlemen without an escort. Even when they did have urgent business.

Pamela shivered, and the woman opened the door wide. "Come in, my lady. How far did you come?"

Pamela shrugged. "A few miles. I really do not know."

"Well, bless you. You must be freezing. I will make you some hot tea. I am Mrs. Smythe, housekeeper to the marquess."

"Thank you." Pamela followed her into a small sitting room and sat with relief on an upright chair. The lodgings were not what she expected. They were not nearly as grand as her father's residence. Indeed, they were rather spare. But a fire blazed in the fireplace and she found a chair near its heat.

When Mrs. Smythe disappeared, she dropped her head into her hands. What had she done? If anyone discovered her here, she would be ruined. Her father would be in a rage.

She still felt the pain from the blow yesterday. She recalled the rumors she had heard. Her father had caused her mother's death. He had openly talked of killing Lord Manchester.

Now that she had disappeared without permission, she would receive no mercy.

She swallowed hard. What if Manchester had been playing with her? What if he took her back?

*What had she done?*

She sat in the chair, leaning toward the heat, praying it would warm her soul as well as her body. She had come to warn him, and in doing so she might have signed her own death warrant.

Pamela realized at that moment she could not go back.

Not ever.

And Manchester? If he was not what she believed him to be? Where would she go? How would she survive?

She stared blankly at the dancing flames. Bright. Cheerful.

"My lady?"

The woman's voice startled her, and Pamela started to rise in a panic.

"It's all right, my lady. It is just me with a bit of hot tea to warm you," the woman said and put down a tray laden with a teapot, cup, thick cream, several pastries.

"Do you know when Lord Manchester will return?"

"Nay," the woman said. "He must have come in very late last night. I made him breakfast, and then he hurried out."

"I . . . I sent a note yesterday," Pamela said.

A look of horror came over her face, then she hurried out of the room and returned a moment later. "It is still on the silver tray. I forgot to tell him about it."

Pamela did not know whether she should be relieved or not. At least he had not ignored her. But what to do now?

Did she dare return home and hope he might stop to visit her? Should she stay here until he returned?

Her father probably knew she had left against his wishes. He'd made it clear last night that she was to stay in her room for her disobedience. Would he forbid her from seeing Manchester? Would he send her back to her aunt's residence?

Should she write something on paper or even tell this woman? Then what if her father learned of it?

Torn with indecision and misery, she looked up at Mrs. Smythe, whose expression went from horror at her own failure to obvious concern for Manchester's uninvited guest.

"You are welcome to stay here until he returns," the woman said kindly.

"My father will . . ."

"Lord Manchester will take care of it," the woman said with the supreme confidence of one who believes totally in someone.

"Can someone find Miss Fremont, the actress?" Pamela said, taking her last desperate chance. She was growing more uncertain and even panicked every passing moment.

"I will ask Sydney," she said. "He has been there. In the meantime you drink that tea," she ordered.

Pamela did as ordered as the woman swept out. The housekeeper obviously had the same kind of confidence in her employer as Pamela had at the beginning of this journey. But now that time had worn on, and her problems multiplied, her fear grew.

Then his valet was standing in the room. He was as large as she remembered. But his eyes were kind.

"My lady?"

"I came to tell the marquess something. He must know. I have not been able to find him." The words came tumbling out of her mouth now. Despite his size, the valet had the same comforting face and words as his mother.

"Lady Pamela," he acknowledged. "Does your father know where you are?"

"No, and he must not."

Smythe looked at a clock in the corner. "Lord Manchester said he planned to call on you later."

"I cannot go home."

She tried to check the tears in her eyes. But leaving the house today took the bulk of her courage. She had been so sure—with no evidence whatsoever—that Manchester would magically solve everything.

Then she stiffened. She was no simpering miss. Just days ago she had resolved to be strong. Just last night, she had defied her father.

He studied her for a long time, as if he wanted to do something but was not quite sure exactly what.

"Miss Fremont will know," he said.

She looked at the clock again and her blood chilled. "When does she go to the theater?"

"I will see if we can get there before she leaves," he said.

She rose. The top of her head came to his shoulders. That gave her comfort. There was a steadiness in him.

"I want to thank your mother."

"I will do that for you later. Your cloak?"

She shook her head.

He disappeared and returned with a worn cloak. "My mother's. It is not what you are accustomed to, but . . ."

"I am very grateful," she said with what smile she could manage.

He did not say anything. He opened the door for her, then followed her down the steps. In minutes he had hailed a hackney and helped her inside.

"I do not have any funds," she said, humiliated.

"Lord Manchester would not want you to pay," he said.

The coach started. If only she was in time.

Daven had news.

Stanhope had barely entered White's and sat at Daven's table when his partner said, "It was the actress."

Stanhope struggled to control his anger. He had not wanted it to be her, he realized now. At some point in the blasted contest, he had started to actually care about her. The realization was galling.

"How do you know?"

"She told the manager of the theater. You are banned from attending the theater, and he has approached Sir Thomas Colley about opening an investigation into Stammel's death."

Stanhope's hands clenched the glass he was holding. "How serious is it?"

"Colley is incorruptible. There is nothing we can do to stop him. I fear one investigation will lead to another."

"We have stopped them before."

"A baron has not been killed before."

"I had nothing to do with that."

Daven was silent.

"You do not believe I had nothing to do with Stammel's death?"

"I am thinking about leaving London for a while. Now that we are no longer at war with France . . ." Daven said without answering the question.

Stanhope stared at him. "This will go away."

Daven stood. "If I were you, Stanhope, I would leave, too." He left the table.

Stanhope sat there blindly. No one spoke to him.

How could everything have gone so wrong?

He had expected to have the betrothal this afternoon and Manchester's thirty-five thousand pounds. That and the insurance money would have been a godsend. Now his daughter was missing, Manchester was proving to be more stubborn than he thought, and a bloody actress was accusing him of murder.

His world was falling apart, and it was all her fault.

Why?

Now that he thought of it, she had targeted him ever since she came to London. He thought back to the times she had dangled herself in front of him, only to back away. Of her strange friendship with Pamela, even Manchester.

*Manchester* . . .

Was he still at his home? Or with Monique Fremont? Or was there another reason?

He jerked away from the table, knocking over a chair as he rose. Goddamn it, no one was going to make a fool of him.

Manchester smoked his cigar and drank some of Stanhope's brandy after the man left.

He wondered where Pamela was. She hadn't appeared to have many friends. Perhaps Stanhope had decided he was no longer useful as a possible son-in-law.

He poured the rest of the bottle of brandy in a spittoon, then approached the door, which had been left open, and looked out. He probably had a few moments before the butler appeared again. He took the forged manifest from inside his waistcoat and wandered over to the desk. Again, he unlocked the drawer quickly and put the manifest at the bottom of a pile in the lower left hand drawer.

He straightened just as he heard the butler again, but he did not have time to lock it.

He moved to the door. "Just looking for you," he said as the butler came through the door. "I am ready for another glass of brandy." He peered at the man with his quizzing glass. "Is Lady Pamela about yet? Dashedly bad manners to keep me waiting."

The butler stalked over to the bottle on the table, discovered it was empty, and left again. Gabriel locked the drawer and sat, stretching out his long legs.

Monica would be on her way to the theater. The Smythes should be packed and waiting for him. If only he could talk to Pamela.

Timing was everything tonight.

*Everything.*

# Chapter Twenty-nine

The theater was full.

Monique had learned long ago to turn her personal thoughts off once she stepped on the stage.

It was more difficult today than it had ever been in her life.

So many warring emotions.

She thought she had made her decision. Yet doubts pummeled her.

Monique had not questioned her instincts or decisions for a number of years, not since she found something at which she was very good, which earned her respect. Which gave her entrée to almost anywhere she wanted to go.

She hadn't wanted more than that, other than to see justice done. But now she realized there was something stronger, something far greater than the approval of an audience.

Should she tell Gabriel everything? Perhaps he would want nothing to do with her then. But at least she would know.

Hope battled despair even as she kept the banter light on stage and responded to the laughter. She wished she could see the audience. She did see Lynch in the curtains. He was beaming. A ripple of guilt ran through her. She *did* have an obligation to him.

Did she have a greater one to herself?

She uttered the last line, and the theater exploded into applause. She knew it had not been one of her better performances. Richard looked at her curiously.

"I'm sorry," she said as they exited the stage.

"No need, love. You are better on your worst day than anyone else on the best day. It is a pleasure being on the stage with you."

The compliment warmed her. She liked him. He swaggered and considered himself a gift to all women, but he was also very professional on the stage and, unlike many actors, ready to compliment his fellows, whether they were in lead or supporting roles.

"Thank you."

"No need. You make me look good." He looked at her closely. "Would you have supper with me tonight?"

"I am sorry. I cannot."

"Refused again. You will destroy my confidence, Monique."

"Impossible," she said lightly, then paused, wondering whether she would see him again. "Good night."

He gave her a curious, searching look. As if he knew something—or perhaps Monique herself—had changed.

She turned and went into her dressing room, where Dani waited. She was on edge too, moving around restlessly, which she rarely did.

Monique felt the weight of other lives on her. She wanted Dani to go tonight. She must go. She might never find another man like Smythe, just as she, Monique, would never find another Manchester.

Monique's housekeeper answered the door when Pamela and Smythe arrived at her lodging.

Mrs. Miller recognized Smythe, who then introduced Pamela.

The housekeeper curtsied. "My lady," she said.

"I am looking for Miss Fremont," Pamela said.

"She has gone to the theater."

Pamela felt the earth move under her. She had depended on contacting Manchester, passing on her news and returning home—all hopefully before anyone knew she was gone. That, though, was impossible now. Her absence no doubt had been noted. Why had she not been patient and waited for Manchester at her home?

She had been rash for one of the few times in her life. She should know it always ended in disaster.

"Come, miss," Smythe said sympathetically. "We will find my lord for you. I know he cares about you."

The housekeeper looked at them with curious eyes.

Pamela wondered what both were thinking. Had Manchester and Miss Fremont confided in them? Did Manchester's valet realize that they were playing a charade?

"And if we do not?"

"I will take you home," Smythe said.

She looked at him. "I cannot return there."

The housekeeper looked distressed. "You can leave a message, but she will not return for at least three hours."

"Thank you," Pamela said politely. But even she heard the weakness, even fear, in her voice. Then, "perhaps I can stay here and wait for her."

Mrs. Miller looked at Smythe, then at Pamela. "I think that would be all right," she said. "You can have some tea, and rest. You look weary and it would not do for you to go to Lord Manchester's residence."

Pamela *was* tired. Exhausted, in truth. She had not slept since she had arrived in London and had not slept well before that, not since Lord Stammel's death. And she doubted her father would look for her here. He could not have known that she had grown close to Miss Fremont.

She looked at Smythe in question.

He nodded. "I will continue to look for Lord Manchester, but I think he planned to come by here tonight in any event. He will look after you," he added with a slight smile.

Pamela turned to Mrs. Miller. "Thank you," she said with heartfelt gratitude. She turned to Smythe. "And to you."

His face flushed slightly before he nodded, turned, and left the house.

Pamela had not returned home.

Stanhope had stopped at his residence, hoping she might

be there. Perhaps she would know more about Manchester than he'd thought. A woman, even a plain mouse of one, could often exact more information than harsher methods.

The longer Stanhope reviewed the past weeks, the more he centered on a conspiracy between Manchester and Monique Fremont. Nothing else made sense. They had appeared at the same time. Seen too often in one another's company. They always had reasons, but reasons were easy to come by.

He had been played for a fool. No doubt about it. The latest blow came when he arrived at his residence. One more note, this one saying there was some question about the purchase of muskets for Ireland.

He'd read it with growing dread. But the threads were coming together in one giant tapestry.

He now agreed with Daven. He had to leave London, and he had to do it immediately.

He'd seen accusation in Daven's eyes. If his partner was questioned, Stanhope had little faith in his ability to keep silent.

But he needed funds to live well outside England. He had some banknotes, but much of his funds had been spent on refurbishing his ancestral home. Manchester, though, had cash. And Stanhope damned well intended to get it.

In the meantime he planned a visit to Monique Fremont tonight. Barred from the theater? The very thought enraged him. Thomas Kane, the Earl of Stanhope, banned from a common theater.

He waited for his daughter to return home. When that did not happen, he sent out his footmen to make discreet queries about her and to watch the residences of both Manchester and Monique Fremont.

As he waited, he drank brandy. His best. He looked around the comfortable room that he might soon have to forfeit. His ancestral home in the country. His roses.

His anger intensified. It was a fire inside him. With each sip, his rage grew. He had befriended Manchester when no one else would. He had been patient with Monique Fremont. He'd helped fill the theater by recommending the play to his friends.

Now they had turned on him. They had caused his friends to turn on him.

They were trying to destroy him, and they would pay for that error of judgement.

The brandy stirred his thoughts. How bad was the damage? If he killed Manchester and the actress, would the trail lead back to him? Or was Stammel's death his noose?

And why was Stammel dead?

A debt to Manchester. Manchester's accusation that he placed a burr under a saddle. Jewels found in his belongings. And where had Manchester been just prior to finding them?

*Manchester. Always Manchester.*

Had Manchester stolen the jewels and planted them in Stammel's belongings? Had the American marquess been a far better hand at cards than he'd led Stammel—and himself—to believe? Blazes, had he killed his partner and friend for no reason?

Manchester? But how could the man have gotten into his safe? And how would he know the combination? Though he had left the man in his office, Stanhope did not think he'd had access to the rest of his house.

*The soiree!* Monique Fremont had spilled something on her dress. Manchester had disappeared then.

Stanhope saw it all now. All the pieces fit into a very tidy package. He had been outwitted by a common actress and an American upstart. He had seen what he had wanted to see.

He had money at his country estate. Enough to see him abroad.

But first he would see to Manchester and Monique Fremont. Monique first. He would force her into sending a note to Manchester. Then a lover's quarrel. Murder. Suicide.

Gabriel waited in the shadows at the back of the theater. He had finally left Stanhope's home, giving up on trying to see Pamela. He'd wanted to tell her she could accompany them to America or, if she wished, stay in London under the protection of Baron Tolvery.

He had made decisions this night. He had heard the rumors

running throughout London that Stanhope had murdered his partner. Gabriel knew exactly where those rumors had started, and so would Stanhope.

Monique was in deadly danger.

No doubt she had known that. So then why had she resisted the opportunity to leave? No theater engagement or contract was worth one's life. Like it or not he was taking her tonight.

They both had started in motion events that could not be stopped. Stanhope was neatly trapped in a pincer movement. And there was nothing as dangerous as a trapped animal.

He looked at his watch. He'd sent a message to the captain of the *Amelia* that he might be late, but most certainly would have his passengers aboard before sailing time.

Thunderous applause ran through the theater as the play ended. He had seen it before, of course, and tonight Monique appeared as effervescent as previously. He stepped out the doors and went for his horse. He planned to wait until she left the theater and follow her carriage to her home. She was not going to be alone this night.

The air outside was damp and the first tendrils of fog crept along the streets. It would not be long before it eclipsed the carriages waiting outside the theater.

He watched from a side street as the carriages left one by one. His gaze was centered on the side door from which the actors entered and left. He finally saw her emerge. Lynch was at her side and helped her into the carriage.

Gabriel wanted to join her, but he wanted more to determine if anyone else was following her.

The carriage pulled out onto the street. Gabriel waited until another one pulled out, then followed.

The fog was growing dense. It blocked the streetlights and masked the people walking in the streets. They were little more than shadows, just as the carriages ahead were barely visible.

But he knew the way. He didn't think anyone else was following, and he closed the distance.

*     *     *

Covered with a long dark cloak and wide-brimmed hat pulled down over his eyes, Stanhope studied Monique's residence from the street. Lights shone from two downstairs rooms. Smoke curled from the chimney.

He had to get rid of the housekeeper first. Then he would wait for Monique and her maid to return.

He looked up and down the street. Residences more than one hundred feet distant faded away in the fog.

Stanhope waited as a carriage clattered by, then went up to the door and knocked loudly. He then quickly went down three stairs and flattened himself against the wall.

The door opened and he heard an exclamation from a woman, then, "Is anyone there?"

He made a small choking noise and bent over. She came toward him. He swung his arm, hitting her on the head. Unconscious, she sank down on the sidewalk. He lifted her, putting an arm around her as if helping, and dragged her through the still-open door into the residence, then down the stairs into the kitchen area. He tied her hands and ankles, gagged her, and pushed her into a storage area.

Everything was silent inside. A fire roared in the sitting room.

He looked around. He had sent flowers, but none were in evidence. Monique apparently had kept none of them.

The anger flashed again, then settled into stone-cold rage.

He thought about going up the stairs, but Monique's maid always went to the theater with her. There had been no lights on above.

He looked through a cabinet, found some brandy, and poured himself a glass.

And waited.

Smythe was as frantic as he had ever been. He could not find his lord anywhere.

His family was packed and ready to leave. He knew the name of the ship, and Gabriel had given him both funds and letters to present to a shipbuilder in Boston.

But he felt responsible for Lady Pamela, and he worried about his master.

Servants everywhere were talking about Lord Stanhope and the possibility he might have killed his partner.

Smythe had left Lady Pamela at Miss Fremont's residence under the care of Mrs. Miller. Miss Fremont would know what to do, and it was far better for Lady Pamela to be there rather than wandering the streets or staying in a male household.

He had gone to the clubs, then waited outside Lord Stanhope's residence before going home to wait. Surely, his master would return before time to go to the docks; Smythe knew from Dani there was still the possibility that both would journey to America with them. If not, they would meet later.

He prayed they would go together. He had never thought to attract a young lady. That someone like Dani had evidently enjoyed his company was an amazing thing.

Smythe did something he seldom did. He paced. He gave himself another hour, and then he would go to Miss Fremont's. He wanted this journey to America. It would give his mother, sister, and himself opportunities he never thought to have. But it would mean little if he lost Dani.

Monique and Dani alighted from the carriage and walked inside her residence. The door was unlocked, which was unusual. Even more unusual was the fact that Mrs. Miller did not greet them. Usually she was waiting at the door, wanting to know if Monique wanted tea or some refreshment.

An oil light flickered in the hallway.

Dani took her cloak and went up the stairs while Monique looked for Mrs. Miller. She wanted to tell the housekeeper that she may be leaving shortly.

If Gabriel still wanted her after he heard the truth . . .

In the past few hours of soul-searching she had come to the conclusion that nothing was more important than Gabriel, that, yes, she could rely on him to make sure Pamela was safe.

But would he feel the same once he knew . . .

Mrs. Miller was not down in the kitchen. Monique came back up the stairs and saw Stanhope blocking the front door.

She lifted her head slightly in puzzlement, a streak of apprehension running up and down her back. "My lord, I did not expect you."

"No, I do not suppose you did," he said. He was wearing a cloak much like she had seen Manchester wearing. His head was bare of any covering, and his hair askew. His eyes were glittering black pieces of coal.

"Where is Mrs. Miller?" she asked.

He shrugged, but his body was rigid with rage.

"You did not harm her?"

"You should not worry about her," he said.

Her eyes reflexively went to the door.

"Is your love expected?" Stanhope asked. "Then I will not have to ask you to write him a note."

"No one is expected," she said.

Stanhope laughed. "Now I know he is coming. You are quite an accomplished liar, Monique. But what I want to know is why?"

"I do not understand," she said in a cool voice.

"You and Manchester. I can guess at Manchester's reasons. But not yours."

"You talk in riddles, my lord. There is no me and Manchester. He is merely an acquaintance."

Monique played for time now. She wondered where Dani was, whether she'd heard voices. She could not get to the back entrance without coming down the stairs, and Stanhope was facing those.

Stanhope grabbed her arm. "You will tell me what I want to know. If you do not, there is your maid upstairs. Perhaps she can."

The malevolence with which he said the words sent chills through her. She tried to jerk away from his hold, but it only tightened.

Two men were outside. The ones that were to take Manchester to the ship if necessary. She had to maneuver her way back into the window and signal them with the lamp. But how?

She looked back at her captor. Rage transfigured his face.

Only one thing might force him into letting her go for even a moment.

"I will tell you," she said suddenly, going still. "If you wish to know so much, then let me go and I will tell you why I wanted to meet you."

"You will tell me anyway."

"No."

"Damn you."

She did not flinch. Did not move.

He suddenly released her hand. His eyes bored into hers. "Do you remember a woman named Mary Anders?"

Recognition flickered in his eyes, then his face paled.

"Do you?" she insisted.

"Yes." Stanhope's words were little more than a whisper.

"She was my mother."

Monique allowed the words to sink in.

His face went from white to gray. "She could not . . ."

"Why? Because you tried to kill her. And me. You thought she was dead."

"Oh my God," he uttered. "You . . . cannot be . . ."

"I am your daughter. My mother survived your attempt. But in doing so, she lost everything. Her dignity. Her health. Her life . . ."

He was staring at her as if she were a ghost. Then, "You are wrong. It was not me. My father . . . he told me she had died. I . . ." Then his gaze went to the bead bracelet on her wrist. His face hardened as he apparently understood what had happened.

"You," he said. "Then it *was* you. How long have you and Manchester . . . ?"

"It was not Manchester. It was myself alone," she said. "I wanted justice. You destroyed her. Not immediately. It was a long painful death, instead. One man after another, each sapping her strength, brutalizing her. She lived in fear, and so did her family."

His face hardened. "My father said it was best that your mother, and you, died. He was right, damn it."

"No!"

Monique heard the cry from above and turned to look at the stairs. Pamela stood there. So did Dani.

Stanhope turned that way, too.

It was time enough to pick up a lamp. If only she could set it in the window. The two men she'd hired to kidnap Gabriel would go to the back and come in. They would be prepared to forcibly take a man to a ship.

But just as she moved toward the window, Stanhope grabbed her again with one hand.

The other held a pistol.

The fog cloaked much of the house. Gabriel had waited as the lights went on inside. Then he saw two men lurking across the lane. They were trying to look as if they were just talking, but they did not look quite right for this respectable section of London.

He moved closer. From an angle he saw Stanhope inside, a pistol in his hands.

Keeping an eye on the two men across from him, he went to the front door. He had his burglary tools with him, since he had not known whether he would need them to get inside Stanhope's home.

Weapons. He had a pistol in the saddlebags of his horse, tied to a hitching post not far away. Did he have time to fetch it? He wasn't going to risk it, nor the two men loitering nearby. He had a knife in a sheath in his waistcoat. That would have to suffice.

Using his back to disguise his movements, he tried the door, finding it locked. He reached inside his waistcoat, and in seconds the lock opened.

Straightening, he sauntered inside as if he had his own key and belonged there. His right hand was close to the knife. He saw Pamela on the steps. How in the hell did she come to be here? And Dani?

His gaze went to Stanhope, who turned in his direction, the pistol moving away from Monique and toward him.

Stanhope's eyes were wild. "Manchester! I knew it. I knew you were in with the bitch."

Stanhope's pistol had only one shot. Gabriel would far rather he expend it on him than either Monique or Pamela.

"It took you a while, though, did it not?" he said conversationally. "You are not nearly as intelligent as you believe you are." He stared at Stanhope. "There is evidence of your crimes now. Unless you flee now . . ."

Stanhope's arm wavered slightly as it moved between him and Monique. It was difficult to determine which he wanted to shoot more.

"You have one shot in that pistol," Gabriel continued. "You cannot kill everyone in this room. Even three women, I believe, can stop you, and you will hang. On the other hand, you can run now. You have a chance. You can leave the country."

"Exile." Stanhope spat it out.

"I expect that is better than a hangman's noose," Gabriel said calmly. He knew Stanhope's fingers were itching to shoot. He was betting on the man's sense of self-preservation.

"There is evidence," Gabriel said again. "I expect authorities are checking the cargo of the *Peregrine* as we speak. You have little time."

"You did this," Stanhope said in a forced whisper.

"I did. And alone. Oh, Miss Fremont was a convenient foil, but I have planned this for years, my lord," he said mockingly. "Everything. Even as I captained an American ship during the war. I wonder if I sank some of your ships."

"God damn you."

"Go, if you want to live," Gabriel said in a low singsong voice. "Go."

"Not before I kill you," Stanhope said, steadying the barrel of the pistol in Gabriel's direction.

"No!"

He heard Monique's voice at the same time he saw her lunge toward Stanhope. She literally flew the few feet to knock his arm just as the pistol discharged. Pain ripped through Gabriel's arm even as he lunged for Stanhope. The man avoided his grasp and slipped away from him toward the door.

Gabriel went after him, slowed by the pain.

He caught him at the door. Stanhope whirled around and hit his wounded arm with the butt of the pistol, dropping the weapon as he did so. Stunned, Gabriel sank to his knees as Stanhope tore open the door and fled.

Monique rushed to him, but Gabriel shrugged her aside, rose, and staggered to the door, only to see Stanhope mounting Specter and disappearing into the fog.

Home. The man had to be going home. He would need money. Weapons. Clothes.

Gabriel ran to the corner, searching for a hackney. Blood streamed from his arm. He felt it dampening his clothes and running down his arm. But he refused to allow Stanhope to escape.

He was only partially aware of the two men he glimpsed earlier coming toward him, and he heard Monique scream out, "No!"

He pushed past them. Monique followed. He turned. "Send someone for Baron Tolvery. On Greene Street. Tell him to go to Stanhope's."

"No," she said. "Your wound . . ."

But he ignored her words. Instead, he stood in the way of an oncoming carriage. As it stopped, he opened the door and peered inside. An obviously inebriated lord stared back at him.

"An emergency," he mumbled to the occupant of the carriage. "Lord Stanhope may be in desperate danger. Take me there." He said it with such command that the man stuttered through the window to the driver.

Monique had reached the door. "Tolvery," he shouted again at Monique. "Reach him."

The carriage lurched forward before she could answer. The jolting of the carriage caused more pain to shoot through him. Blood, he noted, was dripping on the floor of the coach, but the lord was so drunk that he did not seem to notice. "By Jove! Stanhope, you say?" his startled host said.

"Aye," Gabriel said, wishing he had more than the knife with him. Stanhope had left his pistol in Monique's residence, but he undoubtedly had more weapons. He was not going to get away, though.

"I'm Ridley," his host said. "Don't know Stanhope well." He looked down at the floor. "Say, you are bleeding, sir."

"It is nothing," he said.

But the young lord looked less in his cups now. His eyes

went to the blood puddling on the floor of his obviously expensive carriage. "I think I should find a police officer or a Charlie." He started to rap on the back of the carriage, then saw Gabriel's face and sat back.

Seconds later they pulled up in front of Stanhope's town house. "*Now* you can get a magistrate or police officers," he said and jumped out.

Stanhope had a lead of perhaps ten minutes if the earl had raced Specter.

Gabriel didn't see the horse in front. Stanhope had probably ridden into the mews. To go to the front would mean awakening the servants.

Only one light shone from the house, and that was in Stanhope's study. Ignoring the growing pain in his arm, Gabriel strode to the back of the house. His horse was there. He tried the door. It was unlocked. He moved inside and went to the study. The door was closed.

He opened it as quietly as possible and heard the sound of drawers being pulled out. Gabriel stepped inside and saw Stanhope going through the drawers. A valise sat at the doorway.

Stanhope whirled around. "You!"

Gabriel looked at the bottom drawer, where he had placed the forged papers. It had not been opened.

Then he saw a pistol on the desk.

Just then he heard the shouts from outside. Time to gamble a little, to gamble for time.

"It is over," he said.

"I can take you with me," Stanhope said.

"Then you most certainly will have a public hanging."

A pounding was heard at the door. "You have no friends now," Gabriel said. "Just like my father had none. You drove them away. Do you know Baron Tolvery? He is at the *Peregrine* now."

Stanhope reached for the pistol and Gabriel lunged for it as well. But he was weaker than he thought, and Stanhope reached it first.

More pounding at the door. Alarmed shouts of servants.

Clutching the pistol, Stanhope looked toward the door. It opened. Anxious and frightened faces peered in.

Stanhope stood there. Pistol in hand. His eyes fixed on the servants staring at him from the door, then at Gabriel.

The pounding outside was louder.

Stanhope lifted the pistol to his temple. He closed his eyes and pulled the trigger.

# Chapter Thirty

Gabriel leaned against the wall.

The scene was familiar. It had haunted so many days and nights.

He wanted to feel satisfaction. He did not.

Then men pushed inside. Stanhope's hand was still around the pistol. His eyes were open and appeared to be staring.

One man, obviously in charge, stepped forward, "Wha' 'appened 'ere?"

"His lordship shot hisself," a footman, a long shirt hanging outside his trousers, said in awe.

The man who had asked the question looked at Gabriel. Gabriel nodded.

"A young lord said someone planned to kill Lord Stanhope," the policeman said.

"I told him that," Gabriel said. "But Stanhope tried to kill me, and I wanted to stop him from escaping. It seemed simpler to say he was in danger than to try to explain."

"Your name, sir?"

"Manchester. The Marquess of Manchester."

The man's eyes narrowed. "I heard of you."

"I am sure you have," Gabriel said, aware of the hollowness in his voice. "Excuse me but I must sit down."

He stumbled to one of the chairs. He'd been wounded before during a sea battle. He knew there was a period during which pure energy or excitement kept a wounded man going, and then . . .

"Sir?"

Voices began to fade.

"My God, he has been shot."

"Call a physician."

"Help lay 'im down."

His eyes started to close, and he suddenly smelled an aroma he remembered. Loved.

Loved.

A cool hand touched him. He tried to force his eyes open, but they could . . . could . . . quite . . .

He felt someone lift him, and then his world went black.

Monique sat by his bed. She prayed.

She had not prayed in a very long time. She only hoped her prayers would be accepted.

The physician called to Stanhope's home said Gabriel had lost a great deal of blood. His remedy, after pulling out a bullet, was to bleed him to remove the poisons.

Smythe, whom she had sent for, would not allow it. He had seen too many men die. Alcohol, he said. Pour alcohol over the wound. He had seen it work before. And rest. Gabriel needed rest. Nourishment.

*Care.*

Monique could provide the last. She had sat by her mother for days, watching her die. She did not intend to watch another person die.

She'd had him moved to his own residence after authorities assured themselves that Stanhope had indeed taken his own life. She determined that Gabriel was going to live.

And at least Mrs. Miller was safe. She had been found bound and bleeding, but was soon indignant and ready to see justice done. She'd not been mollified to realize it *had* been done.

Smythe helped Monique keep vigil as Gabriel sank into unconsciousness after the bullet was removed from his arm.

He woke for a brief period to ask as to her welfare, and Pamela's. Then he lapsed back into unconsciousness again, his body apparently depleted. Then the fever took over.

He tossed and turned, muttering unintelligible words, evidently returning to that day when as a boy his own father shot himself. Monique bathed his face and body, as his body seemed to radiate heat, then covered him with blankets as he shivered. She forced broth down his throat during brief periods of consciousness and tried to tempt him into drinking water.

His wound was all her fault. If she had left when he'd asked her, if she had been able to spirit him away sooner. If she had not been hell-bent on revenge. Perhaps then he would not be lying in this bed.

"You should get some rest," Smythe said as he entered the room with fresh water and clothes. "I will dress the wound."

She shook her head. "I cannot leave him."

"He is strong and has a will like iron," Smythe said.

"It is my doing."

"No, miss. He knew what he was doing."

"I should have—" She stopped suddenly.

He looked at her with a raised eyebrow.

"It doesn't matter now. There was a ship bound for Boston. I had hoped to . . . see him on it."

"How?" he said, an old gleam in his eyes.

"Kidnap him," she admitted wryly.

He chuckled. "He intended the same thing for you," he said. "The night he was shot. My family and I . . . we were also intended to be aboard. And take you if necessary."

*A few hours.*

A few hours difference and they both would be sailing for Boston. Now he was terribly ill; she had violated her contract by refusing to go to the theater, and Lynch was threatening her; Stanhope was dead; Daven had been arrested and his estate was under scrutiny. Pamela was staying at Stanhope's home, trying to cope with numerous queries and investigations.

Monique had taken a few moments to send a message to Pamela's young man, asking him to come to London. Her sister had dropped by several times. She was pale but steady. She had opened her father's records to the magistrate. They had found papers that proved the earl had tried to defraud the government.

Monique knew it was difficult for Pamela, but she could not—would not—leave Gabriel. Pamela had understood. She had stood beside Monique and watched him as he slept.

"Keep him," Pamela urged her.

"He is not mine to keep. I did not trust him enough. Nor he I."

"You were trying to protect each other," Pamela said gently.

"No, we both wanted . . . my father dead more than we wanted each other."

"Not toward the end," Pamela said softly.

"But then it was too late."

"It is never too late."

How Monique wanted to believe her. But how does one who has lived a life based on the past and vengeance turn to one of the future and hope? She wanted to believe it was possible, but looking at Gabriel on the bed, she truly wondered.

Pamela seemed to have grown years in the past few days, or perhaps she had viewed events from a distance for so long she had little emotional involvement.

After she'd left, Monique studied Gabriel's face. Such an intriguing face. Angular but with a dimple in his chin. The dark eyebrows that now covered those glass-clear green eyes. She recalled his rare smile, the lolling gracefulness of his walk. She reached out and took his hand, a hand marred by calluses. A giveaway of hard work. But now she remembered he always wore gloves in the presence of Stanhope and his friends.

She explored his hand now, then pressed it to her face and kissed his fingers. What would she do without him? He had given her a taste of what love was all about.

She played with those fingers, wishing she could do more. He had rushed into a room, believing she was in danger. He had diverted Stanhope from her. No greater love, she thought, remembering part of a saying she had heard somewhere.

He was so hot. His wound looked frighteningly red and raw.

His eyes opened slowly, then his bloodshot gaze met hers, and he smiled. "I have dreamed of you," he said. "I did not think . . ." His voice trailed off.

"No dream, " she said. "I have been here."

"You are supposed to be in America. Smythe . . . promised."

"He told me," she said with a smile. "By force if necessary."

He moved. Groaned. His voice was raspy. "Water."

Smythe was at the door and rushed over to pour water from a pitcher into a cup and handed it to Monique. She leaned over and put it to his lips.

He drank slowly. His skin still felt on fire.

When he was through, he closed his eyes again. "Thank you," he whispered.

She leaned down. "Thank *you*, my lord."

"Gabriel."

"Gabriel," she said.

He smiled. A weak wobbly smile that broke her heart. His eyes closed again.

"Get well and I will do anything you wish," she whispered. "Fight for me."

Hours later the fever broke. She was half asleep on the chair next to him when she heard Smythe's indrawn breath. She leaned over to see Gabriel bathed in sweat.

Smythe was by her side. "It is good news," he said. "The fever has broken." He handed her some cloths, obviously knowing she wanted to dry him herself.

Any words were stopped by the lump in her throat. She nodded and gently washed away the moisture. His eyes flickered open again, and he moved slightly as she reached his stomach.

His eyes had been dull, and that had worried her more than any other physical sign. They were usually so clear. Now there was a flicker of the old amusement even as a groan escaped his mouth.

"Anything?" he asked in a barely audible voice.

It took her a second to realize he must be referring to her whispered words earlier. She hadn't thought he had heard them.

"You were not supposed to hear that," she forced through that lump that lingered in her throat.

"What day . . . ?"

"Three days since you were shot. You lost a great deal of blood. That was a reckless thing to do, go after him. I did not realize how . . ."

"What . . . what has happened?"

"I do not know. I just know from Pamela there is an investigation of Lord Stanhope's business activities. There is no doubt he shot himself. That is all I know."

"And . . . Pamela?"

"She is coping quite well. I have sent for Robert, though," she said. "If they still want one another, nothing can stop them now."

She continued to dry his body, lingering here and there to trail a fingertip along muscled lines of his chest. It trembled with her touch.

A long breath came from his throat, and she realized how tired he was. His wound was still raw and must be extraordinarily painful, but Smythe said he hadn't seen any infection. She prayed constantly there would be none.

"You should not try to talk," she said. "You need rest."

"I wanted you to be aboard . . ."

"I had the same plans for you," she said. "I had two men ready that night to kidnap you and take you to the same ship."

He gave her a broken smile. "I would have liked waking up with you at sea."

She swallowed hard. *Would have liked.*

"Rest," she said.

"I cannot as long as you do . . . that."

She realized she had gone a bit farther than she had intended. Her hands withdrew as if burned.

"You do not have to . . ." He moved his arm slightly and pain ripped across his face.

"Be still," she said.

"You did . . . not answer my question. You said you would do anything?"

"I did."

"Merry," he said in a voice growing increasingly faint. "I . . . like it."

She started her washing again, but not near the sensitive place. His eyes closed again. She suspected he was at least partially awake. Everything seemed such an effort for him. She leaned down and kissed him. "Anything," she whispered.

Even leave him.

Gabriel felt weaker than he'd ever felt in his life. Every movement took supreme effort. Every word.

His arm was pure agony.

At one time he'd felt himself slipping away. Only Monique's words had kept him from doing so.

He knew the wound had not been that bad. It had been the loss of blood. But he couldn't allow Stanhope to escape.

It had almost killed him.

He felt no satisfaction. Only sorrow that he'd allowed the man to consume his life and almost kill him.

How could anything be built on hate and revenge?

But miracle of all miracles, it appeared Monique had not left his side. And every touch of her hands made him stronger.

He hadn't been able to keep his eyes open, but neither did he drift off to sleep. He drifted in some space, alternating between the world when he was a lad, the scene in Stanhope's home, and Monique's light, which illuminated the area between.

He tried to speak again. To tell her that. But he was so tired. Even now, he was so very tired.

Monique forced herself to eat. His fever had broken, but he still drifted between consciousness and sleep.

There was a little more color in his face, but not enough to cool her fears. Fear for his life. Fear for what would happen when he returned to health. Would he truly want her now that he knew she was Stanhope's daughter? Had he even heard that part of the exchange between Stanhope and herself?

The question kept haunting her.

*Anything.*

She would do anything for him. Even let him return to a life without her. It would break her heart but maybe that's what love was about. Joy. And pain.

The door opened. *Mrs. Smythe.* They were becoming fast friends now. Mrs. Smythe kept a kettle of broth hot for whenever Manchester woke. She had constantly tried to tempt Monique with meat pies and pastries, but she had to force herself to eat even a little. Just enough to stay and care for Gabriel.

Dani had hovered in Manchester's room, along with Smythe. They had sat together in a corner of the room. Holding hands. Exchanging glances both worried and intimate. The few times Monique had left to attend personal needs, Dani had quietly taken her place at Gabriel's side.

Monique had no doubt the two—Smythe and Dani—belonged together.

A knocking came from below.

Mrs. Smythe hurried out the door to answer it.

In seconds she had returned and handed her a card. *Lord Tolvery.*

She gave a reluctant look at Gabriel.

"I will stay here with Lord Manchester," Mrs. Smythe said.

Monique gave her a grateful glance and left the room, Smythe protectively behind her.

"Miss Fremont," the baron said. He was a stocky, older man who walked heavily with the assistance of a cane. "How is Lord Manchester?"

"He is very ill."

"I am sorry to hear that. He is a very unusual and determined young man."

She nodded, waiting.

"He came to me with some information. I passed it on to the suitable people. Evidence of crimes was found in Lord Stanhope's home. They are now looking into old cases, including that of his father. I wanted Manchester to know that."

"*Merci,* my lord."

"You are every bit as lovely as I've heard," he added.

She smiled.

"If Manchester needs anything, anything at all, please call on me. I did his father a disservice years ago. It is a debt I feel deeply. I hope he will stay here in England."

"I do not think he will."

"I regret that." He turned painfully and hobbled toward the door.

Monique closed the door behind him and looked at the card. She remembered now that Gabriel had asked her to send someone for him that night Stanhope had shot him. Instead, she had rushed after him.

She wondered how many other friends Gabriel had. Smythe's family obviously adored him. So did Pamela. She suspected he had many in Boston.

She had only Dani—had never had more than Dani. She had been too afraid to confide in anyone. Too much in a hurry to end a deadly quest. And now she stood to lose everyone.

She went up the stairs, clutching the card in her hands.

Gabriel had won. His father might well be exonerated now. She hesitated near the top, leaning against the wall. Both of them had tried to fight their parents' battles. And they had nearly destroyed themselves in the doing.

She vowed then she would never leave that kind of legacy for her own children.

"Monique."

It was Dani's voice.

She finished the last two steps and ran for the bedroom. Dani was outside.

"He's awake. He is better. He asked for you."

Relief flowed through her. For a moment . . .

She went inside the room. He was sitting up. His face was still pale. New lines made trails on his face. His hair was plastered to his head, and bristle on his cheeks and chin made him look like a bandit. But his eyes had that familiar glint that had been missing.

She leaned over and handed the card to him. "The baron said your father's case is being investigated. You have succeeded."

He dropped it. "It doesn't matter now."

She looked at him, her stomach constricted in a hard knot. "He said he hoped you would stay in England."

"No," he replied.

He reached out and took her hand with his good one. It was unexpectedly strong.

She knew it was time to tell him. There had been too much dishonesty between them already. "Stanhope was my father," she said.

He looked at her steadily. "I suspected as much."

She must have looked as startled as she felt. His fingers tightened around hers. "You and Pamela resemble each other," he said. "And I wondered about your protectiveness . . ."

"How can you . . . care for someone who has the same blood as . . . as the man who is responsible for . . . ?"

"My father was responsible, too," Gabriel said. "He wanted to show *his* father that he could be successful. He was too eager to accept help that should have aroused his suspicions. And perhaps if he had fought the charges . . ."

He was silent for a moment, then added, "I was not responsible for that any more than you are responsible for an accident of birth. But I made myself responsible just as you did."

He moved closer. She saw the edges of his mouth tighten and could only guess at how much even that slight movement cost him.

He fell back, his eyes searching hers. "I don't care what your father did or who he was. I want . . . you to know that."

She wished she believed that.

He took a deep breath, and she knew his strength was still depleted. It was as if he was gathering what was left to say something. Farewell? Her fingers tightened around his.

"The theater?" he continued after a moment. "You have been here with me. Your role?"

That was not what she wanted him to ask. She wanted him to ask her to go with him again, now that he knew she was Stanhope's daughter. "Do you really believe I could perform, not knowing whether you were—"

"It takes more than an English earl to kill me," he interrupted before she could say the word. "I know your career . . . is important."

Her heart dropped. "I can find another part."

"Is that what you want?"

It wasn't. She wanted him. But though he'd said he loved her, he mentioned nothing about the future.

But their lack of honesty before had led to disaster. "No," she said softly.

"Does that mean you might like to see new places?"

"Boston, in particular," she said, holding her breath.

"I am a sailor," he warned.

"Can I sail with you?"

"Aye," he said. "If you are my wife."

Her breath caught in her throat. After a few seconds she asked, "Is that an offer?"

*"Oui,"* he said with that amused smile she loved so much.

"Then yes," she said. "Yes."

Very, very carefully, she leaned down and sealed the bargain with her lips.

# Epilogue

*Boston*
*1822*

They waited at the docks for the ship to anchor. A runner had reached the house just twenty minutes earlier, telling Merry Manning that the *Monique* had been sighted.

Gabriel would be aboard. So would Pamela, Pamela's husband, Robert, and their two children.

It had been three months since she had seen her husband, nearly five years since she had seen her sister.

Only a pregnancy had kept Merry from this voyage. She had been on grand journeys to China and India. In the past three years, though, she had stayed home after the birth of David, now a toddler three years old. Another new child was due in two months. Even now she could feel her kicking.

She was quite sure that the child was a she, though a second boy would also please them both.

As she reached the waterfront, just minutes from their home, she saw the ship approach the wharf. Gabriel was on the deck, just as she had seen him years earlier. His hair was shorter and glinted like gold in the sun, and his posture radiated the confidence she had always loved.

Beside him was Pamela, waving madly. She held the hand

of a girl that looked about David's age, and Robert—a broad smile on his face—held a younger sibling.

She and Gabriel, Pamela and Robert had been married in the same ceremony in London before she and Gabriel had left for America. Monique had liked Robert immediately. He was a kind and compassionate man who obviously adored Pamela. He had not cared that she had lost most of the fortune accumulated by her father, and the estates as well.

Pamela had used what money she'd been able to save from her father's estate to join Robert in Edinburgh while he finished his medical studies. He was now a physician in the same village where his family lived.

David yelled and waved as he saw his father, and Gabriel grinned back. In minutes Gabriel and her two friends departed the ship. David ran toward his father, who scooped him up and gave him a hug and introduced him to his cousins before setting him down. David shyly ogled his cousins.

Then Gabriel turned to her. The broad smile turned tender as his gaze went to her widening form, then to her face. He touched her cheek as he often did with fingers that adored. Then he kissed her in front of a goodly part of Boston until she thought she would melt into the earth.

His eyes promised heaven a few hours later.

She turned to Pamela, who was watching with amused affection. "I see nothing has changed between you two," she said.

"Nor you," Merry replied. Robert's eyes regarded his family with unmistakable pride and love.

Pamela took Merry's two hands and held them. "A long visit this time."

"Perhaps we can convince you to come to Boston," Merry said. "The city is in need of fine doctors."

Something in Pamela's eyes told her it was not an impossible dream. She knew Robert's father had died, following his mother's death by only a few months. Merry imagined that gossip had not made their life easy.

But that would come later.

Now it was time to return home. Tonight they would celebrate the reunion. Sydney and Dani, who lived several blocks away, were eager, as well, to see Pamela and Robert. Sydney was a foreman in the shipping company and was soon due for another promotion.

This would be Gabriel's last voyage as a captain. Now that Samuel Barker was retiring, Gabriel would assume control of the shipping company. It would mean an end to captaining ships, but Gabriel had assured her he would be content.

"I was restless because I had no home, no anchor," he had told her before this last trip. "You and David and the new one are my home and my life. I have reached my landfall."

She knew they would journey together again. But it would be for pleasure and joy. Just as she had tinkered with a few plays until her son came. She did not miss it.

She'd discarded the name of Monique as well. Merry suited her much better these days.

All those thoughts warmed her as she stood in the loving circle of her growing family. She'd never thought to have such joy.

Gabriel reached down and slyly felt her stomach under her cloak. The baby kicked. "Ah, a little spitfire," he said. "Takes after her mother."

She smiled back. "Or his father."

She offered one hand to him and the other to Pamela.

"Let's go home."

In 1988, **Patricia Potter** won the Maggie Award and a Reviewer's Choice Award from *Romantic Times* for her first novel. She has been named Storyteller of the Year by *Romantic Times* and has received the magazine's Career Achievement Award for Western Historical Romance along with numerous Reviewer's Choice nominations and awards.

She has won three Maggie Awards, is a three-time RITA finalist, and has been on the *USA Today* and Walden's bestseller lists. Her books have been alternate choices for the Doubleday Book Club.

Prior to writing fiction, she was a newspaper reporter with the *Atlanta Journal-Constitution* and president of a public relations firm in Atlanta. She has served as president of Georgia Romance Writers and as a board member of River City Romance Writers, and is currently a member of the national board of Romance Writers of America.

Clan loyalty forced her to marry...
but can it force her to love?

# ISLE OF LIES

# Donna Fletcher

**Tricked into marrying an enemy of her clan,
Moira Maclean finds herself pregnant
with his child, and unable to suppress
her growing love for him.**

"Donna Fletcher's talents are unfathomable."
—*Rendezvous*

0-515-13263-2

Available wherever books are sold or
to order call 1-800-788-6262